"A classic, often considered the best, in the reform movement. With the changing environment, I believe it could become a widely read book, much like Kate Millet's."

—Peter R. Breggin, M.D.,
author of *Toxic Psychiatry*

"One of the greatest works of our time, and without any doubt in my mind, the single finest book against psychiatry ever written."

—Jeffrey Masson,
author of *Against Therapy*

Too Much Anger,
Too Many Tears

Too Much Anger, Too Many Tears

A Personal Triumph over Psychiatry

Janet and Paul Gotkin

Harper Perennial

A Division of HarperCollins*Publishers*

A hardcover edition of this book was published in 1975 by Quadrangle/The New York Times Book Company. It is here reprinted by arrangement with the authors.

HarperCollins books may be purchased for educational, business, or sales promotional use. For information, please call or write: Special Markets Department, HarperCollins Publishers, Inc., 10 East 53rd Street, New York, NY 10022. Telephone: (212) 207-7528; Fax: (212) 207-7222.

First HarperPerennial edition published 1992.

Library of Congress Cataloging-in-Publication Data

Gotkin, Janet, 1943–
    Too much anger, too many tears : a personal triumph over psychiatry / Janet Gotkin and Paul Gotkin.
        p.   cm.
    Originally published: New York : Quadrangle/The New York Times Book Co., 1975.
    ISBN 0-06-097434-6 (pbk.)
    1. Gotkin, Janet, 1943–   . 2. Mentally ill—United States— Biography.   I. Gotkin, Paul, 1942–   . II. Title.
RC464.G68A3   1992
616.89'0092—dc20
[B]   91-50527

92 93 94 95 96 RRD 10 9 8 7 6 5 4 3 2 1

For our daughters,
Miranda and Bethany,
with love

The Invisible Woman

The invisible woman in the asylum corridor
sees others quite clearly,
including the doctor who patiently tells her
she isn't invisible—
and pities the doctor, who must be mad
to stand there in the asylum corridor
talking and gesturing to nothing at all.

The invisible woman has great compassion.
So, after a while, she pulls on her body
like a rumpled glove, and switches on her voice
to comfort the elated doctor with words.
Better to suffer this prominence
than for the poor young doctor to learn
he himself is insane.
Only the strong can know that.

—Robin Morgan

Contents

Acknowledgments

Our heartfelt thanks to the following people:

Jeffrey Masson, whose persistence and unflagging belief in this book led, finally, to its new incarnation.

Hugh Van Dusen, our editor, who made the rebirthing process virtually painless.

Leonard Roy Frank, Judi Chamberlin, Rae Unzicker, George Ebert, Don Weitz, Kate Millet, Marilyn Rice, and David Oaks for sharing their thoughts with us on the current state of psychiatry and "the movement."

Our brothers and sisters in what we still think of as the Mental Patients Liberation Movement for their strength, tenacity, and determination to work for a better world.

And from Janet, special thank-you's to:

Joan Brennan, who taught me about love, courage, loyalty, and trust, and who introduced me, tenderly, to my warrior-child.

Phyllis Mendelsohn, Ray Messing, Mary Bond, Susan Weingast, Carole Breen, Susan Tuckerman, and Marge Davis, for accepting my pain unflinchingly and always being there.

Kavjo Motsinger-Sykes, who quite amazingly assisted at both the birth and rebirth of this book.

The courageous women of ISSUE, who gave me hope, support, and inspiration.

Preface to the HarperPerennial Edition

We wrote *Too Much Anger, Too Many Tears* nearly twenty years ago. In the Introduction to the original edition, we said we were essentially private people who wouldn't have chosen to open up our lives to public view if we didn't believe we had something important to say. We saw Janet's experience—her breakdown at college, the years in and out of mental institutions, the drugs and shock treatments—as "the quintessential psychiatric trip." Sadly enough, after all these years, stories like Janet's continue to be repeated, and what was not unique twenty years ago is even more common today.

Much has changed within the institutional psychiatric system since then. The back wards of mammoth state hospitals have been emptied, although the hospitals remain open; more "community based" services have been developed; and a network of legal advocacy has been created. But for those caught up in the system, the basic experience remains depressingly the same. Entering this world, as Janet did in the 1960s, was like going through the looking glass. Suddenly she was a "mental patient," and words like "treatment" and "help" had new, frightening meanings. Life was never going to be the same.

Too Much Anger, Too Many Tears is not a book that is friendly to psychiatry, not one of those stories in which the "patient" thanks her crusty yet kind-hearted psychiatrist for guiding her back to the clean, white world of sanity. In 1975, this was considered a radical, ground-breaking book—even, by some, a dangerous book, since it raised issues that challenged the legitimacy and morality of the entire institutional psychiatric system. Many publications did not review *Too Much Anger, Too Many Tears* when it first appeared and many television talk shows refused to have us on as guests.

Too Much Anger, Too Many Tears was certainly not the first book of its kind. In fact, we saw ourselves as part of a long narrative tradition. But it was the first book in a long time to give an inside view of what getting caught up in the institutional system was really like. And it combined a personal, emotional story with a radical, political perspective.

Elizabeth Packard was an early activist. Back in the 1860s, she self-published *Modern Persecution, or Insane Asylums Unveiled.* In it she told the story of how her minister husband committed her to the Jacksonville State Asylum because she publicly contradicted him on a matter of Calvinist doctrine. She was taken away on a train, "railroaded," and spent three years trying to regain her freedom and struggling with Andrew McFarland, the asylum superintendent. Finally, after a well-publicized trial, her sanity was vindicated, although she found herself with no money, no home, and no children. In the last years of her life, Elizabeth Packard crisscrossed the United States, convincing state legislatures to overturn laws that made women the legal property of their husbands and gave people labeled "insane" fewer rights than household pets. In the Introduction to *Modern Persecution* she wrote: "In the following narrative of my experiences, the reader will therefore find the interior of a woman's life delineated through the exterior surroundings of her bitter experiences."

Another spiritual ancestor of *Too Much Anger, Too Many Tears* is *A Mind That Found Itself*, a gritty book written by Clifford Beers around the turn of the century about his ten-year confinement in a variety of state and private asylums. Because Beer's views were watered down by the psychiatrist-influenced Mental Health Association that he helped found, people are not aware of how keenly and ferociously he indicted psychiatry and its institutional system. No less a rebel than McQueen from Ken Kesey's *One Flew Over the Cuckoo's Nest*, Beers was an eccentric man who refused to let his spirit be broken. He describes seclusion, forced drugging, sheeting, and other procedures that passed for treatment—all in an unusually modern-sounding voice.

Our own book, and the ideas behind it, grew out of our involvement with what was called, in the language of the times, the Mental Patients Liberation Movement. This was a loose federation of former "mental patients," who believed, as we did, that the institutional system was fundamentally oppressive and that all involuntary confinement and "treatment" should be abolished. To express our point of view and bring about change, we did what people did in the 1970s—organized, picketed, leafleted, lobbied, and talked on radio and television. It is ironic, looking back now, to realize that organizations like the American Psychiatric Association, which considered us little more than disgruntled "treatment" failures, now take credit for many of the ideas we first promoted.

So, this is the context in which *Too Much Anger, Too Many Tears* was originally conceived. We wrote it, to borrow that potent phrase from the 1960s, to make the personal political. Yet, page by page, the book tells a personal story—a romance, an ordeal, a testament to the durability of the human spirit. People who have gone through, or who are going through, an experience similar to Janet's will recognize much of what we describe here—from the bumbling, arrogant "professionals" posing as experts, to that dreadful sense that the nightmare will never end. What makes Janet's story so unique is that, in spite of how much she endured, she survived.

Originally, we described *Too Much Anger, Too Many Tears* as a mystery story. The book begins in 1970 and Janet has just overdosed on an incredibly high amount of Mellaril and is in a coma, hovering between life and death. "Something profoundly important happened inside Janet's head during a deep five-day coma that followed her last suicide attempt," we wrote, "some inner struggle was won, some revelation realized that changed her from a half-alive, hard-core mental patient into a joyful, animated human being. The clues to what occurred are scattered throughout the narrative and at the end of the book we've done our best to pull together these clues and reveal our own solution."

A lot of time has gone by since *Too Much Anger, Too Many Tears* was published, and since we are different, we look at what we experienced in a somewhat different way. One criticism leveled against us was that we didn't wrap up our story in a neat way. It was fine to say we had written a mystery, but couldn't we have done a better job unraveling it? Why did Janet crack up in the first place? How did she recover so completely? In 1975, an editor of a major book club went so far as to say he would use the book as a selection if we changed the ending. Our reaction: How do you change your life?

Yet, over the years we've come to understand this criticism a bit better and to be more gracious about accepting it. And, to be honest, questions have haunted us as well. In the new Epilogue to this edition of *Too Much Anger, Too Many Tears* we have done two things: catch the reader up on what has happened to us in the intervening years and deal more directly with why Janet became who she became.

Still, a mystery will always remain. How easy is it to categorize a human being, after all? As we said originally: "The mystery of pain and growth and profound change remains locked in Janet's head and heart. And the ultimate unanswerable solution to the mystery of spiritually dying and coming alive again is perhaps the theme and focus of our book."

In preparing the new edition of this book, we wrote to ex-psychiatric inmates still involved in the struggle for patients' rights, asking them what changes they saw in the institutional system in the past decade and what problems still remained.

George Ebert, an ex-inmate activist with the Alliance in Syracuse, New York, talked about "the myth of deinstitutionalization." Referring to New York's massive dumping of institutionalized people into substandard board and care homes, single-room occupancy hotels, and street corners, Ebert commented, "Removing the institutionalized person from the institution does not remove the institution from the individual. More and more people are being institutionalized, broken, reprogrammed, and dehospitalized into an institutional framework."

In New York State, for example, not a single state hospital has been closed, and while the permanent incarcerated population has decreased, the number of people processed through the system in outpatient clinics, municipal hospitals, psychiatric wards, and as shorter term but repeat in-hospital patients has increased. While traditional long-term commitment may be less common, it has been replaced by pernicious practices like "outpatient commitment" and by the enforced use of injectable drugs like Prolixin, whose effects last as long as three months. Leonard Roy Frank, a former psychiatric inmate and activist and editor of *The History of Shock Treatment*, rejects the term "deinstitutionalization" as misleading, and instead refers to the large-scale transfer of incarcerated people into smaller facilities as "trans-institutionalization."

Frank, who lives in San Francisco, believes, along with most of the other activists we corresponded and talked with, that while public awareness of the human rights issue in psychiatry has certainly increased over the last twenty years, "Main-Street people are still in the dark about the purposes and practices of institutional psychiatry." Frank believes, too, that "the dirty business of psychiatric deception and violence has been sanitized," and therefore made acceptable, by the token efforts of legislators and lawyers to provide a meager framework for advocacy and protection.

David Oaks, a veteran ex-inmate activist who now lives in Eugene, Oregon, where he edits a publication called *Dendron News*, commented on the new "respectability of mental patients," who are now invited to participate in scientific seminars and are employed as advocates and peer counselors. He expressed a widely shared dismay about the cooptation of ex-inmate groups that receive federal funds; he feels saddened, too, as we do, at what appears to be the loss, or at least the temporary obscuring, of a vision of radical change.

Rae Unzicker, an ex-inmate activist from Sioux Falls, South Dakota, who heads the National Association of Psychiatric Survivors (NAPS), expressed a widespread concern about "the re-emergence of the medical model...evidenced at the National Institute of Mental Health, where the 90s has been declared the 'decade of the brain.'" Unzicker powerfully explored her thoughts on the issue of the "medical model": "It frightens me," she wrote, "to hear the thirtysomething generation talk about 'chemical imbalance' as though it's the newest health trend....I often ask them how they know they (or, more frequently, the other person) have some chemical imbalance—is there a blood test, an X-ray, a CAT scan? Nope. But they hang on to this myth because it somehow legitimizes their suffering." Without question, as our book asserts, this myth continues to legitimize involuntary commitment and violent, punitive procedures like electroshock, drugging, and the use of physical restraints.

Perhaps most disturbing is psychiatry's continued reliance on physically intrusive methods to subdue its unwilling charges. The drugging of psychiatric inmates is more pervasive than ever, and the newest chemical armamentarium includes increasingly powerful brain-damaging compounds. Tardive dyskinesia, an irreversible brain damage syndrome that is caused by taking psychoactive drugs, is a rising scourge among psychiatrically-labeled people; estimates of the numbers of people afflicted with tardive dyskinesia *start* at 10 percent and go as high as 70 percent, but volumes of documentation about this completely avoidable, doctor-induced disease have not deterred the dramatic rise in the use of psychoactive drugs.

And electroshock, that nearly incomprehensibly barbaric procedure that was first used to subdue pigs in Fascist Italy in 1938, is steadily increasing. As a result of some bad press in the 1970s, the small cadre of active shock doctors organized themselves into a highly effective public relations operation in the early 1980s, taking on the task of convincing the public that shooting electricity through someone's brain was a safe, smart, caring, therapeutic endeavor. For the most part, they seem to have succeeded. The National Institute of Mental Health and the American Medical Association have endorsed the use of ECT and, after years of efforts on the part of the American Psychiatric Association, the Food and Drug Administration appears, at this writing, to have caved into pressure to "declassify" electroshock machines. This means that ECT devices would move from Class III, where they are now described as posing significant risks to life and limb, to Class II, where their use would be less circumscribed and scrutinized.

One would think that ECT is truly a throwback to the days when mental patients were dunked in ice-cold water, or stuffed, face up, in the wooden torture device called the "Utica crib." One would think there would be an enormous outcry against the barbarity of shooting electricity through the most delicate and complex part of a person's anatomy and calling it "treatment." But there is very little outcry, except among the survivors, and their accounts are almost universally discounted by ECT practitioners as being "anecdotal."

David Oaks struck to the core of our concerns in his comments on ECT. He wrote, eloquently, "Eliminating electroshock is not just done by banning it by law. We must look for the reasons why society and even some individuals turn to brain damage as an answer. Certainly, there will always be emotional pain in society. But massive social change must give birth to a vision of empowered communities, where people are truly equal and cared for, where the environment is nurtured, where emotions and differences are valued, where support skills are widely accepted and developed....Then we will be able to comfort each other in times of inevitable pain, we will challenge the roots of unnecessary pain caused by society, and fewer people will 'choose' the brain damage of psychiatry as a solution."

Things change and things remain the same. The world is vastly different now than it was when we wrote *Too Much Anger, Too Many Tears*. Judi Chamberlin, a long-time activist in the ex-psychiatric inmates movement and author of *On Our Own: Patient-Controlled Alternatives to the Mental Health System*, summed up the current state of the "movement" like this: "In spite of the changes," she wrote, "the key issues have not changed. We are still struggling for the right to be heard and to represent our own interests." And this, from Leonard Frank: "We need to get on track with greater militancy and more energy devoted to closing down institutions, ending forced treatment, demythologizing the medical model."

And Rae Unzicker's view: "Our greatest hope lies in changing people's minds before they ever reach a psychiatrist, and making them think about the issues involved in giving one's self over to another person for 'help.' We may not keep people away from 'help,' but we may educate them to take charge, recognize inherent power imbalances, confront unethical practitioners, and ask cogent questions about drugs and other 'treatments.' At a more subtle level, I hope we are able to educate people about the value of pain, that emotional suffering is a normal, natural part of living."

When we wrote *Too Much Anger, Too Many Tears* we worked hard to re-create, as truthfully and as fully as we could, a painful ten-year period in our lives. Looking back now at what we wrote, we find some clunky sentences and awkward phrases, and even a couple of embarrassingly personal moments we might want to redo, but there isn't a single idea expressed in this book that we feel any differently about. At its core this is a simple story of a young woman who went for help, what she found, and what she became. Our story has a happy ending, not because of psychiatry, but in spite of it.

We offer you our story and our thoughts about how this story happened to come about and why it continues to be repeated, hundreds of thousands of times each year, mostly without a happy outcome. And we offer you our belief that if we are ever to achieve a just and equitable society that cares for its most vulnerable and wounded members, what we need is what we have always needed: a revolution of the heart and of the spirit.

September 1991

Introduction

There has been a considerable number of sensational books written about people in the throes of what is called mental illness—people with split personalities, people with no personalities, people who have ultimately been guided into the clear white world of sanity by dedicated professional help. This book is not exactly one of these.

In one sense, ours is the story of the quintessential psychiatric trip. Unless someone has endured years of what is referred to as madness and years of treatment and confinement, much of what follows will seem exotic and sensational too. But, according to the National Institute of Mental Health, one person in ten will enter a mental institution at some time in her or his life, half of them to be labeled, like Janet, by the modern catch-all phrase, *schizophrenia.* For these people and for their families, our story, although different in detail and perhaps different in its resolution, should be recognizable.

Our book is written in hindsight, with an admitted perspective of bitterness and irreverence, and it is ultimately a condemnation of the waste, medical arrogance, and bumbling psychiatric pretensions that, in different ways, dominated both our lives. It is an attack on a growing pervasive belief in this country that science can wipe away misery or crime or distasteful behavior, a belief that has called forth a new, ever-hungry monster of mental health care which, like George Orwell's vision of psychological tyranny, is beginning to wind its way into every facet of our day-to-day lives.

Essentially, we are private people. We would never have decided to hold open our lives and experiences to public scrutiny if we weren't convinced that our story was in no way unique, and that other people might benefit from our hard won insights into the exploitative and political nature of much of psychiatric practice.

We have tried to be as honest as we possibly could, concentrating on what we thought and how we felt during the past ten years of our lives, as well as on what has happened to us. We've worked hard to recreate the three-dimensional feel of our experiences, to make our narrative, an inward/outward view of that quasi-mystical state called madness, scrupulously true; or, at least as true as any two persons' vision of reality can ever really be.

Whenever possible, we've searched back through old medical receipts and bills, so that we could tell our story with factual accuracy. But we were frustrated in our search for complete accuracy by the refusal of the hospitals that had confined Janet to release her psychiatric records to us. Their rationale, as we gather from their letters to us, is that the release of those records is not in a former patient's best interest, although why privacy is suddenly so jealously guarded when records are open to academic study, staff who never knew the patient, government and law enforcement agencies, and the courts, is beyond us. Another, more insidious motive for the fearful secretive aura that surrounds psychiatric data will reveal itself as our story unfolds.

Because we wanted these hospital records to help us put together this book; because the stigma of psychiatric labels manages to follow a person through his or her life; and because we believe that secrecy in general, whether in government or in our public institutions, serves only the people who hold the secrets, we have instituted a class action suit in conjunction with the Mental Health Law Project and the New York Civil Liberties Union, to overturn the various directives and statutes which have traditionally kept mental patients from discovering what has been written about them. This suit, which involves legal and ethical principles that have never before been challenged, moves into the United States Court of Appeals, in the early months of 1975.

But apart from whatever political overtones are present in our narrative, this book is still basically a story of personal experience. On its deepest level, we look upon it as a mystery story, involved with the romantic ambiguity of what it means to come fully alive. Something profoundly important happened inside Janet's head during a deep five-day coma that followed her last suicide attempt; some inner struggle was won, some revelation realized that changed her from a half-alive, hard-core mental patient into a joyful, animated human being. The clues to what occurred are scattered throughout the narrative and at the end of the book we've done our best to pull together these clues and reveal our own solution. But the mystery of pain and growth and profound change still remains locked in her head and heart. And the ultimate unanswerable solution to the mystery of spiritually dying and coming alive again is perhaps the theme and focus of our book.

In order to protect the privacy and innocent feelings of the friends, relatives, and fellow patients that appear in this story, we have changed their names. In order to protect the guilty, we have changed the names of the psychiatrists, hospitals and other mental health workers, as well.

—Janet and Paul Gotkin
November, 1974

Prologue

A Day in the Life: a.m.—Janet

Even though it was September, it was still summer. The sheets were soggy and wrinkled from a night of restless, summer sleep; my pillow had fallen to the floor and the wet pillowcase lay in a ball under my cheek. The telephone rang; it was seven-thirty. Just like every other working day. Paul's father was calling to wake him. In fifteen minutes he would be dressed and out of the house, riding down Bedford Avenue in the bright warm morning. He would fight off his sleepiness, make his way across Brooklyn through the Flatbush Avenue traffic, and in three-quarters of an hour he would be drinking black coffee and eating a fried egg on a roll where he worked. He must have kissed me good-bye as I lay asleep. I didn't notice. He was already gone.

My nighttime pills wore off close to eleven o'clock. It was past the time for my morning medication. I had been asleep since ten o'clock the night before. Another hot day. Another long day. Stretching empty and long and hot, the day seemed a tunnel. At the end was Paul, coming home exhausted and hungry. He would hold my tight, shaking body while I sobbed and sobbed. Steady, strong, he would hold me and try to ease the pain. Wordless, I would try to bury myself in his body. After awhile the sobs would subside, the pain recede. We would have dinner. And by ten o'clock, drugged and exhausted, I would fall asleep with a cigarette in my hand, the day ending like every other.

In between was the tunnel. Each day it seemed to stretch out longer, the lights getting dimmer. "I can't bear it," I screamed. And, as despair rose in my tightened throat, the tears poured out.

"You must keep busy," Dr. Sternfeld said. "Don't take yourself so seriously." Dr. Sternfeld said that too. "I love you." That was Paul. "Sweet spring is your time." e. e. cummings. "Oh, God, please help me." That was me.

I knew I had to get up. It was almost twelve and I was supposed to take my medication at ten. But I was sleeping at ten. Which pills was I supposed to take? Two Valium? Three Thorazine, two hundred milligrams each? Paul had counted them all out the night before, I remembered. As I stood outside the closed bedroom door, he had taken out the hidden bottles, counted out my daily ration, and hidden the precious containers. I wasn't supposed to listen. It would give me a clue. But I had listened. "Oh, who devised this childish game?" I almost cried again. It was two Valium and two Thorazine. I figured it out, swallowed them in one gulp in the bathroom, and went to find my glasses and make coffee. I had already smoked three cigarettes and my throat ached.

The elders were waiting in the kitchen. I knew they would be. They always were. In their long white robes, mist swirling at their bare feet, the elders had become an inescapable part of my life in the past months. Sometimes they would recede so far into the mists I would think they had gone away, back to wherever they came from. I would be free again! But suddenly they would emerge behind me, to the side, on a mountain in my bedroom, laughing, taunting, or so thunderously forbidding in their silence I would clutch my ears and close my eyes for fear I would be blinded.

Today they were in conference and didn't seem to notice me. "Have they forgotten?" I silently wondered. Quickly scanning the living room for the girl with the sunglasses, I opened the refrigerator door, took out a pitcher of orange juice and, not taking my eyes off the whispering, long-gowned group, let the door shut with a bang. Nothing! No one had even blinked! My heart began to beat faster. I could hear its thumps, irregular and excited. The room was getting brighter. And a voice inside me chanted, "Going home, they're going home. You will be free, they're going home. Going home, going home. To misty lands, they're going home."

"Paul," I thought. "I must tell Paul. He won't have to come home early any more to take care of me. They're leaving." My excitement grew. "Maybe I can even drive the car. And Madelon. I can go and visit Madelon now. They're taking the girl with the sunglasses with them too. Oh, thank you, God." The words came fast and faster, silent, swirling in my head. I held my ears and closed my mouth to try to keep them in, just to be safe. But joy and relief came flooding out. I held the orange juice pitcher as if it were a baby.

Something made me look up. The mist had cleared. Tall, oh, so so tall the elders stood, their faces long and gray and lined, their hands outstretched and pointing, pointing sparks—at me. My arms let the pitcher drop to the floor. I cupped my ears to keep out their taunts. "You really thought we'd leave?" they screeched, and pointed, never moving. "Why, you silly, ugly, frightened girl, this is our home now."

"No," I cried. "Leave me alone, please, please, leave me alone."

A Day in the Life: a.m.—Janet

"Nobody ever dies of fear," I told myself. "They want you to think you'll die of fear."

The oldest one stepped forward. "Remember what we said," he warned. "We only want to help you. You fat and stupid girl, you must know you cause pain to others. Why, it is pain to look at you. But we don't mind. Come with us. With us."

I felt like the scarecrow as my body folded to the floor. "Yes," I said, touching the pieces of the pitcher. "Yes," covered with orange juice and the tears making me want to vomit. "I will." Louder. "I will. I will. Just go away."

They disappeared. My nightgown was soaked with juice and tears and sweat. It was just twelve-thirty; if I wanted to speak to Paul before he went out, it would have to be now. I was so exhausted I could barely lift the receiver.

A conversation like any other. We talked. I cried a bit. If I wanted him to come home early I should call again. Would I be all right. Why didn't I spend the afternoon with my mother. Yes, he loved me. Was I certain I was okay; I sounded strange.

Something had jelled inside me. As I spoke, it rounded out, firmer and heavier. In my stomach and spreading out under my diaphragm, my decision was growing; it was turning to resolve. I wondered why Paul didn't hear it as it grew and rumbled. On the edge of my brain a small voice was crying, very low: "Please ask me, Paul, please hear my strong resolve and come and slay it. If you love me."

"I'll be back at two," he said. "And darling, don't be afraid to call."

"Yes," I whispered. "I love you."

The pills were in the bedroom somewhere. "There are a limited number of places they can be," I thought. I felt calm, though excited at the thought of the search. The conflict that had been tearing me apart for months had finally been resolved. It didn't seem to matter why. I knew the time would come. Hadn't I been telling Paul and Dr. Sternfeld that it could not go on forever? The nightly ritual of the pill counting? Paul hated it. But Dr. Sternfeld said it was the only way. "A risk we have to take." It frightened me—I dreamed of pills at night and during the day I stayed out of the bedroom if I could. Or, drawn to it, I lay on the bed and wondered which corner, which drawer or book hid the forbidden capsules.

Without even trying it, I eliminated the closet: the top, too difficult to reach quickly (Paul was usually quite fast); the bottom, too cluttered with shoes and boxes and handbags (not safe enough). Instead, I went to Paul's bedside table. "A logical place," I thought.

"But really kind of obvious." I didn't hold much hope for the bedside table. Nothing. I didn't bother with my night table. Although I rarely opened it, I knew that the accumulated junk in it would come clattering out—too noisy. Paul was very quiet. There was the large aluminum storage box under the bed. A possibility. I pulled it out and looked through quickly. Nothing again.

I sat on the floor for awhile to rest and think. As I lit a cigarette I saw her in the doorway—the girl with the sunglasses. She had first appeared early in the summer and had lately become an almost constant companion. Dr. Sternfeld and I had talked about her at length. I knew she was really me, an embodiment of my unacceptable impulses, an external conscience. I knew all about her—even down to why she wore huge gold-framed sunglasses and had a shadowy face and spindly legs. But she still didn't go away. Today she was bigger, yet somehow vaguer than usual, and her glasses shone blue in the sunlight. There was something reproachful about her expression; she shook her head slightly from side to side. And she never took her eyes off me as I sat on the floor.

She always made me think. And I didn't want to think about anything today. Just find the pills, take them, and come what might. She wanted me to think about being dead; her eyes were making me think about being dead. The huge resolve inside my chest cavity began to crumble as the tears formed in my throat and eyes.

For the first time ever I faced her directly and spoke. "You don't understand. I can't go on," I said. "It hurts too much. I hurt too much. I have no more strength. It's been too long, the pain. Yes, I'm afraid. You ask me about Paul. I love him so much it's like a rubberband across my lungs sometimes. I don't want to hurt him. Don't ask me to explain." My voice was louder, getting shrill. "I don't know if I'm doing the right thing," I shouted. "I don't know. I have no other choice; don't you see?" She turned her back and disappeared. "Go haunt someone else," I screamed.

After ten more minutes of looking in drawers, under rugs, and behind books, I found the cache. Paul had hidden the bottles inside the metal radiator shield. A very clever spot. I tried to put him out of my mind. I took out a bottle so large it could almost have been a cookie jar and brought it into the kitchen. I washed my hands and face, combed my hair, and changed into a loose blue linen smock and sandals. I made the bed, cleaned up the kitchen, and stood for a minute or two at the front door, feeling my arms get warm in the sun and listening to my landlady scream at her three-year-old granddaughter. Turning towards the living room, I thought the house was rather pretty in an ordinary way and clean enough to satisfy even my mother-in-law. A picture of my mother filled my mind. I was supposed to call her this morning. Well, she knew I slept late. Heavy tears came up behind my eyes.

I couldn't remember when I had been so calm. I stood and watched myself walk. Some dignity left, I thought. "We might be able to make you into something acceptable, yet, Mrs. Gotkin. We haven't much to work with, it's true, but modern science does work wonders, you know." Picturing the scene, I laughed in spite of myself. I wished it was still really summer and Paul would come home early and we would go swimming at Neponsit Beach as the sun was sinking and walk along the cool afternoon sand and drive home in the dusk and . . . The nicest times of the whole past year had been those afternoons. Interludes of peace between pain and pain. But you cannot live in interludes, and anyhow, the summer was over. I was going to take the pills and put it in God's hands. Whoever He was, He couldn't do worse than everyone else who had tried to run my life. "I don't know if I'm doing the right thing," I whispered. I was on my knees in the living room. "But I have no choice anymore. Forgive me for being weak," I sobbed. "I've tried. I've tried so hard."

I didn't want to go into the kitchen yet. Instead, I took a small foil packet of grass from a hidden drawer in the desk and rolled a joint. I hadn't smoked in a long time. I almost always crashed badly on grass. I hallucinated, I thought. But it was a nice high and today I wouldn't have to crash. The smoke was rough and hot. I felt angry at getting high alone. I let the joint go out half-finished. Between the living room and the kitchen was the telephone. Border between two countries. Should I announce my intention of crossing? I dialed Paul's number. It was two-thirty and he would be back from lunch.

We spoke for a short time. As in the morning, he seemed preoccupied, tired; the effort to enter my head was too great for him, I thought. But my resolve thundered and quaked; the crying voice was weak. "Yes, I'll try to take a nap," I heard myself saying from the distance. "Good-bye. I love you."

For a long time after the click I held the receiver against my chest, my arms crossed over it. Maybe two minutes. Deep sobs shook my body. All cried out, I stopped and put the telephone back in its cradle.

On the counter, immediately to the right of the kitchen sink, the large brown bottle was waiting. Without even drying my face, I filled a glass with cold tap water, opened the cap, and began swallowing the small, smooth, yellow pills by the handful. After years of practice, I was expert. I filled the glass again and again.

PROLOGUE

There seemed to be thousands of pills. But they slid down cool and smooth, never sticking in my throat like the Doriden. With half the bottle gone, I stopped and sat down at the kitchen table. I had a vision of my stomach filled to bursting with smooth, yellow pills that would not dissolve, and a wave of panic flooded my body. What if I didn't die? The possibility had not occurred to me. This was not an *attempt;* I was going to kill myself. If someone intervened, it would be God, and I would accept that too. But to face Paul's sadness and reproach and Dr. Sternfeld's rage? I was nauseated and scared.

A few more swallows, another fifty pills, and I lay on the floor, waiting to sleep. "Please," I prayed to someone, "let me die now, let the poisons fill my body and make me sleep." I was wide awake, without a hint of drowsiness, after several hundred pills. The floor was cool in the late afternoon and my resolve was a heavy, decaying mound in my stomach. "I'm not going to die," I thought, more and more terrified. "It doesn't matter what I do."

I stood up, took a long, serrated knife from the silverware drawer, and began to cut parallel lines on my inner arm, being careful not to go too close to the old wrist scars. We had no razor blades, nothing very sharp in the house. Outside it all, far away and temporarily safe, I watched myself cut, not feeling a thing. The tears rolled down my cheeks and mixed with the blood. A dull knife that couldn't find a vein and tranquilizers like M&M's—the irony was unbearable. In the gray chamber in my brain I had a vision of myself, the immortal woman scarred from head to foot, forever seeking death and begging a white-robed doctor to set her free.

I lay down the knife and picked up the phone. The nearly empty bottle was as large as the door and the knife shone like silver. I wanted Paul to come through the door more than I had ever wanted anything except to die. When Dr. Sternfeld answered, I began to cry, shallow, coughing sounds from lips I didn't feel. I told him about the pills, my bleeding arms, and how I couldn't fall asleep. I was thinking of the future and a new vision of doom was forming. "Don't be mad at me," I sobbed. "Please don't punish me." "I'm not," he said. "You almost didn't get me in time. I was just leaving." "In time," I wondered, "for what?"

"The silly man must think I called him to save me," I thought, incredulous. "He doesn't understand at all."

Begging for forgiveness, I listened as Dr. Sternfeld told me his plans. He would call an ambulance and meet it at my house. I should just sit down quietly and wait. There was nothing to worry about. "Where will they take me?" I asked. "Don't worry," he said. "I'll be there."

As I hung up the phone I looked at the knife on the kitchen table and the brown bottle of pills on the sink. More than anything in the world I didn't want to go to the hospital again. Angry tears were forming now. "It isn't fair," I said quietly. "It just isn't fair." But I wasn't even feeling angry anymore. My eyes were getting bleary and my fingers numb. The outlines of the room were fading. "Please God," I prayed, "help Paul to understand. He can't, but help him just the same. Please let him know I love him; in spite of this, I love him." I was drowning in tears, again fighting off the dark, chaotic pain I had tried to lose forever.

As the bell rang, two policemen crashed through the front door and came running into the kitchen. Roughly, one said, "Come on, let's go." Dr. Sternfeld had said he would meet us, I remembered through the haze. My voice distant and tinny, I told them I was waiting for the doctor; he would be here any minute. He had told me. Would they like to sit down and wait? The kitchen darkened as two more men entered. "Can you walk?" one asked. "Of course," I said. "If I couldn't walk, you wouldn't be here." But he didn't understand.

"Okay. Let's go." The voice was deep. "But my doctor said he'd be here." I heard a mumble; laughter. Through the blur of blue and the clatter of boots, panic touched my arm. "You walking or we have to carry you?" "But my doctor . . ." I began, faltering. No answer, just a tall, blue shape, pressing my arms to my body. This was a new nightmare, and my stomach turned to hot liquid. "It is not in my hands anymore," I realized. "Even God has forsaken me."

"I'll come," I said.

Slowly, supported on both sides by blue towers, I walked into the late afternoon shadows. The ambulance loomed huge in front of the house. Bedford Avenue was lined with spectators. "The silly, nosy sons of bitches," I thought. "I wonder what they see." Inside the ambulance I sat, a blue hulk on either side of me. I was dizzy and my legs and arms were numb. Suddenly, up the steps and into the ambulance, shrill and angry, came my landlady. "What's going on here?" she demanded. She wasn't going to stand for it—her tenant in an ambulance! Through my growing numbness, I felt a surge of fury. The nasty, ugly, old bitch. Always screaming at her granddaughter. "Mind your own fucking business, for a change," I yelled. Two years, and I finally said it! Mrs. Kramer seemed to shrivel in surprise. The engine started and everything slipped out of focus.

PROLOGUE

"Where are we going?" My lips were moving by themselves; my body was heavy and gray and sick. "Don't worry, you'll be all right." A voice inside me tried to scream. "I don't want to be all right. Don't you understand? I want to die!" But no sounds came out.

The car stopped. I was lying on my back and I was being carried somewhere. That smell! Those sounds! Immediately I knew. I was in a hospital. "O Lord, why have you forsaken me?" But no one answered.

In the emergency room a class was in session. The lesson for the day was stomach pumping. A doctor was demonstrating the procedure. The group of interns seemed interested, but slow. Their English was poor, and the doctor had to explain each step a few times to make sure they understood.

As I lay on the table, my arms and legs strapped down, someone thrust a large, cold, metal and sponge instrument down my throat. I coughed and tried to scream. "I can't breathe. I can't breathe. Help." "Do you understand the method of insertion?" I heard. "Any questions?" My mouth and nose were filled with vomit, as my body tried to loosen the metal in my throat. Each time I tried to scream, I seemed to drown in metal, sponge, and vomit. "Why is the spasm in her chest?" I heard. The doctor explained, again, the function and nature of the stomach pump. I closed my eyes and prayed to die, old at twenty-seven. All questions answered, I was wheeled away. The dark was closing in, the noise was dimming. "Paul, Paul, where are you?" I cried inside. In my mind, I saw a vision of the electroshock machine. And all went blank.

A Day in the Life: p.m.—Paul

The New York Mets were losing on the clear September day Janet took her overdose of Mellaril, but they were rallying in the ninth inning. I dawdled while Tommy Agee danced off third base and Wayne Garrett continued to foul-off pitches. When I parked my car in front of my office, the Mets had lost. Not even a lousy ball game could go right for me. It was four o'clock in the afternoon, and in an hour I would be going home.

Dr. Sternfeld had left a message for me to phone him. I settled into my swivel chair and dialed his number from memory.

"I'm glad I finally reached you," he said. He sounded weary and distant, as if he were throwing out his words from across some blurry chasm. "I don't want you to get upset. I want you to sit down and listen to what I have to tell you."

"What are you talking about?"

"Janet called me a half hour ago. She's taken an overdose of tranquilizers. I don't think we have anything to worry about, though. I think we've caught her in time. But, of course, with any kind of overdose, we can never predict what will happen."

I reached for a cigarette, stared at it, wondered what it was doing in my hand, and flung it back across my desk. The late afternoon sun flowed through the low dusty windows near my chair. From outside my office, I could hear the thundering of fifty-five sewing machines.

"What's happening now?" I asked, mentally patting myself on the back for the surprising calm in my voice.

"I think she's okay," Dr. Sternfeld answered. "I've told you that I don't think we have anything to worry about. I've just spoken to the police for a second time. I want to make certain that they get her to a hospital as fast as possible."

"Where are they taking her?"

"The nearest city hospital. What is it? Fairview Hospital? Do you want me to call Janet's parents?" he asked.

"I'd appreciate it. I don't want to talk to them right now."

We endured a long, tense silence.

PROLOGUE

Finally he said, "Are you leaving for the hospital now?"

"I suppose I will."

"Just take good care of yourself," he said. "Drive carefully. I'll meet you there in about forty-five minutes."

My hands were shaking so badly I could barely hold the steering wheel. In shock, my thoughts reeling out of my control, I couldn't really comprehend what had happened to Janet. I had actually shut off a part of my mind a long time before, and it was to be some time later, long after my initial shock had worn away, that I would be able to open it up again.

I kept wondering why she had phoned Dr. Sternfeld instead of me. But I knew the answer already. I had lived with her for five tortured years, and I knew that if she was going to look for someone to save her life, it wasn't going to be me.

I parked my car in the hospital parking lot, in one of the chalked-off spaces reserved for doctors. I slid through a chain link fence, climbed up a row of concrete steps, and entered the emergency ward. From the outside, Fairview Hospital was deceptively pleasant looking. Surrounded by dense stately trees and rambling private homes, its tall whitewashed buildings seemed graceful and airy. But inside, the emergency ward was crammed with all the misery of city living—the belching alcoholics, the victims of muggings and rapes, the fidgety addicts, and the wheezing feverish children.

I ignored the insistent queries of the hospital receptionist and marched past her into the medical ward. The long corridor was blurred with motion; nurses and aides rushed across the littered floor, as if someone had just told them that the building was on fire.

The doctor who had pumped out Janet's stomach was a grim-looking man with oversized owl-shaped glasses, patent leather hair, and a mask of vagueness in his pale brown eyes.

"I'm looking for Janet Gotkin," I said.

"Who?" he said softly.

"I was told that you were the doctor who treated her. Only a half hour ago."

He regarded me blankly, bobbing his head up and down so that his owl-shaped glasses rattled against the bridge of his nose.

"How is she?" I asked.

He nodded again.

"Is she all right?"

"I think so."

"Don't you even know?" I asked, getting angry.

He lifted his bony shoulders. "You're supposed to ask the nurse at the desk if you want any medical information."

A Day in the Life: p.m.—Paul

I peered into Janet's room. She was sleeping on a high metal movable bed. With her hair matted against her forehead, the front of her blue paisley dress stained with blood and spit, she looked rigid and strangely unreal, a death mask image of my wife. I was overcome by a terrible sense of sorrow, a sadness that was focused on me rather than on Janet. I felt old and worn, as if the five years of effort and passion I had thrown into our marriage were symbolic of the futility and waste of my twenty-eight years of life.

She stirred. I entered her room and stared down at her, searching her face for a signal of familiarity and connection that could somehow pull together my deadened emotions. In sleep, her narrow face seemed exquisitely fragile. The softness of her cheeks, the upright angle of her pointed nose, the easy pulsing of her thin chest, all called forth in me another terrible sadness—loving her. I reached out my arm to touch her forehead, but my hand lingered in midair and finally I pulled it back against my chest and turned away. I couldn't absorb all the memories of the past five years, all the hospitals, drugs, doctors, and treatments that had led to this ultimate life and death moment. Janet's suicide attempt seemed now to be the climax of her long psychiatric trip, and I, who had stumbled blindly into the middle of this trip, felt that her overdose was the climax of our relationship as well.

I couldn't possibly know, yet, that her suicide attempt was going to pull us into a startling mystery of rebirth and self-discovery that would soon radically alter our lives. I just stood by her bedside, thinking about the strange fragile bond that had kept me with her these past five years. I thought that whether she lived or died, our relationship had broken apart. In taking the pills she had finally destroyed the balance of trust that had always held us together. When I turned away from her, filled with my feelings of bitterness, waste, and regret, I thought that I wouldn't have minded dying myself.

A burly, red-haired policeman appeared in the doorway and motioned me outside.

"Are you her husband?" he asked, waving his hand in Janet's general direction.

I nodded.

"I'm one of the policemen who brought her to the hospital." I stared at him, wondering if he wanted me to thank him. But he wagged a leather notebook at me and said, "I want some more information from you."

A fat silver-haired nurse careened an empty wheelchair down the hallway, and we flattened ourselves against the peeling wall.

PROLOGUE

"I have her name and address here," the policeman said. "How old is she?"

I told him her age, her maiden name, and the name and address of her doctor.

"Why'd she do it?" he asked.

"Do what?"

"You know. Try to take her life?"

I looked down at my shoes.

"I can't really tell you why," I said. "She's been feeling suicidal for a very long time. I suppose her pain just built up and she couldn't bear it any longer."

"They're all fucking weird, these women. I haven't seen my wife for four months now. She keeps telling me she's sick and she can't go on living anymore. Her doctor keeps telling me she's schizophrenic and she doesn't know what she's feeling. And then one day she picks up and goes wandering off to Europe."

"Then you know what I'm talking about when I say the pain builds up."

He ran his fingers across a long red mark underneath his hairline, where the sweatband of his helmet had bitten into the white skin of his forehead.

"I don't know what to do anymore. She left me with four fucking kids to take care of."

"I can sympathize with you," I said, eager to reach out for a connection with him. But he shook his head wearily, as if we weren't connected at all.

Trying to avoid Janet's parents, I walked outside. I met Dr. Sternfeld as he arrived at the hospital.

"What do we do now?" I asked. We paced back and forth across the gray cement of the parking lot. The weather had turned cold, but as we shuffled about, shoulder to shoulder, neither of us seemed to notice it. The air was thickening, threatening rain.

"In the long run or the short run?" he said.

"Both."

"Right now I'd like to get her out of here and into Monroe Park. I don't know if Fairview will release her. If anything happens on the way to Monroe Park, they'd still be responsible."

"And in the long run?" I asked.

"I don't know. We'll have to wait and see."

While Dr. Sternfeld attempted to get Janet released, I entered her room again. She was still sleeping, but her eyes were blinking open and shut as if she was actually coming in and out of slumber. She shuddered, widened her eyes, and catching sight of me, she reached out her arm. I held her hand, not knowing what to say to her.

"I'm sorry," she whispered.

"Don't be sorry," I said. "You have nothing to be sorry about."

"I didn't want to hurt you," she said. "I couldn't help doing what I did. I just couldn't stand living anymore."

I heard the cool rational part of me telling her that I didn't take her suicide attempt personally, that I understood that it had nothing to do with me. But I knew that only part of me was talking; I wasn't telling her the whole truth.

"Is Dr. Sternfeld here?" she asked.

"He's outside, on the ward."

"Is he angry at me?"

"Why should he be angry at you?"

She looked down at the series of red welts across her upper arm.

"I cut myself with one of our old steak knives. I don't even know why I did it. All these years of wanting to cut myself and not being allowed to do it. But I broke my contract with Dr. Sternfeld."

"I thought the contract said that you wouldn't cut your wrists. Technically, you didn't do it."

"I know. I cut myself this way on purpose."

She closed her eyes again and I released her hand. But she opened them again and said, "Please don't leave me now, Paul. Please don't ever go away from me."

"I won't," I said, knowing that I might very well be lying. "I promise I won't."

In my father-in-law's car, driving to Monroe Park, I sat in the back seat, holding Janet tightly against me. A windstorm raged, sweeping a nightmare wash of rain across our windows. Janet kept slipping out of my grasp, sliding limply down the car seat. "Poor baby," I said as I propped her up against me. But I didn't know whether I was talking about her or me.

Squashed between a series of decaying tenements, as new and sparkling, as filled with glass, plastic, and tile as a Holiday Inn, Monroe Park dominated its street. The squat building was very familiar to me. I had come and gone from it many times before.

We double-parked at the entrance and we tried to haul Janet out of the car. But we couldn't even rouse her from her slumber. In the driving rain, two husky white-coated aides struggled, then finally lifted her into a wheelchair. It was like handling a corpse, I thought, or a piece of meat.

She was unable to go through any of the usual preadmission

rituals. I scribbled out her admitting forms, prepaid her first week of hospitalization, and sat through the formal psychiatric examination for her. The admitting resident, a lanky dull-eyed young man, looked at me nervously across his wide polished desk. He was a few years younger than I, well-trimmed, bearded, with a clump of unmanageable blond hair that floundered across his forehead like a flattened pompadour.

Janet had always found it grimly funny that no admitting psychiatrist had ever looked her straight in the eye. They read from their printed papers, she told me, buried their heads in their piles of forms, and rattled off their list of prepared questions. Anticipating disregard, I was not prepared for the resident's obvious nervousness. He fidgeted with his pen, twirled his college ring around his finger, and squeaked his shoes against the shiny linoleum floor.

"I'm not the patient," I offered. "It's my wife."

"I know. I know," he said, wiping his wave of hair away from his eyes. "Do you hear voices?"

"I'm not the patient."

"I mean, does your wife hear voices?"

"Yes."

"What do they tell her to do? Do they tell her to harm herself?"

"No. I don't think so. I mean, they never have."

"Does she hallucinate?"

"Look, I can tell you how she's been diagnosed. She's been admitted to this hospital almost a dozen times."

"Does she hallucinate?"

"Yes. Look, what the hell. You already have her diagnosed as a chronic schizophrenic. Do we really have to go through this again?"

"How does she relate to other people? Does she sometimes think people are plotting against her?"

Janet was officially diagnosed and admitted. I gathered up her few personal possessions, presented them to Lucy, the property clerk, to be labeled, and pocketed her clothing receipt, the carbon copy of her admitting form, and the printed sheet of paper that listed all of Monroe Park's rules and regulations. I stood in the lobby, watching her being wheeled into the elevator. Still soundly asleep, her frail body was grotesquely twisted against the canvas safety belt that held her securely in place. Her head spilled backward across the wheelchair's metal wing and as I stared at her strange lifeless features, I tried to pull her back toward me, to lift into my mind some of my old, familiar, intimate feelings toward her. But I could barely recognize her. Exhausted, drained of emotion myself, I thought, at this moment, that I wouldn't even have been able to recognize my own reflected image. It was almost midnight, and I wanted only to be home and asleep myself.

Driving back home, I didn't even try to be sociable with my in-laws. Our relationship had been strained for a very long time. I settled wearily into the back seat of their car, stared abstractly at the shadowy outline of my mother-in-law's round head and thought about how, when Janet and I had first met in the summer of 1966, they had made their disapproval of me very clear. In fairness to them, they had found themselves in a terrible predicament. Although Janet had suffered for the five preceding years, they still clung to their old memories of her, to their vision of the high school golden girl who had seemed to slide so gloriously through the adolescent miseries of coming of age. Somewhat ragged looking and socially erratic, I was not what they wanted for their daughter. I suppose I wasn't smooth enough or bright enough or personable enough to prop up their dream of her, the illusion that she would one day be the same golden person she had once been. But over the years, her parents and I had been forced to learn to live with each other; we had needed each other very badly.

I stared out the side window, into the fog and rain, and I thought about Janet, where she was right now, on the seventh floor of Monroe Park, the most-disturbed ward. Although I had already endured two of Janet's hospitalizations, and although the image of a mental institution was no longer fearful or exotic to me, I was struck by a sensation that Janet was heading off in a new and startlingly different direction, going someplace I couldn't accept or comprehend. Her suicide attempt had created a wall between us, for she had chosen the fearsome option of trying to die. I attempted to picture the seventh-floor ward in my mind, the long pale yellow corridors, the stark rooms, the padded isolation compartments, but I shook my head and finally closed off my thoughts. Despite my earlier comforting words to her, I had actually taken her suicide attempt as a personal affront to the love between us and as a betrayal of my trust. It would be a long time before I could make peace with the ramifications of her final suicidal act.

My mother-in-law twisted around to look at me. In the dim light of the passing street lamps, I watched her eyes study my face.

"You can't give up faith now, Paul," she said. "You have to hold yourself together and keep up your strength."

I was surprised at how easily she could read my thoughts. I had grown up in the late 1950s when a modern jazz, beatnik aura of cool was the raging fashion. I always thought of myself as stoical and stone-faced, able to control and hide my emotions.

PROLOGUE

"Where are you going to sleep tonight?" she asked. "Do you want us to drop you off at your parents?"

"No. Just take me back to my car. I'm not certain where I'll sleep."

I swallowed two Miltowns that evening (I almost never take drugs), and fell into a dark, forgetful, drugged sleep. At eight-thirty the next morning, the hospital phoned. At first I couldn't understand what the doctor was telling me. He wanted me to arrange for round-the-clock private duty nurses for Janet. During the night, she had descended into a deep coma.

And so I waited. From morning until evening in the brightly lit lobby of Monroe Park, I swiveled endlessly on plastic chairs while Janet lay one floor above me, machines monitoring her strange, inscrutable sleep.

I was haunted by a sense of unreality. I couldn't understand why I was waiting, what I could expect to accomplish. Yet, I couldn't help it. I had to wait. I suppose I had to wait for what my grandmother had always called Mr. Malakh-Hamoves, the angel of death.

In the beginning, I hadn't wanted to wait. On the first morning of her coma, I stood outside her hospital room, discussing her medical prognosis with Dr. Caine, her internist. With his gray silk suit and diamond pinkie ring, Dr. Caine was the smoothest of a team of four doctors. He introduced himself to me, pressing my hand with such a proper amount of warmth and firmness that I was immediately intimidated, and asked me if I had any questions about Janet's condition.

"I'm really totally ignorant about everything that's happening to her," I said. "I'm not sure I even know what a coma is."

He laughed good-humoredly and poked me on the shoulder.

"When it comes to a coma, you're only a little more ignorant than anybody else. It's basically a state of deep unconsciousness. But what exactly does that mean?"

I shrugged my shoulders. "I don't know. What *does* it mean?"

"Let me put it this way. I can best describe it by saying that the body, because of some kind of shock, or in your wife's case, because of the sudden discharge of toxins into her system, pulls back into itself. The brain closes off its conscious awareness of the world, almost as if it wants to devote its full attention to the business of healing its body."

"It's not like sleep then?" I said.

"Not exactly. No. Interestingly enough, in a shallow comatose state, one can distinguish between periods of sleep and wakefulness. Some people have even broken out of their comas claiming that they were aware of everything that went on around them, but just couldn't manage to reach out to the world. There's nothing particularly dangerous about the coma itself. The danger is in the weakened condition of the body and the inability of the patient to tell us what's happening to her. That's why we have so many machines monitoring your wife's condition."

"How long will her coma last?"

"There's no way of predicting. Some people have been in comas for years. But in your wife's case, I wouldn't say we have long to wait. As long as her kidneys continue to function, as long as they keep pumping the poisons out of her system, she'll be steadily rising toward consciousness."

"And suppose her kidneys begin to fail?"

"That's a difficult question. The nearest artificial kidney machine is at a hospital a few miles south of here. But I don't think I'd move her."

"Why not?"

"There'd probably be more danger in picking her up and carrying her there than in letting her system adjust by itself. I'd rather pull out all the tubes and let her fight off the poisons without any artificial help."

The thought that her system could function without medical assistance was shocking to me. But, of course, it was true. What did people do in the past?

"Can her system bear all the strain on it?" I asked.

He shook his head. "We're watching her constantly, which is really the most we can do. As you can imagine, we're experts at handling overdoses."

"It's old hat to you?"

He looked at me queerly. "I wouldn't quite put it that way. Let me just say that we've dealt with thousands of similar cases. And most of them survive."

"Then you think she has a good chance of coming out of this alive?"

"I don't like to make predictions. She's taken an enormous number of pills. I have no way of knowing how seriously her system is damaged. Or even what's going on inside of her. We have to depend somewhat on her will to live. The real business of healing is directly related to the toughness of her body and mind. If you back me into a corner, I can only say that she has a seventy-five percent chance of surviving."

He ran his fingers over his sleek black hair, his diamond ring glistening in the dull, fluorescent, overhead light. Across the corridor, a nurse was motioning for him to approach the nurses' station, but he held up his hand and waved her away.

"Would you like to look at your wife?" he asked.

I peeked around him into the mass of wires and tubes that surrounded Janet's bed. I shook my head. I could see no purpose in looking at her. All I could think of was a line from Ernest Hemingway's *A Farewell to Arms*: "It was like saying good-bye to a statue." I was afraid it would be.

I wanted to be someplace else. Over the years, I had held up under terrible strains and pressures, but I couldn't bear the senseless burden of a deathwatch, waiting for Janet to live or die.

I walked down into the lobby and sat off in a corner by myself. My mind focused on Janet again, but I didn't want to think about her. I searched the cheerful looking lobby for something to take my mind off my own pain and confusion. All I could see were the contorted trappings of illness and despair.

In the early afternoon, when my mother-in-law arrived at the hospital to hold her own personal vigil, I drove home. In the early evening, as I ate dinner at my parents' apartment, she phoned me.

"When are you coming back to the hospital?" she asked. Her voice was cold.

"I don't know. I thought I'd drop by later this evening. There's really nothing I can do for Janet right now."

"Well—" she hesitated. "I just spoke to one of the doctors. There's some problem with Janet's heart. He said to me, 'Where's her husband?' I'm just repeating what he said. He said, 'Where's her husband? This is a very critical, dangerous moment, I think he ought to be here.' "

I phoned Dr. Sternfeld.

"I know," he said, his mellow voice weary and solemn. "I just spoke to the hospital. They seem to be worried about her heart starting to fail."

I tried to keep my own voice calm. "I'm leaving now."

"Do you want me to meet you there?" he asked.

"Of course I do," I thought. "Why the hell do you think I called?"

"Yes, I do," I said.

As I drove back to Monroe Park, I thought about Janet dying. At this moment her death seemed certain to me. I thought about our good moments together, our moments of blinding pleasure and love, as well as the dark overwhelming memories of our years of pain. I was sentimental. For a man brought up on John Wayne movies, tough guy heroes, and barroom swagger, I cried easily. But I felt only a vague numbness now. As if in mock parallel to Janet's comatose sleep, I was preparing to withdraw into myself and concentrate only on my own survival. A forbidden feeling was rattling around in my brain. I thought it was relief.

I parked in front of the hospital and I tramped inside, waiting in the lobby for Dr. Caine to come down from the medical ward, shake his head sadly, and tell me that Janet had passed away. But my anticipation of her death was premature; there had actually been little to worry about. Her heart had, in fact, momentarily faltered, but someone had rushed in with an injection of adrenalin and had saved her life with a routine technique. It had been a moment of true danger, but the danger was only fleeting and, in perspective, rather trivial.

And so, as I sat puffing cigarette after cigarette, I was forced to look into myself. After Dr. Caine assured us that everything was still going well, Dr. Sternfeld told me a long funny story about his tape-recorder answering machine breaking down and about calling the repair service and being annoyed at receiving a tape-recorded message in reply. I looked at him in surprise.

"You don't really expect me to laugh," I said.

"You look absolutely devastated. I thought I'd try to cheer you up."

"I am devastated. I feel like my whole life is crumbling."

He waved his cigarette at me. "I don't like to work in my off hours," he said. "Of course, in a sense, your life really is falling apart. But I'd be betraying my professional ethics if I didn't throw out the idea that a great amount of your pain involves your conflicting feelings toward Janet, as well as the reality of her physical condition."

Later, I thought about what he said. I was slowly making peace with the possibility of Janet's dying, opening up the part of my mind that was eager to rid itself of all the past years of doubt and pain. But Dr. Sternfeld couldn't know that he was as much involved in the reassessment of my thoughts as Janet. He had treated Janet for nearly ten years, and he was as firmly wedded to her as I was. The three of us were tied together in a new image of the nuclear family—the husband, the wife, the psychiatrist—and I was as anxious to throw off the doctors, hospitals, drugs, and psychiatric jargon that had dominated my life as I was anxious to throw off the burden of my painfully disabled wife. But I couldn't really erase another part of my mind that was still connected to Janet by intimacy and deep feeling, and I continued to suffer under the weight of my affection for her.

PROLOGUE

While Janet suffered with her coma, my emotions were pulled up and down. Each day was its own peculiar nightmare. I was helpless to do anything but wait for her to live or die. As long as her kidneys continued to function, as long as her lungs remained clear, there was little anybody could do for her. The danger of a coma was the dull menace of the unknown; nobody could say when or why or how or even if she would ever break out of it.

I tried to separate myself from the rest of the world. My mind created its own adventures. Sometimes I created great pillars of optimism and tumbled them down, or I convinced myself that death was imminent, watching my spirits soar again when I realized she was steadily moving toward recovery. I lived mostly in my own head. To give up my fantasies was to give up the substance and control of my life. I wasn't yet willing to admit how helpless I truly was.

There was always a reason to worry. One day, Janet was jaundiced; on another, pneumonia was suspected. One evening, the staff doctors couldn't reattach the intravenous tube, and a surgeon had to be called in to lift out a section of collapsed vein. In hindsight, the problems were never really serious, but in my mixed state of panic and despair, the smallest change was catastrophic.

One morning I wandered down to the waterfront, sitting on a bench in a little concrete park that bordered a highway, watching the polluted river rush downstream and the factories across the bank belch great swells of smoke into the blue-gray sky. I thought about the question the policeman had asked me a few days earlier: why had Janet attempted to take her life? I had given him a glib quick answer then, but I had wondered later whether my explanation of too much emotional pain was an accurate or complete description of her motives. I could only look at her suicide attempt, as I had looked at other fragments of her behavior, as being sick or pathological and having nothing to do with me.

Whatever I thought or felt during the five days of her coma, the facts were that she was slowly and steadily coming alive again. On the second day, she responded to a pin prick; on the third day, the doctors were able to distinguish between periods of wakefulness and sleep; and now, on the fourth day, she was beginning to stir.

"Does the stirring mean she'll be waking up soon?" I asked Dr. Caine when I returned to the hospital.

"It should mean that," he answered. "But with something as complicated and unknown as a coma, you can never tell for sure."

"She can't go deeper again?" The worst fear is of regression.

"No. I wouldn't think so. Let's just wait a few days and see what happens."

On the fifth day, September 15, 1970, she broke out of her unconscious sleep.

There is a theory that talking to someone in a coma helps them strain toward consciousness. Everybody spoke to Janet—the nurses, the aides, the housekeeping staff. And so I talked to her also, sitting by her bedside, watching the Mellaril that still poisoned her system flow out steadily through a catheter and settle, as a dull muddy liquid, into a clear plastic container beneath her bed.

"Did you hear that?" the nurse asked me.

"Hear what?"

"Didn't you just hear it? Your wife just said something."

I looked down at Janet. She was muttering unintelligibly, as if she were talking in her sleep.

"I want you out of here," the nurse said.

"What?"

"Out. Out. Out. I want you out."

I lingered in the corridor, watching Dr. Caine rush into Janet's room, and a moment later, rush out again. I caught up with him at the elevator.

"I'm sorry," he said. "I really can't talk to you now. I'm late for an appointment and I have to hurry out of here."

"What's happening with Janet?"

"Don't you even know? She just came out of her coma a few moments ago."

"Then she's all right?" I said.

He flashed me a wide dazzling smile. "I think we've done rather well. Don't you? Just a few days more, and she'll be out of bed and up and walking around. I think we can safely say that we've saved her life."

I rode down to the lobby and told Janet's parents and my parents the good news. My father walked with me into the street.

"You know, at a moment like this you can really tell how you feel about a person," he said. "I've had up and down feelings toward Janet over the past years. But when you told me she was going to survive, I felt single-mindedly happy."

"I understand what you mean," I said. "I feel the same way."

I strolled down the street, rounded the corner, and entered a dimly lit bar. In the evening, this fashionable saloon would be crowded with the airline stewardesses, young professionals, businessmen, and career women who made up the well-to-do singles population of New York. But now it was dotted with only a few solitary professional drinkers. On the color television set, Howard Cosell was explaining, in his rasping nasal manner, that no matter how many boxing commissions stripped Muhammad Ali of his title, he would always remain the world champion until someone beat him in the ring.

I swallowed one glass of tap beer after the other.

I was light-headed and somewhat unsteady when I walked back to the hospital. The beer had amplified my good spirits, but it had also opened up a knot of dread inside me. I entered Janet's room and stared down at her. With her eyes closed, her breath whistling slowly through her parted lips, she looked no different to me than she had the evening before. But the nurse assured me that the medical signs were clear: she would sleep for a long time, but she had officially broken out of her coma.

I suddenly couldn't bear the thought that my life was again renewing itself. The time-stopping adventure of waiting for Janet to live or die had ended, but I had no reason to believe that the drudgery of the past years, the whirlpool of doctors and diagnoses and hospitals and mind-deadening drugs would not just go on and on again.

But in this last thought I was wrong.

Janet

PART 1

Camp Woodland

I spent the summer of 1960, the two long months before beginning college, as journalism and French counselor at Camp Woodland. I spent my days in a one-room pine cabin called Walden House, teaching ten-year-olds how to type and use a mimeograph machine and how to say, "My name is" and "The weather is beautiful today" in French. I hadn't wanted to spend the summer at Camp Woodland; I had spent too many miserable summers there as a child.

When my parents mentioned Woodland as a possible place to work after high school, I was flooded with memories of morning line-ups and flag-raisings, compulsory swimming, sports competitions, group sings, bugle calls—and the overriding memory of sneaking off into the woods behind my bunk to be alone, to laugh out loud by myself, to cry for ten solid minutes into the damp leaves, to make up for all the being alone and crying I had not been able to do in a whole summer. I was eleven years old.

My parents were insistent, although their arguments were weak: The city is hot and dirty, camp is cool and beautiful. Perhaps even then they sensed the turbulence under my calm. Perhaps they thought hard work, sunshine, and scheduled activities would maintain order. Certainly, being a counselor at Woodland would be fine preparation for college.

I didn't argue with them or even protest when my father spoke to his friend, Jack Gross, the director of Woodland, to ask if there was a job for me. To have protested, to have said no to my parents, would have been to plant dynamite in a natural gas tank. Or so I thought.

I had just been graduated with honors from high school. Larry Rosen, my boyfriend of three years, had been vice-president of the school and was a prelaw student at an Ivy League school. I had been accepted for early decision at Ellis College. I had never failed. I always smiled and I breezed through adolescence with almost no acne. My parents loved me. My teachers loved me.

But I felt as if there was a bomb planted deep in my insides; and I couldn't say no to my parents.

JANET

"Jack says he'll be very glad to talk to you," my father reported after his telephone call. "I made a date for you for tomorrow."

I couldn't form the words that would say "I don't want to go to Woodland," just as I couldn't say, "I don't want to go to Ellis." So I nodded. "Thanks for calling."

Two weeks later I was in Lakeville, Pennsylvania and the world began to grow dark.

Although I slept in a bunk with fifteen twelve-year-olds, I didn't have any direct responsibility for caring for them. I taught French to eight- and ten-year-olds and produced a slick newspaper and yearbook to impress the parents. The children who came to work in Walden House reminded me of myself when I was a camper at Woodland: lonely, hungry for understanding and love. We had fun when we worked together, though by mid-August almost all pretense of work had stopped. My campers would come early in the day, begging the free time from their counselors. We would sit on the porch and read; they would tell a little about themselves, confide their jealousies or fears. Sometimes we closed the little house and walked together into the woods until Camp Woodland, its shaven lawns and pebbled paths, its brilliant flower beds, luxury cabins, and whistle-blowing staff, had disappeared like a dream.

Sitting in the woods behind Walden House, I could hear the muted, familiar camp sounds. I felt alone and strange, isolated in the semidark. I wondered if anyone would miss me if I never came out, but just melted away to become part of the wet leaves and decaying trees that covered the ground where I sat.

I wished Rachel could be with me. But I knew she would be at the lake with the rest of the camp, supervising the afternoon swim. In my mind I could see her standing on the dock, tall and brown, outlined against the sun.

Rachel and I were graduated from high school together, but for four years we never said more than a vague hello in passing. Our mutual misconceptions kept us distant.

When I arrived at Woodland for the week of precamp counselor orientation, I saw Rachel Luce standing in the middle of a small group. Her laughter gurgled up, filling the room. I felt small and mousy, afraid of the laughter and the milling people. I was only a day late, yet everyone seemed to know each other. No one noticed me as I stood and watched from the outside, fear growing in me that I could never share in this casual friendliness. As their intimacy grew, I would be left behind, always unfamiliar, a stranger.

Yet if someone had walked over to me at that moment I would have retreated at the first tentative touch. Reflexively, I would have shrunk back like a snail, back where it was dark and alone, with the sound of my own heartbeat in my ears, in the distance, everywhere. No one approached me.

Self-conscious and near panic, I sat alone during the first counselor's meeting, trying to look composed and wishing Rachel would notice and recognize me. She didn't.

As I watched Rachel sitting across the room, Jack Gross's admonitions about loving discipline and the need for structure and clean bed linens filtering through my brain, a realization took shape. "I'm invisible," I thought. "The invisible girl. That's why she doesn't say hello." But I knew it wasn't true. Nothing invisible could hurt like me.

As the voices of the girls' and boys' head counselors droned on I could feel myself slipping off the wooden bench onto the floor. "O Lord, please don't let me make a noise. Don't let me fall here in the middle of this meeting." I tried to regain control of my body, but it didn't seem to be mine. I felt myself melting away.

"Hi, Janet! I didn't know you were here."

It was Rachel. The pieces in my head clicked together and my limbs were my own again. Startled, I looked up.

"Hi," I said. "It's so good to see you."

"C'mon. Let's walk up the hill."

We walked together, not saying much, exchanging comments about Jack Gross, camp, and the weather. As we stopped, separating to go to our bunks, the tears I had been holding behind my eyes poured out.

"Janet, what's the matter? What's wrong?"

"I don't know," I said. I couldn't stop crying. The words lurched out. "I don't know. I'm so frightened."

Silently, she put her arm around me. We walked up beyond the circle of girls' bunks.

"It's okay," she said. "I'm here. Don't worry."

Little words, comforting, quieting words. I knew she understood. Relief that I wasn't alone made me weak, as the tears poured out.

The nightmare of my senior year of high school haunted me. I hadn't told anyone about it. Just Mr. Arlen, my chemistry teacher. While my family, my world, was splintering apart, I got A's in school. But I cried alone at night and in long afternoon walks on the docks of lower Manhattan. I lied to my parents about my activities so that I could cry my hurt alone and not be discovered. While war raged between my brother and my father, with our kitchen table as the battlefield, I scrunched into my closet, muffling my cries in the clothing. While my mother grieved for Matthew, her lost beatnik son, and gathered her dreams and plans around my life, I was disappearing deeper into a private nightmare.

But no one noticed. And I didn't say a word. I smiled and applied to Ellis. They didn't want to know of the hours I sat alone in the deserted stacks of the Donnell Library. While my sister-in-law Sara sat catatonic at Oceanville Hospital and Matthew came disheveled, always needing a shave, to weekly dinner confrontations with my father; while my parents clung to me, gaining strength from my life, I tried to hold myself together.

"Sometimes I couldn't feel anything at all," I said to Rachel. "My whole body would go numb. When I was with Larry, it was like I was dying inside. It was awful."

"You always looked so happy at school," Rachel said after I had quieted myself. "Everyone envied you. My friend Diane used to say, 'Don't you wish you could be like Janet Moss?' 'I guess so,' I'd say. But I wasn't too sure. I mean, I thought it must be hard to be the best, always. Never to stop."

We were sitting behind the circle of girls' bunks, in the shade of the trees where the woods began. I was squeezing Rachel's hands so hard my fingers were cramped. But I didn't let go.

"What does she really think of me?" I wondered.

"I thought," Rachel went on, "that maybe you might be lonely sometimes, in spite of all your friends. I don't know why I thought that. Just something about you. Something sad that I saw in your eyes sometimes when you thought no one was watching. When you came to meetings your eyes looked hot—do you know what I mean?—as if you had been crying. Diane said, 'Janet Moss crying? That's ridiculous!' You looked afraid, too, sometimes, even when you were laughing."

She stopped, looking at me with questions.

"I didn't think anyone noticed," I said. "I tried very hard not to let anyone know I was having trouble."

"Not even Lisa?" Rachel asked, incredulous. "Not even your best friend?"

"No one," I whispered, beginning to cry again. "All year I thought I would die and no one knew."

"I know now, Janet," Rachel said, very low.

"I feel like a fraud. Everyone thinks I'm an ice cream cake. But inside, under the icing . . ."

I stopped short. I had never articulated any of these feelings before. The prospect of hearing the words, of making concrete the mass of anguish inside me, was terrifying.

"Yes?" Rachel said, encouraging me. "You can say it."

"Inside—" My voice was barely audible. "Underneath was—not cake, but shit."

I covered my face with my arms. I didn't want her clear blue eyes to see me, to see into me. Now I knew she would hate me.

"That must hurt a lot," Rachel said slowly. "To hate yourself so much."

I had said it. Shit. Me. A fraud. And she hadn't left. It was getting darker.

"Hey," Rachel said. She stood up, smiling. "Come on. It's almost time for dinner. We'll be late."

Nothing had changed. The sky was intact, the grass still green. My father once told me how he had expected the world to fall apart or a thunderbolt to hit him the first time he ate bacon. Coming from a kosher home, it was a dreadful sin to eat pork. And when the sky did not cave in, he was surprised and confused. Had his mother been wrong? That was a disquieting thought. Or were the gods just taking their time to punish him?

I had just tasted bacon and it scared me. I had opened a tiny hole and let a stranger in. I had told about my family.

"I love them, Rachel, but they're driving me mad. I love them even when I hate them, but they won't let me be me. They pretend nothing is wrong, that we're still the perfect family. They play this awful game of masks, only they never take them off. I played it all year. I kept my real self hidden. And now I don't know where I am or which voice to answer with."

I said it all. I committed the unpardonable. The Mosses are human. They hurt and they fumble and their lives are a tangle—just like everyone else's.

I waited for the sky to fall. But nothing happened. With a mixture of relief and anxiety, I heard Rachel repeat, "Come on, Janet. It's time to eat. Let's go."

The summer seemed endless. I would look at the clock on the wall of Walden House and find that not even an hour had passed. I checked the time constantly, waiting for the summer, like a long, sleepless night, to be over. Often I felt as if I wasn't even in the cabin, but outside, watching. In my mind I would stand in the woods and look in the back window at the campers working away and singing, like Walt Disney's dwarfs.

It was the nights, though, that held the real terrors for me. Rachel spent some time with me, but often she went into town for beer and ice cream, to hang around outside the drugstore, to laugh and relax with the other counselors. Then, I was alone.

JANET

Every night, dinner and evening activities over, the children in bed, a senior boy would blow taps from a high hill overlooking the camp and the lake. I didn't have to help in the bunk and I could stand on the damp, dark campus, listening to the clear notes of his trumpet.

> Day is done. Gone the sun.
> From the lakes.
> From the hills.
> From the sky.
> All is well. Safely rest.
> God is nigh.

I thought of the children sleeping. I thought of Matthew and my parents. I thought of myself squeezed to desperation in the middle of their triangular struggle. I thought of Larry and how he loved me and couldn't understand my frightened body. I thought how I didn't want to go to Ellis and how I could never face my parents if I didn't. I remembered Matthew's weekly visits, he and my father facing each other across the dinner table, my mother crying while the air between them seethed with accusations and insults.

"Stop it, please stop yelling at each other," I would beg. They never listened. I would slip off to my room, close the door tight, and bury myself deep in my closet so I wouldn't have to hear their screaming. But nothing could drown them out.

I cried every night as I listened to the sound of taps over the silent camp. "He is playing death notes," I used to think. "And everyone thinks it's a lullaby. A goddamn lullaby."

Taps was over; it was Rachel's day off; there was a counselor's dance scheduled in the social hall.

As I had many times before, I stood in the dark outside the lighted building, listening to the music and laughter drift out into the night. It seemed to me the other counselors were always laughing, sharing plans, complaints. Their intimacy frightened me. But I was excluded as much by my own fears as by their lack of interest.

"I don't belong," I thought, and, afraid of being as isolated amidst the noise as I was outside it, I walked on alone, with no place to go.

I climbed the hill, past the semicircles of boys' and girls' bunks, past the red and white stone administration building. The laughter from below and the night sounds around me mingled, enmeshing me as I climbed.

"In three weeks I have to go to Ellis," I thought. "I can't. I can't be what they want. It's no use. Oh, Rachel, where are you? I'm so afraid."

Camp Woodland

I was still walking, beyond the campfire site to a wooded place I knew overlooking the lake. I sat on a tree stump and watched the water far below. It was an exotic substance, that black, undulating mass, reflecting the full moon.

"No one knows where I am," I whispered. "No one."

I lay on the ground, my face in the musty-sweet grass and cried. The year had finally caught up with me. I couldn't run any more. Alone and frightened, I felt tiny and full of pain. I was as black as the night and the points of light that were the stars felt like pin pricks in my mind.

"Please let me die, God," I prayed. "Please, please let me die."

"I'll lie here," I said, "and my tears will melt me. If I lie long enough the dew and my tears will make me part of these leaves and grass."

I wanted just to stop being. Dying would be no more struggle, a stopping. It didn't seem too much to ask. I wasn't doing violence to myself, no one could accuse me of that.

Every muscle in my body was tensed, trying to become permeated with the cold and wet of the ground. I concentrated my cells and heartbeat on becoming the ground.

I wanted to catch pneumonia; then it would all be over.

"Oh Lord," I prayed again. "Please let me die. They're tearing me apart. I can't go on. Please."

"If I wish hard enough, it will happen. It *will* happen. No one will miss me. They won't even know I'm gone."

My clothes and hair were wet and icy cold. "Be still," I told my frozen, squirming body. I tried to monitor the insects and night animals in the grass around me.

I had resolved to be calm, to have faith, and to wait for death.

But the tears kept coming and the sobs shook my body until I felt the whole earth was quaking. For the first time all year I didn't try to stop them. Wave after wave of cries. My body heaving with cries. "No place to go. Alone. Why, oh, why?"

Then nothing. More black night, cold body. Quiet.

Perhaps I had been lying on the ground for an hour. Perhaps four. A shape was blocking out the moon.

"Janet. O my Janet."

"Rachel?"

A half thought, that maybe I was dead, jiggled around in my brain.

"My Janet," she repeated. "Oh, why are you so sad?"

It wasn't really a question, more a litany, as she sat next to me and closed me into her warm dry arms.

JANET

"I'm not dead," I said slowly, each word precise, blunt.

Rachel held me close. "I was in Lakeville, at the movies, with Carolee and Ellen. I left them and came back. I knew something was wrong; I knew I had to come back to camp." She was talking fast, running the words together in a stream.

"Why?" I interrupted her.

"I just had this feeling, a push in me, that I had to come back. When I got to the administration building, I knew. Suddenly I said, 'Janet.' I could almost hear you crying."

"How did you know where I was?" I asked.

"I don't know. I didn't, really. I just walked. And stopped. And listened. And I came here."

"I wanted to die so badly, Rachel. Why did you look for me? Why didn't you let me die?"

"'Cause I love you, baby. And anyhow, it's not so easy to die."

"But how did you know?" I asked again.

"I don't know. I just did, that's all. You're wet, let's go back to camp."

"I can't." I wanted to scream it, to lacerate the night with my pain. "I can't, I can't. Rachel, I'm tired and scared."

She held my face between her hands. In the moonlight her eyes were dark and shining.

"I know you're scared," she said. "All those feelings turmoiling around inside you. Who wouldn't be scared? You want to be what your parents want and you want your brother too. And you want to lie down in a froggy ball and be a baby. You want to be a woman and conquer the world. You can't do them all; you're filled to bursting with love and fury, so you're shaken and exhausted."

I wanted to believe it was so simple. But the forces pushing me seemed unrelated to the mundane facts of college and family or to anything on earth. They seemed cosmic, eternal. If I tried to tame them, even to touch them, the full force of the gods would come down on me.

"But you're strong, I know you are," Rachel said. "No matter what you think, you're strong and you'll be okay. I know it."

"I need help, Ray," I said. "Whatever it is that is tearing me apart—I need help to make me whole again."

"I know you do, Jan. But I'm here with you now. Can you wait till you get to Ellis?"

"I guess so," I said.

"There'll be someone there you can talk to," she said. "Someone to help you."

"I wanted to do it myself," I whispered.

"I know. I know," she said.

"Maybe it will work out now—Ellis, and everything."

"Yes, yes."

I was falling asleep on her shoulder. "Let's go," Rachel said. "It's almost morning."

Ellis College

The freshman annex of Forest House at Ellis College was at 100 Front Street. An old, narrow, five-story colonial building with a patch of scrubby lawn and a creaky porch, it was wedged between two hulking Victorian mansions, and surrounded by tall trees. It seemed almost pitiful, with its peeling white paint and its black shutters askew. "I don't want to live here," I thought when I first saw it. And I wished I hadn't been so adamant when I requested a single room.

Inside, 100 was actually quite charming in a shabby sort of way. There was an airy living room with a brick fireplace and a tattered, stringy rug that almost invited you to drop bits of wool and cigarettes on it. There was a small study room that smelled of smoke even when it was empty. The kitchen held an ancient gas stove, a tiny refrigerator, and could accommodate one and a half normal-size people at one time. Stephanie and Laura, two sophomores who served as surrogate house mothers and received a cut in tuition for their sacrifice, shared a sunny square room right off the living room. All the rooms on the three upper floors were singles.

Mine was at the top of the house, tiny and atticlike, with sloping ceilings, peeling walls, and splintery floors. Almost no light came through the one round window. There was a small bathroom but no other bedroom on the floor. Even in September the floors were cold. It was dark, picturesque, and claustrophobic. I felt like Rapunzel.

"How cozy," my mother had exclaimed. "I'm sure you'll love it up here. Don't you think so, Janet?"

If the college authorities had tried, they couldn't have picked a more unfortunate room for me. Small and isolated, in a small and isolated house, it was the perfect place to withdraw to. Without articulating my fears, I knew I would be more alone than ever, out of the mainstream, with no entry available, should I want to join in.

I hadn't wanted to come to Ellis. I knew an all-girls college in a small New England town was wrong for me. My first glimpse of the sea of blond heads confirmed my fears. "What am I doing here?" I had thought the first day. It seemed as if I was the only short person on the campus. I felt like a small brown bug, common and unappealing, amidst masses of tall blond willows. It seemed ironic and yet fitting that I should be housed in the oldest, most dilapidated and isolated house on the campus with twelve other insecure freshmen, all wanting single rooms above all else.

Sitting on the bed in my attic retreat I felt like crying. I wanted to say, "Mother, take me home, please. I don't want to stay." But I knew she would chide me for my doubts and fears.

"It's a great room," I said lightly. "Quiet. It'll be really pretty when it's fixed up."

"Now don't go spending too much time by yourself up here," she said laughing, as if the very idea were almost too silly to mention.

We both chuckled and went to buy furnishings for my room. My mother chose a green cotton spread, curtains, and rug, and a dull gold triangular corduroy pillow. They wouldn't get dirty, she said, and would provide a restful, understated background.

"For what?" I wanted to shriek. "A funeral?"

But I consented, following her mutely as she hopped from store to store, choosing, buying, exclaiming. A second hand bicycle, a green book bag, a plaid scarf, red tassels for my ice skates. All the trivial paraphernalia that would proclaim unmistakably, "Look, that is my daughter. She is an Ellis girl."

Back in my room my mother paced the short length of the floor in an effort to calm herself. She was exhilarated from the shopping. I was exhausted; my muscles felt as if they were disintegrating from overuse. I sat on the green bed, my body slouching into the corner near the mustard pillow. We weren't supposed to smoke in the rooms because of the danger of fire, but I lit a cigarette just the same.

I knew my mother had something to say. I waited, looking hard at the glowing tip of my cigarette.

"Janet, dear." She said my name as if it were a key that would unlock me. I felt the doors closing in my brain.

"Why doesn't she just say good-bye and leave?" I thought to myself.

"Jan." This time there was a tentative, questioning tone in her voice.

"What does she want?" I wondered. "Isn't it enough that I'm here at this place, that I've done what they wanted? Now why can't they go away and let the steel doors close behind them? Why can't she leave me alone?" I felt myself hardening inside toward my mother. I was afraid I would not be able to contain my growing anger.

"We have to start for home now," she said. "Daddy is getting the car."

Was she waiting for an answer? I didn't know.

"Yes. Oh, is it that late?" I managed.

"Janet." Her voice was rising, with a nervous, desperate edge, as she encountered me closed and unresponsive.

I looked up from my cigarette for a second. My mother was biting her bottom lip and twisting her hands into snaky patterns. Her face was tense. She didn't know I was watching her.

"I know she is trying to say something to me," I thought, "but she doesn't know how. She is frightened. She loves me."

I didn't care. I wanted to be alone, to try to gather my strength for my first dinner at Forest House.

Suddenly, as if she had come to a decision, she stopped pacing, quieted her hands, and sat down on the edge of my bed. She appeared to be looking at me, but I felt as if she were focusing on a point on the wall, directly behind my head.

"Janet," she said, this time softly. "We love you very dearly. We are going to miss you. Try to take care."

There were cracks and tears in her voice. It went through me, this warm voice, into my hardening heart, like a knife.

I felt the need to console her as I had many times in recent months.

"Oh, I'll be fine, Mother," I said. "Don't worry."

"Worry?" She was indignant at the suggestion.

"We have faith in you. We always have. We know you won't let us down."

"Let *you* down. Let *you* down." The words, the absurd, unimaginable words made circles in my head.

There had been a moment of electricity between us, an instant when perhaps we could have spoken. It was over. I was closing up again. She was moving off. She couldn't show her real self to me; she never had. Nor I to her. We were frozen and it hurt.

"I know you must be tired and we really do have to go," she said, as if nothing strange and poignant had happened between us a moment before.

"Be careful with that cigarette, Janet. I wish you wouldn't smoke in your room, especially in bed, dear."

My throat was tightening. I pressed my lips together hard.

"I just wanted to say how much we're going to miss you and we know how much you're going to love school." She stopped. "I'm very excited for you, Janet," she added solemnly, not making any move to leave.

It seemed as if I would never be alone again.

"Excited? Oh, so am I, Mom. It's going to be great. Really. I'm just a little tired, that's all."

The words sounded shallow, unreal, as if they were coming from somewhere distant, not my own mouth.

But my mother smiled. Perhaps that was what she had been waiting for—reassurance. She wanted me to tell her that I was happy, that I didn't blame her for anything, that she was the best mother, as always.

Tears of anger and helplessness welled up behind my eyes. They seemed to fill my body until I felt my head and stomach, legs, toes, fingers, and lungs—every limb and organ was nothing but hot black tears.

I was afraid they would overflow, that I would turn into a huge lake of tears in front of my mother, that she would have to clean me up. Then she'd never leave. I'd have to tell her how it wasn't her fault and console her that her daughter was a pool of tears and try not to do it again because of how much it upset her. I couldn't hold myself together for much longer.

"Helen! Janet!" My father's voice came up from downstairs, breaking the silence.

I touched her hand. It was cold and limp. I was frightened at how suddenly she had moved away from me.

I wanted to apologize to her, to tell her that I really loved her, that it was nothing personal, my preoccupation. I wanted to say, "I love you even though you're pushing me too far. Can't you love me even if I don't want to go to Ellis?"

She stood up to leave.

"I'll come to the car with you," I offered.

"Remember what I said, Janet, please." Her voice was brittle, wavery.

"It's too late," I thought. "It's all over. I can't tell her now."

We said good-bye and I watched the green Plymouth moving away up Front Street. I was on my own.

Afraid to go inside, wanting to run away but with no place to go, I stood for a moment on the green New England street, almost rigid with a sense of utter aloneness. There was no way out.

I took a last look up the broad street, drew a deep breath, and turned back to 100.

A tall blond girl was trying to drag a huge brown suitcase onto the porch.

"Can I help?" I asked, feeling nervous quivers in my stomach.

"Thanks. I sure need it," she answered.

Together we got the suitcase onto the porch, into the front hall, and finally, to the first floor landing and into No. 2, a large and sunny corner room, painted white with windows on three sides. I thought about my dark hole upstairs and shivered.

"Hey," she said, "thanks. My name's Mary Boyd. I'm from California."

"I'm Janet Moss," I said. "I come from New York. Brooklyn." I expected her to laugh when I said Brooklyn, but she didn't even seem tempted.

"I didn't really expect this to be such a tiny house," she said doubtfully, echoing my feelings.

"Well, Forest House is just down the block." I felt knowledgeable, more confident. "It looks like a gothic horror house," I said laughing, "but maybe it's not that bad inside. Dinner's in about twenty minutes."

Suddenly I felt shy and awkward. I wanted to ask her to sit with me at dinner, but I was afraid she wouldn't want to. Even if she said yes, it would only be because she didn't know anyone else. After she was settled she wouldn't even want to know me; I was sure of it.

"I'll meet you downstairs," Mary said, catching me by surprise. "Let's go together."

We all walked the half block to Forest House in a group, the twelve of us almost clinging to each other to gain confidence. I was the shortest, I noticed, Mary the tallest.

Forest House was almost as dilapidated and ornate on the inside as it was outside. We walked through a tremendous living room, furnished with deep old chairs and dark thick rugs, into an enormous dining room. The upperclassmen hadn't arrived, and except for the welcoming committee, we were the only ones in the dining room.

We ate dinner self-consciously, our smacking, clinking sounds echoing off the walls. I sat next to Mary, but neither of us seemed able to manage the appropriate small talk.

"Mrs. Macauley's coming," one of our hostesses whispered as I was trying to wipe the congealed blueberry pie and hard sauce off my upper lip. The French doors leading off the dining room opened noisily and the house mother appeared. She seemed all bosom, covered in navy blue chiffon. Two tiny eyes peered out from behind ancient rimless glasses, while we waited, not breathing.

"I will see you all at tea," she proclaimed slowly, in a booming voice.

Perhaps it was the way she leaned heavily on the door frame;

perhaps it was the deliberate, distinct way she spoke each word. I knew Mrs. Macauley was drunk.

Many weeks later, she had me in with three other freshmen for our formal introduction tea. Perched uncomfortably on a faded green loveseat in Mrs. Macauley's suite, balancing a china teacup on my knee, praying I wouldn't spill it on the lace or velvet, I thought how ridiculous it all was. The ritual appearance before this absurd, sad old woman.

"And when did you have your *paahty,* dear?" she asked, turning unmistakably toward me.

I had been at Ellis long enough to know what she meant. Not my prom or sweet sixteen, but my coming-out party.

"I didn't have a party," I whispered into my teacup, feeling a blush of shame creeping up my neck to my cheeks and forehead, angry that I should be feeling small and ashamed, and unable to stop myself.

That first dinner at Forest House, however, I knew nothing about parties or Mrs. Macauley, except that she was drunk and that I felt sorry for her.

Later that night as I lay in bed in my dark room, looking at the slanting ceiling above me and listening to the unfamiliar creaks and night sounds of 100, I felt calmer than I had in many weeks. I had gotten through the ordeal of leave-taking with my parents. I had survived my first day at Ellis.

"Maybe it won't be so bad, after all," I said to myself, wanting desperately to believe it. More than anything else in the world I wanted to believe that here, in this strange place, Ellis College, I could start new, become someone independent. I could forget about Matthew and my parents, forget about Larry, erase the despair that had haunted me when I was home.

Part of me was already deep in this fantasy of new freedom. But not all.

"No, it won't work," I said out loud to myself, as if to confirm the reality of my life as it was. "I know I need help and I'm going to get it."

As I turned to my side, ready to sleep, I noticed what seemed to be a large, black mass in the middle of the room.

"It must be a trick of the shadows," I thought, closing my eyes. I was asleep in a moment.

The next morning, after chapel, I called the counseling office.

Listening to the buzz on the phone, I wasn't sure at all that this was what I wanted to do. "But I can't make it alone," I whispered.

"Yes," a sharp voice answered. "Counseling office."

JANET

In a few moments it was over. Dr. Kurtzman would see me at eleven o'clock on Tuesday.

"But I don't need a *doctor*," I said slowly, my hand still on the cradled receiver. "I'm not *sick*."

I walked upstairs to my attic room, my head ringing and brilliant colors dancing before my eyes.

"At least I don't think I'm sick. Oh, who knows?" I said. "I just don't understand anything."

Dr. Kurtzman

Dr. Kurtzman was an ugly man. The first moment I saw him slouching into a large soft leather chair I knew I wasn't going to like him.

I knocked three separate times on the door to his office, waiting nervously between knocks for a response. On the fourth, a lazy voice drawled, "Come in." My stomach felt like molten lead, churning and hot. As I sank into the carpet I felt a wave of panic, as if I were getting in too deep, above my head. I closed the door behind me, quaking as it clicked shut.

From the floor-to-ceiling bookcases and muted curtains to the shiny oak desk and leather recliner, everything in the tiny office spoke unmistakably and self-consciously of professionalism. It was designed to impress.

Behind the desk, empty of everything but a clean leather-bound blotter, a glass ashtray-paperweight, a black leather-trimmed appointment book, and a telephone, Dr. Kurtzman sat in his creamy leather chair.

I wondered if he was going to stand up to greet me, or at least nod. He wore a gray tweed jacket with leather elbow patches, and his fat manicured fingers were laced casually across his belly.

I looked at his face. It was soft and unfocused, almost as if there had once been sharp contours and character lines but they had melted, like the details on an ice cream cake, leaving an expressionless mask behind. A pair of heavy tortoiseshell glasses made his eyes seem larger than they were. His hair was brown, combed meticulously across the top of his head. He held an unlit pipe between thick lips. Although he couldn't have been more than thirty-five, my first and lasting impression was of a sloppy, sated, lewd, old man.

I stood unsurely at the door, waiting for him to acknowledge my presence.

"Dr. Kurtzman?" He was still staring at the opposite wall.

"Dr. Kurtzman?" I said louder, trying to muster courage and volume. "I'm Janet Moss. I have an appointment with you." It was more question than statement.

I seemed to have startled him. He took his pipe from his mouth, putting it in the glass ashtray on the spotless orderly desk, cleared his throat, and swirled the leather executive recliner until he faced me directly, composure regained.

He didn't say a word, but looked me up and down appraisingly, short brown hair to moccasins. I felt as if he were undressing me in his head and I shrunk back into myself, toward the door, pulling my raincoat tighter around my body.

He lifted his pipe from the ashtray, lit it with two matches and leaned back into his luxurious chair.

"Won't you sit down, Miss Moss."

It was a line; he said it confidently, professionally.

"Yes, I—thank you," I mumbled.

"Why don't you take off your coat?" He was smooth.

I settled into the small square chair across the desk, lit a cigarette, and studied my fingers. I wished I had worn a blouse instead of a sweater.

I wished I had never come.

"What exactly was it you wanted to speak to me about, Miss Moss?"

I thought of Larry, of myself lying stiff and frightened in his arms while he tried to soothe my cold body. I thought of Matthew, sad and alone, waiting for his wife to speak again, lashing out at my father as if he were to blame for the unfairness and pain of growing up. I thought of my mother and the way she looked at me with eyes that said, "You are my last and only hope." I thought of how I had tried to die. Of always saying yes. And dreams of blood.

"Miss Moss?" His voice was sharp, pinning me down.

I knew I had to say something.

"It's very hard for me—" I began, still looking at my hands. "I wanted—" The sentence hung in the air; I sensed his annoyance as he rustled in his chair.

"How on earth can I tell this sloppy self-important stranger about my pain?" I wondered. "He is impatient with me; he will never understand."

"I'm usually very articulate," I said apologetically. "I guess I'm just a little nervous today."

"Miss Moss," he said abruptly, disregarding my attempt to lighten the atmosphere. "You have something on your mind. I can tell that."

"Yes, but I'm nervous, I guess," I said, beginning to feel defensive. "I mean, I don't know you and it is always hard to talk about private things with a stranger."

Dr. Kurtzman

"I am a doctor, Miss Moss," he said, as if that excused his strangeness, his rudeness, or the lust in his shifting eyes. "You can tell me anything, without fear. I am not here to judge or punish you. I want to help you."

It was the first time I heard those ominous words, "I want to help you." I watched him run his tongue in a caressing circle around his rubbery lips as he spoke.

"A certain amount of reticence is natural in these circumstances," he said, pausing dramatically. "However . . ." He let the sentence hang.

I looked guiltily at my fingernails.

"I cannot treat you if you don't tell me what is bothering you," he said with the assurance and arrogance that come from power. I was angry and frightened.

There was nothing understanding or compassionate about the man sitting across from me. I didn't like him; I saw no reason to trust him. He hadn't once looked me in the eye, although he had been trying to look through my clothing since I came in. I found him personally repulsive. Wasn't that reason enough to account for my reticence in confiding in him? And yet he was implying something much darker, I thought—that it was not personal preference that was keeping me silent, but something wrong, something abnormal in me. It was absurd, yet the implication, or was it accusation, was there as clear as a jellyfish, for me to see. I brushed it aside, but it clung, tenacious, prickly.

"I just wanted to talk to someone," I tried to explain. "Someone who would understand." I was wishing I had the strength to tell him he was obviously not that person, but I continued, fumbling for innocuous words.

"I've been upset. There were problems in my family last year. My brother left home. I was having trouble with my boyfriend."

"Your brother left you and then you had sexual problems with your boyfriend?"

I thought of how much I missed Matthew; of Larry's touches and the terror of suddenly going numb, not being able to feel anything. In one sentence Dr. Kurtzman had made it all seem pathological and dirty.

"I guess you could say it that way," I admitted unwillingly, feeling like crying.

"Do you have trouble talking about sex?" he asked loudly, leaning forward.

"It's not that," I said, wanting to explain what it was like to know you are utterly alone for the first time in your life.

"Were you close with your brother?" He was almost leering, shooting sparks that were questions at me.

"Not really. He's six years older than I am. But that's not why I came to see you." I was in too deep to back out now. I wanted to try to explain about the blackness inside me and the tears I couldn't control.

"But he won't understand. I know it," I said to myself.

"I didn't want to come to Ellis," I said. "I was afraid to tell my parents because they were already upset about Matthew and I thought I would really kill them if I didn't go to college."

The words were coming fast, but as I listened to them they sounded peculiar, trivial, stripped of the love and conflicted pain that gave them meaning. Dr. Kurtzman was writing in a small black book as I spoke. He never looked at me.

"That would have made you very powerful, to be able to kill your parents," he said. "Do you believe you have that power?"

"No. No," I said giggling self-consciously. "Not really *kill* them. Just make them very unhappy. You know what I mean."

"But you used the word kill."

"I didn't mean it literally."

"Really!" He was still writing rapidly in his little book. The air between us was silent, heavy.

"Last summer," I went on, continuing where I had left off, "I tried to kill myself."

"Oh."

"Well, not really. I mean, I lay on the grass and tried to catch pneumonia and die." It sounded so silly and puny as I recounted this episode of articulated despair.

"Suicidal." He spoke the word triumphantly, as if he had been waiting for it, knowing it was there all the time. "I think we can set up a treatment schedule now, Miss Moss. What day would be most convenient for you?"

"I don't know," I answered, bewildered, thinking, what is he treating me for?

"You don't *know* what days you are free, Miss Moss?"

He was gaining momentum. It was almost funny, this pathetic effort of his to find me mentally incompetent.

"He's probably got a fresh Ph.D. in his drawer and I'm his first case. No wonder he's a bit overeager," I thought later as I sat in a luncheonette on Green Street, drinking black coffee.

"I don't have my program yet," I explained. "Sorry to disappoint you, doctor," I said tartly, gaining in a spurt of nervy confidence. "I may be suicidal, but I still have all my faculties."

Dr. Kurtzman

Dr. Kurtzman's face turned gray, his heavy mouth and jaw hardening. He did not see the joke.

"Call me when you get your program, Miss Moss," he said stonily. "I'll see if I can fit you in."

The interview was over.

I gathered my coat and pocketbook, cigarettes and matches, conscious that he was watching every awkward movement, positive he was storing it all up to use in his "treatment."

"Thank you for seeing me," I said, wondering what I was thanking him for, wishing I could walk out and say, "I don't need you, you unfeeling, vain son of a bitch." But I needed someone, badly, and it seemed as if Dr. Kurtzman was the one. My attempt at humor had only alienated him; his displeasure frightened me.

He rose a few inches from his chair, reaching his hand toward me across the desk. I leaned over and clasped it. It was moist and soft and fat. I gulped down a wave of nausea, turned, and left the office.

I didn't go to Forest House for lunch, but wandered around the campus alone, stopping at a small counter restaurant on Prager Street for coffee. I tried to make some sense out of my morning interview with Dr. Kurtzman.

He looked like a pig. "Not his fault, really," I thought, though his physical flabbiness and vanity sickened me. He had no manners and he practically drooled when he looked at me. "A *lewd* pig, into the bargain." Of all the things I had said or tried to say, only the words sex and suicide had interested him. I was looking for someone to help me find my lost self and he was looking for a case.

"Don't go back," I told myself. "You'd be better off without anyone than with someone you have to pretend with. You've pretended long enough."

I knew I could convince myself not to go back to Dr. Kurtzman. In a way, I knew I might be better off. This man could never help me find peace in my life. But he had planted a seed of doubt in me—maybe there was something wrong with me that required "treatment," a need that superseded likes and dislikes.

Everything in me rebelled against that idea. But I needed someone to help me balance my tenuous way through the year.

"We are the only counseling service on the campus," the woman had said over the phone.

Alone, I walked slowly across the campus to register for my classes; I watched the quick purposeful steps of the other girls. Striding past me, they seemed boundlessly energetic and confident.

"They would probably tell him to go to hell," I thought enviously.

"They probably wouldn't need him to begin with," I added, ashamed of my confusion, my weakness, and my need.

That night, trying to fall asleep, I thought about Mary Boyd. I had never known anyone who even looked like her: I couldn't imagine that she would want me for a friend. Me? The city mouse? She could have all of Ellis College to choose from, even the upperclassmen in fancy houses like Raleigh and Simpson. They would come swarming to kneel outside her square sun-drenched room with its red and white curtains.

I put a heavy clamp on my rioting imagination.

"What would she say if I told her about Dr. Kurtzman?" I wondered, afraid she would no longer want to know me, aware at the same time that I would have to tell her if we were ever to be close friends.

Dr. Kurtzman. The name sounded like a death knell in my head. "I'll call him tomorrow," I said to myself. I felt angry, defeated, more hopeless than I had before my interview.

Turning over in bed, I saw a strange black mass in the center of the room. The night before, when I noticed it, it had seemed like a trick of the shadows, shifting and amorphous. Now, it was somehow solidified. All the darkness in the whole room seemed concentrated in that one spot, the size of a beachball. But it wasn't shadow or light. No. It was real, substantial. And it was moving—this *thing* in the middle of my room. Moving toward my bed in a rolling, silent, slithery motion.

I shrank back to the wall, my eyes wide. The rounded black mass undulated toward the bed. I grabbed the corduroy pillow, holding it at arm's length in front of me. But the thing had stopped a few inches short of the bed. In the dim light I could see it, swaying back and forth, shiny, smooth, a solid mass of black jelly.

"What is it?" I couldn't even say the words out loud.

The thing was settling itself on the floor. It was not just an undifferentiated blob, I saw. I held my breath, watching in frozen horror as it waved one squirming tentacle after another, making writhing patterns in the air. I could feel the motion of the air as it waved its tentacles—there must have been ten, fifteen of them—twining and intertwining them in a squirmy dance. The underside of each one was lined with disclike suckers, the size of dinner plates. Two enormous brilliant green eyes shone from the deepest center of the black body. I held my arm over my eyes.

"A squid," I said. "It's a squid!"

Dr. Kurtzman

In a sudden uncontrollable movement my stomach heaved. I had vomited on the bed.

I watched, fascination mixed with terror, as the squid settled itself in the middle of the room, retwining its tentacles about its body until only a single, shining, swaying black mass was visible.

"It can't be," I whispered, as it faded again, becoming more and more shadowlike. "It can't be real. I must have made it up. I must be dreaming."

But there was nothing dreamlike about the vomit on my bed. I turned on the light, still shaking, cleaned up the mess, changed my nightgown, and went to the john. The room looked perfectly normal in the light; I was afraid to turn it off.

"Are you going to let some dumb nightmare throw you like a little child?" I scolded myself.

I turned off the light, carefully keeping close to the wall and climbed into bed.

It was still there, barely perceptible, an undeniable accumulation of rounded, shiny blackness. It could almost have been a trick of the shadows. I watched it for close to two hours, hardly breathing. I closed my eyes tight, trying to make it go away. Still there, swaying slightly now and then, it was in a quiescent phase.

I fell asleep at two-thirty.

The squid came out only at night. I don't know where it went during the day. I would go to sleep after watching it dance and sway in its self-circumscribed area of floor. In the morning light it was always gone.

I knew it wasn't really there, not in the sense that my desk and chair were there. Yet it wasn't a dream or a fantasy either. It was both inside and outside myself, urgently present, strangely dependable, consistent. I came to accept its presence, but I tried not to think about it or dwell on its origin. It was my black secret, a shame that I hid, like Matthew's leaving home, his wife's hospitalization, or my weekly visits to Dr. Kurtzman.

Every Tuesday afternoon at four o'clock, after an art history lecture, I rode my bicycle to the gray stone building that housed the counseling office; each week I stood outside the doctor's office, not wanting to go in.

I rarely spoke about what concerned me: my loneliness, my trouble going to the art study room, the feeling of hopelessness that was engulfing me, the squid. Near the end of the semester, on an icy gray day when I was so full of fears and feelings I thought I would explode, imminently, into fragments, I opened myself to him a bit, out of desperation, not trust.

I told him about Mary, our Friday night dinners out, her acceptance of my going for help with my problems. I told him of the letters I had been getting from my parents urging me to become involved in extracurricular activities. I was continuing to wear the mask of perfection for them; underneath, I was crumbling. I couldn't tell them, though. I knew the time would come, it was near, when play-acting would have to stop, and I dreaded that time. I told him how, even when I was with the girls in my house, I felt alone, encapsulated, untouchable. I had breakfast alone, doughnuts and coffee in the basement, an agony of silence in the midst of chatter and laughter. I was moving away from the world, into a darker private realm, inside me; I was frightened. My voice sounded distant to me; my body, alien. I was never hungry, eating only to avoid questions from the other girls.

"Why are you telling me these symptoms of yours?" Dr. Kurtzman asked, looking through the tent of his fingers at the wall. I had never thought of my unfamiliar and unhappy feelings as "symptoms," and I was startled, a bit confused.

"Do you want me to feel sorry for you?" he continued. "That is not what I am here for." He was bored. I didn't understand why he should be so aggressively indifferent to my pain.

"No," I said, anger coiling in my stomach. "I don't want you to feel sorry for me. I want you to listen to me, help me."

"I do listen to you," he said, his voice lethargic. He added bitingly, "*When* you speak!"

"Your round," I thought.

We sat silent, the air heavy with pipe and cigarette smoke.

"We'll talk more next week," he said briskly.

"My exams begin next week," I said.

"Then I'll see you after vacation." He was writing in his black notebook as I walked out.

It was snowing when I left Dr. Kurtzman's office. I climbed onto my bicycle. In less than a minute my fingertips were red with cold; I had left my mittens upstairs. The heavy flakes landed on my eyelashes, making the world look fuzzy and white as they partially melted from my body heat.

"Why didn't I tell him about the paintings in the art study room?" I moaned out loud. "Why didn't I tell him how frightened I was of them?" The term was nearing its end and I couldn't go to study the pictures.

The irony of having help so near, yet so unreachable filled me

Dr. Kurtzman

with anger and self-pity. As difficult as it was to cope alone, it was ten million times harder to face Dr. Kurtzman's predictable reactions to my pain: sexual intimations and cold, mocking, humorless indifference. I wasn't sure what he thought of me but I was certain he was anxious for a chance to use his training to make a case out of me, and that scared me more than all my own peculiar thoughts and dreams and impulses wrapped up together. I kept silent out of fear. But I was also afraid to be completely alone. I believed, perhaps, in the magic of his *doctorness*. As a man he might be despicable; but as a doctor . . . no, he must have *some* judgment, *some* insight. He must know something more than I did about what was making me into a wreck of a frightened, paralyzed, desperate human being. That seed of a doubt, that despite all my deepest feelings and beliefs he *did* know, was what kept me going back.

I didn't tell him that the squid had been acting up. After the first few devastating weeks, we had learned to live with each other, on an understanding of mutual noninterference, because there was no other choice. He stayed in his place, on the floor; I stayed in bed. But lately he had been cavorting around the room, green eyes aglimmer, lashing out of his territory into mine, flapping his strange, hoselike tentacles, reaching for the blankets, sucking them in part way, then letting them go back, leaving them wrinkled and damp on the bed.

I couldn't sleep. My strength was failing, oozing out of me like blood from a wound.

I still hadn't told Dr. Kurtzman what had happened in the art study room. The art history final exam was only five days off. I had tried for three weeks to memorize the pictures, but I had given up. The last time I went there the art study room was filled to bursting with girls jostling each other for positions, all gazing at the pictured walls as if they would imprint the images on their brains. It had been stiflingly hot and close. I was caught in a narrow aisle between two ceiling-high partitions covered completely with pictures. I was surrounded by hundreds of Byzantine Christs looking down on me. I was impaled on their stern, unforgiving, knifelike gazes. Gathered from myriad churches, brilliantly tiled, they stared at me from the wall. Pale faces, fierce black beards and hair, eyes afire with dark fervor, they furrowed their brows and stared, nodding slightly in unison, became still, then nodded again, accusing, always accusing.

I shook my head to clear it. "It's not possible," I said. "Pictures don't move."

I had tried to make my way out of the aisle; it was too crowded.

Unperturbed, the other girls were studying, writing notes, whispering about color gradations and the lost mosaic craft.

JANET

The pictures were looking at me! There was no doubt about it. Dark and fiery, eyes narrowed, bearded and vengeful, they were watching every move I made.

It wasn't possible!

But it was true. I had to get away. I had to get out.

"Let me through," I shouted, closing my eyes and charging the crowd of serious students. Mouths open in surprise, they parted, leaving me to tumble forward through a narrow path, out the door, into the cold, cold New England winter.

I never went back to the art study room, carrying with me the hideous memory of the Almighty's judgmental stare, trying in the oppressive aloneness of my green room to decipher the mystery of the moving pictures.

"They *did* move," I told myself. "They looked at me. I saw them. I felt them," I said. I remembered the stabbing pain from Christ's black eyes.

"O Lord, what's happening to me?" I whispered. "Am I hallucinating? Am I going mad?"

There it was, finally. The real fear that had been plaguing me and that had kept me from severing my relationship with Dr. Kurtzman. I was afraid that my mind was disintegrating, my perceptions clouding into insanity.

Yet this was the one fear I would never reveal. "Dr. Kurtzman would be eager to pounce on this," I thought, achingly aware again that the one person I was supposed to confide in was the one person who would tear me down, doom me to fulfill my own worst prophecies. So I said nothing.

As I left that last session with Dr. Kurtzman I thought, "I could stop, lie down, and let the new snow cover me forever. No one would see. They would find me when it melted—stiff and dead."

At least dead would not be this perpetual looking for exits, this walking into walls.

It seemed as if I was locked in a triangular room. Dr. Kurtzman guarded one corner door, the stern, accusing Byzantine Christs, another. At the third corner stood my parents, their encouraging smiles fading into stony disapproval when they saw my failing grade in art. All the exits were irrevocably blocked.

I moved on, the white whirling world getting grayer and grayer, less and less real. My body was an ache, a sob, and a yearning, a huge black bubble of pain, growing and growing.

I passed Mary and some girls in the living room of 100 as I entered, my eyes fixed straight ahead, seeing only grayness. I turned the key in the rotted door to my room, locking myself in.

Dr. Kurtzman

I cried and cried, knots of pain heaving and quaking, my body a tight ball in the corner of my wet green bed, as the salt tears came and came from my depths.

"Why? Why?" I pounded my forehead with tightened fists, hearing the punch, feeling only the roaring turmoil that filled my body as I cried.

Exhausted, I fell spent into sleeping, waking slowly to gray morning light filtering through my eyes as through depths of water.

I was flooded with tears, my body wracked again. "Won't it ever be over? Ever?"

I didn't know why I was crying. It wasn't me who was crying, but the pain and the blackness imprisoned inside me. It was the pain that cried and wailed.

The walls were filled with black-bearded Christs looking down on me, burning me with their eyes.

"Go away. Please go away." I begged. But they stayed, impassive yet angry, watching me cry and die in my green corner bed.

It was night again, the dim light had grown dimmer. I heard a knock on the door.

"Janet, it's Mary. Please let me in."

I shrank deeper into my corner, praying she would go away.

"Leave me alone," I said, trying to disguise the tears in my clouded voice. Part of me yearned to run into her arms and cry while she held me and told me it would be all right, everything would be okay, baby.

"I want to speak to you, Janet." She sounded anxious.

If I saw her I knew I would break. I would never finish the letting go. There was a sea of tears still locked in me, pushing against my eyes to escape.

"I'm okay," I said. "Please go away. I want to be alone."

She was hesitating, sensing the contradictions in my voice. "Promise you'll call me if you need me."

"Yes," I whispered.

"I'll see you in the morning, then." Her voice was doubtful, still anxious. I heard the old floor boards creak as she went downstairs.

It was as if my last support had disappeared. I pulled the pillows and blankets over my head, as the cries came again from their ever-renewing source deep inside me.

For the next three days there was nothing but blackness. I slept, waking with sobs, sleeping again when exhaustion overtook my aching body.

I cried and I slept.

Through the thickness in my head, I heard a knock, then a voice.

JANET

Mary.

My eyes were needle slits, swollen so that I could hardly see. I touched my cheek and nose: the skin was soft, painful to the touch, puffy and damp.

"Open the door, Janet." Mary's voice was firm and worried.

"Go away. Please go away." I was spent. I couldn't ward her off forever.

"Laura's with me," Mary said. "Please let us come in. Janet, I love you." I heard a crack in her voice.

I crawled over to the door, my leg stiff.

"Promise you won't make me come out," I said.

"I promise," Mary answered.

I stood up, fumbling with the key as it creaked in the lock. I opened the door slowly, my arm over my face, backing up toward the bed as Mary and Laura entered.

Mary reached for me, her eyes huge with sadness and compassion. I fell on the bed, crying again, as she held me, wordless, comforting.

"The pictures in the art study room . . ."

"It's okay, Janet," Mary said. "Don't try to explain."

"No. I want to tell you." Between sobs, my voice came rusty and teared. "They were moving, the pictures. Looking at me. I couldn't study. I'm going crazy."

I was weak from days of crying, as I screamed, "Please go away and let me die."

"I called Dr. Kurtzman," Laura said steadily.

"What can he do for me?" I asked, months of frustration and bitterness welling up.

"At first he said he wouldn't see you—"

"Who cares?" I interrupted, my voice dull.

"I convinced him to see you. This afternoon, at two."

"No," I cried. "I can't."

Mary's voice was like a salve, warm and flowing, entering the center of my pain. "It's beautiful out," she said. "The snow stopped. It's a white world." She paused. "We'll go with you, Janet. Don't be scared."

I was, though; scared of the crazy sad confusion in my head and the tears that were still coming. I felt as though my life and I were somehow becoming separated, and I was afraid of what would happen to my life, now that I was relinquishing control of it.

I remember stumbling through the knee-high drifts, Mary and Laura supporting me on either side. The wind and sun, reflected on the crystallized snow, burnt my swollen eyes, even behind sunglasses. Under my stinging skin I felt old, as if I were stuffed with gray tissue paper, instead of living, self-renewing flesh. My legs were rubbery and I kept falling.

Dr. Kurtzman's eyes looked pink, as if he had just gotten out of bed. He didn't even try to contain his annoyance at being roused on a Saturday.

"What do you want?" he demanded. I had not had time to sit down.

Trapped in the darkness behind my sunglasses, weak from days of crying and not eating, I heard a small, tinny, distant voice telling Dr. Kurtzman of my ordeal. He listened impatiently as I recounted my story of despair, hallucination, and fear.

He pounced on a moment of silence.

"If you're telling me all this so I'll get you out of taking your exams, you can forget about it," he said, angrily. "I don't know what you expect from me, but I will not be used so that you can shirk your responsibilities."

I was astounded.

"Do you think that's why I came to see you?" I asked. "Do you really think I made this all up to get out of taking my examinations?"

He didn't answer.

"I'm going mad and I come to ask you for your help and you're worried about being 'used.'" It was wild, absurd, unbelievable.

"You must take the consequences of your actions." He was speaking to the wall again.

"You goddamn, cold, unfeeling, self-righteous, egotistical son of a bitch," I said through my teeth.

"He wouldn't help me," I told Mary and Laura outside. I was still trying to take in the scene. "He thought I wanted him to get me out of my exams and he was very righteous and angry as hell. My God, would you believe it?"

I was furious and it felt good, blood surging again in my body, fight and strength returning.

"Maybe you ought to go see Dean Pynchon," Laura said.

"I can take my exams." I was defiant. "That's not why I went to see him. You made me go, anyhow. I knew he'd never understand."

"I know. I know," she answered. "But still . . ." Her voice was hovering uncertainly in the air above my head.

"You can't wage war in secret forever, Janet," Mary said very softly.

"I know. Of course. You're right."

JANET

My parents would have to know. They would be broken, pride hurt at my secretiveness, reproachful and defensive, as if my breaking down were a direct accusation of them. They would want to pretend I had never cracked up, they wouldn't be able to, and they would never forgive me for reminding them of their own fallibility.

Was this my life, I thought, this twisted, intense, bizarre tapestry?

I knew I would do whatever was demanded of me; I would do it passively and uncomplainingly, as always, holding my anger and my desperation, all my real feelings, close and private so *they* could not touch me.

I would watch *them* manipulate my limbs and my life and not protest. But let *them* dare to violate my private secret place and I would kill. I didn't know whom.

How unexpectedly things grew out of control, how like a cancer my life had become, sprawling riotously away from me, propelled by its own force.

I knew it was a tenuous balance I was striving for; to sustain two people in one body.

But I was going to try—again.

I went through the second semester as my parents begged, even excelling in some courses. When Dean Pynchon heard of my problems, she insisted that if I was to remain in school, I see a psychiatrist. My parents paid for it, angrily, hopefully, confusedly.

Soft-spoken, tall, almost completely gray, Dr. James Wyatt was a gentle, innocuous person with a leisurely psychiatric practice consisting largely of misfits from Ellis, like myself. He wore impeccable Ivy League tweeds and had a perpetually vague, questioning look in his cloudy blue eyes. Twice a week, for almost five months, I taxied to his office in the three-story building where I sat for forty-five minutes, my legs curled under me in a large chair upholstered in burlap, looking at him across twenty feet of bare, polished floor, saying very little. Occasionally he would ask how I was feeling or make a desultory attempt to draw me out.

He seemed like a kind enough person; perhaps, if he had shown any real interest in me, I might have opened myself a little; I might have dared to expose my incipient madness to him. Certainly, I was yearning for someone to help me salvage my sanity in the growing chaos of my mind. But he didn't seem very concerned about my silences or very interested in hearing me when I did speak. And the occasional hint of irrational thoughts or extraordinary experiences made him more vague than usual.

Dr. Kurtzman

He was marking time, it seemed, watching that I didn't crack again, babysitting almost, calling it therapy, so that I might finish the year. We were both relieved when the semester was over.

I felt drained, triumphant. I had done everything everyone had wanted of me; I had even come through the year with a B+ average—while I was cracking up. Could there be a more poignant demonstration of loyalty and quiet than that?

But suddenly they wanted more. I had to take a medical leave for a year of treatment—if I ever hoped to return to Ellis. No one consulted me; the decision was made by Dr. Wyatt and Dean Pynchon. And no one questioned that I would need treatment during my year's leave.

Dr. Wyatt gave my parents a list of six psychiatrists the day I left Ellis.

"No, I don't know any of them personally," he admitted, answering my parents' question about which of the psychiatrists they should choose for me.

"But they're all fine professionals, experienced, highly regarded," he added quickly. "Any one would be fine, I'm sure. Why don't you just start with the first." The names were listed alphabetically. "That's David Berman. A good man. He's very, very busy. But you couldn't do better. Good man."

My parents were impressed and relieved. With an outstanding professional like that, how could we go wrong? Or so they wanted to believe. Desperately. They were adrift, too. I was their daughter, cherished, beloved. And I was suffering and acting strange beyond their comprehension or experience. They wanted to know why. They wanted to know how they could make it all better again, make the hurt go away.

No one said to them, "You cannot make hurts of the soul go away. The best you can do is love her. Perhaps this will end in tragedy, perhaps not." Instead, the magicians who were called doctors told them I was "sick" and if they did what was necessary, I might get "well." If they didn't—no one painted in the details, but the implication was clear.

No one had the balls to tell them that human misery of the spirit was a mystery, and that the life force—or the death force—could not be directed with certainty.

It was terrible for my parents to accept this sickness of mine. But at least it was specific. They could read about it, talk about it, listen to the professionals who had made careers out of it. They could know that status and reputations would help their daughter. They grasped onto Dr. Berman's title as onto a piece of flotsam—and they clung to it—to assure themselves that they weren't drowning.

I reserved judgment, though the attributions of sickness had begun to take their toll.

Dr. Berman

Dr. David Berman was a tall, stoop-shouldered man. Our interview, the week after I returned from Ellis, in his luxurious mahogany-panelled office, lasted fifteen minutes, during which time he made it clear he was doing Dr. Wyatt a professional favor, using time he really couldn't spare.

My father sketched in the events of the past year: the distress leading to my consulting Dr. Kurtzman; my failure to progress; my hallucinations and crack-up at the end of the first semester; my informing himself and my mother of my emotional difficulties; my decision to finish the school year; my semester of therapy with Dr. Wyatt; my realization of the need for a year's leave and for more intensive treatment. My father spoke articulately, in an even, controlled voice.

"Who is he talking about?" I wondered. "Not me. It wasn't like that at all; it wasn't a logical, simple progression."

I hadn't said a word.

Dr. Berman swiveled in his chair. Behind him, through a large picture window, I could see the early summer greenness of a park. I wished I could fly through the window, over the trees, and never land on earth again. Away from my mother and father, Dr. Berman, Ellis, myself.

"And do you want to go into treatment?" he asked me sharply.

"Yes, of course," I mumbled.

"Why?" he asked, thumping his fingers on the shiny desk.

"I want to go back to school after this year," I said. But I didn't know if that was true. I had said it to myself so many times the past months that the words came automatically. By June, when my medical leave became inevitable, I had felt an aching, ironic desire to stay at Ellis. I hadn't wanted to go to Ellis in the first place and my freshman year had been a disaster. Yet, the prospect of not returning in the fall, and especially the loneliness I would feel not seeing Mary anymore, left me desolate.

Dr. Berman did not seem convinced that wanting to return to school the following year was sufficient reason to enter into treatment. He was frowning.

JANET

"I've been very confused and unhappy," I said, wondering if that would do.

"You mean you wish to get well?" he asked.

"Yes," I said meekly. But a voice inside me was angry at his words and his tone.

Dr. Berman rose from his chair and shook hands with my father. "I'll be away for two months. I'll see her in September," he said.

The summer was a steamy nightmare. Each morning during the rush hour I rode to secretarial school in the packed subway. I spent eight hours a day taking orders from a hidden microphone.

"Ready for dictation? Ready for dictation!" the recorded voice would intone.

"No, no," I wanted to scream. But I didn't; and the voice wouldn't have heard anyway. It didn't even know I was there.

I ate lunch in Bryant Park: cream cheese sandwiches on raisin nut bread from Chock Full O'Nuts. Alone, I watched the drunks crumpled in the heat on their benches; I watched the secretaries hurrying in and out of Stern's department store. I rode home on the sweltering subway during the evening rush to eat a silent uncomfortable dinner with my parents and do two hours of shorthand homework.

I was going mechanically through the expected motions of living, feeling little beside a spreading numbness in my body, only partially sensing the storms gathering below the surface of my mind.

"I'm supposed to be sick," I thought sometimes. "What am I doing going to school in this intolerable heat? I should be in bed."

It was absurd and sad.

"I'm supposed to be so sick I have to take a medical leave from Ellis for a year; but I'm not too sick to ride to Manhattan and go to secretarial school in this awful hell of a summer?"

Or was "sick" their way—Dean Pynchon's, Dr. Wyatt's, my parents'—their euphemistic way of saying, "Go away and come back when you can behave the way a good Ellis girl should. Good girls, good Ellis girls don't go around making everyone uncomfortable and scared by showing their demons and despair in the light of the day."

Perhaps they all thought they were being kind. Perhaps they got comfort from thinking I was ill—or even believed it somewhat. Perhaps "sick" was a euphemism to them!

To me, my sickness called forth visions of wild-haired women raving behind bars in lunatic asylums. Sick-houses!

In September 1961, it was still hot. The Indian summer heat that barely stirs the leaves was stirring memories for me. All of my friends had left for school. I was alone, riding into the city on the subway, trying to learn to read *The New York Times* standing up, trying to look like a secretary, wanting to tell everyone I met that I wasn't really a secretary, but an Ellis girl in disguise, a poor sick Ellis girl with a mysterious ailment requiring that I work and be treated by a specialist for a period of one year.

My parents told their friends I was sick; that was why I had taken a leave of absence. "Sick" was somehow respectable, though they continued to whisper it and no one asked for details. I thought my parents' friends were unusually solicitous to me when they came to visit, and it infuriated me and confused me. They spoke softly and slowly, asking how I liked my job. "Isn't it wonderful, Janet is working?" my parents would say, while their friends nodded approvingly, saying, "Just wonderful, dear." And I would think, "Last year they were impressed that I was accepted to Ellis College in the spring; now they think it's fantastic that I work four hours a day in a shoddy office as a small-time clerk."

Dr. Berman's office was on the fourteenth floor in a luxury building in Manhattan. There was a doorman and an elevator man each attired in a gray double-breasted military-style uniform with many shiny gold buttons, a gold shoulder braid, and a stiff, peaked cap. They stood ramrod straight, showing a wisp of a sneer when I asked for Dr. Berman's office.

I was twenty minutes early, alone in the waiting room. It was a sunny, many-windowed room with molded plastic chairs, Matisse prints on the wall, a brown and beige shaggy rug, and current issues of *Today's Health, Better Homes and Gardens, Life, Newsweek, American Heritage,* and MD scattered casually on low tables. A small bathroom, with a toilet with a can of room deodorizer on it, a dry spotless sink, a new cake of soap, paper towels, a Dixie Cup dispenser, a freshly laundered floor mat, and an empty wastepaper basket, led off the waiting room. I wondered if anyone ever used it, or if they did, why they never washed their hands; or if they washed their hands, whether Dr. Berman crept out between patients to change the soap, dry the sink, and empty the wastebasket.

I tried to stop thinking my silly thoughts. I sat tense, small, and tight-kneed in a hard chair, holding a magazine in my lap for show. I clenched and unclenched my hands, pursed my lips and swallowed hard to force the growing lump of anxiety down my throat and back to my stomach.

All summer I had been hoping that somehow I wouldn't have to see Dr. Berman. Perhaps he would never return from his vacation; perhaps that whole first interview had not really occurred, I had made it up; perhaps I would receive a letter from the dean inviting me to return to Ellis and I would room with Mary. But the fall semester began and I was still in New York, pretending I was alive, wishing I was dead.

Sitting in the waiting room I thought with a shiver of the June meeting with Dr. Berman. I had felt like screaming, "Hey, this is *my* life you're deciding about. Doesn't anyone want to consult *me? I* think he's a little creep with no manners and I don't like him!" But I hadn't said a word.

I stared across the room at the sensuous curves and colors of a Matisse print, letting my mind float out of my body into an undulating world of reds and yellows. It felt so good.

"Miss Moss."

Dr. Berman stood in the doorway, a tall figure with straight black hair. He was dressed in a conservative dark suit, a stiff white shirt and a nondescript tie. He wore a gold pinkie ring with a tremendous diamond. Even while he stood still, his hands were moving, fidgeting and darting, like quicksilver.

I shook my head to clear it of the pulsing Matisse colors and stood up, dropping the magazine off my lap onto the floor, and tripping over the edge of the rug. His face, as he watched my embarrassed clumsiness, was immobile. I followed him into his cavernous office, wading through the carpet. As I looked at the walls of bookcases, I had an uncontrollable vision of a newspaper headline, "Earthquake Buries Psychiatrist Beneath Books." The image of Dr. Berman flailing his arms and legs helplessly against a mighty shower of psychiatry texts tickled me.

I passed a smooth leather couch on my left, tucked unobtrusively away in a dark alcove. The right-hand wall was bookcases from floor to ceiling, except for a small area near the window; in front of them were three upholstered chairs in a casual group. That was where my parents and I had sat in June. Dr. Berman's mahogany desk, as large as a banquet table, took up two-thirds of the width of the room, standing majestically before the picture window that was the facing wall. At our first interview, Dr. Berman had sat behind the desk, dwarfed by it, speaking to us across its rich expanse, his back to the sun, the park, and the city. There were a few exquisite Japanese vases and modern sculptures placed casually on occasional tables or shelves throughout the room. The carpet was a thick brilliant oriental.

Today he moved toward an upholstered easy chair, which I had not noticed before, to the left of his desk, directly in back of the brown couch. He settled into its depths, while I stood in front of him waiting, like a small naughty child, for instructions from the teacher.

"As you no doubt know, the treatment will be psychoanalysis," he began matter-of-factly, looking over my head toward the door. "You will come five times a week, fifty minutes each session. I will give you a schedule of appointments today. Do you have any questions?"

Questions. My head was awhirl. Psychoanalysis! I only had until next June and psychoanalysis took years. I couldn't carry on the prescribed psychoanalytic monologue anyway. I needed someone to talk *with*.

I *wouldn't* lie down while a strange man sat behind me watching every twitch of my body, analyzing every wish and hate and dream. A man, moreover, whom I barely knew and had disliked on introduction. "I won't," I said to myself. "No."

But his imperious manner left no room for doubt or question. Take it or leave it. Psychoanalysis or nothing. Dr. Berman held the key to Ellis, and we both knew it.

I was still dumb, trying to quiet the racket in my head and calm my thumping heart, when he said, "No questions? Then please lie down on the couch, Miss Moss, and tell me whatever comes into your mind."

I moved mechanically, my legs feeling wooden, hoping I wouldn't crack when I bent a limb.

The leather couch was cold and smooth; my ninety-five pounds didn't make the slightest impression on its overstuffed contours. I lay arched with discomfort on the ungiving surface, holding my arms straight and close to my sides, fingering the heavy old leather, finding a worn spot here, a rough spot there. The wall was to my right, giving some comfort; the gaping room to my left, leaving me unprotected. I could not see Dr. Berman where he sat in his deep comfortable chair, a foot behind and slightly to the left of my head. I couldn't see him but he could see me. It made me uncomfortable.

I tried to find a more congenial position, shifting my body slightly, crossing first one leg then the other, to the creak of the old leather—but the couch would not accommodate me.

"What are you thinking about?" Dr. Berman's cool voice interrupted.

"It's none of your goddamn business," I thought angrily. "You put me squirming on your analytic slide and then you have the nerve to expect me to help you find my secrets? You're nothing better than a psychological Peeping Tom."

"Miss Moss," Dr. Berman's unperturbed voice sounded again, "we have fifteen minutes left. This is your time you are wasting."

I leaned awkwardly over the side of the couch, fumbling in my pocketbook on the floor for a cigarette and a match. There were no ashtrays.

"I prefer that you do not smoke during the session," Dr. Berman said. And I realized, again, that he was watching me carefully.

"I have to smoke," I said.

"I am sure you can survive for an hour without a cigarette," he retorted, his cool voice crackling with impatience.

"I have to smoke," I repeated. "I can't lie here without smoking."

"My patients do not smoke during their analytic sessions," Dr. Berman said.

"I'm the boss around here," he was saying, "and you're just a puny, sniffling subject."

"I can't lie here anymore," I said.

"Please lie down, Miss Moss," Dr. Berman commanded. "The session is not over."

"Please," I begged. "Let me get up." My whole body was shivering. "Don't make me lie here. Please."

Dr. Berman was unruffled, stonily silent.

"I feel naked," I said, "there's nothing to hold onto."

I could feel his cold eyes examining me minutely; I could hear the scratch of his pen as he recorded his observations.

"You're not even human if you can sit there like that and watch me suffer," I said, abandoning caution. "Why are you doing this to me?" I felt the panic of a pinned insect, the anguish of the pin, the frenzy, and the helplessness.

Dr. Berman watched me flail and twitch. For an instant I wondered if his face showed interest or pleasure, if he was enjoying my agony.

"You may get up, Miss Moss," he said brusquely. "The session is over. I will see you tomorrow at the same time."

He had released the bonds. I stood up, surprised. I had thought it would go on forever. Still shaken, I gathered my pocketbook and my sweater together, put on my shoes and straightened my dress.

I was embarrassed at the display I had made of myself, angry at him that he should have caused me to relinquish my self-respect, all because he had something I wanted badly.

Ashamed and enraged, I focused my eyes on the rug, glancing up at him for only an instant. He was reading his appointment book.

Dr. Berman

The year dragged on like a sleepless night. I saw Dr. Berman every weekday after work. My life seemed bounded on both ends by the subway, dirty, frantic, noisy, and crowded, smelling of sweat and garlic in the summer, wet wool and garlic in the winter. I still couldn't read *The New York Times* standing up. I felt, in fact, like a sleepwalker—moving wraithlike from Brooklyn to Manhattan and back again, making stops each day at my office and at the office of Dr. David Berman, practicing psychoanalyst.

"What am I doing here? This can't be *my* life," I thought sometimes. "It must be a dream."

"Janet is working as a secretary," my mother would answer a friend's query. "Isn't that fine?" There was always a desperate note of challenge in my mother's voice and the touch of a crack as the disappointment and misery crept through. Sometimes she cried; and I felt so guilty and angry and sad, I wanted to scream until I would never scream again.

I didn't understand why they should say they were proud that I could hold a menial position that demanded virtually no intelligence or skill. It had something to do with my being "sick," but what?

"Do they think some mysterious and potent forces have taken me over, impaired my mind, and doomed me to a life as a clerical worker? Do they think I'll never be a poet, that it's all over for me?"

Perhaps they thought they had no choice. I was conscious that they saw me differently than ever before; to them, I was a broken dream. They couldn't look me in the eye. It was as if they were afraid of me. Afraid of *me.* I wanted them to love me, to say I was all right, and they were afraid to come close. They were very unhappy. It made me sad.

We rarely spoke, eating strained, silent dinners together each night. I would help my mother with the dishes, excuse myself, and go to my room. Even facing the squid was easier than coping with the empty look in my father's face and the deep sighs of weariness, self-pity, and reproach that issued from my mother.

"I'm sorry," I wanted to yell at them. "Whatever I've done, I'm sorry. If I've cracked your dreams, I'm sorry. I'm sorry. I'm sorry."

They seemed to have pinned all their hopes on Dr. Berman. They had met him only once, at the June interview. Yet, in a few months' time he had become a powerful figure in their minds: the magician-healer who was going to cure their sick daughter and return all of our collective lives to a state of harmony, security, and predictable achievements. He was going to transform their unexplainably sullen and withdrawn child into the vivacious, charismatic leader of former years. Whatever mysterious illness she had that was making her act peculiar and unhappy, Dr. Berman would cure it.

It didn't matter that the hope and theory could not stand up to nonideological scrutiny. They believed it. It was all they had.

I don't know what they imagined took place at my daily sessions with Dr. Berman, but they were hungry for information and reassurances. I answered them in monosyllables, more and more painfully and ironically aware of the gap between their fantasies and expectations and my reality.

Dr. Berman had won the battle of the couch. It had been an easy victory for him, though an agonizing defeat for me.

The second day I had sat myself nervously on the edge of the couch, diagonally facing him. He looked at me, surprised.

"I don't want to lie down," I said drawing courage from unsuspected depths.

Dr. Berman frowned slightly and shook his head with the kind of quick, short motion you use to get a mosquito off your nose.

"If you can help me, you can help me as well if I sit up or if I lie down," I continued.

I couldn't see why he should object. But Dr. Berman's frown had deepened to a black and angry expression.

He didn't even bother to acknowledge what I had said.

"Please lie down, Miss Moss, and tell me whatever comes into your mind." His words were iron thrusts into my body.

"I *am* telling you," I said shrilly.

"Lie down first," he said imperturbably, "you must lie down."

"But . . ."

"Miss Moss. I am losing patience." His voice was well modulated and icy.

"I told you that if you came to me, the treatment would be psychoanalysis. It is an integral part of the psychoanalytic technique that the patient lie on a couch, without viewing the analyst. As analyst I must be objective and removed from the patient's personalized problems and experiences. If the patient has a pathological aversion to lying down as you do, it would seem appropriate to examine the distorted perceptions and feelings that are giving rise to the anxiety."

"I don't have a pathological aversion to lying down," I said angrily. "It just makes me very queasy that you are sitting up and can see me while I am lying down and can't see you. That's a fact, not a 'distorted perception.' It's a question of being in a disadvantaged position."

Dr. Berman

Dr. Berman rose from his chair. "There is nothing to discuss, Miss Moss," he said pausing emphatically between each word.

"Will you lie down now?" he bellowed.

His voice and his presence towered above me. I knew I had lost.

Dr. Berman was red in the face as he stood over me.

"All right," I said. "You win. I'll lie down."

I reached for my pocketbook.

"No cigarettes," he growled.

It was a fine crackling autumn afternoon and I had entered his office feeling invigorated from my crosstown walk. The trees in the city were afire with fall colors. I felt tingly and alive with optimism for the first time in months. Maybe things might work out, after all.

"It's a beautiful day," I said as I lay down. I wanted him to understand how the day had made my spirit rise and poetry sing in my body; how glorious it was to *feel* something good again.

Dr. Berman was silent. Why didn't he respond?

"The air is crisp and everything smells good. In the park, it was like—like—being born again." I was trying to ignore his silence.

"We were discussing your brother yesterday when the session ended." Dr. Berman interrupted blandly. "I am interested in the connection between Matthew and today's odd enthusiasm for walking in the park." His voice was soft and smug.

"It's not odd," I cried. "It's perfectly natural. I'm young and it's a gorgeous fall day. I've always loved autumn. Believe it or not, I'm a whole person, not just a mass of unconscious sexual fantasies."

I paused. Dr. Berman didn't say a word. I wondered if he even heard me.

"You're a cruel cold man," I said, shaking with rage and indignation.

"Are you finished, Miss Moss?" he asked sarcastically.

"Yes," I said, quieting. "I'm finished."

If there had ever been a spark or a flicker of trust or hope, it died forever that autumn day.

I continued to see Dr. Berman, spending my hours lying silent and distraught on his couch while he watched me, sometimes commenting on the sexual implications of my silence or my movements, implying that my behavior was pathologically disturbed; most often saying nothing, for days on end.

Winter had come and New York was cold. The occasional snows turned quickly to slush. The cold seemed to penetrate my bones.

JANET

Each day I rode to work, went to see Dr. Berman, and rode home. My father picked me up at the subway station.

Dr. Berman had become a menacing specter in my life—a stony, judgmental, presence. Only if I offered him a dream or a fantasy was he appeased. He would not tolerate talk about my job or my parents, my loneliness or my sense of aimless isolation. To my parents, he was a saviour—they were waiting for the imminent miracle. For myself, I endured him, harboring a waning, though present hope that if I did, I might still return to Ellis in the fall. I couldn't even contemplate what would happen if I refused to go to Dr. Berman.

I felt as if I were living in a room in a house where the shades were always drawn and sounds came through muffled and distorted from the outside world. I had not spoken about my real feelings for so long that they had begun to recede further and further, eluding me as I tried to grasp them. I was living in an alien body, threatened by darkness and rumblings in the interior. I had a sense that if I could speak to someone I might see through that darkness, reestablish contact with the rumblings inside. I knew I must be feeling something; if only I knew what.

The squid was more real to me than everyday.

Dr. Berman, when he spoke to me, seemed convinced that I was very sick. He never directed his attention toward curing me, though; rather, he sat back and watched my sadness and disintegration with silent disapproval.

"He'll keep treating me forever," I realized. "What does he care? Fifty bucks a throw and he sits on his ass and watches the show. He's so goddamned unconcerned he'd probably sneak out when I was talking if he could get away with it."

Once I had mentioned to Dr. Berman that his unresponsiveness made me feel he wasn't there.

"That's an interesting paranoid fantasy, Miss Moss. Tell me about it."

I wanted to cry.

By January I knew I was not going back to Ellis. Dr. Berman would never okay it. I was too "sick."

I felt condemned to a future of utter, desolate aloneness, working as a menial clerk, boarding at my parents' home, a patient of Dr. Berman forever and ever.

The possibility of finding out what was troubling me was pure fantasy.

One afternoon, before my session, I went into a drugstore and bought a package of razor blades.

Dr. Berman

"I'm going to cut my wrists," I said after fifteen minutes of silence. "I bought some razor blades and I'm afraid I'm going to cut my wrists."

"Oh?" Dr. Berman said serenely. "What makes you think of that?"

"What's better to do on a nasty winter afternoon?" I thought bitterly.

"What does it mean to you, cutting your wrists?" Dr. Berman asked.

"I don't know. I just want to do it."

"Why?" he asked.

My life had crumbled down around me; I was helpless and in despair; I had no future, no friends, a present that was agonizing, and he wanted to know why? It was so pathetic, it was almost laughable.

"Can't you guess?" I asked. "Can't you even try to guess?"

"I want you to tell me," he said. "What do you imagine when you think of cutting your wrists?"

I was afraid to tell him.

"Pain," I started, hesitating. "It would hurt—a lot. And blood—it would bleed." I stopped, picturing my cut-up self in my mind.

"I've been thinking about it for a few weeks," I said. "I don't know what made me think of it first. But now it seems like I have to do it. I wouldn't mind the pain." I stopped again.

"In a way it would be good, a relief to feel something real, instead of this black chaos inside me; to bleed real blood instead of feeling my soul ooze out of me invisibly." I wondered if he heard anything I said.

"I want to do it, but I don't want to also. Do you know what I mean?" There was no answer.

"I'm afraid I will cut my wrists; I'm afraid I'll do it and I won't want to."

I was lost and very afraid, pleading for help to stay whole from a man I feared and despised; there was no one else.

"That is a highly charged sexual fantasy. Tell me more about it."

"O God," I moaned to myself, "he doesn't understand at all. Not one bit."

As the weeks went by Dr. Berman continued to probe my feelings about cutting my wrists. To him, it was nothing but a vivid sexual fantasy with aggressive elements directed, in reality, toward my brother.

He was angry when I spoke literally of my real and pressing desire to cut myself.

JANET

"You are extremely stubborn in resisting treatment," he said one day.

"No," I screamed. "It's you who is stubborn. Stubborn and blind. I'm asking you for help. I'm frightened, and all you can do is talk about sex."

I carried the razor blades in an inner zipper compartment in my pocketbook. I knew I would use them someday and I was terrified by that knowledge. I didn't know why I wanted to cut my wrists, only that the circle of my life had grown unendurable, my head was filled with images of blood, and I ached to be held and comforted and loved.

"I can't go on, it hurts too much."

"What hurts?" said a voice in my head. A very real voice.

"Oh, I don't know!" I screamed. "Me!"

I didn't think what would happen after I cut my wrists; I only knew I had to do it. I had to.

Wet stinging rain was falling as I ducked under the green awning of Dr. Berman's building. I nodded familiarly to the military doorman, wondering if he noticed anything unusual about me. He was busy trying to hail a taxi.

For an instant, I thought that the elevator operator gave me an unusually penetrating look. I clutched my precious pocketbook tighter under my arm, trying to look casual. My stomach was a roller coaster of bubbling liquid.

"One more floor, just one more floor," I said to myself as I watched the flashing numbers above the elevator door.

"Fourteen, miss. Here you are."

It was a day like any other. I stepped off the elevator and walked into Dr. Berman's waiting room. I had ten minutes to wait.

It looked the same as it always looked—airy, plastic, clean. I had read all the magazines that were piled on the low tables.

The tiny bathroom looked unused and new, just as it had when I first saw it seven months before. I closed the door behind me. That voice in my head spoke loudly.

"You don't have to do this," it said. "There must be another way."

"No," I answered, looking hard in the mirror at my unfamiliar face. "I have to. I have to."

I unzipped the inside compartment in my pocketbook and removed the thin package. I unwrapped a razor blade, holding it gingerly in my right hand.

There was nothing but the blade, shining and pulsing. My hand felt soft, a doll's stuffed hand, as I held the glimmering blade.

"You don't *want* to cut yourself," the voice spoke again. "Why are you doing it?"

"I don't know. I have to," I said. With a swift downward move, I made the first cut. Then another.

Sharp pain lined my arm as the blood poured from the cuts. Out of my arm and onto the floor of the small clean bathroom; I watched my blood, red liquid staining the tiles.

I was breathing very rapidly, watching as I took the bloody razor blade in my left hand and began to cut my right wrist. A sharp, swift motion, more pain, blood.

"My God, what am I doing, what am I doing to my poor arms?" I thought.

The bathroom door rattled.

"Miss Moss. Are you in there?" It was Dr. Berman. The door wasn't locked; he had only to turn the knob.

In a moment Dr. Berman was standing in the doorway, his face white, his mouth agape, fear in his cardboard eyes. He seemed rooted to the spot. Blood was dripping from both my arms; I still held the razor blade in my left hand, poised in the air as if to strike again.

It took him almost a full minute to regain his composure. He straightened his jacket and closed his mouth, pursing his thin bloodless lips. His eyes were narrowed, granite, his forehead deeply furrowed.

"Come with me, Miss Moss," he said, his voice crisp and businesslike.

Meekly, the blood congealing on my burning arms, I followed Dr. Berman into his office. He went to his desk, and took a roll of gauze and some adhesive tape from the bottom drawer. I wondered if he always kept gauze in his drawer, just to be prepared, or if he bought it especially for me.

Grimly, with nimble professionalism, he bandaged first my right, then my left wrist, covering the red marks with gleaming white bracelets, sealing each with a piece of white tape. He worked swiftly, his lips set in a tight hard line. This time he did not ask me what the blood meant; but he wiped his sticky fingers with disgust.

I sat on the edge of the couch; he didn't seem to notice. The days of lying down were over. I waited for him to speak. When he did, his voice was even and expressionless; a shadow of fear flickered across his eyes as he faced me, looking, as always, past my head to the wall beyond.

I felt calmer than I had in many months, lighter, relieved finally of the hovering specter of the razor blade. I had done it, it was over.

JANET

Now I waited, not knowing, almost not caring, what would happen to me. At least it would be something different. The circle was broken.

"It can't be worse," I thought. "Or can it?" I was lost in my own thoughts when Dr. Berman's voice interrupted.

"You realize, of course, that I cannot continue to treat you under the present circumstances."

"All this blood on the floor," the voice in my head mocked him. "It's just not good for business."

"I do not know why you have—indulged yourself in this manner."

"You *still* don't know?" This time I interrupted him. "What do you think I've been telling you these months?"

"However, unless you can assure me that a similar incident will not occur . . ." His voice trailed off; he still did not look at me.

I rotated my arms slightly, feeling the pull of the cuts under the gauze bandages. I couldn't assure him of anything and he knew it. God, not psychiatrists, controlled the future. Perhaps he didn't realize that.

He was waiting, watching in fright and fascination as I turned my bandaged arms. I recognized the emotions in his naked fearful eyes: I had felt the same way when I first encountered the squid.

With a decisive movement, Dr. Berman got up.

"You give me no choice," he began pompously. "I shall do my best to find an adequate place for you as quickly as possible. There are usually long waiting lists everywhere, but I do have some small influence with boards of directors." He was preening.

He never mentioned the word hospital, just as he had never mentioned blood or razor blades, but I knew instantly what he meant. Dr. Berman was a man who preferred not to deal directly with the more physical aspects of emotional upheaval.

"I shall want to see your parents as soon as possible," he said. "Please have your father call me tomorrow to make an appointment. I shall want you to be present also. Good night, Miss Moss."

"So that's it," I thought. Strange. Bare. Somehow a fitting end, though. "Good night, Miss Moss."

I walked out into the dark, rainy New York evening and onto the crowded train. A rush hour like any other rush hour for everyone else. For me, I rode a ghastly corridor to nowhere, and I couldn't turn back, ever.

I held *The New York Times* in my wet gloves; my pocketbook, with its opened package of razor blades, under my arm. At the end of this ride was Brooklyn. My parents. Beyond that, who knew?

I called my father from the station, my voice quivering.

Dr. Berman

The wet black gutters shone slimy under the street lamps. I got into the front seat of the car.

"Daddy," I said, praying he might understand and not be angry.

"Daddy. I cut my wrists." Four small words; a bomb.

He smashed his foot onto the brake. I fell forward against the dashboard.

"That wasn't very smart, was it?" His world had crumpled, too.

"Smart?" I whispered, so angry, disappointed, unbelieving, and ashamed I could barely breathe, feeling my unwashed cuts pulse with pain.

"No. I guess it wasn't very smart," I said.

His face was grim, his jaw set in a jutting, hurting line. I thought he might hit me. Or cry.

My mother seemed to shrivel up when he told her, her face growing gray with her own grief. My father put his arms around her, comforting her, and led her away.

We ate dinner in silence.

"Dr. Berman wants to see you," I said, watching their ravished eyes fixed on my white wrists.

They did not speak to me, did not even ask why. Though I couldn't have given them an answer if they had wanted to know.

"It was me who cut my wrists, not them," I thought. "Not them. It was me who hurt enough to want to die. But they don't care a bit about me."

Or maybe they did care, but hadn't the strength or means to step out of their private hells and show it.

Too much raging, too much sadness. No way out. I went into my dark room and watched the squid and the changing patterns on the ceiling.

My parents and I had our final interview with Dr. Berman three days later. We huddled in our circle of easy chairs while the doctor sat ensconced behind his fortresslike desk. The scene was eerily reminiscent of our first meeting; only this time my sentence would no doubt be stiffer. The crime had been greater.

"Well, what's the verdict?" my father asked numbly.

"She must, of course, be hospitalized as soon as possible. I have tried to help her," Dr. Berman said gravely. "But, as you can see," he added, gesturing toward my still-bandaged wrists, "she has been most unresponsive and uncooperative."

"Of course," my parents mumbled. It was almost automatic, their agreement.

If Dr. Berman, from his heights of professional wisdom, had

prescribed joining a chain gang to "cure" my illness, I think my parents might have consented. Would the doctor do anything to hurt their daughter? Didn't the doctor know best? Wasn't the psychiatrist privy to information about his patient that the lay person couldn't begin to understand? This wasn't a matter of choice; it was a question of a sick person and a doctor's informed diagnosis and prescription. Wasn't it?

Of course.

My parents must have had their doubts about putting me in a hospital; just as they must have had their doubts about the wisdom of my five-times-a-week psychoanalysis. But they respected achievement and professional expertise. To have admitted their doubts would have been to open a chink in the iron edifice of psychiatric omniscience. Then what would they do? Flounder and drown. And I might still be in pain and confusion and distress. Love might say, "Don't lock her up"; but what did love know? The expert said, "Lock her up." The doctor had to know best. The doctor always knew best. I was sick. I was mentally ill. I needed "help."

They were desolate, inconsolable, so deep in their own pain and self-doubt they barely saw me at all. Horrified by the depth of my despair, unable to face the implications of my misery, they wallowed in guilt and helplessness, gratefully embracing Dr. Berman's considered professional judgment.

No one asked me what I wanted to do, if anything; where I wanted to go, if anywhere.

The unanimous opinion was that my opinion, if I had one, was worthless. The moment I lifted my hand against myself, the instant I violated the suicide taboo, I relinquished all rights to speak in my own behalf.

No one questioned for an instant the assumption that my violence against myself was irrational and "sick." No one asked, for even a moment, if that act of desperate self-destruction could have been a logical reaction to a barren, dead-end, lonely life. That was unthinkable.

Dr. Berman hid his anger under the cloak of objective psychiatric evaluation and sent me away with a smirk and a sigh of relief.

"I don't know if I can do it," he said vaguely, "but I'll try to get her on the emergency list at Oceanville Hospital. There's usually a three-month wait, but . . ."

My parents looked waxen, miserable, melted small from the tensions of the situation. They looked at me, their looks filled with pleas for understanding, reassurance, forgiveness. I couldn't blame them, but I couldn't support them in their decision, either. We were all on our own.

I listened to them making plans for my life. They were terrified, I realized, by the single physical fact of the cuts on my wrists.

"Haven't they ever wanted to hurt themselves?" I wondered. "Everyone does, sometime or other. The only difference is, I *did* it."

They were so terrified they wanted to get me put away quickly so they wouldn't have to face their own madness and violence as it was mirrored on my arms.

My mother and father wanted me to feel glad again—they loved me. But they could not cope with the explicitness of my desperation. They thought I would get help in the hospital. They were innocents; they had no real reason for believing otherwise.

Dr. Berman, on the other hand, was speaking of other things when he assured my parents I would get the help I so urgently needed. When I emerged from the hospital, I would no longer cut my wrists; I would be helped. Subliminally, if not consciously, my parents must have understood his message and been glad. Glad for me; but glad for themselves.

The interview was over. Dr. Berman shook hands with me. I watched his eyes darting covertly back to my forbidden wrists. He looked guilty, as if he was afraid his mama was going to discover him looking at dirty pictures.

That weekend my father received a call. Dr. Berman had worked with speed and efficiency; his influence had never served him better. Two weeks later he was through with me and the threat of blood on the carpets forever.

I entered Oceanville Hospital, Belville, New York, in Spring, 1962. My career as a full-fledged mental patient had begun.

Oceanville Hospital

Oceanville Hospital was described in its brochures as a "therapeutic community" for young adults. Situated in a residential area of upstate New York, on several gently rolling acres, green even in early spring, its low buildings melting into the contours of the land, it could easily have been mistaken for a country club complex or a suburban-style research institute. But despite the architectural and horticultural illusions and the obstructionist word play, it was, simply, a mental hospital: a repository for well-to-do misfits.

I don't know precisely what I had envisioned, but this was not it. No mad shrieks issued from decaying buildings; no wild-eyed Medusas howled obscenities from behind barred windows. In fact, the buildings were new, bright-looking brick structures, and there were no bars that I could see on any windows. We passed nine people playing volleyball in the blustery afternoon air; groups of young men and women in twos and threes strolled around the lushly landscaped grounds. They didn't look crazy. They didn't even look odd. It was very quiet.

My father carried my small suitcase as we looked for the admissions building. He held his free arm around my mother. I walked close but alone, continually conscious, as I had been in the past few weeks, that I was the cause of their dreadful pain.

My own fears and anxieties, in fact all of my feelings, seemed to have receded so far away that most of the time I felt nothing but an emptiness, resembling hunger, verging now and then into the yawning desire to kill myself, retreating again to become an irresistible fatigue of body and mind. I would wake from dreams more vivid than wakefulness, my wrists throbbing with pain, my body wracked with sobs to face the light, my parents, and my imminent hospitalization—and the emptiness would return. It blotted out everything and left me dull, unable to articulate any words through the tissue paper haze in my head. I acted drugged, but no one seemed to think it odd. My parents watched me with dry-eyed sadness, whispered to each other, cried, and spoke in funereal tones. But they didn't seem surprised.

I couldn't even gather the strength or clarity to run away or cut my wrists. The world was made of gray cotton. The administrative processes had been set in motion; there was no way to stop what was happening; all the rueing in the universe could not turn time back to pre-Dr. Kurtzman. Through the mists in my head I tried to pinpoint the exact moment I had lost control of my life. Was it when I accepted Dean Pynchon's judgment of my disability? When I gave in to Dr. Berman? When I cut my wrists? "It must have been the wrists," I thought. But why did they all come down on me with such a vengeance? It was *my* wrists, after all. My blood. My cuts. My life.

I lost the hazy train of my thought, reemerging to face a robust, pleasant, plumpish woman with gray hair, a starched white uniform, and the largest bosom I had ever seen.

"Mrs. Rooney will take you to your ward," I heard a saccharine voice explain.

"Where have I been?" I wondered, frightened that I had withdrawn from the admissions ordeal so completely, at the same time impressed by my ability to do so, storing the knowledge away, certain I would use it sometime.

"What a pretty petite young lady," Mrs. Rooney said, taking my hand. Her voice was honey rich; her uniform crackled as she moved.

I withdrew my hand with a jackknife pull.

"I can walk by myself, thank you," I said. "I am not a child. Or an invalid."

My parents sat near the desk, watching me with unconcealed misery. Two shadowy figures, encapsulated in their private pain, they were the authors of the scene, yet they seemed unable to bear that truth. Or perhaps it was the knowledge of their unwilling role that was causing them such grief.

Mrs. Rooney was unruffled.

"Of course you can walk by yourself," she said, gathering together assorted receipts, papers, and a manila folder with my name on it, bustling all the while.

"Come with me, Janet." She seemed genuinely warm, if a bit condescending. I was terrified. The door from the admitting office opened onto a hallway that branched off immediately, leading in several directions to the unknown recesses of the hospital.

I hung back, still holding my violated hand against my chest, fighting off the acid-sharp tears and swells of nausea that were rocking my body. "Where is she taking me?" I thought, unable to visualize anything but a black cold death pit.

"Say good-bye now, dear," Mrs. Rooney's cheerful voice directed.

Mrs. Lester, the admitting lady, was looking with pity and empathetic concern at my parents. My mother had begun to cry.

JANET

"When will we be able to see her?" my mother asked pitifully. They were waiting, I realized, for me to be taken away.

"That will be up to her doctor," Mrs. Lester answered. "Usually new patients don't get any visitors for at least two weeks. We want Janet to adjust to her new home."

New home! The euphemism made me want to puke.

"Two weeks!" my mother sobbed. My father held her tighter.

"Now that's not so long, Mrs. Moss," Mrs. Lester reassured her. "It's all for the best."

"But two weeks!"

I couldn't watch any longer.

"Thank God," I heard my own true self say. "Thank God I won't have to see them for two weeks." Even the clay of the death pit would be a relief after that closed web.

I heard my father say to my mother, "Try to keep calm."

"My pocketbook!" I stopped, realizing its loss kinesthetically. "Where's my pocketbook? And my suitcase?" Everything I cared about was packed in the suitcase—my e. e. cummings anthology, my Paul Klee postcards, all of my earrings, letters, and notebooks. My English hairbrush and my black turtlenecks. And the pocketbook. That big, floppy, worn, leather carryall—with its endless supply of cigarettes and its treasure pockets filled to bursting with papers, keys, pictures, and books. I never stirred without it. It had disappeared.

"We have your things dear," Mrs. Rooney cheerily assured me. "We have everything right here." She was pointing to the corner of the room where my valise, pocketbook, and coat were piled.

"Well?" I asked, annoyed. "May I have it please?" How dare they take away my pocketbook like that.

"Oh no, dearie," Mrs. Rooney answered. "Everything must be checked and marked first. You'll get it later, when the clothing room sends it up to the ward."

"But why?" I demanded.

"Everything must be checked," Mrs. Lester intervened, "to make sure you have nothing you could hurt yourself with."

I glanced guiltily at my wrists.

"But there's nothing in my bag," I protested. "Look, you can see for yourself."

"Also," she continued, "it discourages stealing to have all personal possessions clearly marked."

My mouth was open, my jaw slack.

"Don't bother your head, dear," Mrs. Rooney said. "You'll get it all later."

"But my cigarettes, can't I take my cigarettes and lighter?"

"Sure you can take your cigarettes, dear." Mrs. Rooney was like a big mother bird. I was her chick and she seemed to hover with growing maternity as the situation worsened for me.

"Not your lighter, though."

I felt a growing edge of panic. "Where are they taking me?" I wondered again.

"I always carry my lighter," I said, feeling petty in my protests, yet sensing that I was fighting to retain something larger than a cigarette lighter.

"If your doctor agrees, you can have your lighter."

The subject was obviously closed. I felt powerless and somehow naked without my pocketbook. All I could think of was how I would wipe my nose if I sneezed or cried: the tissues were in my bag.

I gave a last look at my parents, a somber and pathetic pair, mourning my demise prematurely, I thought. It was with relief that I allowed Mrs. Rooney to guide me out of the room.

"You'll like Mid II," she chattered, as we walked through the maze of halls, passing in and out of several different buildings, all named Middleberg Something, containing doctors' offices, a gymnasium, a game room, an occupational therapy area, a cafeteria, and more offices. "There are lots of people your own age." Mrs. Rooney, I noticed, carried a large ring of keys attached to her belt, but she never used any of them. All the doors were open.

"Hi, Rooney," a young girl called. She was sitting on the floor outside the door that said Middleberg II.

"I didn't know you got your privileges back, Carol," Mrs. Rooney said, stopping to speak to the girl.

"Well, I didn't—exactly," she answered mischievously.

"Then what are you doing out here alone? Does Mrs. Petra know you're here?"

"Oh, come on, Rooney. I'm just sittin', that's all."

"Let's go, Miss Carol."

The girl got up in one jerky movement. She could have been beautiful, I thought. Her hair was thick and black, her skin white. But she was very thin and her exquisite black eyes seemed pushed from her head. Her hands were like birds—darting and tiny—in perpetual fidgety motion. I saw, with a lurch of fascination, that she had gauze bandages on her wrists.

> *Rooney, Rooney, stern and stable,*
> *Wished that she was Betty Grable.*

Carol giggled, as she mocked Mrs. Rooney.

"You better be careful now, Miss Carol Cohen." Mrs. Rooney was serious, but I could sense the humor and affectionate concern in her tone. "Or you're going to be in *real* trouble one of these days. And I don't mean just having your privileges taken away."

"Why, what do you mean, Mrs. Looney Rooney?"

Carol was dancing around us, giggling. But there was such pain in the hushed velvet depths of her eyes, it made me want to cry.

"Never you mind now. You know what I mean."

I didn't, though the hint of dark threats hung in the air.

"Who's your friend, Rooney?" Carol asked in a singsong voice. "You bringing us a new victim?"

"This is Janet Moss. Try to be nice, Carol. Remember how scared you were when you first came? You were shaking all over."

"Hi! I'm Carol Cohen, resident hebephrenic. What are you?"

"Carol, don't scare the girl!"

"I'm not scared," I said defiantly, summoning up my courage.

"Well, what are you?" she demanded again.

"What do you mean?" I asked. "I don't understand."

We walked through the front corridor of Mid II, Carol jogging alongside. Ahead of us I could see a large open area with people milling about. There were doors, some closed, some partially open, on both sides of the hall. Bedrooms, I guessed. The corridor extended to the open area and continued past it, ending, in the distance, in a door with a lighted EXIT sign above it. Halfway down we passed a double swinging door on the left. I caught a glimpse of white tile and a row of sinks.

"Your diagnosis. What's your diagnosis?" Carol asked impatiently.

We were approaching the open area and the milling people.

"I don't know," I said, confused. "I mean, I don't have one—I don't think."

"You don't *have* one?" Carol's voice reached a near-shriek. "Hey, you guys." She spoke to the group of people clustered around a tremendous circular wooden desk with chairs and tables in the open center. "We have a real novice; she doesn't even have a diagnosis yet!"

Two women in stiff nurses' uniforms sat, judiciously writing in notebooks with green lined paper. They were either deaf or extraordinarily absorbed in their work, I thought, because they didn't seem to notice the hullaballoo around them. A serious young man with a moustache was writing in a looseleaf book with aluminum covers; when closed, it said "Orders." I wondered who he was, what kind of orders he was writing and for whom.

We stopped at this oddly shaped desk while Mrs. Rooney walked through an opening in its side, past the nurses and the serious young man, into a room with a clouded glass door that said "Nurses' Station. Staff Only."

"I have to see my doctor today," a tall, distraught woman was saying.

"Are you sure I didn't get any mail?" a girl asked.

"Dr. Zeno said he would order my pass," another girl said insistently. "Come on. Check again. I know he said it."

"Do I have full grounds yet?"

"I'm not taking my sleeping medication tonight."

"What's for dinner?"

"Who's on rounds tonight? I have to see a doctor," a red-haired young woman with a lined face was moaning.

"O God, O God, O God." A young girl stood with her back to the desk and her eyes closed, repeating the cry over and over.

No one seemed to notice me except Carol, who kept jiggling around, shrieking with laughter, and trying to attract attention to herself.

Finally, she took my arm, pulling me toward the quieter open area across the hall from the nurses' station. The three walls were lined with couches and easy chairs. A television set that no one was watching, played from a precariously angled shelf, high on a wall. Occasional coffee tables held magazines and overflowing ashtrays. Late-afternoon sun slanted through the beige patterned curtains, making shifting ghostly designs on the scuffed linoleum. Impressionist prints hung on the clean, green painted walls. Every effort seemed to have been made to make the room homey and comfortable. Yet, in spite of everything, a loveless, institutional air pervaded it like the persistent odor of a public toilet.

At least it was quiet, removed from the noisy group that was trying vainly to get the attention of the starched scribes behind the desk in the nurses' station. "Why don't they answer?" I wondered.

"Esther, Jessie," Carol called to two girls who were sitting on the floor sharing a box of cookies and a cigarette.

"A new patient. Rooney just brought her."

They looked up, vaguely interested.

Carol pushed me over toward the girls. "She doesn't have a diagnosis," Carol whispered, waiting for their reaction.

"Then how'd you get here?" the shorter girl asked somewhat challengingly.

JANET

I was suddenly aware that I was an outsider and that I would have to prove myself acceptable and trustworthy. This was going to be my new home, this hospital, and it was urgently important that these people like me. What would make them like me? I felt like a stranger in a foreign country, moving tentatively, on instinct alone. Not knowing the language or the customs or the unique prohibitions of the land, I was praying I would not make a fatal error and irrevocably alienate the people.

"I cut my wrists," I said, "and my doctor didn't want to treat me anymore."

"Let's see," the other girl said. This was Jessie. She was pretty, in an earthy, freckled way.

I turned my wrists upward, exposing the slim, brownish scars.

Two more people, a young man with red hair and a beard and a heavy, sallow-skinned girl, had joined us. Everyone was looking at my wrists.

"They put you in here for *that?*" Jessie said with a deprecating wave. "For a couple of scratches? Jeezus, you must be pretty fragile." She laughed but it came out as a snort.

"It was more than just scratches," I said defensively. "They're healing now. But they were deep cuts. And they bled a lot."

"You call that cuts? Even I've got better than that."

She thrust her arms toward my face. There were shiny short scars, each one in a hollow of skin, all over her lower arms. I imagined with a shiver the sharp jabs that had made those marks. Before I could say anything she pulled her arms away.

"Even Carol has scars," said Jessie. "But you haven't seen anything yet. Show her your arms, Sandy. Come on, let her see a professional job, show her your arms."

The tall, brown-haired girl with the drab lifeless skin shook her head. She wore blue jeans and a faded flannel shirt. Her hands were dirty and the ends of her fingers were raw where she had bitten her nails almost to the cuticles.

"Did you have stitches?" Jessie's friend Esther asked.

"No," I had to admit.

"The first time you cut your wrists?" Carol asked.

"Yes," I said, aware that their intense and undisguised interest in my wrists was an exquisite relief after the weeks of silent avoidance and guilty looks. They were trying to underplay it, trying to test me; I could tell that; trying to make my scars seem insignificant. But I felt I had gained a certain entree among them just the same. Instead of the mark of shame they were at home, to be hidden and whispered about, these cuts of mine were almost a status symbol here.

"Did you pass out?" Jessie asked.

"Who found you?"

"What did you use? A blade?"

The questions came in a torrent as three more patients joined the group.

Piece by piece I told my story. They were really interested! I was staggered, thinking, with a mixture of pleasure and anxiety, that I felt as if I belonged. I felt at ease with these people. When I told about Dr. Berman and how he sent me home on the subway alone, Esther burst out, "The cock-sucking bastard. He ought to be hung by his balls." Everyone laughed. It was the first time I had even smiled in weeks and my facial muscles felt stiff from disuse.

"But he never tested you or anything?" Jessie asked, still skeptical, returning to the earlier question of how I had arrived at Oceanville without being diagnosed.

"I guess they'll give you the full treatment, then," Esther said thoughtfully. "You're uncharted territory, a real challenge."

"What do you mean, 'the full treatment'?" I asked, frightened.

"Oh, it's nothing. Just tests. Hours and days of weird tests. Drawing pictures, telling stories, matching words. Then all the doctors get together and add up the results and find the category they like best and give you a case number and whammo: you're diagnosed. Forever and ever. A new identity. A new you."

Jessie's voice was bitter and sarcastic; no one was laughing anymore. Suddenly Carol burst forth.

"What do you think they'll give her, Sandy?"

Everyone turned to the large-boned girl with the coarse skin who would not show her arms. She had not spoken at all.

"Too early to tell," she answered. "Probably some kind of schiz."

They all nodded, some more doubtfully than others.

"No," I wanted to scream. "I'm not. I'm not anything but me. I don't want to be diagnosed."

My knees felt wobbly, the walls were swaying. I wanted only to sink to the floor in a limp mound, fold up my body, my arms above my head, and release the rumbling storm of tears that swelled inside me; go to sleep, and wake in my own bed to find the interrogation over, my arms flawless and Oceanville Hospital only a bad night dream.

"Okay, girls, don't suffocate her." Mrs. Rooney pushed her way through the group. She was holding the folder with my name on it.

JANET

"Come with me, Janet," she said with bright authority. "The doctor will examine you now."

"What doctor? Why?" Questions buffeted each other in my head. "There's nothing wrong with me," I said.

"Come, dear. It's late in the afternoon and the doctor is very busy. We musn't waste his time."

My heart was thumping, resounding with such force in my chest, I looked to check if anyone had noticed. The group of patients had melted off. I could see only Esther and Jessie back in their spot on the floor, eating cookies and smoking cigarettes.

I followed Mrs. Rooney nervously into a small, white room opposite the nurses' station. It had a thick wooden door with an upper and lower section, each hinged to allow it to be opened separately. Mrs. Rooney opened the whole door. There were three locks. I could see a possible purpose in opening just the upper part; but unless there was a speakeasy inside, I couldn't conceive why anyone would use the lower. "Maybe they employ midgets?" I thought. "Or it's for the ward dog? Or Stuart Little has his medical degree?" I felt like laughing. The image of a minuscule white-coated doctor slipping into his undersized office was very comical.

The doctor was the tall young man who had been writing orders in the metal-bound book a few minutes before. He asked me to take off my clothes, put on a hospital gown, and sit on a cold metal chair while Mrs. Rooney stood by the locked door. He tried to conceal his unease with a self-conscious chatter that made him sound like a wind-up toy. He was very young, I thought. In his late twenties probably, and he used his stethoscope and tongue depressor with earnest absorption.

He took my pulse, trying not to touch the healing scars while at the same time pretending they weren't there. Eyes, ears, nose, throat, chest, heart, respiration, reflexes, blood pressure—all normal. I could have told him that and saved all this trouble.

Had I ever had chicken pox? Mumps? Other childhood diseases? My appendix removed? Tonsils? I revealed my medical history, my childhood of constant sore throats and colds. "Oh yes. I had dysentery when I was three years old."

"Dysentery?" the doctor repeated. "Where did you get dysentery?"

"In Pennsylvania," I answered, "from eating dirty berries."

Rooney and the doctor exchanged doubtful looks, nodding slightly to each other. They didn't believe me.

"I had mononucleosis, too. In high school," I said.

"Are you sure it was mono, not just another sore throat?"

"Yes, I'm sure." I saw Rooney make a question mark on the paper.

"Do you have any scars?" the doctor asked.

"No. I mean, I guess you'd call them scars." I reached out my arms.

"How did you get these?" he asked, his eyes riveted on the floor.

"I cut myself with a razor blade," I said.

"How long ago?" he asked.

"A few weeks ago."

He cleared his throat. "They're healing nicely. In a little while you'll hardly be able to see them. Do you have any other scars?"

"No," I said. Rooney and the doctor examined my body, finally satisfying themselves that there were no secret scars anywhere.

"Please lie down on the table, Janet," the doctor said, indicating a long metal examining apparatus in the middle of the room. "Put your feet in the stirrups. I won't hurt you. Have you ever had an internal examination?"

"No. I don't want to," I said. Stirrups? What was I? A horse?

"Now, dear," said Mrs. Rooney, standing on the right side of my chair. "It will only take a moment."

"No." I started to scream. "Don't make me. Please." Panic at my helplessness, remembrances of the torture of Dr. Berman's couch, all the anguished fears about my body and my nakedness poured forth like the eruptions from a volcano.

"Don't make me do it," I was crying, as I plummeted through the swirling space of the chrome and white room.

The snap of a lock. The door opened and shut. The snap of a lock. Another white-clad woman, Mrs. Rooney's mirror-image, on my left. Another doctor, robed in white, standing, sober, at the foot of the long gleaming metal table.

Everyone was clothed, standing, in white. They all wore heavy rings of jangling keys. I was naked except for a grayish diaphanous hospital gown, sitting, tiny and cold, amid the towering white figures and the glass cases of sharp polished instruments.

"They're going to hold me down on that table while that man sticks that huge shiny thing up my vagina," I thought. "They think I'm crazy. I can scream and scream and they're still going to do it."

I closed my eyes, taking deep, deep slow breaths. The accumulating oxygen made my brain light and floaty.

I could feel the two uniformed women leading me to the table. I could feel the legs moving woodenly under me. They weren't mine.

"Now you just lie down, dear. That's a good girl. It will be over in a moment."

JANET

The table, through its rough paper covering, was cold. High in the air they fitted my feet into the unyielding metal restraints. The two nurses each held one hand in an iron grip. "An animal ready to be butchered, that's what I am." My eyes were closed, my senses blurred from my deep, concentrated breathing. I was trying to blot it all out the way I had in the admitting office a few hours earlier.

It wouldn't go away.

I heard, in the distance, a single-noted wail, high, prolonged, a cry of agony and loss. It was coming from me.

"What are you doing to me?" I whispered.

"Nothing."

It's all in your mind they cried in unison.

"O God, please forgive me if I've offended you. Please help me," I cried to the encroaching walls.

"This won't hurt," I heard.

"Please let it be over," I prayed.

A column of ice moved through me. One sharp, slicing pain. "Damn it," said the doctor. Fire between my legs.

A scream.

"It's all over, dear," Mrs. Rooney's voice came motherly and concerned. "Now that wasn't so bad, was it?"

"What did you do?" I gasped. "What did you do to me?"

"It was nothing," he said. "Nothing."

"Here's your blouse, dear. Let's get ready for dinner. I'll show you your room. We'll do the rest tomorrow."

"The rest?" I thought. "What have I done to deserve this?"

I emerged from my examination shaken and disoriented. The pain in my lower abdomen had subsided, though I continued to bleed slightly and have occasional cramps for a few hours.

I was leaning drunkenly on Mrs. Rooney's broad shoulder, as she supported me in the walk down the hall, past the nurses' station, to my room. The hallway ended in an exit that was locked at night.

"What did he do to me?" I kept asking.

"Now don't you worry your head, dear," she kept answering. "It was nothing."

"It wasn't nothing," I mumbled. "He hurt me. That's not nothing."

My room was green. Green bedspread, green curtains, green lockers. The walls were painted green, that special sour color that depresses the senses and sickens the heart. It is the color of hopelessness. You can see it in hospitals and institutions and tenement hallways, wherever people are in pain. I had seen it only when I visited my grandmother in the hospital when she was dying. And in the toilets of the New York City subways.

There were two single beds in the room, their metal headboards against the right hand wall. I chose the one in the corner, farthest from the door. Two low wooden tables stood between the beds. Small lamps, attached to the wall, provided individual light for each person. Several feet away from the beds, a mirror hung on the wall. A series of drawers on each side of it served as a dresser. There was one window, thickly screened, on the same wall as my bed. No closets, I noticed. Just two green metal lockers, on the right hand wall, near the door as you entered the room, parallel to the beds.

Mrs. Rooney unlocked one locker although I had nothing to put in it.

I lay down on my hard green bed, crying from the relief of being alone, finally, refeeling the unexpected pain that had seemed to shoot from my groin through my central intestines.

"What did they do to me?" I whispered to myself again and again.

A voice, close, at once husky and melodious, said, "They must have taken a Pap smear. It's a scraping of your cervix to test for cancer. It's not supposed to hurt at all, but some of the young doctors aren't very skillful and they hurt a lot."

A young girl was standing near my bed. I hadn't heard her come in.

"Who are you?" I asked, half afraid, but sensing somehow that she was not an enemy.

"Oh, I'm sorry," she answered. "Maggie Ellman. I heard you crying. Thought I'd come in. Tell you what happened. You're not alone, you know."

She seemed shy, yet oddly forward, matter-of-fact even, as if the fact that we were in a mental hospital and that I had just had my insides assaulted didn't faze her very much. I wanted to hug her for the humanness that had pushed her to come and comfort me.

"It was awful," I said. "They wouldn't tell me what they were doing. They wouldn't listen to me. They kept saying, 'It's nothing, It's nothing,' and then they held me down and put that icy cold thing in me."

"A speculum," Maggie said. "Are you a virgin?"

"Yes," I answered, embarrassed and ashamed. "Did I make an ass of myself with all that screaming?"

"Oh, no. You weren't bad. Sometimes, with new patients you think there's really esoteric torture going on in there."

JANET

"Couldn't they have told me what they were doing? I mightn't have been so scared. Couldn't they have waited till I was a little settled?"

" 'Course they could," Maggie answered shortly. "But they didn't have to, so why should they? It would be more trouble for them to examine you the next day, though Lord knows it's trouble for them to hold you down, screaming and squirming. Maybe they enjoy it."

She looked thoughtful. "This way they can say you acted irrationally. You screamed and cried for a dumb internal exam. But what do you expect from a mental patient anyway?"

I didn't quite know what she meant, though the sarcasm and bitterness in her words hung like mourning curtains in the room.

"Well, now you're initiated, anyway. Welcome to the club," she said wryly.

She smiled, a crooked, mournful smile, full of warmth and sorrow. "See ya around," she added and disappeared out the door.

I lay alone again, feeling the darkness inside me softening and the terrors of the hospital lessened by Maggie's comfort and the knowledge that someone cared and didn't think I was crazy, part of me knowing above all that I had to keep myself intact in this bizarre and terrifying world called a mental hospital. How?

I realized I had only one hope for survival. I must reweave my cobweb world. I had let the cottony gray cushion unravel and I was hurting again from the attacks of the world.

"Stay apart. Don't let them touch you. It's the only way," I told myself. "You can do it."

I slept in a white hospital gown, a loose, shapeless, gauzy garment without sleeves, that tied at the neck and hung open to the knees. It could be worn with the opening in the front or the back. Either way, it was humiliating to be seen even by the other patients. A pair of paper slippers had been folded alongside the gown in the green metal locker in my room. I thanked someone that I had my own sandals to wear.

By nine o'clock I was alone, lying in the unfamiliar, rubber-sheeted bed, watching the shadows on the ceiling, listening to the strange hospital sounds. I fell asleep in ten minutes, and awoke, with a jerk, to find the room totally dark, shadowless, and the air hushed, deathly. It must have been deep night.

Walking in my gown past the nurses' station on my way to the bathroom, I had the sudden unmistakable sensation that I was a ghost, a floating, diaphanous creature in a nether world of amber light and silent, white-suited figures who were always writing. This was not a real place—how could it possibly be? Some maniac had dreamed it in a fevered night and I was part of her creation. I could continue down the hall, floating past the nurses' station and the deserted dayroom, past the silent bedrooms and the lit bathroom, down to the door that would lead back to the real world. I could just slip out. It was locked! The heavy door was locked! I was not a ghost. I was a prisoner! The fantasy dissolved abruptly with the noise of running white-shoed figures.

"What are you doing here?" a faceless woman, an aide on the night shift, demanded.

"I was only going to the bathroom." I stood with my back against the wall, trying to conceal my nakedness beneath the open, fluttering gown.

"The bathroom's over there." She pointed down the hall. "Not here," she bellowed.

"I couldn't sleep. I was taking a walk," I said.

"Well, walk the other way, where we can see you." It was an order. "I want you in bed in five minutes." She looked at the heavy round watch attached to her arm.

I was frightened. For the first time since I had arrived I was truly, deeply afraid. A prisoner in the place they called Oceanville Hospital! I would not allow my mind to dwell on what might happen if I did not obey. I had never felt so alone in all my life.

Back in my room, I stared at the squid, a heaving black lump illuminated in the amber light from the hall. It was almost comforting to have him with me; at least he was something predictable, something familiar.

My brain had melted into stew meat. My head was a bubbling mass of questions and unarticulated dreads.

Someone had pulled over a chair and was sitting outside my door, guarding the entrance. I could see her fingers moving as she knit in the golden hall. "I must keep watch myself," I thought. But sleep came and took me away.

I awoke in the morning to a shape looming over my bed. It was still dark. What time was it? They had taken my watch.

"Temps," the voice of the shape boomed forth. "Morning temps. Are you Moss?"

She was talking to me.

"Yes," I said, still protected by covers up to my nose.

"New patient? Admitted yesterday?" she questioned in her booming voice.

"Yes," I answered. "What does she want?" I thought. "Who the hell is she? I've heard that voice somewhere. I know it."

JANET

She was night shift, I learned later. The twelve-to-eights, who nodded in their chairs keeping watch over the sleeping inmates and the ghostly halls. They were all fat and lethargic, mostly women, people who emerged only at night, returning to their homes to sleep away the sunlight hours.

"I know that voice," I thought again, trying to concentrate my sleep-ridden brain on remembering.

"O my God." The words escaped my lips but were lost in the bedclothes. It had been last night, only last night that I had met her. At the door. She was the mountain who had blocked my passage, forced me back to bed with threats. She didn't seem to remember the incident at all. I pulled the covers up to touch my bottom eyelids.

"I have to take your temperature. Can you do it yourself?" she asked, thrusting a rectal thermometer at me. Her voice seemed more of a roar than a human tone.

"Won't she wake my roommate?" I wondered, and I remembered that the second bed in my room was empty. A three-month waiting list! Ha!

I inserted the thermometer in my rectum, in the dark, under the covers, while the woman took my pulse, holding my wrist with her large, pancake fingers, pressing on a half-healed scar for a minute that seemed a year, counting the seconds on the heavy, round, luminous-dial watch I had noticed the night before. Then she left. The ward was still quiet, though early morning stirrings were beginning to impinge on the block of nighttime silence. A rustle here, a cough there, the clink of bottles, rusty early-morning voices, the closing of a door. Morning light was creeping through the heavily screened windows in my room, diluting the night. I still had the thermometer in my rectum.

The previous day, as Mrs. Rooney followed me like a shadow, I had made a vow: I would stay apart and not let them touch me. I would be busy and vigilant, build an ever more secure cocoon to protect myself while I learned the subtle ins and outs of survival on Mid II.

I was on "restrictions," I had learned from Mrs. Rooney. All new patients were, until their doctor changed their status. That meant I couldn't go anywhere off the ward without a staff member. There were other categories limiting freedom of movement. It was totally at the discretion of the individual doctor which category you were in. After restrictions, if I was good and my doctor approved, Mrs. Rooney told me I could have limited grounds privileges. Then I would be able to go to meals, to doctor's appointments, and to scheduled activities by myself—as long as I signed in and out. If I was especially good, I might get limited in two weeks.

After that, the status everyone sought was full grounds privileges. I would be able to come and go as I pleased, signing in and out, of course, even to the extent of roaming freely on the beautifully kept hospital grounds. Once I had full privileges I would be on my own, Mrs. Rooney said, because "we trust you to take care of yourself. But you must earn our trust. That is the philosophy here at Oceanville. Freedom is a privilege. You must learn to care for yourself. We are only here to help in that end, not to do it for you."

I remembered my nocturnal walk through the ghostly corridors, my meeting with the angry aide on the night shift, and my growing realization that I was in a true sense a prisoner, locked doors or no locked doors, and that everyone thought I was crazy.

Under the covers I fingered first one wrist, then the other.

"Four little cuts have led to this," I said. "It's not possible. But it's true."

By the time the night nurse finally came to take the thermometer my room was gray with morning light and the corridors were alive with activity. I reached for a cigarette, remembering with a curse that I wasn't allowed any matches, and got out of bed.

I dressed in the only clothes I had—the blouse, skirt, underwear, and sandals from the day before. Standing in front of the full-length mirror, I looked for a long time at my reflection, trying to be objective, trying to find what had changed. There was nothing unusual. I saw a short, slim, nineteen-year-old girl with some pimples on her face, bangs and light brown hair reaching just to her waist; hazel-green eyes, very changeable, usually obscured by large, dark tortoiseshell sunglasses; ordinary clothes—a gray pleated skirt and yellow button-down shirt—worn to impress the admitting office; nose, slightly Semitic, longish, but not grotesque by any means; legs, fair; hands and feet, small, bony, not unattractive. Interests: poetry, French literature, Renaissance music, folk dancing.

I looked again at my eyes reflected in the mirror. They looked big, frightened, almost furtive—the way a rabbit looks when you've caught it and taken it out of the fields to play with in your bedroom, to take care of and give a new home to in a box your mother brought from Macy's; but it is confused and only wants to go back to the fields and it doesn't understand why you've taken it away; but it can't speak.

Why? Why was I here? I looked in the mirror for signs of madness, whatever they might be. But all I could see was me.

JANET

When my parents came to visit me two weeks later, they had already been warned by ferrety Miss Wexler, my social worker, not to pay any attention to my complaints or pleas. My dissatisfaction, they had been assured, was only part of the normal process of adjusting to hospital life. Of course no one *liked* being in a hospital, but it was necessary. I would have to learn that I was not the best judge any more of what was good for me, that the people at Oceanville were there to help me, and that the more I resisted their efforts to help me, the longer I would have to stay in the hospital.

I had spoken to my mother once on the telephone, when Dr. Steber, the hospital physician, had given me permission to make calls. I had received several letters and cards from my parents, all designed to cheer me up. They had contained bits of gossip and news from Brooklyn and repeated assurances that every one of their friends loved me and knew I was going to get well soon—that, despite the fact that their friends didn't even know I was in the hospital, just that I was "away." As for my parents, their faith in me never faltered, and they knew I would be healthy and back home very soon. The letters, produced from love and fantasies, were so sad they made me cry.

As visiting day drew closer, I felt more and more urgently that I did not want to see my parents. Dr. Steber had given me limited grounds privileges, though, and I was afraid that he might take them away if he thought I didn't want to "get well." Not wanting to get well was a serious sin for a patient to commit. Being hostile was another. But harboring suicidal thoughts was *the* primal sin at Oceanville, and even a hint that self-destructive forces were working could call down the retaliatory forces of the hospital, ranging, I gathered, from revocation of privileges to shipment to a state hospital.

My first two weeks at Oceanville had shaken up my life and my concept of myself beyond recognition. To my surprise, my anguish and loneliness had been somewhat tempered by my parents' absence. For the first time in many months I hadn't had to live with the silent accusations that I was the cause of their sorrow and the devastation of their lives. When I cried, no one was laid low by the tears. I had faced a bit of my anger toward them for putting me away, and reached inside myself to touch some of my resentment toward them for their selfishness. They had never let me have anything of my own, not even my despair.

Our meeting, in the dayroom, was awkward to the point of being palpably unpleasant. My parents were the first visitors to be admitted when the doors to Mid II were opened at two o'clock. They clutched their pink visitors cards in their hands, relinquishing them to the aide seated at the door. They seemed to be tiptoeing down the hall, looking nervously from side to side as if they were expecting an attack, or at least some outward sign that they really were in a mental hospital. I waited, with the other patients who expected visitors, in the dayroom next to the nurses' station.

"Darling," my mother embraced me as if I had been missing for years.

"How do you feel, Janet?" my father asked.

"All right," I said, swallowing hard my desire to ask how he would feel if he were locked up with a bunch of crazies.

"Do you feel better?" my mother asked anxiously. "A little better?" She had to know that she had done the right thing in putting me away. I wouldn't, I couldn't, give her that satisfaction— not when my anger was raging inside me like a swollen river.

I turned my eyes away, shutting them out.

"We brought you a carton of cigarettes," my mother said. "And plenty of matches."

"I'm not allowed to have matches," I said fiercely. "I'm crazy, or didn't you know?"

"Now, Janet, that's not why," my mother said. "They just don't want you to hurt yourself."

"Well, they can't stop me. If I want to hurt myself I can find a thousand ways to do it. They won't stop me by making me beg for matches."

My anger was poison, flowing from my mouth.

My mother seemed struck; her face was carved from stone.

"Tell us about your doctor, Jan," my father said.

"His name is Dr. Steber; he's tall, dark, and handsome. Okay?"

"Do you like him?" my mother asked tentatively, recovered.

"Yes, I *like* him," I retorted. "I see him three times a week, a half hour each time. And I'm lucky. Most of the other doctors give fifteen-minute appointments."

"Well if you like him," ventured my mother, "maybe he'll be able to help you."

I couldn't play question and answer games any longer.

"I want to get out of here," I said, trying to keep my voice low. "I want you to get me out of here." My teeth were clenched and the virulent words came out hot and explosive.

"Now, Janet," my mother began. "I thought we had settled this. You must stay in the hospital until you are well. Then you can leave. We are only trying to help you."

"They've tested and diagnosed me," I said, my voice peaking in a screech. "And they won't tell me what I am, what class of maniac I am." I started to laugh. "You didn't know there were different classifications of crazies, did you? Or did you? Well, I'm a special kind. But when I tried to look at my folder and see, the doctor said, 'It isn't good for you to know. You're too sick to know.' And he threatened to put me on restrictions for two weeks or more. He said I had 'morbid curiosity' and he wrote it down on my record."

"Janet, calm down," my father said.

"Oh, but that's nothing," I said, the words mingling with laughter that was twisted pain.

"You should see us when the whole bunch of doctors come on rounds twice a week. They're a team; this is a team effort, see? And there's Dr. Maynard in his gray striped suit with his gray eyes and gray hair and gray mind, followed by his five puppy dog residents. They're our doctors, they're studying at Oceanville, they're using us to learn from, isn't that cute?"

"Janet. Stop!" They didn't want to hear this. I knew it. I knew too that I would gain nothing lasting, nothing but the momentary satisfaction of forcing them to see the ugly truth I faced every day.

"They stop in every room, stop every patient, because it is important that the whole team be aware of the individual's progress and problems. Ha!" I was paraphrasing the hospital line. My parents couldn't miss the sarcasm; but they were confused. And, it seemed to me, frightened, as they looked at me. Perhaps they thought I *was* crazy by now? Everyone else did. And, after only two weeks, even I had begun to doubt the wholeness of my sanity.

" 'And how are you this morning, Janet?' Dr. Maynard asks, trying to make his mousy voice sound impressive and resonant.

"He turns to his followers and whispers, 'She's a ———, extremely ———, suicidal ———, delusions of ———, inappropriate ———, reaction.' They all nod knowingly, scrawling notes on their pads while I stand and listen to them talk about me as if I weren't there. Maybe I'm not. 'I'm fine,' I say meekly, humbled by the presence of the great healers. Dr. Steber is among them, but he doesn't even nod or indicate that he knows me. He's not supposed to. I'm just another case.

" 'Have you been going to your activities?' the gray doctor asks.

" 'Yes,' I say.

" 'She is taking music and dance therapy.' Dr. Maynard is speaking to the team. I can't hear all of his words, but he is pointing at me and talking, while the doctors nod with comprehension.

"At first I thought they really wanted to know how I was feeling.

It was humiliating, being treated that way, but I tried to ignore it. Maybe they didn't realize how humiliating it was." I stopped. "Didn't realize it! Oh, that's a joke."

"Janet!" My parents spoke together.

"So one Monday morning when they came on rounds and Dr. Maynard asked me how I felt, I said 'Well, I don't feel too good. I've been sort of depressed.' They all watched me, expectant. I had been feeling so bad, I just wanted to die. I thought they'd help me understand why I felt so bad. That's what they're there for, to help me."

My parents' eyes were wide with listening and compassion.

" 'I started thinking about razor blades again,' I confided. And you know what he said, the bullshitting bastard? He called the charge nurse and said, 'Put this patient on fifteen-minute check.' Dr. Steber had just given me limited grounds privileges and he put me on fifteen-minute check. I opened up a little of the pain in me; I asked for help the way they keep telling us we should. And he put me on fifteen-minute check. That was his 'help.' So stupid. Why do they punish you when you feel bad?"

For an instant, musing, I forgot that my parents were there.

"But I got off in a day and a half," I told them. "It came to me in a flash, how to get off. Just tell everyone how good I felt, eat my meals, participate in my activities, seem cheery. That's what they want. So I did it. And the stupid bastards believed me."

I started to laugh and sob, a throaty anguished sound.

"Janet." My father's voice was panicky. "Stop."

"But Daddy, I thought you wanted to know about my doctors and how everybody is trying to help me." I was playing it to the hilt, I realized, pulling out the stops and playing the crazy sick-in-the-head mental patient. It was exhilarating, like riding on a roller coaster. And why shouldn't I enjoy it? I didn't have anything more to lose. What else could they do to me? I was already in a mental hospital.

"Well, are you going to get me out?" I asked.

My mother tried a new tactic. Reason with her. Be conciliatory. "Sweetie," she started. "It's just that you're in a new place and you don't really know anybody yet and of course it's strange, but soon you'll like it here. Miss Wexler says you're really doing well for the first few weeks."

"Who's Miss Wexler?" I asked. I almost didn't want to know.

"She's your social worker," my mother answered. "A lovely young woman."

"I didn't know I had a social worker," I said. "And if she's mine, what is she doing talking to you?"

"Well, the social workers try to help the families of patients adjust to the hospitalization of their loved ones. That's their job."

"More official bullshit," I thought.

"Oh, that is priceless. That is just priceless."

"Visiting hours are over," a voice resounded through the halls.

"I left the clothes and books and things you asked for with the aide. They will have to get checked and marked," my mother said apologetically, almost as if she expected me to forgive the hospital routines as easily as she did.

"Good-bye, dear." They both kissed me hard, but I turned my head.

"Bye," I said. "See you next time."

I went into my room and cried, my head buried under the pillow. I cried because I loved my parents and I hated them and they didn't know me at all. I cried because I knew I would never go back to Ellis and because I missed Mary so much I could feel it as an empty aching place. I cried because the confusion in my head seemed more confused than ever. I wanted to cut my wrists and I didn't want to—and no one but a few other patients, all experiencing their own chaos and helplessness and pain, seemed to understand how trapped you had to be, how much you had to hurt inside to want to cut and scar your own body.

The doctors spoke deprecatingly of "suicidal gestures" or "pleas for help." They called it "acting out" and punishment was swift.

But it was dumb, screaming torture of your heart, or your soul dying, or the panic of being backed in a corner, that made you raise your hand against yourself to disfigure the only body God would ever give you.

And the pain of the cuts was almost a relief after the other agonies you felt.

Sometimes, as the months wore on, I felt, fleetingly, that Dr. Steber understood what I was trying to communicate about being lonely and hopeless and wanting to cut my wrists. He was, as I had flippantly told my parents, tall, dark, and handsome. In fact, he looked like William Powell when he played opposite Myrna Loy in all of those Thin Man movies. His eyes were brown-black, impenetrable behind his glasses, though I could tell they were eyes that had known pain and would know more. His hands were narrow, his fingers long. He wore understated brown tweeds and smelled of aromatic tobacco even when he wasn't smoking his pipe. I liked him; perhaps I even had a crush on him. I believed he might help me, because I believed he saw *me* behind the symptoms that were reported to the never-ending joy of the psychiatrically trained nurses, and Dr. Maynard and his team.

Three times a week, after picking up the paper slip that said *D. A.* (Doctor's Appointment) at the nurses' station, I would go to see Dr. Steber in a small sunny cubicle of an office on the fourth floor of the main building of the hospital. He was usually off schedule after speaking overtime with a patient, but I didn't mind, because he offered the same privilege to me. He never stopped our sessions just because the time was over. Sometimes I stayed only twenty minutes; once I stayed an hour.

I told him my story, piece by piece, from the desperate summer after high school through my experiences at Ellis with Dr. Kurtzman, the school authorities, Dr. Wyatt, Speedwriting school, and Dr. Berman, filling in family stories along the way.

I told him of the Paul Klee postcards that adorned my walls and the e. e. cummings poems I was memorizing. I told him at length about Mary and Rachel and Larry, and about my growing friendship with Maggie Ellman, another patient on Mid II.

I did not tell him about the squid or the cocoon of separateness that was drawing itself tighter around my neck, though at times I longed desperately to confide in him. He was a quiet man, who used his intense talent for listening deeply to enable me to listen to myself. I heard a very frightened little girl, trying to act grown up. A voice inside me repeated and repeated, "Separate. Separate. Do Not Trust."

No doctor had ever affirmed that there was a person, a unique me behind my symptoms. Dr. Steber seemed to understand that I was more than my history, and he listened intently to everything I said. "Perhaps he could help me untangle myself," I thought, "Lord knows, I'm messed up. But at what cost? My freedom?"

Again and again, I swallowed the aching want to pour out my pain. Instead, I started a campaign to convince Dr. Steber that I no longer needed to be hospitalized.

"You mean you don't think you will cut your wrists again?" he asked one morning.

I couldn't look him in the eye.

"No," I said, my voice quavering in spite of my efforts to keep it calm. "I realize now that it was a sick thing to do and that I only did it to get Dr. Berman to pay attention to me."

JANET

I didn't believe a word of what I was saying; every taut fiber in my body was inflamed at the indignity of having to lie to gain my freedom.

"The nurses' reports for the past week seem to show that you've been depressed. You haven't been going to meals—"

"I wanted to lose weight," I interrupted quickly.

"Mrs. Rooney says that you've been staying in your room, alone, and that she's heard you crying."

"But that doesn't mean I'm going to cut my wrists," I argued.

"No," Dr. Steber admitted slowly. "But it does mean that you aren't feeling as good as you're pretending to me."

I paused for a weighted moment.

"I want to get out of here," I said. "Please let me go."

"What would you do? Where would you go?"

"It doesn't matter," I said.

"Yes it does." He spoke in a deep, certain voice.

"The longer I stay here the worse I feel," I said. "And don't hand me that bullshit about being allowed to be as sick as you really are, in a controlled environment."

Dr. Steber smiled wryly, as I paraphrased a favorite Oceanville homily.

"Everyone keeps telling me how sick I am. When I say I'm not sick, those saccharine busybody nurses explain how that shows how sick I am. It's mad. But you know what the really scary part is? Sometimes I believe them."

Dr. Steber was listening hard. I continued.

"If I stay in my room they tell me I'm withdrawing and that's sick. If I join the girls in ward activities and start to have fun they tell me I'm being manic and that's sick. They want me to have friends but they say my relationship with Maggie is sick. They won't even let me speak to Sandy Steinberg because the contact is not therapeutic. And when I get angry and tell them to mind their own fucking business they say I'm being hostile. And you know, only sick people are hostile. Nobody takes you seriously, that's the worst part of it. And it's the most demoralizing experience in the world not to be taken seriously."

Dr. Steber didn't say a word.

"Listen," I said. "I am not a disease and I'm not a child and I'm tired of being humiliated and talked down to and turned into a helpless invalid. This place is a goddamn school for psychosis. If you didn't know the symptoms before you came in, you learn them, fast. And you adopt them, you start acting sick because you want to fit in and after a while this is the only place you have any hope of fitting in. If you're not suicidal when you come, it doesn't take long to get that way."

Dr. Steber was still silent. I blessed him for letting me finally say what had been building inside me and for not insisting that my perceptions were distorted.

"If I stay here any longer, Dr. Steber, I'm really going to go mad," I said. "And I know how much better it is than other hospitals. But you know something? I don't care. I still can't take a shower when I want to or smoke a cigarette in my room or go out for a walk. I still feel like a visitor to the world when I do go on a 'trip' with the other patients. Do you know how awful that is, grown people being checked on and herded to the movies. Oh, the nurses and aides wear street clothes, but you think everybody in Belville doesn't know who we are? We're the sickies from Oceanville Hospital."

"I understand how you feel, Janet," Dr. Steber said.

"No you don't," I shouted. "You can't. Ever. You're on the outside. You can go home at night. How can you possibly understand what it's like to be condemned to a mental hospital–prison because you did something society can't accept?"

"I really want to help you, Janet," Dr. Steber said.

"Then let me out of here. Give me a chance."

"To do what? Kill yourself? I can't let you do that."

"But it's my business, not yours."

"I can't discharge you until you're much less depressed than you are now," Dr. Steber said. "I think you've been holding back your real feelings just to convince me how good you feel. Is it really in your best interest to do that?"

"I don't know," I said. "But one thing is certain, it's not in my 'best interest' to be here. Because if I stay much longer, I'm really going to give up hope. I'm beginning to believe maybe I really am mad. Maybe you're right and I'm wrong, maybe I really do belong here."

"The hospital is not perfect, but please try to trust me, Janet."

"How can I?" I asked. "You say you want to know my real feelings, you want to know if I feel suicidal. But if I told you, you'd put me on fifteen-minute watch or special to stop me. I'm here because I cut my wrists and you're going to punish me for even *wanting* to do it again. You won't release me until you're convinced I won't ever do it again. You think I'm sick because I want to die. But you want me to trust you?"

It seemed as if the session had gone on for hours; I was exhausted.

"I know it's hard to believe, Janet," Dr. Steber said, "but I do understand—at least some of what you're saying. I understand the double pulls you feel. And I do want to help."

"Yes," I said. My throat felt choked with tears. I wanted to believe him. "I think I'd better go. Can I still go bowling with the group tomorrow?"

There it was again, another time I had to ask for a privilege the rest of the world took for granted.

"Are you sure you feel able to go?" he asked.

"Yes," I lied. "I'm sure."

I had heard Sandy telling Maddie Jacobson and David Silver how she stole razor blades from the drugstore in Belville. I wondered why she didn't buy them outright, but I realized almost immediately that the storekeeper would not have sold them to her.

I asked Maggie if she thought I was crazy, or did outside people somehow know we came from a mental hospital.

"Oh they know," she said. "I don't care how much the staff tells you you're being paranoid."

We laughed.

"How, do you think?" I asked her. Maggie had a certain fineness of perception and exact way with words that made her explanations pointed and true.

"There's a strangeness about us all," she said, thinking while she spoke. "A—you might call it—an unused quality. Almost a dustiness. As if we had been put away in a trunk and just taken out. We don't feel quite at home in the light; we act somehow awkward, self-conscious. They sense all that, immediately, and they know we're from a different world. And we are, of course."

No one could dispute that. We were the misfits, the angry, the ugly, the fat, the unpleasant, the eccentric, the sad people—the ones who just couldn't keep to the straight and narrow. We couldn't make it on the outside so they called us sick and put us away.

But it wasn't easy to make it inside either, I was learning.

"He wouldn't even talk about discharging me," I told Maggie after my appointment with Dr. Steber.

"I didn't think he would," she said sympathetically.

"I think in a way he really wants to help me feel better," I said. "But he thinks I should be helped here."

"They all say that," Maggie commented. "After all," she added succinctly, "if we weren't here, they wouldn't have a job. But who cares anyway?" she added irrelevantly.

"Don't you ever want to go home?" I asked.

"Like this?" she pointed in an all-embracing gesture, to her agonizingly blemished and bloated face and her heavy body. Maggie's doctor was giving her large doses of a tranquilizer called Mellaril which was causing her face to break out in angry red sores. Her metabolism had been slowed down to such a degree that she had gained close to thirty pounds and looked more like a zeppelin than the lovely seventeen-year-old girl she was. As a final indignity the drugs made her ravenously hungry. She seemed almost dopey, her sharp witty perceptions emerging only occasionally from the drugged fog of her mind.

There was a resignation, almost a dullness in her tone that was elusively familiar.

Suddenly, I knew why. Centering my life around the hospital, I was beginning to talk that way myself.

The next day, after I had bowled two games and begged off a third, I excused myself, and slipped out of the bowling alley. The aide in charge hadn't noticed me go, or if she had, she would think I was in the bathroom or the snack bar.

The drugstore was down the block. I was panting from nervousness, my legs weak under me as I walked in, trying to look casual, ordinary, and calm. Sandy had said it was important to divert the woman's attention. How could I do that? I was alone. She, at least, had had someone with her.

"Yes? May I help you?" The round, rosy plum of a grandmotherly lady was speaking to me from behind the counter. My mind was as empty as a night beach in winter.

"I have a sore throat," I said. "My mother used to give me something called Lozilles—flat, greenish things—to suck on. Do you have any?"

"Well now—I'll take a look," she said, turning her back toward me while she searched the shelves behind her.

With one quick motion my hand shot out from my jacket pocket and closed, like a trap, on a package of razor blades I had been eyeing. It shot back again, the precious loot secure in the blackness of my pocket. Just in time. The drugstore lady turned back to me. I was panting with a nervous anxiety so keen it reminded me of a time when I was a child looking breathlessly through *A Stone for Danny Fisher* to find the dirty parts and hiding it just an instant before my mother came.

Only this was a different kind of hide and seek. A grown-up, bizarre game that wasn't a lark, but an irreversible rite of initiation.

"I can't find any Lozilles," she said. "I think the company may have stopped manufacturing them."

"Then I'll take something else," I said very quickly. "Anything that will help my throat."

"You could try these," she pointed to a yellow package. "Or maybe—"

"I'll take them," I said, cutting her off. Time was passing; I had to get back to the bowling alley before I was missed.

When you live in the closed world of a mental hospital, you learn quickly not to take any pleasure for granted. You learn the skills of survival, and the rules of reward and punishment, and the high comic art of playing the fool.

"The only choice you have here," one girl had said, "is the kind of insanity you choose."

"I must write that down," her doctor said. "Otherwise, I might forget it. It's very profound."

At Oceanville, activities include occupational therapy with knitting, tile work, ceramics and lanyard-making among the most popular time-killers; sports therapy, particularly directed to those patients whose sickness is overaggressiveness; dance and music therapy: everyone is either drugged or stoned in their own misery and preoccupation so no one can keep time. But it doesn't matter, so long as it is therapeutic.

Entertainment is limited: Friday evening movies, bowling trips, Bingo or Saturday night dances replete with pretzels, Coke, and crepe-paper streamers.

That lured you when you were in the eighth grade, you say? But you're a mental patient now, and that makes all the difference. You're not bored, you're dissociating. The old rules don't apply.

You say you have nothing to talk about but the hospital when you go home on a weekend pass? You say your friends are busy growing and doing and you feel useless, and stagnant and downright peculiar? You say everyone you used to know looks at you with pity and barely concealed unease? And you feel more and more sure you'll never make it in the outside? You say each time you venture out and see the widening gap between your world and theirs, between inside and outside, you come back to the hospital feeling so bad you want to kill yourself?

"Well, that's your illness," a doctor would say. "That's why you're here—to be cured of this depression, these feelings of unworth, and this morbid preoccupation with death."

You say your mother looks at you funny and doesn't trust you alone in the bathroom?

"It's all in your head, dear," you're told. "Your poor, sick head."

Happy? No. You're manic.

Sad? No. You're depressed.

Angry at your shrink? Resisting therapy.

Like your doctor? Positive transference.

Nurses piss you off? You're hostile.

Cut your wrists? Acting-out again.

Not hungry? Could be anorexia.

Listening to the summer birds sing? Hope she's not going catatonic!

Can't stand Bingo? Antisocial.

Won't be intimidated? Dissociative reaction.

Make a joke your doctor can't understand? Thought processes disturbed.

Think no one takes you seriously and they're condemning you to a life as a social outcast? Paranoid and more paranoid!

We Only Want to Help You—It rings like an ironic anthem of despair, over and over, in your ears and head, until you choke and gasp from the help and scream, "Okay. You win. I've no more heart to fight."

You turn your eyes inward, away from the temptations of the world. They're not for you. Your center of gravity has changed. The focus is reversed. Hospital is home; the outside world, your parents and friends, is the place you visit.

You find you've changed. You talk about suicide, comparing experiences and methods, as if this was the norm. It is. Everyone else's symptoms and pathology become a source of endless interest and conversation.

You revel in the little games of sabotage you can concoct—crack the Ping-Pong balls, switch the clock, jam the TV. No one is surprised to see you acting like a child. The staff had been wondering when you would come around to accepting your true nature.

You take your precious moments of privacy, your friendships, your soul truths, and you guard them as if they were drops of water in a desert. And they are.

You plan, you wait for the moment you can kill yourself, because you know that's the only real way out of this world called a mental hospital.

For a week I carried my secret treasure, the razor blades, concealed first in my pocketbook, then in my sunglass case. No one had searched me when I returned to the hospital because I had full grounds privileges and was considered responsible and nonsuicidal, although the potential was always there.

I had gathered during my months at Oceanville that the entire staff—doctors, nurses, aides, and therapists of every description—all conceived of what they called "suicidal impulses" in the same way. The "suicidal feelings" or "impulses" were lurking inside us, rather like ferocious animals, crouched and ready to spring. The person who harbored these exotic impulses was considered to be sick and at the mercy of them, at all times.

Although it was not *you* but the *impulses* which were truly to blame in the cases of suicide attempts, it was still your responsibility to control them. You were punished for not doing so, often threatened when you continued to refuse to control them. Interestingly, the same refusal to control these impulses that had gotten you into Oceanville in the first place could get you out of it—only into a worse place, a state hospital. The doctors set the standards; I learned, as time wore on, that you had no choice but to conform, eventually.

Sometimes the same doctors indulged themselves, with impressive gravity of countenance, in the fantasy that patients were cutting themselves up and taking overdoses solely to provoke their keepers. Sometimes, to further confuse things, the suicidal impulses themselves were thought to be sick. In order for the person to become "well," the impulses had to be totally eliminated or exorcised, banished from your psyche forever. I came after awhile to believe that this was truly possible. And I paid, many years later, for my naïveté.

It was often difficult to convince staff that the lurking animals in you had been fully tamed. The nurses and doctors would remain vigilant, waiting in terror for your mad beast to reemerge. Mine, it seemed, was accepted to be in a harmless or sleeping state, so no one searched my hair or my hem or pockets for hidden weapons.

At the end of the week, Sandy cut her wrists and security was tightened.

Between the hospital-wide interrogation and the personal search, I managed to open the package and separate the individually wrapped blades, hiding them variously behind a postcard on my wall, in the hem of a curtain, in a torn spot on the bottom of my mattress, behind the wall mirror, and under a corner of curling linoleum near my bed.

"What are you doing?" Eileen asked. She was my new roommate. Four feet ten inches, hair dyed the color of dried apricots, heavy makeup, and golden-jeweled frontless and backless three-inch platform heels, she was an unaccountable oddity on the ward. She had arrived in fine spirits, settled in easily and gone about her business with brisk, unwavering cheerfulness. I had never seen her cry, or even frown. We couldn't figure out what, if anything, was wrong with her—or why she was in the hospital.

"Eileen must be suffering from the happiness syndrome," Maggie said one day. "A serious ailment, quite rare. Difficult to treat." Everyone laughed, except Eileen, who seemed confused, unsure if she should be pleased or distressed to be the object of universal mirth.

Naive, almost simple, she thought razor blades were for shaving and pills for headaches.

"What are you doing under the bed?" she asked.

"Just looking for something I lost," I answered. She had not seen the blades and I didn't want her to. She would report me, without a doubt.

"Eileen, be a love and get me a Coke? Please? The money's in my locker," I said.

She tottered off to the dayroom on her glittering platforms while I hid the other razor blades. For all her cheeriness, she never made any friends in the two months she was at Oceanville. She had tried to become friendly with me, but her constant squeaky chattering made me want to scream. This time I was taking advantage of her, and I felt bad.

When I finally cut my wrists, a week and a half later, I knew I would not die. I knew the cuts were not deep enough to cause death, although the blood flowed like liquid velvet from my arms, the life stream released before my eyes. I knew someone would find me. But it didn't matter.

Leaning against an oak tree in a thickly wooded section of the hospital grounds, feeling the burning pain, the lines of pain crossing my wrists, watching myself in the ritual act of release and retribution, it didn't matter if they found me. Nothing mattered. Not even why.

Summer was coming; the blood poured from my screaming arms; the old oak felt rough and reassuring as I leaned my cheek on a gnarled root that grew twisted and perverse from the ground.

I held my arms in front of me crying, "Look, look, what you've done to me." Who was I calling? It didn't matter. Only the pain was real, the blood, and the tree. I would cover myself with scars and they would move me further and further into the dark depths of the hospital till I was nothing but one enormous interwoven scar, alone in a cell in the intestines of the earth, with no human contacts but the doctor who still came each week to try to help me to get well.

I was faint, moving through blurred frames of the endless and repeating film that was my life.

A doctor was stitching up my arms. I watched, fascinated. He held a curved threaded needle and he was taking small, looped stitches in my arms, sewing the cuts as matter-of-factly as if they had been a torn seam.

I started to laugh; three nurses and one doctor-tailor all working on me!

In ten minutes the five black lines on my arms were covered with rounds of white gauze and sealed with tape.

"You may have something for the pain and to help you sleep, Janet, if you need it," the doctor said. "Now where did you get the blade?"

I didn't answer.

"Where did you get the blade?" he repeated louder.

"I didn't get it from anyone else, if that's what you're worried about," I said.

"I want to know where you got the blade," the doctor said, his lips set grimly.

"What does it matter where I got it?" I said. "I got it."

"Where?" Three voices chimed in and I was surrounded by inquisitors.

"In the drugstore," I answered. "The Belville Drugstore."

"How many did you buy? Where are the others?" a nurse asked immediately.

"I didn't buy them, I stole them. And I flushed the rest down the toilet," I lied.

"You didn't give them to anyone else?" a nurse asked.

I was indignant. Did she really think I would give somebody a blade? What did she think I was? "Of course not," I answered.

"And you didn't save any either, Janet?" another nurse asked.

"No." I lied again.

I had emerged to an anxious group of patients from the treatment room, that same room where I was examined, crying, the first strange distant day I came to Oceanville.

While I waited near the nurses' station for my room to be searched, I answered the barrage of questions concerning method, timing, weapon, and extent of injury. We discussed possible retaliatory measures.

"You'll be on special, for sure," Maddie said.

"You won't get a warning, though, I don't think," Una said, " 'cause it's only your first time. In the hospital, I mean."

Oceanville Hospital

"Do they hurt?" Carol asked, eager, as always, to hear stories of pain and disfiguration. There was nothing personal in her enthusiasm for blood and gore; it was just her thing.

Karin, a wrinkled, harrowed thirty-four-year-old refugee from Germany, wept quietly in a corner.

Seena sat on the couch a few feet away, knitting with flying fingers. She seemed not to have heard a thing.

Someone had put meatloaf behind the television set, the aides had not discovered it yet, and an odor of putrefaction filled the air.

I looked around the room for Maggie, hungry for someone who would sympathize, without clothing their tragic understanding in the paraphernalia of fetishism. True, no one had asked *why* I cut my wrists and that was a relief after the probing interrogations of the staff. No one ever asked why. If we shared anything as patients it was a common understanding of despair. Only Maggie had the grace—or was it the love?—to understand in complete silence.

I needed her, but she was nowhere around. Probably she was sleeping. I was alone, the frame of desolation repeating and repeating itself.

The search of my room yielded nothing and I felt weirdly and frighteningly triumphant as I pictured my five razor blades, each cleverly concealed in its undiscovered hiding place. I had fooled them once. And I would do it again.

Mrs. Rooney put me on special that night, her attitude a bewildering mixture of sympathy and reproach. When I couldn't sleep she came with me to the silent shadowed dayroom and took a break while Mrs. Petra made me hot milk.

Mrs. Petra was the night-shift charge nurse, a woman who exuded an almost palpable aura of strength and concern. Many, many nights she had sat with me in the dark dayroom, made me warm milk, listened as I talked of my pain, and when I couldn't speak, held me while I cried. Unlike the other night staff, she never slept on duty.

"I'm sorry, Mrs. Petra," I blurted out.

"No, Janet," she said, "don't apologize to me. It was yourself you hurt."

"You mean you're not mad at me?"

"Mad? No." She put her arm around me. "I'm not mad at you. Sad, yes. Sad that you wanted to hurt yourself. And sad that you were unable to tell me before you did it."

"But I couldn't," I cried into her shoulder, soft under its crisp white uniform. "I wanted to. But you would have stopped me, wouldn't you?"

She nodded. "Yes. I would have tried to stop you."

"And I wanted to do it. So I couldn't tell you. Don't you understand?"

She held me as I cried. Would nothing relieve the pain inside me, the gnawing, screaming pain that was eating my heart, my guts, my brain? My life?

"Am I crazy, Mrs. Petra? Do you think I'm crazy?"

"No," she answered. "And I think I do understand, Janet. I've never felt quite the feelings you describe, but I've felt similar things, less intense. I don't think they're really as strange as you and everyone here would like to believe. There are some things in life you just have to go through, trying to be strong, praying for the luck to make it."

"I can't stand the pain," I cried. "I won't make it."

"I think you will," she said. "You're stronger than you know. You'll make it—if you don't kill yourself first. Was it hearing about Dr. Steber that made you so depressed?"

"Hearing what? I don't know what you mean," I said, feeling a shiver of apprehension.

"Weren't you on the Mid today? Didn't you go to community meeting?"

"No. I can't stand those meetings. All that talk about who should clean the ashtrays and whether we should serve potato chips or peanuts at the next dance. Dr. Maynard saying how we must take responsibility for our lives. It's a farce! We would take responsibility, if they'd let us decide something other than great issues like whether the television is too loud. But what about Dr. Steber?"

I knew I would have to face him the next day and try to explain my duplicity. I did think our sessions might begin to make an impact on me. I was beginning, fleetingly, to open myself to him; if only the facts of my life—the daily humiliations and indignities of hospital routine, the boredom, the discontinuity and the isolation of being in a mental hospital—were not so devastatingly pervasive. It was hard to begin to have hope in a changed future when every day was a study in hopelessness, when every action was scrutinized and analyzed, when you knew, even when no one said it outright—that you were being kept in this dressed-up prison because there was something deeply, essentially, *wrong* with you. Everyone called this wrongness "sick"; even Dr. Steber.

Recently he had begun to say I didn't have to settle for a pseudolife; he thought I could get "well."

"You can make it outside, Janet. That's where you belong. But you must try."

Oceanville Hospital

It was futile to try; I knew I would never make it on the outside. And if I had ever had a chance, the months of incarceration and living death had dispelled it utterly. The separation between myself and my life that had begun at Ellis felt almost complete. I had been passive; I had watched the doctors mangle my life. I had let them put me here and condemn me to this farcical representation of living. My dreams were out of reach. Would Ellis College take me back? It was absurd. I had only to destroy the inner me, the silent me that had sat, enwebbed, and watched these men destroy my future.

Dr. Steber had said, "No, you must have faith in your powers of regeneration. I do."

"I'll try," I had said.

But I had weakened. I had cut my wrists, and tomorrow he would have to know.

"There's going to be a change of doctors in two weeks," Mrs. Petra said. "Dr. Steber is leaving Oceanville. He's going to take his last year of residency at Mt. Arlen Hospital."

Leaving? Dr. Steber was leaving? He couldn't leave. He had pushed me to begin to feel again, to be real again. He had promised to be there if I was frightened, to be strong if it hurt.

"I don't believe you," I cried, turning my disappointment and grief into fury at Mrs. Petra.

"It's true, Janet. It happens every June. I thought you knew, you poor child."

"Why, Mrs. Petra? Why is he leaving me like this? How can he do it? I trusted him. I believed in him. All the rebirth shit he handed me. I believed it. I was going to try to get well. He said he'd help me. I thought he cared, he made me think he really cared."

I was shaking, but no tears came to my eyes, just deep cries from my depths—sounds that a cat makes when it's sick and it tries to puke, and the puke won't come but it heaves and bellows just the same.

"Janet, he's not the only doctor who can help you. It's really what's inside you that counts. You'll have another doctor."

She was trying to comfort me, I knew. But her words sounded thin; I don't think even she believed them as she held my erupting body.

"I don't want another doctor," I screamed. "I've had too many doctors already. That's why I'm here, because of doctors. If I'm so sick they should let me die already. Have they no pity, these doctors?"

I took the yellow sleeping capsule Mrs. Petra offered and I let her take me to my room. Only a few muffled cries and sighs and varied deep rhythmic breathing could be heard in the ghostly corridor of the ward.

"I wish I had died," I said. "I wish I had cut myself bad enough to die. Next time I'll do it right. Next time they'll never find me."

"No, no, don't say that, Janet. It'll be better, you'll see."

She sat with me, stroking my arm and forehead, listening to my cries, until I fell asleep.

Dr. Steber had helped me start to rebuild my fragile world; he had been its main support. He must have known that. Now he was going away, leaving me with the rubble, to survive as best I could. It didn't seem right, it didn't seem fair.

But then, whoever said life was fair?

I remembered my brother saying that when I was eleven. He was seventeen and I had thought, with a delighted, horrified tingle, how grown-up and exquisitely cynical he was. I wondered if I'd ever see him again.

Dr. Steber left and the few doctors who remained at Oceanville switched to other wards in order to vary their experiences. The administration did not think it was healthy for the patients to become attached to a single doctor, anyway. It fostered unreal dependency situations, they said. Comfortable in the certainty of their ideology, they removed the anchors from our lives, and watched our flailing desolation, taking notes, and discussing its therapeutic significance. Only Dr. Maynard remained, familiar, gray Dr. Maynard, initiating another group of novices into the intricacies and satisfactions of treating the mentally ill.

My wrists healed, old patients left, new ones arrived, the summer wore on, the heat relieved only by an occasional group trip to the beach.

Dr. Arthur Jarrow was my new doctor and when I first saw him I laughed out loud. I don't think he ever forgave me. He was averagely tall and averagely built. In fact, he was so superbly average, he was almost a composite, not an individual at all. And very proper, humorless, and self-important in his blue and white cord suit, his white oxford-cloth shirt and striped tie, his cordovan moccasins. I didn't like him. Not only did he not like me, he disapproved of me and within our first week of mostly silent sessions, he suggested I change my dress into something more tidy and feminine. He himself was an extraordinarily tidy person.

"You think I'm a beatnik?" I asked.

He frowned, finding the word unpleasant.

"What's wrong with my clothes?"

"Haven't you anything *brighter* to wear?" he asked.

"I like black," I answered.

"All the time?" he asked.

"All the time," I said. "Look, Dr. Jarrow, I don't tell you what to wear, do I?"

He humphed, "That's different. I'm your doctor."

"Well, when my clothes get sick, I'll bring them to see you. Dr. Steber never saw anything wrong with what I wore."

He winced.

"You haven't taken off that black turtleneck and black pants in two weeks," he complained.

"Dr. Steber never cared—"

"Dr. Steber's gone," he interrupted in a whine. "I'm your doctor now."

"I know," I said. "And you don't understand me at all." The session wasn't over, but I got up from my wooden chair, turned, and walked out of the room. I didn't want him to see me crying.

After requesting an interview for two weeks through the nursing staff, I finally got to see Dr. Maynard.

"I can't talk to Dr. Jarrow," I told Dr. Maynard. "He doesn't understand what I'm saying."

"I knew you were distressed about Dr. Steber leaving," Dr. Maynard said.

"But I was willing to try with someone else," I explained. "Only it just won't work with us."

Dr. Maynard regarded me with disinterest.

"I don't like him; he doesn't like me," I blurted out. "If we knew each other outside we'd probably never even say hello. That's how different we are."

"You don't have to like him," Dr. Maynard said. "You just have to work with him. He's your doctor, not your boyfriend."

"But I can't *talk* to him," I repeated, frustrated at the inadequacy of the words.

It seemed simple enough to me: How could you have therapy with someone you couldn't communicate with? With an alien? Why didn't he understand? I was afraid Dr. Maynard was like Dr. Jarrow, only older. That's why he didn't understand.

I tried again.

"I think he's afraid of me," I said, deciding to risk his disbelief. "Whenever I talk about cutting my wrists, he looks scared. He thinks my friendship with Maggie is sick and my clothes are sick and my hair is sick. And he doesn't understand how you can feel so sad and lonely that you want to die, but that it doesn't mean you're sick. Dr. Steber understood. At least he thought there was something to me that wasn't diseased. Jarrow doesn't even like me. We're like Martian and Venusian—no contact."

The moment the words were out I knew I had made a mistake. Dr. Maynard's face had turned papery at the mention of wrist-cutting and by the time I spoke about Martians, he looked positively corpselike—except for his left eye, which was twitching from anxiety. A former female patient of Dr. Steber's had committed suicide within two weeks of her discharge. (On Mid II we had all grieved her death. Imagining the depth of her despair, our sympathy was mixed with a considerable amount of awe and envy at the strength and courage it had taken for her to make the final move.) It was Dr. Maynard who had discharged her, at her request, and the phantom of what he regarded as his misjudgment must have haunted him continually.

"As if you can ever keep someone alive against their will," I thought.

"You are going to enormously complicated lengths to avoid involving yourself in your own therapy, Janet," Dr. Maynard said. "And I will not be party to these manipulations. Dr. Jarrow is not an ogre."

"I never said that he was," I answered curtly. "I just said I couldn't talk to him and I wanted to change doctors."

"This is the second request I have gotten for a doctor change this week. Maggie has similar complaints about Dr. Marin. She says they 'operate on different wave lengths.' " Maggie's apt phrase oozed off Dr. Maynard's tongue, clothed in his disdain. I knew of Maggie's problems with Dr. Marin, a dull, vulgar, insensitive man from all reports.

"I told her, essentially, what I am telling you. I am not making a threat, but a statement. This is a hospital, not a country club. You will begin to cooperate with your assigned doctor and with the staff, you will begin to participate in the daily life of the ward and in your own scheduled activities and jobs or we will take disciplinary action. I am late for a meeting. Good-bye."

"No go," I told Maggie as we sat in an open field on the grounds. "And he even threatened disciplinary action if I didn't shape up."

"You too," she said glumly. And, opening her notebook and perking up, she added, "Let's finish the poem we were working on."

"Which one?" I asked.

"The one about the roustabout, remember? It had the lines,

The ibson volunteer abstracted molars by the score,
Complaining that his stigma lay encrusted by the door.

> *He oscillated putridly and limped a somber grin,*
> *"My trauma cannot function," he confided to his kin.*

"What came next?" I asked.
Maggie read,

> *Although you feign aghast, my friends, do not belie my dude,*
> *For pumpernickel bables are a most nutritious food.*

"That's where we stopped."
"What's a 'bable'?" I asked.
"A newborn bagel?" she volunteered. We both laughed. Maggie and I had started writing poems together several weeks before; we had found an outlet for the creativity that had been bottled up so long it was going moldy inside us. We wrote together, alternating couplets, keeping to a prescribed rhythm, but letting our imaginations romp unrestricted with the words. The staff called them our "nonsense" poems.
"I've got it. Listen," I said, grabbing a pencil. "Dedicated to Lester Maynard!"

> *And then he sipped his anthem with occasional disgust*
> *In enigmatic grandeur, shouting, "MENTAL HEALTH or*
> *BUST."*

"Perfect. Fantastic!" Maggie said.
"Did you see Jarrow's face when I recited the verse at the community meeting?" I asked. "He was an absolute potato. He's such a prig."
We both collapsed with laughter, rolling in the grass and giggling. The residents and Dr. Maynard had sat together, of course, in a somber line, apart from the patients. It had been a special two-hour community meeting called to discuss proper moral conduct and the necessity for sexual abstinence in a mental hospital.
"Recite it again, Janet," Maggie begged. "You were so funny." She started to laugh again.
"You be Maynard," I said.
We both stood up in the knee-high grass.
"It has come to my attention," Maggie spoke in a thin voice, mimicking Dr. Maynard's vacuous pomposity. "It has come to my attention that some patients, a very few I'm sure, have been taking advantage of their privileges and the warm weather and engaging in promiscuous activities on the grounds of this hospital."
"No!" I imitated Carol's faked outraged exclamation.
Maggie, as Dr. Maynard, ignored it.

"As I have said before, this is not a country club. Freedom comes with responsibilities, or there can be no freedom at all. I understand a certain young man and a girl from Mid II were found, only partially clothed, in the bushes near the tennis court."

"Horrors!" came an unidentified voice.

It was at that point in the meeting that I had stood up, paper in hand, and recited,

> Oh ripe flesh hanging everywhere in evanescent white!
> "The transcendental joys of love," she belched, "are sheer delight!"

The meeting had broken up with the patients' appreciative laughter and Dr. Maynard had put me on restrictions for a week. I almost didn't care. I had no place to go anyway. In an act of sympathy and friendship, Maggie had stayed with me on the ward for the week, causing Dr. Maynard to walk around in a glower of frustrated anger. She didn't even go to her doctor's appointments.

Now, with Dr. Maynard's final refusal to change our doctors, it seemed as if our last hope of ever getting out of the hospital—and our last reason for staying sane—had vanished. I was angry, I was bitter, I was lost. Knowing that we were without recourse or power, we tried to salvage something from what we felt were life sentences. We tried to wring some humor, mental-hospital humor, from a situation that was bleak and desperate beyond belief.

The next day Maggie hung a sign that said "Abandon Hope All Ye That Enter Here" above the entrance to Mid II. It was down in an hour, but she had made her statement.

Without quite realizing the moment of transition—perhaps it was when Dr. Steber left—I had passed from a state of passive acceptance and suffering to a state of actively seeking revenge on my torturers. I'd be damned if I'd let them see me in pain. Damned if I'd shuffle for them.

Maggie and I were like starved children in a pastry shop. Unrestrained, we broke down; we ran free and wild.

For three weeks we hid, with a growing number of followers, in the bathroom during doctors' rounds—until there were only a tiny number of patients, all new, to submit to case-history questioning from the team. We sent letters, sarcastic, important-sounding but virtually incomprehensible documents written in flowery, pseudo-business/academic prose to all the ward doctors. It was harassment, plain and simple. And it was exhilarating.

David Silver's brother had smuggled some marijuana onto the ward, and we smoked in the backyard of Mid II, getting so high we stumbled around gloriously, but no one even noticed. It was the first time I ever smoked pot and it tickled my fancy that we could turn on, unobserved, in this fortress of professional behavior watchers.

Maggie and I continued to write our poems, tacking them in the bathroom and on the bulletin board, alongside such comments as "Persecutors will be Violated," "You Can't Have Your Hog and Eat It Too," or "Down in the Mouth is Worth Two in the Bush." The doctors were infuriated, but impotent. And we revelled in it all.

But there was a recklessness, a childishness, an abandon to our pranks that tempered the satisfaction we got from expressing our outrage. Where would it all end? For myself, I felt as though I was rushing uncontrollably forward on a track that was programmed, at a time I couldn't predict, to self-destruct. It was inevitable. But why shouldn't I get some kicks along the way? Why shouldn't I have some fun, however small, before the final blow-up?

But inside I was dying and crying; the whole world was blacking out.

Jessie had razor blades; I heard her bragging how she had copped them from the nurses' station in the adolescent pavilion. They were single-edged, too, the best kind because you got more leverage, without nicking your fingers.

"Let me have one, Jessie, please," I begged.

"No, Janet. They're mine. Get your own."

"Come on Jessie, just one. I won't cut my wrists," I lied. "Don't worry. I just want to have it, you know, sort of for security."

"You promise?"

"I promise."

She gave me a razor blade; I slipped it into my cigarette pack. "What an obvious place," I thought with satisfaction. "But they're all so dumb, they won't even know." I heard a very real, small, frightened voice inside me crying, "Help. Help me. Please." But I closed my ears. I didn't want to listen.

I stood near my window, looking out at the summer world, distorted by thick security screens.

When Dr. Steber left, I recalled, I had written a series of letters to Dr. Simmons, the hospital director, requesting that I be discharged. They were well-reasoned and respectful letters, not at all like the bitter satiric documents Maggie and I had recently been creating from our frustration. I had calmed my acute sense of loss, and had explained that rather than begin a relationship with a new doctor in the hospital, I would prefer to continue therapy outside. I wanted very badly to leave. I felt I could control my self-destructive urges despite recent indications to the contrary; I had already been at

JANET

Oceanville the requisite three months; there were people waiting for admission who needed and wanted the hospital; I didn't. Would he please consider my request? Bring it up at staff meeting? Respectfully yours.

I waited; no answer.

When I met Dr. Jarrow for the first time, I renewed my requests. No answer.

After several more letters, Dr. Maynard told me that Dr. Simmons felt it was premature for me to leave.

"But you can't keep me here against my will," I had screamed.

"We only want to help you, Janet; be assured, we know what's best."

I slipped my razor blade out of the Marlboro pack and unwrapped it, holding it up to the waning, filtered sunlight.

"Fuck them all, the bastards," I said, shaking my head.

Was this really me standing here with this blade, was this me cutting myself deeper and deeper into the pit that was waiting? Me—Janet Moss—a mental patient?

"It must be me," I said. "Who else could it be?"

I seemed to hear laughter; the room seemed filled with doctors and nurses, looking at me, shaking their heads gravely.

"The prognosis is not good," I heard. "Not good, not good, not good."

It was a familiar motion; it got easier each time; I didn't care that people were passing back and forth in the corridor outside my room and that someone was bound to enter momentarily. I wasn't trying to kill myself. It was the cutting that mattered. Those sharp, searing pains into my flesh, that bright red blood that stained my jeans. At least it was real, it was mine, the only freedom I had left. I looked at the blood and at myself watching myself, cool and removed. I felt like a stranger, fascinated yet puzzled by an alien ritual of blood-letting.

"I must be sick," I said to myself, "to be doing this."

"Don't adopt their view," a voice in my head warned. "If you do, you're doomed."

"I am sick," I cried. "Sick. Sick. Sick. Crazy. Sick." In an orgy of self-recrimination, I screamed the words at my mangled arms. "No matter what I do, I'm *sick*."

Two aides on the afternoon shift, stumbling over each other, appeared breathlessly at the door. I was still holding the blade and blood dripped from my wrists.

"I'll be on special again," I thought. "I don't think these cuts will need stitches. Just dressings and bandages," I said out loud.

Oceanville Hospital

Several weeks later, I cut my wrists again. This time with one of the blades that was still hidden in my room from my first attempt.

By the time October came, I was almost a legend. Next to Sandy Steinberg, I had the most hours on special and the most scars in the hospital.

I was one of the sickest patients on Mid II; everybody said so.

I had become addicted to razor blades.

"Where will it end?" I asked myself. "God, I can't go on like this. Please make it end soon."

But God wouldn't; I had to act myself. Pills would be better, I knew, but since I was not taking any medication, I didn't have access to anything sufficiently potent. It would have to be blades. I had one left, hidden behind the reproduction of Paul Klee's *The Twittering Machine*, hanging beside my bed. This time I would not be cutting for the satisfaction or need to cut; this time I would not use the excuse that I was so sick I couldn't control my self-destructive impulses. This was a logical, well-reasoned decision. I had weighed my choices: continued hospitalization, a half-life with my parents as my guardians, or suicide. I chose the only viable alternative. Life was unbearable, there was too much pain.

This time I would not be discovered. I would make sure of that. There would be no morning light.

I came to the final decision by lunchtime, and I went calmly through the day, trying to be cheerful and not arouse suspicion. When the midnight shift came on, and made their first check, I pretended, successfully, to be asleep. The check over, I sat up in bed; the blade was under my pillow.

I thought of my mother and father and their grief. "I don't want to hurt you," I whispered, crying into the night. "Please try to understand, I have to do this." I thought of Mary and my brother. The blackness of the night was seeping into my brain as people's faces became blurred. I knew I had to act. Quickly.

So I cut, hard downward thrusts, deeper and deeper, until the blood from my core was running out. I had never cut like that, ever—deep angry cuts into my flesh. I was weak, nauseated, and I lay in a growing pool of blood. I pulled the covers over my head, curled myself up and waited to die. I couldn't feel the individual cuts. Just a kaleidoscope of pain, undifferentiated, that encased me; I was in a box of pain. The bed was whirling, I could hear the whoosh of the sheets against my nightgown. I began to vomit; I couldn't breathe. It was dark, darker.

"Thank God, it's finally going to be over," I thought.

JANET

Mrs. Petra did the three-o'clock check. Everything was quiet. Too quiet, she may have thought. And why was Janet completely buried, in a massive lump, under her covers? I had already passed out when she found me.

I remember, through a red blur, having my wrists sewn and bandaged in the medication room, by a doctor I didn't know. There were a lot of cuts and they were deep.

"She has always healed well," I heard Mrs. Petra say. She was holding my other hand, as I regained consciousness.

Dr. Maynard came to see me in the morning. He didn't even say hello, but stood gravely by my bed, anger making his left eye twitch.

If I did not shape up immediately, he explained, and stop cutting my wrists, I would be shipped to a state hospital. Oceanville with its therapeutic permissiveness could no longer be responsible for me.

"Why didn't you let me go five months ago when I wanted to?" I asked him miserably.

"Obviously, you were too sick. We are doctors, we have a responsibility." He was so smug it was sickening.

"And you still won't let me go, right?" I demanded.

"We have tried to help you, within the framework of the hospital. But you wanted to do it your way. We went along; we cannot stand by any longer."

"And if I stop cutting my wrists," I asked with a dawning perception, "will you let me go then?"

"If you demonstrate some improvement and a desire to be well, yes, we will consider discharging you."

He looked distastefully at my heavily bandaged wrists. "You will need a few days in bed and special for a week. After that, we'll see." He turned and left.

So, they were going to punish me again. Only this time it would be for keeps. A state hospital. Legal commitment. "Well, at least this time they're not pretending it's for my own good," I said out loud. "My poor parents," I thought. "They don't deserve this."

I thought of Sandy, and the last time I had seen her, a bleak, rainy Saturday afternoon in early autumn. She was being shipped to a state hospital; no one knew which one. Her suitcase was packed and she was sitting on it. Her room looked bombed out: the mattress stained and torn, papers and cigarette butts on the floor, the walls filthy and marked with crayoned curses, the curtains ripped. There were no pictures, no color in the room. It smelled of misery and total, utter desolation. It was hard to believe it had been lived in by a human being. I stood at the door.

"I came to say good-bye, Sandy," I said.

She didn't move or blink; her vacant eyes stared into the grayness of the room.

I moved closer.

"Maybe you won't have to stay too long," I offered, trying to be cheerful. "We'll come to visit; David said so. And Maddie."

"Maddie's being shipped away tomorrow," Sandy said tonelessly.

"Sandy," I started.

She stood up and grabbed my hands.

"Don't let them do this to you, Janet," she said fiercely. "Get out when you can. Or you'll never get out. You're intelligent. You're pretty. They'll get you. Be smart. Cool it with the blades now. I wish I had."

She was clutching my hands till her knuckles were white. Her eyes were bright as she pleaded with me, her cracking voice revealing the sensitivity I had always known was there.

"Your life isn't over, Sandy," I said.

"Don't waste your time on me," she interrupted harshly. "Take care of yourself. No one else will. I was strong and tough; you're not. I thought they couldn't touch me. But they got me. I'm warning you, Janet. Listen to me." She was shaking me. Tears were rolling down her sallow cheeks.

She sat down abruptly, letting me go. The tenseness, the fight in her seemed to have flowed out. She was small, vulnerable, terribly resigned.

"Please listen to me, Janet," she whispered hoarsely.

"I will, Sandy," I said. "I promise." I wanted more than anything else in the world to take this large-boned roughneck of a sad girl and hold her and comfort her and tell her it would be all right, that I loved her, and everything would be okay. I moved toward her, but she held her arm out stiffly, pushing me back. She seemed embarrassed at her show of weakness.

"Take this," she said, thrusting a worn book into my hand. "It's mine. I want you to have it. It's called *The Sibyl*."

Tears were clogging my throat and eyes.

"I—Sandy—" I began.

"And get out, please. Just go now. Leave me alone." She had turned her back and was looking out the window.

"Take care, Sandy," I whispered. And holding the book tight against my chest, I left.

In the three months that followed, I hadn't listened to her, though the memory of that day was etched in my heart. She had wanted so badly to give me something, not a book, but the advantage of her experience, so that she might have comfort in the knowledge that at least her suffering hadn't all been wasted.

Sitting in bed now, my wrists in fiery pain, I thought again of her warning. I hadn't believed it could happen to me, but it was coming true now. Did I still have time to change the plans that were being made for me? If so, it would be my last chance. Once in a state hospital, I would be doomed forever.

"They would rather release me," I thought, "than commit me. But they have to cover themselves against malpractice or negligence suits. They don't want a postdischarge suicide to deal with. But they do want to get rid of me, that's for sure." I laughed bitterly to myself. "They must rue the day Berman pressured them into admitting me."

It was a question of timing, self-control, orchestration, and credibility. They had to believe I was repentant and that I was really getting well. They wanted to believe it, so I would be playing to a receptive audience. I would become the model patient: cooperative, submissive, and cheerful. I would admit my mistakes, bow to their wisdom, demonstrate my good intentions and promise to behave and continue to pursue the path of mental health. They would write it down for their records, I would submit to the humiliation of a formal staff hearing, and they would let me go—a fair exchange.

"The hypocritical bastards!" I said, when I unfolded my plan to Maggie.

"You're just finding that out?" she countered.

"No," I said. "But I'm going to put it to work for me for the first time."

It took two months to fully implement my plan, two months of silent hidden suffering, during which a new Janet emerged. Dr. Maynard smacked his lips in satisfaction; he was taking credit for the transformation, I could tell. And in a way, he was responsible. After my failed suicide attempt, he had said, in effect, "If you continue to act in accordance with your deepest feelings, we will send you away to a state institution. If you stop acting on the truth of your despair, we will give you your freedom."

Good mental patients please their keepers and are rewarded.

Bad mental patients are punished.

Good is happy.

Bad is sad.

It was a simple formula, so simple I wondered why it had taken me nearly ten months to understand it.

Oceanville Hospital

I stopped sending abusive letters to the doctors. I faithfully followed my activity schedule. I participated in community meetings and spoke to the team on rounds. I received permission to go to school and enrolled in an aesthetics course at a nearby college, traveling an hour on two buses twice a week to get there. I hated it, it panicked me to travel at night, alone, with the lights flashing and the unfamiliar sounds and sights and expectations of the outside world making me shrink like a snail deeper and deeper into my frightened self. The staff was very proud of me.

I thought about razor blades, I dreamed about razor blades, I stole razor blades from drugstores and hoarded them in my room, waiting for the time I could be free to use them again. I told Dr. Jarrow how wrong I had been to want to cut myself up, and he communicated my change of heart to Dr. Maynard, who smiled benevolently at me in the halls, patted my head paternally, and moved on, self-satisfied, smug, all-powerful.

Inside my body, I crouched, a knot of anguish, watching my outside self perform to the doctors' delight.

"I must be very sick to be playing this game," I thought. "Very sick to want to cut myself so badly."

In some ways, the indoctrination had been a success.

"You'll be leaving anytime now, Janet, I bet," Mrs. Rooney said. "It's a joy to see you feeling good."

She meant it, and I wanted to scream, "No, no, I feel so bad I want to die!" But I couldn't, because to do so would have meant months—maybe years—more of hospitalization to get me well. So I kept my silence and smiled.

Only Maggie knew of my double life and the pain I was enduring.

"You can't go on forever pretending to be one thing and feeling another," she said.

"Not forever," I answered. "Just long enough to get sprung."

"Then what?" she asked.

"I don't know. But at least I'll be free."

She looked doubtful and concerned. "I know what you mean, in a way, Janet. But I think you're playing with fire."

"I have no other choice," I said. "Except to be buried alive."

Jacob Sternfeld had treated my brother after he left home and during the time of his emotional distress while his wife was in Oceanville. I had phoned him and visited him once, without my parents' knowledge, when I was at Ellis. His advice, on hearing my problems, was that I go back to school and try to work with Dr. Kurtzman, since, although I wasn't very sick, I obviously needed professional help. He couldn't really see me more than once because he was seeing my brother and that would be unethical.

But he was no longer seeing my brother, who had fled the city with his wife and was hiding out at a university, taking a post-graduate degree. Perhaps Dr. Sternfeld would take me as a patient.

I had no particular fondness for him and no particular reason to believe he was a good doctor. Judging by the outcome of my brother's therapy, the very opposite conclusion could be drawn. But I needed a doctor. Oceanville Hospital, still not absolutely convinced that I was trustworthy and well, though anxious to get rid of me just the same, had consented to discharge me only if I could find a psychiatrist who would take me into treatment and who would effectively take responsibility for me and my actions.

My parents, holding firmly to their belief in Dr. Sternfeld, called to ask if he would treat me.

I called him to ask if he would treat me.

He wavered.

We pleaded.

He finally consented.

On a winter's day in 1962, Dr. Sternfeld sent the following letter to the director of Oceanville Hospital:

> *Dear Sir:*
>
> *Your patient, Janet Moss, has arranged to continue her treatment with me after she leaves Oceanville Hospital. I would very much appreciate if you could send me as soon as possible an abstract of her hospital record, including data obtained from psychological tests.*
>
> > *Very truly yours,*
> > *Jacob Sternfeld, M.D.*

The following week I was discharged, regaining my freedom after ten months of noncriminal incarceration.

Dr. Sternfeld / Monroe Park

Dr. Jacob Sternfeld *was something* of a quasi-legendary figure in New York, particularly among the intellectual Jewish middle class from whom his private patients were drawn. Eclectic eccentric, the Boy Scout of shrinks, he exuded an aura of self-confidence that verged on the aggressive. Above all else, he was Benevolent and Concerned. From the first moment of our relationship he intimidated me; and I felt guilty about it. In a sense, he sprung me from Oceanville; I was bound in gratitude to him. And, of course, unspoken, there was the ever-present reality of rehospitalization if I didn't behave.

Eight years later, our intensely complicated relationship was still defined by the facts of its beginning. He called me Janet. I called him Dr. Sternfeld. Wordlessly, he offered himself as Savior, Rock, Father, and Friend. No one human being could accommodate that diversity of roles, but he thought he could; and I wanted him to. Alternately, he played Supreme Judge, Exterior Conscience, Punishing God, Reproachful Father, and Thwarted Lover, though he did not admit to these less than flattering portrayals. And all this on demand, at thirty-five, then forty, then forty-five dollars a performance. It seemed somewhat humiliating to be paying for friendship, love, and comfort; and uncertain what would happen to his wellsprings of compassion and caring if my parents' money ran out.

Dr. Sternfeld had approved of my plans to spend three weeks with Mary and her family at her home in California, at Christmastime to ease my transition from Oceanville back to the world. We would start treatment when I returned.

"Take these with you, Janet," he said, handing me a white palm-size cardboard box which he had just finished filling with blue tablets. "If you are very anxious, or if you feel suicidal, take one. Don't hesitate. You may take up to four a day. They may make you a little drowsy, but that's nothing to worry about."

"What are they?" I asked. Even though I had spent almost a year in a mental hospital, I knew next to nothing about drugs. I had taken an occasional Nembutal capsule to help me sleep. Nothing else.

"Stelazine," he said easily. "It is a remarkable drug, something called a psychic energizer. It is related to Compazine and Thorazine, in the same family so to speak, but it is not a tranquilizer." He spoke articulately, if a bit condescendingly.

"Is it habit-forming?" I asked him uneasily. I was standing in front of him holding the little white box, as he sat in a swivel chair at his desk. The bottom drawer of the massive antique desk was open; it was two drawers high, crammed full with bottles and boxes of pills, more kinds and colors of pills than I had ever seen. There must have been thousands of them. Reaching over, he shut the heavy drawer. "Habit-forming," he repeated, as though the idea were vaguely humorous. "Not at all. Of course not. Just take them whenever you need them. We don't want any accidents. You are out of the hospital, and I trust you will stay out."

He stood up and put his arm around my shoulder. I was shivering. His arm was strong, warm, muscular, and unthreatening. "He doesn't want anything from me," I thought.

"I'm so afraid," I whispered, starting to cry.

"Of what, Janet?" Dr. Sternfeld asked.

"I don't know." My body was shaking with all the fear and tears I had subdued during the past months of my pantomime of health at Oceanville. "What am I doing on the outside?" I thought, panicked. "I'm too sick, I should be in a hospital."

"It's okay to cry, you know," Dr. Sternfeld said, wrapping me in his strong protective arms. I buried my face in his chest. How good it was to feel safe. Or at least to have the illusion of safety, if only for a moment.

"Everything's going to be all right," he said, reassuring me. "I'll be here when you come back from California. If you need me when you're away . . ." He pointed across the room to the telephone. "You can call. Anytime. I'll give you the numbers."

"I'm afraid I'll cut my wrists," I said, falling into his chest.

"No, you won't," he said. "You *can* control your impulses. I'm here to help you learn to control those impulses. But if you're afraid, you can always take a pill; that's what they're for."

What kind of magic was in these pills? I wondered. Once swallowed, did they cause paralysis in my fingers so I couldn't hold a blade? I didn't care. Dr. Sternfeld was there; he was going to take care of me.

"The hour is up, Janet," Dr. Sternfeld said, glancing at the antique

French clock hanging above his desk. It read one forty-five. I had come at one o'clock.

I felt a surge of anger in my chest. He had held me, comforted me; he had said, "It's all right to cry." And now I had to turn off my pain, turn away from his comfort—because the "hour" was over? What did he think I was, a machine? Could my crying mechanism be synchronized with his clock? I swallowed my anger hard, as I heard a voice inside me say, "Aren't you ashamed of yourself, you ungrateful girl? To be so picayune? After how he's shown his caring for you?" I couldn't answer the voice or tell Dr. Sternfeld about it. My shame flowed through my body, a sticky melted mass covering the anger that stuck like a bone in my throat.

I disentangled myself from Dr. Sternfeld's body, and wiped my eyes and nose with the tissues he offered. He was smiling.

"I have faith in you, Janet," he said.

"You don't even know me," I answered.

He waved away my response with his hand. "You'd be surprised how much I know about you," he said, a touch of mischief in his bright blue eyes.

"What do you mean?" I asked.

"I treated Matthew, you know," he said. "I've spoken to Dr. Berman, and I got a report from Oceanville. So I'm not as ignorant as you think."

"Good Lord," I whispered to myself. "They've got a dossier on me, and they send it to anyone who wants to see it. And I don't even know what kind of crazy they've called me. And Matthew! My God, what can he have heard from Matthew?"

The illusion of safety had dissipated completely. I clutched the packet of pills tighter.

"Have a good time in California. Relax, and I will see you in three weeks." He handed me a small white card with his home telephone number, his office number, and his hospital number on it, and walked across the room, opening the heavy carved sliding oak door. "Call me when you get back," he said. I still stood near the desk, questions and doubts playing hide and seek in my aching head.

"I have another patient," he said, pointing to the waiting room across the hall.

"Oh, yes, of course, I'm sorry," I said in a flurry of apology. I walked past him through the doorway and he reached out, stopping me as he took my hands in his.

"It may be a long struggle, Janet," he said, "but you're going to be fine. I know it. And remember, I'm always here."

JANET

I could feel the tears coming again, but I stopped them, pulling my hands away.

"Thank you," I said, my eyes on the floor. "Thank God I'm wearing my sunglasses and he can't see my eyes," I thought.

I rode home on the subway, my mind in confusion and distress. This man, this stranger, had taken me in his arms and said in action and in words that he would care for me, help me; that he would *be there* for me. Why? He barely knew me. Yet, he had unerringly touched my need, and I had crumpled like a rag doll into his arms. He had said he believed in me. How could he? No matter what second-hand information he had, he still didn't really know me at all. Yet, it was good to hear that declaration of faith. Good, and disconcerting at the same time. Because how could it possibly be true? But would he lie? And the pills. I was glad for the sense of security they gave me. If I needed one, I could take it. But how did he know what pills to give me? He didn't examine me. In fact, he knew almost nothing about me. "Remember," he said, "I'm always here." No one had been *always there* for me for a very long time. I was clay in his hands, I thought a bit cynically. And he can play with me—if he wants to. Did he do that today? He holds out his arms. I cry. He says, "Time's up." I must stop. He did it twice. I mustn't let him do that to me. The voice of mine I first heard in Dr. Sternfeld's office spoke: "Shame, shame. The man tries to show concern and you suspect him. It's not his fault there was a patient waiting. Are you so sick you can't respond to another human being's authentic concern for you?"

"Shut up," I said. "I have enough problems without you telling me to feel guilty. I probably have enough guilt so I could give a little to every person in Brooklyn and still have some left over to spread around in the other four boroughs. So just leave me alone."

The next day I flew to Los Angeles. Mr. and Mrs. Boyd and Mary welcomed me warmly into their home. "So glad you've come, Janet," Mrs. Boyd said. "Mary's told us so much about you."

"Has she told you I'm crazy?" I thought achingly to myself, as the sun streamed through the white curtains of the flowery front room.

Mary had told them about Oceanville, and they seemed to accept me completely into their life. I had nothing to hide. But I couldn't help wondering if they trusted me completely. Mrs. Boyd seemed always to be the last one in the kitchen—so she could lock up the knives? The medicine cabinet contained nothing but aspirin and milk of magnesia. And I knew, too, that their acceptance of me was predicated entirely upon the normality of my behavior. What would happen if I suddenly started to scream during dinner? Or if I mentioned the gargoylelike creatures I saw each night peeking from the corner of my room?

I couldn't keep up my pretense forever. I wasn't normal, I was sick. Why pretend that I had a chance to have a life like other people? Why not just give up now?

Through my despondency and isolation, Mary seemed extraordinarily lovely, unreachable. At Oceanville my friend Dina and I, commiserating, had described ourselves as small, brown, and mousy with tall, golden creatures for friends.

What did Mary want with me, I thought again and again during the endless three weeks. She asked me here from pity. She is ashamed of me.

"This is my friend Janet, from New York," Mary would say, introducing me to one of her family or friends.

"Do you go to Ellis, too?"

"Well, not exactly," I would say, swallowing in panic.

"Oh? Do you go to another school?"

"No."

"Oh." Silence. The strangers exchange glances. I want to disappear in a puff of purple smoke, forever.

"Then you've graduated. And you're working in New York City? How exciting. Are you on vacation from your job?"

"I'm between jobs."

"Oh." A silence as black as a tomb.

It was written in the turn of their lips and the clouds in their eyes; they didn't believe me. I wasn't one of them. What sort of twenty-year-old girl doesn't go to school or work? What kind of a weirdo has Mary brought home?

It was no use. I could never pass. The pain would go on and on and on, forever. I knew it as if I had already lived through the panic and despair of a lifetime of waking-sleeping hours.

The night before I was to return to New York, I sneaked into Mrs. Boyd's sewing room. I opened her sewing box. Inside was a single-edged razor blade, shiny and new. It transfixed me. I couldn't move, only stare at it, visions of my arms and throat mutilated by the hot blade flaming before my eyes. I wanted to take it and cut and cut myself until there was nothing left of me but ribbons of bloodied flesh, piled on the floor.

"Why not?" I said. "Why not get it over with now?" I stared at the gleaming blade; it seemed almost alive.

JANET

I slipped it into my cigarette pack and turned, abruptly, to find Mary standing in the doorway. She had just come in.

"Janet," she said, her face tense with concern. "Are you okay?"

"Oh, Mary." I fell into her outstretched arms. "I'm so scared. What's going to happen to me? I want to go back to Oceanville now, where it's safe, and I don't have to pretend; and that's sick, sick. I know it, so I'll never get better."

"You're going to get better," she said. "Dr. Sternfeld will help you. You'll be better soon. I know it."

"No," I said. "No, never. I'm too mixed up."

The next day I took a plane to New York, the vision of Dr. Sternfeld's comforting presence buoying me. I almost couldn't wait until the following morning to see him again.

Dr. Sternfeld greeted me with a distant coolness that contrasted sharply with the open fatherly affection he had volunteered the day before I left to visit Mary. I had been waiting for fifteen minutes in the red-carpeted waiting room, examining the paintings, splashes of color on the walls. I was nervous and twittery, clutching and unclutching my cigarettes, monitoring every small sound that drifted down the elegant staircase and through the windows. Through the doorway, across the rubbed parquet floor of the narrow hall that separated the waiting room from the office, I saw the heavy carved doors slide open and a dark-haired young girl emerge. She looked about my age; her eyes were swollen.

"I don't know how to thank you for seeing me," she said, turning to Dr. Sternfeld. Watching her in her unhappiness, I felt an inexplicable shock of jealousy through my body. Would he ever see me if I were upset, I wondered.

"It's all right," he said. "I hope you've learned something."

"Yes, oh, yes." As she pulled her gloves out of her coat pocket, a small white cardboard box fell on the floor. She bent to pick it up.

"I'll see you at the regular time next week," Dr. Sternfeld said, watching her put a fuzzy plaid hat over her head. She opened the door to the front vestibule, rattling its brilliant old stained glass.

"I'll be with you in a few minutes, Janet," Dr. Sternfeld said. I nodded, my smile cut off as he left his office and disappeared down a hallway. I heard voices, scurrying feet, angry tones.

All I could think of was the open office, the heavy old desk, its vast recesses filled with pills. I had seen them; I knew they were there. If I took some, would he miss them? Probably not, there were so many. Did I have time? Did I dare? My heart was beating a wild tattoo of fear and excitement. But I couldn't move toward the drawer filled with forbidden treasures. Pills of all colors danced a witches' ritual in front of my eyes.

"Come in, Janet." I jumped, startled. His voice had punctured my dreams.

He watched me walk. I held my hated body tightened, my shoulders hunched, my face all but obscured by sunglasses. He closed the doors. Immediately to the right, along the rose-colored plaster wall, was a couch, a leather couch. It could have been a twin of Dr. Berman's. A big lazy old easy chair sat behind the raised-pillow part of the couch, in a small alcove with a bay window. A low coffee table was parallel to the couch.

"I don't have to lie down, right?" I asked. Dr. Sternfeld had already settled himself in the soft depths of his chair and lit a cigarette. He didn't answer; he watched me. Tentatively I walked to the couch and sat down on the edge. He was waiting, his face set in a semismile that suggested infinite time and patience and a certain godlike immovability.

My lips felt fused, my tongue a stone lump. I lit a cigarette, looked at the red carpet at my feet and directed every living cell in my body to disappear. "Go away. Go away," I told myself. "And whatever you do, don't cry." To cry was to let the sap drain from the body. I was vulnerable and that was dangerous. But crying was the only thing that relieved the terrible shaking tensions in my body and my brain, if only for a short while.

Dr. Sternfeld sat silent, watching.

"I stole a razor blade," I burst forth, the words exploding uncontrollably, "from Mrs. Boyd's sewing box. And I took three dollars from Mary's wallet. She's my friend. I stole money from her." I was screaming and the tears were forming hulks of building pressure behind my eyes and in my throat.

Dr. Sternfeld was unmoved, waiting.

"What are you staring at, a freak show?" I sobbed.

"Did you use the razor blade?" he asked quietly.

"No," I said. "Not yet."

"I want you to give it to me." He was firm, sitting forward in his chair.

"No." I shrank back. "No. It's mine."

"Give it to me, Janet." His voice was warm, sinuous.

"I'll just get another one," I said, beginning to cry.

"I want you to give me the blade." His hand was extended across the coffee table.

"Why?" I cried.

"Do you trust me?"

"Yes," I answered automatically, though it wasn't entirely true.

"Then prove it. Give me the blade."

"It's not fair," I screamed. "It's not fair." I was crying, my body shaking. "I want to trust you. I want to believe in you. All the while I was away I thought about you and how you said you'd always be here for me. But that's not being here, taking the razor."

"I don't want you to hurt yourself," he said.

"But if you take that, I have nothing."

"The razor can't give you security," Dr. Sternfeld said. "Not really."

"I know, I know," I screamed. "But it's all going to end in death soon anyway, so what's the difference?"

"There won't be any difference if you kill yourself now. We have a lot of work to do unraveling the past. But we can't do it if you're dead."

"I don't want to die. I just want to cut my wrists."

"The razor, Janet."

I threw my pocketbook on the table. "Take it, it's in my wallet," I said.

"You don't understand at all," I whispered. "You're no different from all the others." I drew up my knees, crossed my arms over my head, and buried my face in my lap. Hollow, barking sobs came from my body. I was empty, except for tears and pain.

"Would you like me to sit down next to you, Janet?"

"Yes," I managed, muffled between cries.

I felt his body, a warm weight on the couch beside me. He held out a box of tissues. Gratefully I took some; my nose and eyes were dripping, my whole face was wet and swollen. He sat for a few minutes watching me cry.

"Would you like me to put my arm around you?" he asked.

"Yes, yes," I cried out. "Yes."

He held me in his arms, his strong warm arms, as I howled and cried and shook. He was steady, unyielding, *there* as he had promised. I collapsed in his arms with a relief that shook me to the core. I was scared at how much I needed his warmth and his protection, scared at how easy it had been to relinquish control and cry.

"I'm going to fall apart," I said, still crying. "I'm afraid if I really let go, I'll fall apart in pieces on the floor." He was still holding me.

"Don't be afraid," he said.

"You're keeping me together."

He didn't say anything. I felt my body growing whole as he held me, his warmth calming my tense, suffering self. It felt so good to be there, to be held like that. It was terrifying how good it felt. What would I do if he went away? I didn't want to think of that, but it was there, the danger, and it was always going to be there. The shadow, the uncertainty, the other side of complete safety and dependence. I closed my eyes to it, to everything but the holding and the safeness.

Beyond the circle of his arms and the glow of his *there*-ness was the blade.

I stopped crying, occasional residual sobs making my body shiver involuntarily.

"I'm going back to my chair now," he said. I watched him mutely. He looked across the room to his desk, lighted with a brilliant fluorescent lamp. "We only have a few minutes left," he said.

The latch was opened, the spring released, the bottom was gone from under me, I was falling. He didn't seem to notice.

He asked briefly about California, whether I had taken the Stelazine.

"Once or twice," I said; my voice echoed through the tunnel as I fell.

His voice came through, filtered and alien.

Now that I was back and in treatment, he could start me on a regular medication. The other had been just an emergency measure. He would give me a tranquilizer, not a very widely used one, called Taractan. It had few adverse side effects and would not make me very sleepy. He opened the bottom right-hand drawer, rummaged around and came out with a fistful of sample packages of Taractan. The pills were red and looked like M&M candies. We would start at four hundred milligrams a day.

"Why not?" I thought. "If it will make me feel better."

"This should calm you down a little." Dr. Sternfeld said as he handed the samples to me.

I stuffed the bulky cards with their cellophane-wrapped pills into my pocketbook as Dr. Sternfeld stood. The time was up. He was looking at me oddly; I felt as if he was assessing my chances of ultimate salvation. Would I make it? Would I be a good patient? There was an undefinable smugness, though, almost a pride in his narrowed eyes, as if he were saying, "Yes, I'm pleased with the way things went today." I was horrified at the idea that he might have wanted me to break down the way I did, that perhaps he could even have tried to maneuver me in that direction. He was smiling, his arms outstretched.

"We have a lot of work to do, Janet." With a sentence and a

gesture, he had allied us in the struggle. I wasn't alone. I fell again into the inviting warmth of his arms; he patted my shoulder.

"I'll see you on Thursday. Four forty-five."

I went to see Dr. Sternfeld at least twice a week, usually three times. It was virtually all I did, except lunch occasionally with a friend, listen to the radio, write letters, and try not to fight with my mother. My house was crowded with memories of a childhood and adolescence of achievement and joy, enriched in the remembering, offered to me by my mother, to look at, digest, suffer. Her son had left her, and I was all but gone. She was bitter, sad, lonely. I was so sorry she hurt, but my own pain was more than I could deal with.

There was no place to go, no one to trust, but Dr. Sternfeld. I fled to his office, an island of safety. He welcomed me. But he had his own trips, though he never admitted to them, and I never saw them myself until many years later.

Dr. Sternfeld was totally unpredictable, presenting himself at one moment as my friend and champion, turning the next instant to sarcasm and mockery in order to shake me from my stubbornness. He invited me to call him anytime, at any hour, then berated me for conceiving of myself as "special" or "privileged."

It was difficult for me to talk to him, and I spent hours at home writing the things I was afraid to say. In many ways Dr. Sternfeld made me feel helpless and angry; often, when I was with him, I doubted my reason, my perceptions, my honesty. At the end of one session, after a particularly trying week, I handed him a piece of green-lined paper. "Here. Please read this," I said. "I wrote it yesterday."

Why is it so very important that I not cut my wrists anymore? I don't plan it. It happens. Alone in a room. Noise intrudes. So afraid. Think. Can't think. Room is swarming with bugs. No awareness of anything but me and the razor. No significance. Must. Must. It isn't fair. I believe in you. I trust you. You make a tiny part of me have hope and no way to hold on. . . . I become more confused after you talk. I become confused because you seem to put words in my mouth and they seem perhaps right and I just don't know. Yes, your voice echoes in my head, terribly loud, with ringing and screeches. Mocking, threatening words and sounds. And I am uncertain of what you mean and suddenly I am afraid of you, too. That same cringing freezing fear that turns itself into hate hate hate and desire to kill and there is no way out—of anything. . . . Yes, you put me on the defensive and then you tell me that you are not sarcastic and

*impatient. It is in my mind, my sickness. I feel that you are accusing
me of something when you say I must be irreproachable only to
maintain a semblance of self-respect. And you make me feel
ashamed because I cannot stop thinking about Matthew. I keep
sensing, in spite of not wanting to, that you are mocking me,
making light or pat decisions and judgments about my life. What
did I learn with Dr. Wyatt? At Oceanville? With Dr. Berman?
Nothing?! That is what you ask. Well, I did learn something, but
maybe I cannot say it; it is too important. Please, please don't
become sarcastic in contrast to my stubbornness—my inability to
think, talk, and cooperate. There are sirens ringing in my ears, a
constantly changing scenario of horror and unimaginables and
everything scares me. . . . You will still the inner hush, and I am
frightened.*

He didn't return my writing or even comment on it. I never asked
him if he had read it; I was too afraid.

After two months, the tensions in myself, my home, and in my
relationship with Dr. Sternfeld had become excruciating, and I stole
a package of razor blades from a neighborhood drugstore. One
weekday, after my parents were asleep, I cut my wrists. I didn't cut
very deeply, just deeply enough. I watched the blood; it was me. I
could still control me. After a few minutes, I bandaged my own
arms, cleaned up the bathroom, took a Nembutal, and went to sleep.

Two days later, as the first gashes were beginning to heal, I cut
myself again.

Dr. Sternfeld was grim. In less than two months, he had tried
several different drugs on me, including Tofranil, a popular antide-
pressant. The Tofranil had made my whole body shake and my
pulse race at one hundred thirty beats a minute..I was seeing bugs
crawling on the walls and I was palpitating and frenzied. He had
stopped the Taractan after only a couple of weeks because it didn't
seem to be doing anything. Nor did Stelazine have a positive effect
on my state of mind. Dr. Sternfeld had started me on Thorazine, the
granddaddy of tranquilizers. But even that had not worked. I had
cut my wrists. And he had stated his concern. I had done it again.
As far as Dr. Sternfeld was concerned, there were no choices left for
us. Or rather for him—in his treatment plan for me. He wanted me
to go into Monroe Park Hospital. And he wanted me to have
electroshock treatments.

"No," I said. "I won't go. I don't want to go into another hospital."

"Monroe Park is very different from Oceanville," he explained.
"It's a short-term hospital. People go there for a rest. Sometimes a

week or so. You'll be going in as my patient. I'll prescribe your medication; I'll be treating you."

"I don't want to go to a hospital," I repeated.

"You can't stay home in your present state," Dr. Sternfeld said.

"Why not?" I asked.

"I'm afraid someday you're not going to just scratch yourself with the blades. You're going to end up dead. I can't treat you if you're dead."

"I won't kill myself," I said. "That's not why I cut my wrists. I can't help it. The impulse comes over me. It blinds me. I don't feel anything; it's not me who's cutting. It's so frightening. I'm so scared."

"That's why I want you to go into the hospital. So you can have a rest from these compulsions and fears for a while, Janet." He spoke softly, almost cajoling. "Why not be good to yourself, for a change? Treat yourself to a rest. Don't deny yourself the luxury of being taken care of. Don't be ashamed of needing help." His words flowed out smooth and persuasive. "It's sort of like going to a hotel," he said. "A special kind of hotel. And I'll be in to see you regularly to take care of anything you need."

A hotel. This hospital was like a hotel? I couldn't believe what he was saying. I was feeling used; anger was turning to blackness inside me, blotting out my thinking and my words. And I didn't know why. But I was frightened. All I could see were the razor blades, the relief of the cutting. Where was he pushing me? Could I ever return?

"But the shock treatments?" I asked in a small voice. "I don't want to have an electric shock put through my brain. It's too awful."

"There's nothing to it," Dr. Sternfeld said blandly. "You'll get an anesthetic before, and you won't feel a thing. The whole procedure takes only a few seconds. And it is also entirely safe. There is no danger whatsoever." He spoke calmly, easily, the earnest clichés flowing into my head and circulating, like an unbroken electric current in my brain.

"No," I said vehemently. "I don't care what you say, I don't want to go into the hospital. And I won't have shock treatments. I don't need them. Shock treatments are for people who are in deep depressions. I'm not; you told me."

"Janet," Dr. Sternfeld said as he moved to sit beside me on the couch. "Janet, I only want what's best for you. Think about it. If there's a chance that the treatments will help you, they're worth a try."

Dr. Sternfeld / Monroe Park

The hour was over. The hour was always being over. I wandered through the cold streets, praying for a bus to run me over. I didn't want to go to the hospital. I had just gotten out of a hospital two months before. It wasn't the right thing for me. I knew it. But as Dr. Sternfeld said, what else was there? And shock treatments? No, never. I couldn't even contemplate that horror. What if I didn't go to the hospital? What then? More wrist-cutting. I knew it. And more. And eventually, Dr. Sternfeld would say, "I'm sorry, Janet, but I cannot treat you anymore." He had as much as threatened that already. Without him there was really nothing. He was the only line to life or a future that I had.

"I have to call Dr. Sternfeld," I told my parents after dinner.

"It's Janet," I said into the phone. "I'll go."

"I'll make the arrangements for your admission and I'll call you back. I'm glad, Janet. You've made the right decision, a positive decision. For yourself. For health."

"I don't know," I said as I put down the receiver.

"I'm going into the hospital again," I said to my parents. "Monroe Park. Dr. Sternfeld wants me to."

"Janet, why?" they asked in unison.

"I don't know. Oh, Mother. Daddy. I don't know."

A street in New York City. Monroe Park Hospital. Seven stories of loonies. A modern brick building, it didn't look like a hospital. More like an elementary school built in the 1950s. But then Oceanville hadn't looked like a hospital. What did a mental hospital look like anyway?

My father pulled the car to the curb. It was late winter, 1963. Dr. Sternfeld had telephoned to see if there was a bed; they knew I was coming. Two young nurses in spanking white uniforms emerged laughing from the front door. I looked upward: there were no bars on the windows. But, of course, bars on a residential street would never do. The community wouldn't like it. They probably had triple-thick screens—like at Oceanville—that were very strong and effective, probably as good as bars, and cosmetically more appealing. "They should try them at the zoos," I thought. "What's going on in the darkness behind those screens? How many suffering people are locked in there?"

"I'm afraid, Mother," I said. I pulled at the neat sleeve of her tweed winter coat. "Mother!" She hadn't heard, and looked without seeing down the windswept street. Maybe it would all go away for her if she stopped hearing or seeing—me, her pride, the hospital, Matthew, ambition, love, her memories. "I'm so scared," I said, and the winter wind wrapped my words around my body, knotting me in swirls of litter, dust, and fear. I moved into the brightly painted lobby, my head low, my shaded eyes nervously following the green carpet patterns under my feet. It was a trap, I knew it. And I was walking into it, freely, uncomplainingly. A tidal wave of shame flooded me; I gasped for breath.

"I'm a mouse, a toad, a bug," I thought. "I deserve what I get. I'm bad, ugly, bad."

"Stop thinking that way." It was my own voice, coming anguished and hot from my dry lips.

Everyone in the lobby turned to me. I could almost hear the jaws of the trap click shut; darkness began to close in like fog.

"This way, please," came a voice.

I walked, without seeing, propelled by a hand that felt like my father's, small and knotty.

A fog had enclosed me and I felt held aloft, as unreal as a dream you try to remember in the morning. I tried to see through the gray; there was someone with me, I could make out the outlines of seated figures. Yes. A man, across a desk. The lines sharpened. He was rustling papers, holding a pen.

Questions came. He was asking about me. Who was he asking? He was asking me.

"Why did you come to the hospital?"

"I don't know," I said.

"You must know." He was impatient, sharp.

"My doctor wanted me to come."

"Why?" he said.

"He wanted me to stop cutting my wrists."

"When did you cut your wrists?"

"I don't remember."

He was writing fast.

"Why do you want to die?"

"I don't want to die. I just want to cut my wrists."

"Why are you depressed?"

"I'm not depressed." I felt on solid ground now. "Dr. Sternfeld says I'm not depressed."

"You cut your wrists, but you're not depressed?" He looked at me as if I were a unicorn.

"Yes," I said defensively.

"Are you taking any medication?"

I told him about the Tofranil, Stelazine, Taractan, and the Thorazine. He wrote.

"Do you hear voices?"

"I don't know what you mean." He was trying to get me to incriminate myself. It wouldn't work. I was too smart.

"Do you hear voices?" he repeated.

"I hear your voice."

"Other voices. Voices that tell you things they don't tell other people."

"Sometimes. But," I added quickly, so that he wouldn't get the wrong idea, "Dr. Sternfeld says they're not real hallucinations; they're projections from my unconscious." I wanted him to understand. I was not crazy.

"Do you see things? Hallucinations? Visions?"

"Yes," I said. Why didn't I lie? "But, Dr. Sternfeld—"

"Skip it. I know. I know. Dr. Sternfeld says they're not really hallucinations. Right?"

"Yes," I said. He didn't believe me. "Why?" I demanded. "Look at me, for God's sake. You don't have to touch me. Just look at me. You won't catch anything if you just look at me."

I felt like the worst leper of the world. What was wrong with me that I was being treated like this?

"You're sick," a mocking voice chirped in my head. "You're sick in the head and you're going to a head hospital to get well."

"I'm scared," I whispered to no one. "I'm so scared."

The doctor got up. "That's all. You can go now. Mrs. Arnold," he called. I pushed my wooden chair away from the desk.

"Come with me, dear." A fat efficient-looking woman in green jersey was spread out near my chair. I backed away, repelled, as she took my arm with a flabby hand.

"Don't touch me," I said.

She looked quickly toward the doctor who nodded.

"I don't like strangers touching me," I almost shouted, desperation making my voice jagged. The room was a tomb; only the eyes of the stone figures were alive as they met in the air above my head, exchanged doubts, and returned home.

"Of course, dear," she said, her voice and manner dripping with condescending consideration.

"Just a few papers to sign. Nothing much," she said liltingly. "And we'll be all ready to go."

The fear was rising in me, changing to panic, infiltrating my brain so I couldn't think. Where were they taking me? I wanted to be calm, but I knew I was going to scream. Kick my feet. They were taking me away, locking me in a tower. "I'll never get out," I whispered.

The Thorazine was making me fuzzy. I tried to remember that. I had to control myself. The one thing they were waiting for was for me to lose control and go berserk.

"So if you'll just sign here," the woman cooed.

"What am I signing?" I asked. "I want to know what I'm signing."

"It's just a formality."

"I want to read what it says," I said, blood rushing through my head, a bloodfall of panic.

I tried to read the tiny print, but the words were little birds' feet before my eyes. I couldn't even read a large-print book with all the Thorazine in me.

"It's okay, Janet," my mother said. "We signed it too. It's a release so the hospital can give you medication and treatment."

"Shock treatments?" I asked quickly.

"Yes, dear," the woman said. "But only if your doctor orders them."

"He won't order them without telling me," I said, staccato. "He said he wouldn't do anything without telling me." I was saying the words to convince myself. The others looked on: the woman curious, my parents pitying and grieved.

"And I can leave if I want to?" I asked.

"Yes. This is a voluntary hospital. You can leave whenever you want."

"Mother? Daddy?" I looked pleadingly at my parents. Their faces were ashen. "Is it true? I can leave whenever I want?"

"Yes, Janet."

"You promise?" I was so, so scared. I could write my name, my tiny, scrunched up, ant-print signature, and that could be it; that could be it forever. But they said no, it wasn't true.

"Don't sign. Don't go in." I heard a voice in my head, comforting, firm. "Leave now. You don't have to do this. You're a free agent."

I wanted to listen to the voice. I wanted to be strong and say, "I've changed my mind; I don't think I'll check in here after all. Good-bye."

"We cannot wait all day, Janet." I heard the hard impatient edge, a completely inarticulated, yet unmistakable threat in the fat lady's voice.

"What are you afraid of?"

"I'm not afraid. I—I— Okay," I screamed, my body stiffened, then suddenly went limp like a rag. "I'll sign your goddamn paper."

"Janet!" my mother said, protective, angry, embarrassed, afraid for me.

"I'm all right. I'll be good. I won't make a fuss. Don't worry, Mother."

Dr. Sternfeld / Monroe Park

"Irene will check your suitcase and mark your clothing. May I have your pocketbook, please?"

So, they started the same way here as at Oceanville. Stripping you bare. Making you a name, a number, a case. I watched a short ducklike woman look swiftly through my pocketbook. "You better take these," she said handing my wallet and keys to my mother. "She won't be needing them here." She giggled to herself. "You can keep your cigarettes," she said, handing me my Marlboros. "Not the lighter. These other things," she pointed to my notebook, comb, brush, and assorted cosmetics, "I'll check them on through with the rest."

"That's me," I thought, looking at the scattered trivia from my purse. "It's me, but that lady doesn't know it or she doesn't care that she's taking it away."

I felt crumpled up and parched.

"Someone will be down to get you in a few minutes," the fat admitting lady said briskly. "You'll be on seven. No telephone calls for a week, first visiting next Sunday from three to five. Mr. Moss, Mrs. Moss, won't you say good-bye now?" It wasn't a question. The fog had closed in again. I could barely see anything, barely feel the icy clinging kisses that my parents gave. They were gone.

And I? I was going to seven.

"You absolutely must get me out of here," I wrote to Dr. Sternfeld.

The only why being that the ceiling is swimming, that these hands are not mine, not anyone's for that matter, and I feel as though I am being choked, suffocated, and I cannot cry out, can only hold back tears in a continuum of burning and imagined fear. The aloneness of being afraid. But we cannot sit as the lives fall below level, watch the trays fall and clatter and not try to catch the pieces, not try to do the carrying. Fitzgerald–the inner hush. It is too insane–fear and pain. I feel the Thorazine almost as a presence, a person. And it does not stop these awful feelings that I am going out of my mind–just holds them at bay, barely. You are my jailer and my single hope for freedom. That can't be. But it is. There is no difference between my imaginings and reality–here. Sirens ring in my ears, a constantly changing scenario of horrors and unimaginables, and everything frightens me.

I was on seven, the Tower next to the Unit, the top floor of Monroe Park.

A long, long hallway; halfway down, a glass cage. In it, people in

139

uniforms, people with keys, people with needles, bottles, pills. Writing all day, about us.

Lena bangs on the glass. Harder. "My clothes. Where are my clothes?" she screams. Inside, the nurses write.

Ruthie picks up her grayed hospital gown, waves it and howls, showing her belly, a vast white mass of loose flesh, and her crotch, hairless, sexless, looking like the bottom of a newly plucked chicken. She dances and laughs as the young nurse approaches her with a loaded hypodermic. "Be good now, Ruthie. Be a good girl." She yowls obscenities at the nurse.

"Don't touch me with that," she howls.

"Did you make doo-doo on the floor again, Ruthie?" The nurse moves steadily, her voice calm. She has the needle.

"I couldn't help it. Please." Ruthie has backed herself into the corner. "I'm going to tell my daughter about you when she comes."

Ruthie's daughter hasn't come in two months. The staff thinks Ruthie is crazy, but funny. They laugh at her. "Poor Ruthie," they say. And they laugh. Ruthie is a comedian, they think.

"This will make you feel better," the nurse says. Jab.

"Owww," screams Ruthie, as the liquid Thorazine sears its angry way into her flabby old muscle. The young nurse leaves her in a pile in the corner on the floor. Where does the raggy gown end and Ruthie begin?

No one, it seemed, was wearing clothes. But that was an impression, not a fact. I was wearing clothes, each piece marked with a white tag and magic marker. My four roommates in the dormitory at the end of the hall were wearing clothes. Mostly, it was the old women wandering in perpetual search of their glasses and their teeth who wore the gauzy hospital gowns, tied at the neck, open the rest of the way down to reveal their shriveled, sunken buttocks and their veiny legs. A few young girls who would not quiet down no matter how much Thorazine was injected into them, stood at the one door to freedom next to the nurses' station, a door that was double locked, that led to the elevator, the street and freedom, waiting for a doctor.

"My teeth," Mrs. Lesser lisps. "Where are my teeth?" The nurse took away Mrs. Lesser's false teeth in the morning, before her shock treatment, so that she would not swallow them during the convulsion. The teeth were supposed to be marked, kept in a special place. But the nurse had been busy; she had misplaced the teeth. Perhaps she had thrown them away. It was always happening. So Mrs. Lesser, in a post-ECT fog, stumbles, lost and frantic, unable to speak or eat, in a losing fight to retain a shred of the dignity and self-respect that has sustained her for seventy-five productive years.

The girls, three of them, kept managing to get out of the dayroom. Ordinarily, the dayroom was locked. We, the patients, were inside. It was a huge room with couches, dining tables, and a pool table. But when it was locked, as it was from early morning to late afternoon, it seemed smaller than a gopher hole. There were no activities off the floor for the seventh-floor inmates. No recreation, no occupational therapy. Nothing but the locked dayroom, from morning to night. You couldn't go to your room to lie down, not even when the drugs had made you as heavy as a pregnant bear, and you lumbered, eyes closing, falling into people and walls, wanting only sleep.

"Lie on the couch," an aide would say.

All day long the television blared. And the cigarette smoke accumulated. If no one had a lit cigarette, you had to beg a match from an aide. She'd jingle her keys and pretend to search for the precious sulphur-tipped flare. You'd writhe and wait, anger rising.

"Sorry, Miss. I just can't find a match." You'd walk away, disappointment engulfing you like a cloud.

"Oh, heeere it is. Ha, ha, ha!"

So you tried to light one cigarette from another until your mouth, dry and cracked from the Thorazine, felt like a desert canyon, burning.

Three young girls—they couldn't have been more than sixteen— had become expert in sneaking out the door when a staff member entered or left. Marie Jane had cornered a young resident, grasping his white coat as he locked the door behind him. We could hear her all the way in the dayroom.

"Get me out of here," she begged. "They're keeping me here against my will. There's nothing wrong with me. They have no right to lock me up. You're a doctor. Please help me."

Her voice had risen to a shrill plaintive hue.

"Speak to your doctor about it," was his curt, bored answer.

"My doctor?" Marie Jane's voice was a high shriek. "My doctor is the Wizard of Oz!"

"Marie Jane!" We heard scuffling. Screams. They were dragging her kicking body down the hall. "Are you going to stop, Marie Jane?"

"It's not legal. They're keeping me here against my will," she repeated. "They said I could get out any time I wanted to if I signed papers. It's a lie."

"Do you want to go to the Unit, Marie Jane?"

JANET

"I don't care," she wailed. "I don't care what happens to me. I'm in hell now. How much worse could it be?"

The Unit was worse. Worse even than the burning agony of an intramuscular injection of Thorazine. The Unit was a room at the end of the corridor. It had a tiny barred window in the door and a mattress on the floor. It was Monroe Park's ultimate in punishment —a padded cell. The doctors and nurses called it a "therapeutic measure for disturbed patients."

I tried to close my eyes and ears, kill my senses, withdraw from the nightmare. Why hadn't Dr. Sternfeld told me it would be like this? A kind of hotel, he had said.

"I didn't know you were going to seven," he said when he came to see me. We were sitting in pink plastic chairs in a small conference room off the locked dayroom. He seemed deeply sorry that I was on seven. It was a relief to be out of the dayroom.

"This floor is for very disturbed patients," he explained. "I wanted you on four. You don't belong here."

"Then get me transferred," I broke in, hope appearing for the first time in a week.

"I'm sorry, Janet," he said. "But I can't. I'm not on the staff. I am just allowed to have my patients admitted here, and I retain the final say in your treatment. But I can't influence hospital policy."

He seemed genuinely dismayed at his own helplessness and at the implied idiocy of bureaucratic practices. Somehow, knowing that he would return to his elegant home that evening while I fought to survive in the world of dayroom/dormitory, this closed-circuit world of misery and no recourse, I couldn't summon any pity for his plight.

"My hands shake so much I can't hold a pen," I said, changing the subject. "And I can't read, my vision is blurred."

"That's the Thorazine," Dr. Sternfeld said. "Don't worry about it." Easy. Flip. You can't read or write? Pfui, that's nothing to worry about. I felt a turbulence rising in my chest, an undifferentiated rumbling, chaos, and thunder. It was fury, rage, and it turned and stormed, until I screamed, "I want to cut my wrists!" Something in me was crying for blood.

"I'm going to reduce your medication. You can't be on medication when you have shock treatments," Dr. Sternfeld answered.

"But you said you wouldn't give them to me without talking about it with me first." A wrench of fear in my heart made me suddenly sober.

"I am talking to you about it now, Janet," Dr. Sternfeld said. "I just want you to have a few—a short course of treatments. Maybe they'll be just the thing to knock you out of this compulsive pattern. And then we can do some work."

He was looking at me, smiling.

I needed him so badly it hurt like a new wrist cut, three feet long and two feet deep in my insides, from my neck to my crotch. I was torn and split, and I hurt from the pain of needing him and wanting to die.

I hated him; he had locked me away in this tower of grief, this mad house of pain. And he had lied to get me to come in, "voluntarily." That was a real laugh. There was no such thing as voluntarily, I was learning. The paper I had signed had committed me to Monroe Park for thirty days. After that, if I wanted to leave, and the hospital wanted me to stay, they could have me legally committed. Voluntary! Ha! Marie Jane had been voluntary and now she was in a state hospital. And now Dr. Sternfeld was lying about the treatments, saying I wouldn't be disoriented or confused. I knew I would be. Anger surged and swelled in me again. Dr. Sternfeld was smiling at me, benevolent, patient, his round face in gentle creases, his eyes crinkled with appreciation of my pain.

I reached into my pocket and slowly took out a cigarette. I looked at it for a whole minute, counting to sixty. "Would you like a cigarette?" I whispered, as I held it out to Dr. Sternfeld. I was choking on my helplessness, my self-effacement, and my need.

"Yes. Thank you," he said. That had become our agreed cue. If I offered him a cigarette, he would come sit next to me. Dr. Sternfeld sat down beside me on the pink plastic settee, his strong arm circling my shaken body, as I leaned gratefully on his shoulder, crying my helplessness and rage into his rough tweed shoulder. I *was* weak. There was no hope for me. Disgusting. But it felt so good to cry and be held, I couldn't resist.

"You'll tell me when I'm going to have the first treatment, won't you?" I asked between sobs.

"Of course, Janet. Of course I will."

He left for home, dinner, evening patients.

I returned to the dayroom, heard the door lock behind me, and waited for dinner to come up on the mobile steam table. Then television. Medication. Sleep.

Dr. Sternfeld was very busy; the trip from his office took over an hour. He called almost every day, though, the nurses told me.

"You're very lucky to have a doctor who cares so much about you," they said.

JANET

I nodded, as the lurching of anger and abandonment ballooned inside me.

My parents came to visit twice a week, bringing cigarettes, newspapers, clothing, books, and admirable attempts at good cheer. They always looked ill, as if they felt like suddenly grasping their stomachs and puking on the floor, but were controlling themselves —for my sake, of course—as we sat, patients and visitors, locked in the dreary seventh-floor dayroom. No visiting in the rooms. Just as there was no smoking in the rooms. That month at Monroe Park I was in a perpetual state of raging vulnerability; I was always locked in somewhere. When I was in the dayroom I couldn't get to the Tampax or tissues in my room—not without begging the privilege from an aide or nurse. When I was in my room at night, I couldn't get to the dayroom to smoke; I would just fake needing to pee and grab a smoke in the bathroom, where the doors to the toilets had no locks and where you could expect someone to come barreling in anytime you were on the pot. "Just checking," they would say.

What? What were they checking?

To see that you didn't get too much privacy. Privacy was nontherapeutic.

Since I couldn't see Dr. Sternfeld I wrote notes to him, notes which I never sent; but the writing gave me an illusion of contact. Contact with something solid, real, and verifiable—paper, words— something outside myself.

Everything is a trap. The simplest situation is designed by the soul-devil and there is no way out, ever, but the one wrong way I am taking. No doors. Yes, a lot. But they are all locked. I wish I had a typewriter here, but they won't allow it on seven. Can't hold my hand steady enough or see the paper clearly enough to write. With a typewriter sometimes I can make believe it isn't me who's writing at all—some one thing, inside, that must come out and be manifested in print on a page. That isn't sick, I don't think. I want to be a writer. Then there are words, I am not afraid, and it comes quite easily, making sense from my non-senses, at least for a while.

I spent two full days, with time out for lunch and medication, of course, with Dr. Heinz Gutterman in a small sunless room on the main floor of the hospital, being tested.

Dr. Gutterman wore shiny blue suits and heavy cologne. And in the airless space of the room, his smell was overpowering.

"I feel nauseous," I said after an hour.

"Nauseated," he corrected me. "Nauseous means repellent, sickening. It is perhaps what you feel about yourself?"

144

Dr. Sternfeld / Monroe Park

"I feel like I'm going to vomit," I said.

He leaned back in his chair, gold filigree, ruby-adorned cufflinks protruding from the shiny suit.

"We have much to do," he said.

"I'm going to puke. For Crissake, let me go to the bathroom!"

"There is no one here to take you," he said.

"I can go by myself. My God. It's just across the hall."

"You are not supposed to go anywhere without an aide; instructions from your doctor."

"Look, you can watch the door to see that I don't escape," I said. "And I can't lock myself in—there's no lock. There's no window, so I can't climb out. I was searched before I left the ward. I have no weapons on me. What could I do in two minutes? Flush myself down the toilet? Bite myself?"

Dr. Gutterman either missed my sarcasm or chose to ignore it. He was a serious man. Very literal-minded, too, it turned out.

"All right," he said finally. "But be quick."

I practically hurled myself out the door, across the narrow hallway, and into the john. I thought the entire contents of my body were coming up, not just the food in my stomach, but the stomach itself—and the other organs too. I had never felt so sick in my life.

Dr. Sternfeld said my attacks of nausea were a physical manifestation of extreme tension and anxiety. He was going to prescribe a stomach tranquilizer for me, Compazine, when I got out of the hospital. Meanwhile, I vomited. The whole first floor of clerks, doctors, and new patients must have heard the retching. I felt weak, drained. Back to the tests. Maybe Dr. Gutterman would leave the door ajar, or open a window—anything to get some fresh air.

For two days, I drew pictures. Man. Woman. Child. House. I told him stories about pictures that he showed me. I counted backward by sevens from one hundred.

"You know I've had all these tests before," I said. "At Oceanville Hospital." He wasn't interested.

I played word associations, opposites, synonyms. I looked at ink blots and identified ravens and dragons and tiny babies hidden inside the eyes of Medusa. I touched my finger to my nose and my finger to my finger. And a hundred other inane tricks and games. While Dr. Gutterman got more serious, taking notes and looking at me with a combination of fear, suspicion, and pity.

I was nervous and exhausted. "He's a fuck," I thought. And trembled before the black gaze that pierced me whenever I tried to make a joke, or point to an inconsistency in the sacred tests.

"You think you'll have me down pat—mentally drawn and

quartered, so to speak—after you interpret these tests, don't you?" I asked him halfway through the second day.

He didn't answer. His black eyebrows almost met and made a single thick dark scowl line across his face.

"Well, you won't," I said. "Because the real me can't be pinned down and analyzed. You'll never touch it."

He moved away. Just slightly, as if he were afraid that even this close contact with my sickness could infect him.

"I will give you a proverb," he said, "and I want you to tell me what it means." He was waiting, pen poised.

"I'm not very good at proverbs," I said.

A muscle twitched in his fat right cheek.

"A rolling stone gathers no moss," he said ominously.

"I told you, I can't do proverbs," I said. At Oceanville they hadn't made me do the proverbs; they had just skipped that part of the test.

"What does it mean?" Dr. Gutterman boomed, his pouchy face turning red.

"It can mean a lot of things, that's the point; depending on what moral value you give the 'moss,' or to 'rolling' for that matter. I don't like proverbs; they're too moralistic, too vague."

Dr. Gutterman's red face was flushing deeper, turning quite purple.

"Look," I said, "if you want to see if my thought processes are disturbed and if I can reason abstractly and ascertain symbolic relationships, I'll do something else to show you. I'll explicate Wallace Stevens's poem, *Sunday Morning*. I have the book upstairs in my room. It's much more complicated and symbolic than a rolling stone. Okay? But I won't do proverbs. It begins, 'Complacencies of the peignoir.' " I began to recite the poem.

Dr. Gutterman looked murderous. Suddenly, I was very scared.

"That will be all; we are finished," he said. With awkward uncontrolled movements he gathered his papers, stopwatch, pictures, and plastic shapes. "I will call for someone to take you back to your floor." He disappeared, slamming and locking the door behind him.

It is very dangerous to antagonize the influential powers in a mental hospital; it is unwise in the extreme to cut off access to what might someday be a court of appeals. Dr. Gutterman was powerful, respected, even feared a bit by the nurses and aides at Monroe Park. He had left in a rage. I had made a fool out of him. I had thwarted him. I had refused to succumb to his will. Would he retaliate? What kind of report and diagnosis would he write? Why had I been so stupid and stubborn? I could have interpreted his silly proverbs if I had really wanted to. True, they were vague to all but unoriginal one-track minds. But that was what they considered normal, anyway—a mind that accepted judgments without questioning them; a mind that would conform to standards and behaviors undeviatingly. To Dr. Gutterman, everything I said was probably an indication of how sick I was. Who, in her right mind, couldn't—or wouldn't—give the meaning of "A rolling stone gathers no moss"? "Me," I thought despairingly. "Me."

I was so shaken by my encounter with Dr. Gutterman that I called Dr. Sternfeld as soon as I returned to the ward. I was no longer on any medication; I needed something to calm me down. I was allowed one telephone call a day, at the pay phone in the hall just outside the door to the nurses' station. Dr. Sternfeld had always said to call him, anytime, if I needed him. I needed him. He listened, as I faltered out the story of myself and Dr. Gutterman and the proverbs. I told him how scared I was, how my heart was pounding—an anxiety attack—and how I was seeing dripping red swords hanging on the walls and ceiling over my head.

Dr. Sternfeld was furious.

"You are in the hospital now; if you are upset, use the resources of the hospital. You cannot come to me to bail you out."

"But they won't give me anything unless you order it," I reminded him.

"Then have the nurses call me. That's what everyone else does. What makes you different?"

The bottom of my life had been whisked away; I was falling, falling again. Where would I land?

"You said I could call you if I needed you."

"Yes, if you *really* needed me. But you call in a panic because you did something stupid and now you want me to protect you from the consequences of your act. That is neurotic need, not real need. And I will not cater to that need."

I was so confused the hall and my head and body were whirling in circles, intertwined like the rings in a puzzle. Was this the same man who encouraged me to "fall apart," to cry in his arms?

"But what if they can't get you?" I asked. "I have to have something."

"You'll wait," he said. "Like everyone else. And if you are very upset, at least you are in the best place you can be: a hospital, where you can't hurt yourself."

"But they can hurt me," I blurted out, thinking of the long Thorazine needles and the Unit.

JANET

"That's absurd and you know it, Janet," Dr. Sternfeld said sharply.

"Yes, yes, of course," I whispered. "It's all in my head."

"I'll try to come on Sunday night, if I can," he said. "And Janet—" he paused. "Try to be good to yourself."

All three nurses behind the glass wall had stopped writing their notes and were staring at me. I hung up the receiver.

A few days later I got my first shock treatment.

The air in my room was thinning, graying, as early morning light filtered through the thick screens. I was no longer in the dormitory; my roommate was still sleeping.

"Moss!" I heard my name, a trumpet call, as a very short, brisk woman appeared silhouetted in my doorway. She stood in a pool of night-light yellow from the corridor, a sheaf of white papers in her hands. Her voice was piercing.

"Moss," she repeated. I felt a rod of fear shoot into the center of my body. I clutched my stomach where I had felt her penetrate me. I couldn't close my eyes; they seemed welded to her small muscular frame.

"No breakfast for you, Moss," she said into the smoky light of my room.

No breakfast. I repeated the words to myself; they were nonsense syllables; I wouldn't hear what they said. No breakfast. That meant shock. I was on the shock list.

"No!" I screamed, hurling the thin beige hospital blanket off my rubber-sheeted bed. In an instant I was by the door. "There must be some mistake. I'm not supposed to get treatments." How many times had I seen other people perform this same panicky charade? How many times had I heard the frantic terrorized cry? Not me, not me. There must be some mistake. Now it was me, in a frenzy of survival fear, crying the futile cry, clawing on the twelve-foot wall.

"No mistake," the little woman said calmly. "Here's your name, right near the top of the list."

"But my doctor said—" I started to explain. She interrupted.

"No breakfast," she said again. "I'll be back to get you in a few minutes." She turned, as smartly as a new private, and I heard her raspy voice with its message for the doomed, as she moved from room to room. "Heidler, Smythe, Reiss . . ." And on until the litany of names was indistinguishable from the pounding of the blood in my head.

We would go together, victims of our genes, our dreams, our hurts, and tough stubborn angers, casualties of a vast clean-up campaign. They would burn it out of us—whatever *it* was that made us all possessed, or heavy with the pain of being, or odd beyond endurance, or "sick." They would set fire to our heads, convulse our poor bodies, befog the brain that screamed and wept and would not interpret proverbs.

> *Beauty is momentary in the mind, the fitful tracing of a portal*
> *But in the flesh it is immortal.*

Wallace Stevens. There he was again. Wallace Stevens, insurance salesman, poet. He never quit his job, led an exemplary life, was never locked in a hospital, his brain incinerated of its passions. But he had his poetry. We had only our suffering.

I leaned my forehead on the cold paint of the door. I felt a moan inside me, rising, pushing against my throat to escape into heaving, a moan of sorrow and betrayal. He promised, he promised. Why are you going to burn my brain, burn up the poetry in my brain?

I tightened my lips; I wouldn't let it out. I wouldn't let them know.

"Oh God, I'm scared," I whispered into the fuzzy pink sleeve of my nightgown. "I'm so fucking scared. Don't let them kill me. Please."

The nurse returned as she promised, followed by a scraggly group of bathrobed patients. Uncombed, disarrayed, shuffling behind her, faces as gray as the predawn light, eyes vacant, empty even of fear. They had all been through it before. Dumb acceptance had been branded into them, all fight sizzled out of existence. They wouldn't give trouble; they were tame. Shuffling along. Good little crazies, do what the master says. And maybe we'll let you out. But no backtalk, you understand. You gotta know your place. "Take your psychodiagnostic tests and shove them." Don't you badmouth me, you little sickie. I'm gonna teach you a lesson you'll never forget. A happy smile, a bowed back, shuffling feet—that was what they wanted.

"Moss, stop dawdling. I haven't got all day."

"Yes," I mumbled. "Yes, sorry." And I stepped into line.

Open the heavy ward door, the double locks yield to the magic of keys. Oh, how glorious to carry keys.

Into the elevator; there are eleven of us—and the nurse.

Sixth floor. Door opens. This must be it. Only one level down, one level below hell.

As we emerge from the elevator, the nurse checks us off as we pass her sharp bird eyes and turn to the left; there are only old men. There is a pervasive sickening smell of urine and old age. Decay and despair surround me like a dust storm. No one is clothed; they are in hospital gowns and paper slippers, or seersucker robes, these wraithlike old men. I hear coughs, hollow coughs from old used bony chests, and the high whining feeble sound of a child-man whom no one minds. My stomach is empty, but my body heaves with an uncontrollable retching at the indignity, the odor, the sadness, the horror of it all.

Turn left, move beyond the green vinyl partition that divides the floor. Move into the shock part of six; leave the old men behind, leave them to their grayness and their quiet coughing despair.

There are two empty high-wheeled stretchers. White-suited attendants, men and women. We are a small huddled group, as the nurse confers with another woman.

"No. No. I won't let you!" I hear. A scream, it pierces my head and floods my mind. A scream from behind a closed door. Then nothing. A door opens, the last door at the end of the corridor, and a stretcher is wheeled out. A girl is sleeping on it; she couldn't be any older than I, maybe younger. I don't know her; she must be from another floor. Was it she who screamed? What did they do to her to make her scream? And to make her stop? The stretcher, pushed by a large black woman, disappears into a room.

"In here," the nurse said, pointing to a small bare room on the right. "Wait here." She was still clutching her papers, the papers with the names. Her keys jangled as they hung heavily on a ring at her waist. It was how they identified each other, without uniforms, how they knew a friend went there—by the keys. Patients—the crazies, the sick ones—never had keys. They might wear street clothes, they might even have a two-hour pass, say, or hold a coherent conversation. But they never had the keys.

We wait in the bare room with its peeling stained walls and its torn plastic couches and filthy foul ashtrays. We wait, not speaking, each one of us living out the contortions of our private nightmares, prisoners in a communal hell. Silent. What is there to say?

One by one we are called. There is no system to the order; you never know when you'll be called.

Two and a half hours. Three of us are left. I am empty of everything but a longing to be dead. My body is heavy, dry inside, like adobe, my brain a solid, claylike weight. My mouth burned out; a pack of cigarettes—gone.

"Moss. You're next." The words come through the thickness of my mind. I think I feel a stirring again, deep, deep inside; it flutters—they couldn't kill my fear. It is alive; alive and trapped and very real.

I intone, my lips moving only barely, words of Hart Crane, that mystic suicide, the poet of convoluted thoughts. Maybe the words, the rhythms, and the richness of the language will make it all go away. The heavy deadness and the fluttering fear.

> There is the world dimensional
> For those untwisted
> By the love of things—irreconcilable

Again I say it. I repeat the somber tapestry of Hart Crane's words. My lips are moving. People are tying me down. A strap across my chest. I am moving backward, on silent wheels, my lips moving barely, my hands clutching the cold metal of the stretcher cart.

There is a brilliant light, the world goes gleaming, a riot of white as the door to the scream-room opens and I move, on oiled wheels; the moment is near. It is surrounded by white.

There is a smell I don't recognize. Four doctors. I am melting, melting with fear. "Lord God of my salvation, what have I done to offend thee?"

A short nervous man moves behind me. A rustle. Clicking. Clink of metal. Whispers.

"How much for her?" I hear.

"Fifteen. Let's try her at fifteen."

Fifteen what? What are they talking about? I don't know. O my God, yes I do! Electricity. Volts for me, for my brain!

"God give me strength to endure it," I pray.

"There's nothing to be scared of," a man says. He is not wearing white and he looks like a Hathaway man. "I'm Dr. Raymond."

He smiles. "Try to relax. We're going to give you a shot. Count backward from ten. You won't feel anything. Just a light, floating sensation. That's all." His voice drones on. "Then you'll wake up; you won't remember anything; just relax."

"What concentration are you using?" someone asks.

I hear a figure. It means nothing.

"Would you like to hold my hand?" Dr. Raymond smiles and reaches toward me.

"Yes. Yes. Please." A hand. A warm human hand. I clutch it, gratified for a crumb. I am helplessness incarnate.

A pinch in my arm; I watch the clear liquid flowing into my vein. Ten, nine, eight. I am feeling warm, a sweet warmness suffuses my body—my head is disattached. I am floating, floating, floating. Seven, six, five.

No. I fight against it. I want to know what they are doing to me. I don't want to sleep. I am afraid to sleep.

But it is sweet, this floating on a bubble; it is seductive, this infinite lightness of floating. Four, three . . . Darkness.

JANET

I awoke on a pillowless bed in a room that smelled of old urine, on gray wrinkled sheets, under a ratty thin blanket, my nightgown wet. My bed was one of several, all lined up, parallel, against a wall in a bare, narrow room. The beds on my right and my left held sleeping forms. I recognized a woman who had come with me for treatments; she had gone ahead of me, I thought. The face of the other body was turned away from me. Where was I? Who were these sleeping people?

In an attempt to see more of the room, I raised my head and then the pain came. My skull had been bombed out. I could almost see the scarred remains left after the rocket hit its mark. No head, just pain in the area that was my brain. It screamed, silent; and the blood flowed, dry. Raw, screeching, violently pulsing pain. "My God, what have they done to me?"

I lay my head down on the hard dirty bed. As the pain subsided for an instant, I began to feel my body. It must have been numb before. Now as I felt it, I knew one vast continuous ache from toe to thigh to chest and elbow. Had I been put through a grinder? Over the wheel? My bones and muscles, every cell and fiber, connective tissue and neuron was a point in the continuous network of pain that was my body. I could not move my hand, bend an elbow, wiggle a toe, without pain shooting through my body's channels. Yet, it was almost a dull sensation, this body-hurt, compared to the electric agony of throbbing pain that was my head.

Why? I didn't know. I remembered only floating in the scream room, as the clear smooth liquid slipped silently into my arm. And darkness.

"You're up. Well, how do we feel, dear?" A fat white-clad woman was standing by my bed. "Did you have a nice sleep?"

"What is she talking about?" I wondered.

"My head," I tried to say, the words coming slowly through my cracked lips.

"Oh, your head hurts? Well, we'll give you something for that headache when you get downstairs. And some breakfast." She was grinning proudly, waiting, I thought, for my—could it be?—thanks. I was only more confused.

"But the treatment?" I said, hesitating.

"You've had your treatment, baby," she said, slapping my leg with an effulgence of her mirth. Pain shot through my leg. She was laughing. I could see the laughs, sharp arrows shooting from her purple mouth.

"I don't remember," I said.

"Of course not." She hit my leg again. Didn't I see the joke?

"You mean it's over?" I didn't understand. How scary that was. They had shot electric currents into my brain and I didn't even know it.

"All over, baby. All over. For now."

"My head," I said again, reaching to touch my pulsing face. It was sticky. Sticky and stiff, where my hair met my temple. "What's that?" I almost didn't want to know.

"Oh, that? That's nothing. Just the jelly. You know? Where they attach the metal. The conducting jelly. Washes right out, so don't you worry."

Conducting jelly. Metal. "O my good God. They really did it."

"My body," I said slowly. "My muscles, my legs, they hurt."

"Why sure, honey. That's from the convulsion." She laughed again.

"The convulsion? Oh, of course, the convulsion." A blue light, growing sharper, seemed to shatter into a million specks in my bombed-out brain. "The convulsion." Suddenly I remembered: ECT, Electroconvulsive Therapy. The electric current made the body convulse. It was like an epileptic seizure. The similarity to epilepsy had something to do with its discovery, I remembered. I would have to find out more.

"No one knows how it works," Dr. Sternfeld had said, calm, smiling.

I shuddered.

"My nightgown is wet," I said.

"You must have urinated during the treatment. Don't worry. It's very common."

"Very common. Very common." I repeated the words to myself. A grown woman peeing all over herself—very common!

"What am I doing here?" I thought. "How did I get here? Where am I going?"

I closed my eyes and let the woman fit my slippers on my cold aching feet. I walked mechanically down the hall, trying to shut out the sight of the waiting white stretchers, the sound of the coughing old men as we walked to the elevator that would carry us upward—to hell.

So that had been shock. I wanted only to sleep. Surcease from the rocket pain and sleep. The ward looked strange—familiar, yet alien—the faces of the patients, blurred, unfocused, odd. I did not know what day it was. Or when my parents had visited me last. Or what hour in this universe of grief it was. Toast and coffee. Warm orange juice. My stomach was greedy, hungry; I was not. But I ate, numbly, unaware of anything but the pain in my head and my body, and the fear that was concentrating, focusing into a black funnel of terror in my mind.

"Dr. Sternfeld just called," a young nurse came to tell me. "He wanted to find out how you were. You're really lucky to have a doctor who's so concerned about you, you know."

I didn't answer, didn't acknowledge she was there. It was easier sometimes to pretend to be beyond their ken, so sick, so crazy that you didn't have to pretend—pretend you cared; pretend you wanted to get well. What was well, anyhow? Well was being on an unchanging plane of placidity. Well was never saying the world sucked. Well was saying this hellhole was a hospital and thank you for giving me shock treatments. Well was crazy. I didn't even blink as she took my breakfast tray.

Two weeks and five shock treatments later I was home again. Released. Fog had settled into the crevices of my mind. I was calm, on the surface. Underneath, a plan was brewing. A final solution.

A Suicide Attempt and Monroe Park, Again

I had always loved the spring. In my deepest gloom, the sensations of life awakening around me, leaves and flowers drawn out by the warmth of the air, had always renewed me.

Somehow, someway, it would all work out; there were buds in me somewhere, too; they would emerge.

But when I came out of Monroe Park, this spring, the fine newly greening world seemed only to intensify the knowledge that I was dying, rotting away. On the side of my head, near my temples, the hair, sticky after each shock treatment, got stiff, and white, and began to flake off and itch. The hospital staff had not let me into the bathroom alone to wash my hair because they said I was too confused and disoriented from the treatments. And since I would only be having another treatment in a couple of days it seemed like a waste of time for them to stand with me while I washed the rotten caked conducting jelly out of my hair.

For two weeks my head collected grease, oil, and white sticky flakes of dried jelly. My hair stuck out straight from the sides of my head. I couldn't get a comb or brush through it.

The nurses had taken away my barrettes, afraid I might leave one in my hair during a treatment. Limp, greasy, rotting.

"They won't let me wash my hair," I had moaned to Dr. Sternfeld when he came to visit, watching his face register in flickering succession: annoyance, anger, and comprehension of my vanity, the pettiness of a mental patient's concerns.

He would not intervene with the staff. It was my problem. I must act in my own behalf, *for* myself.

The electric shocks were burning my brain, I knew that. And the jelly was eating its way from the outside in. They would meet in the middle and my head would be a mass of singed, decayed flesh, nothing human or recognizable. I would be impaired forever. But they were clever; it surely wouldn't show.

Dr. Sternfeld was gruff with me, hurt at the suggestion that he would allow a treatment that might harm me. I was letting my imagination run away with me. The shock treatments were going to make me feel better. He believed in them, though he couldn't say why. I believed in him, though I couldn't say why. There was no one else.

So, it was spring. I was outside again, my hair finally washed. The air caressing the sky, clear blue as it is only in early spring, pregnant with promise and expectation. And my head, invisibly, was rotting away.

I knew I was going to die.

"I want you to take off your sunglasses during the sessions," Dr. Sternfeld said.

It was our first meeting since I was discharged from Monroe Park. I put my arms up over my glasses to protect them. I was terrified. He could have almost anything, but he couldn't have my eyes.

"No," I said, the word sharp, instinctively protective.

"Yes. It is time." His voice was calm, the skin around his eyes wrinkled ever so subtly in a smile of infinite understanding, compassion, wisdom, and irony.

"I can't," I said. He couldn't make me.

"What are you afraid of, Janet?" Dr. Sternfeld said quietly.

"I don't know."

"Are you afraid of me?"

"Yes." The word burst from my mouth, surprising us both.

"I won't hurt you."

"I know. I know. You want to help me."

"Janet. I'll turn around while you take your glasses off. I promise not to look at you."

I couldn't tell if I should trust him. I was afraid beyond reason to relinquish the safety of the muted world my eyes knew behind the sunglasses. They could lock me up, drug me, shock me, humiliate me, but, somehow, with my eyes protected, I felt as though my deepest self was still intact. I hadn't seen daylight unfiltered through dark lenses for long over a year.

"Janet." His voice was a cold knife ripping through my shadows.

"L'essentiel est invisible pour les yeux," I whispered to myself. Where had I read that? One hand clutched to each temple, I protected my eyes from his attack. *"On ne voit bien qu'avec le coeur. Seulement le coeur."* Again, I repeated the comforting words. I was still afraid.

"Janet." A rumble, engulfed by his looming figure. "Take them off."

"I can't, I can't." Whimpering; he had reduced me again to a sniveling snail.

A Suicide Attempt and Monroe Park, Again

"You can. Take off your glasses. NOW!"

I am a mound of stinking rotting earth, I thought. What is this pain in my deepest core? It is a scream. But I cannot let it free. Trapped, it shakes my body, resounds in my ears, fills my chest with furious blackness. If I let it out, it would fill the room, the house, and darken the blue spring sky with a mangled agony of me. It would eat him up, lacerate and torture and eat him. "Oh God (crying from my pain) what sort of sick monster am I to have these dreams?"

"This is the last time I will say it, Janet. Take off your glasses."

Nothing held me together but a gelatinous network of blood vessels and skin. No strength to resist, my fingers, pressed against my head, had melted, weak, uncertain, no longer mine.

Slowly, slowly, I took them off. And more slowly, I opened my eyes, though I shielded them with my weak cupped hands. The light burned through, the colors of the room exploded. I blinked, feeling as though this were a dream—a fantasied world of changing brilliant lights and colors. Looking through the maze of my fingers, I saw Dr. Sternfeld leaning back in his deep chair, his fingers laced across his belly, his expression satisfied, maybe triumphant. He looked as though he had just finished a large heavy meal in the midst of an adoring family. Master of all he surveyed.

I felt more naked before his benign and powerful satisfaction than ever in my life. And the ringing anger in my stomach translated to cut, cut my wrists. It was senseless. But then so was my malleability, my snailness before this buddha.

The rationale—to see the world, to face it, clearly, not to retreat behind my clouded glasses—was clear to me. I couldn't find an argument to refute this step in Dr. Sternfeld's therapy. I never spoke of the helplessness that made me succumb to these things. Just as I never spoke of my feelings about the hospital—or shock. He had let me know that he did not want to speak of it. And I was afraid.

I needed him—the warmth of his body to cry on; the ever-receding, elusive notion that he cared for me, would protect me, forever.

I was allowed to put my glasses back on when the session ended. Thank God. I didn't have to face the fiery world with naked eyes—yet, though the time would come soon enough. It was part of his plan; I knew it. And I knew, too, that I would succumb. Because he supported my jellied self. And because without him, I would have no hope. Because he did what he did only to help me.

"Dear God," I said to myself after Dr. Sternfeld had given me my allotted minute of being held at the end of the session. "I think I am finally mad."

JANET

As soon as the shock treatments were over, Dr. Sternfeld started me on drugs again. It was not a tranquilizer he gave me, but a psychic energizer. Tiny gray-white pills called Permitil, in which he had great faith. So I took them, on a complicated regimen that changed weekly as he increased my dosage. I don't know what they were supposed to do. Lord knows, my racing cavorting mind didn't seem to need energizing. But I took them and believed I needed them—because I was sick. The side effects of the Permitil were not as grossly disturbing as the Thorazine. I did have a parched mouth and knotting shoulder muscles; my vision was blurred and my perceptions vague. But at least my legs and hands didn't shake, and I wasn't gaining weight. I took a muscle relaxant to unknot my painfully tight shoulders; Combid spansules to calm my nausea; Dexamyl to help me lose weight—I had asked him to give me Dexamyl and he had assented, somewhat unwillingly.

And at night, I took Doriden to help me sleep. My mother was the keeper of the Doriden. Appointed by Dr. Sternfeld, she doled me my allotted amount each night, hating herself, and me, and the whole demeaning ritual; sick with the pettiness of it all; doing it, being nurse because Dr. Sternfeld said it was necessary. Round, white, scored in the middle, each Doriden was the size of a dime, one quarter of an inch thick. Each night I was allowed two; the second one if the first didn't work, to sink me into foggy oblivion so that I could fall asleep.

I would take the first at eleven o'clock, then sit with my mother in the den, watching Steve Allen on television. I fought the surge of whirling that attacked me soon after I swallowed the pill, fought to keep my heavy eyelids open and my cottony tongue from flopping out of my mouth. I fought to stay awake, slouched in front of the television, so I could ask my mother for a second pill. She always said, "Do you really need it?" I always answered, thickly, "Yes."

And, after pretending to swallow the second Doriden, as my mother watched, weary misery in her eyes, I stumbled into my bedroom to slip the pill into my top dresser drawer. My white secret—the growing cache of Doriden in the pink satin scarf-container in my top dresser drawer. I had decided before I even left the hospital, before the futile fog of the shock treatments had cleared, that the only way out for me was death. And the only sure way to die—for me—was pills.

Day by week, the pile of Doridens grew. There were twenty, then thirty. Forty pills. Surely enough to do the job. Certainly enough to kill.

New York City was more beautiful than I had ever before

remembered it; the cherry blossoms had flowered and fallen; the hill of daffodils at the Brooklyn Botanic Garden was alive. The air on every street was sweet with ripening buds. "Too sweet. Too beautiful," I thought. And I cried that the dead spot in me should be spreading its numbness, just as the world was being reborn.

"I'm going to the library," I said. My mother, a vacillating figure of anxiety and tenderness, faced me with fear.

"Alone?" she asked.

"I have no one to go with," I answered. No one to go with. No one to talk with. No one to share these agonies. Mary was at school. And Rachel. And Johnny and Laura and Madelon. I saw Ina occasionally. Larry, down from school, came to take me out now and then—a pity call, but welcome. My father left early and worked late. I rarely saw him. There was no one but my mother. And, as our time together grew in tension and abrasiveness, as our endless morning coffeetimes and afternoon shopping trips became harder to endure—perhaps more because of her intensity of hovering love than because of a lack of care, or her panic and her own overwhelming misery—I had to be alone. The look in her sad vague eyes said I was abandoning her. I was accusing her of not being a good enough mother.

"You can't make up for the dull loneliness of my life," I yearned to tell her. "You can't fill the emptiness left by my friends, my atrophying mind, and my cut-off future. Be my mother. God, that would be enough." But, somehow, I never could say it. And she continued to press herself—from guilt perhaps, certainly from love and sorrow—into my consciousness, to try to mold and be my life.

I was grateful for the anonymity of the subway, though the thunderings and lurchings of the train often filled me with fear that Dr. Sternfeld called anxiety, and for which he prescribed drugs.

Forty Doriden in my top dresser drawer. Why didn't I take them? Why couldn't I just end it as I had planned? Why did I continue to make the endless, repetitive plans, decorate and redecorate in my mind, the stage for my final exit?

I had decided, finally, on going to a hotel to take the pills. There, no one could possibly find me in time. I had worked out over and over again the time I would check in, what I would wear, and what I would say. The absolute necessity was to remain inconspicuous. I had decided on the Biarritz Hotel, a scene of luxury.

And the name I would use. I thought and repeated aliases, my mind in search of the perfect name.

Why? Why? Why did I let the trivia of the act force me into paralysis?

JANET

I was sitting beneath an old tree in Prospect Park. I could hear the fragmented sounds of children at play. Otherwise I was alone, watching the sky through the network of small yellow-green leaves.

"This tree must be older than New York," I thought. I clenched my fists in a sudden frustrated movement. What was there about life that you clung to it, in spite of all the beatings and pain? What was there in me, deep beyond my touching, that pushed me to hold onto this life like a baby onto its mother? What? What? I couldn't find an answer—not in the tree or the sky or the scars on my wrist.

Dam up that tenacious source and maybe I could act.

How?

"Stop feeling," a voice in my mind answered. "Feel dead."

"When I have fifty pills," I said, the words coming slow, deliberate, and blank, "I will take them." I paused. "And I will use the name Elena. That is final."

June 11, 1963. I expected to be dead by nightfall. I had never been able to imagine what dead would be like. But it couldn't possibly be worse than my alive.

I remember now only the deliberateness with which I moved through the planned day; I had rehearsed it all so many times in my mind, planned it to the tiniest detail. My father was at work. My mother, reassured by my recent show of cheerfulness, had made a date to meet a friend in Manhattan.

Alone, I packed my small red suitcase with its peeling decal from Wister College. Matthew had given the decal to me many years before.

"Everything must be perfect," I repeated. "Nothing must look suspicious."

My reservation was made at the hotel.

Only the Doriden remained. Where would I put them? Where would they be most safe? In the suitcase? No. In the smart leather portfolio I would carry to impress the hotel personnel? Maybe. My pocketbook? The best place, but the pills were bulky; they would make my chic leather bag bulge. I changed my mind, settling on the suitcase, which I locked with care.

I was swallowing hard to keep the panic from rising into my throat. It was essential to remain calm and in control.

The June air brushed my cheeks like the butterfly kisses my mother used to give me with her eyelashes when I was a small child. Spread before me, surrounding me, the familiar streets of Brooklyn had never seemed so real.

"This is my last day," I thought. And, as the subway thundered under the East River, surfaced at Canal Street, and continued on to Fifty-seventh Street, each noisy moment carrying me closer and closer to the hotel, I couldn't contain the tears that ran down my face.

"I mustn't lose my resolve," I thought. "I mustn't weaken." And, closing my e. e. cummings anthology on my lap, I turned my face to the speeding darkness outside. "Why am I doing this?" I asked myself, and for the last time, argued my right to kill myself, whispering it as I pressed my lips to the dirty glass of the train window. I was crying, crying. My life was nothing but crying.

"I don't know how this happened to me," I heard a voice saying. "How I fell apart so. And where I lost the joy that used to make my heart fly and nest in the clouds. I don't know what happened to *me*. But I am in pain and fear, and I can't even get through the days without my pills and without knowing I'll see Dr. Sternfeld. Maybe I am sick, but if it is a sickness, it has become me, and I am no longer like the rest of the people I knew and know. My world is hounded by mental hospitals, doctors, drugs, and shock treatments. These people who say they want to help me have turned me into—into— an outsider. I have never been so alone in my life." The stations sped by, lighted patches before my eyes. "I have looked for me for a long time, but I have lost myself. And I don't have the strength to care even to try anymore to find me. I can't bear the crying, the pain, the anger anymore."

My suitcase, the fifty Doridens, crushed against my leg with its weight. I was carrying my future—nothing—on the subway to Fifty-seventh Street as the train lurched violently. And it seemed nobody knew or cared.

In the lobby of the Biarritz I saw red velvet wall hangings, dazzlingly brilliant crystal chandeliers, many-faceted, gilt-edged mirrors, deep soft silent red carpeting. I felt smaller, more plain and Semitic and out of place than I had imagined—even with my best Ellis clothes, name, and manner. Everywhere the smell of luxury, the hush of wealth, decadence, and leisure. There seemed to be more uniformed servants waiting covertly, fastidiously attired in suit and manner, than clientele.

"What are you doing here?" I asked myself. It was ludicrous. Then I remembered. I had come to commit suicide.

Elena. I had finally chosen that name for its combination of Protestant-sounding inanity and for the pleasure it gave me to be someone else. I registered at the huge carved desk, watching the fawning clerk as he took my key from the beehive of mailboxes on the wall. I didn't care how much the room cost; I would never have to pay for it.

Ding. A man in uniform appeared, hand outstretched, to accompany me to my room. He had come to carry my suitcase; that was his job and he would expect a reward for it. How could I say, thank you, that case is too precious, I'll carry it myself? I couldn't, unless I wanted to make a spectacle. And that was the last thing I wanted. My heart pounding, I let him take the small red suitcase and I smiled, following him onto the intricately grilled elevator. My eyes were fixed on the suitcase hanging from his gnarled and unsuspecting hand.

We reach the room and he still has my suitcase.

"Is there anything you require, ma'am?"

"No. No. Everything is quite fine." Will he ever relinquish it?

"Just ring if you need anything." He is shifting from foot to foot. Waiting.

"Ring? Yes. Of course." What does he want?

"Nothing else, ma'am?"

Get out. Get out. I want to shout. Then I realize: He is waiting for a tip. The triviality, the banality of it all. I fumble in my big black bag for a dollar, push it into his eager open palm, watch as the precious case drops to the floor.

"Thank you. Thank you, ma'am," he mumbles, an old man, a veteran of many embarrassed foot shiftings. I want to cry—for him, for me, for the world.

"Would you like a drink brought up, maybe?" he asks.

"No." My calm is cracking. "Thank you," I add. "I don't want to be disturbed. For anything." He nods. No hope for another tip. He shuffles off. I put the Do Not Disturb sign on the outside doorknob. I am alone. *Elena* is alone.

There was no more time for thinking, no more room between myself, my decision, and the final act. I released the Doriden from their suitcase prison, walked across the deep carpet into the bathroom, ran the water until it was cold, and began to swallow the pills. One by one, with gulps of cold water, I swallowed the thick, dime-size pills. Fifty times I swallowed until the pink satin scarf-container was empty and my stomach stood out bloated and hard with the water I had drunk, and the fifty heavy pills that were beginning to dissolve, beginning to course their poisons through my waiting frightened body.

It was done. Finally it was done. No more crying. No more pain. No more anguish and shame for my parents. I stepped back from the sink, reeled and fell against the cold tile wall. So quickly they had begun to act? My head felt heavy and it spun around and around. Or was it the room spinning? Or both? I hadn't planned that it should happen so fast. How could I say good-bye to the world this way, as it whirled around my eyes?

I couldn't walk, so I crawled on the red carpet, feeling its soft thickness through my stockings and against my slowly numbing fingers.

> *somewhere I have never travelled; gladly beyond*
> *any experience, your eyes have their silence:*

cummings. The texture of his words, the remembered, loved, endlessly memorized phrases, dropped from my lips.

I am repeating his words, his words that sing of life. Crawling along the red plush carpet, my tongue thick, the red growing gray.

> *dying is fine) but Death*
>
> *?o*
>
> *baby*
>
> *i*
>
> *wouldn't like*
>
> *Death if Death*
>
> *were*
>
> *good*

Even as the world goes gray and imprecise, I can repeat the words. I am crying, so afraid. Can I go on dying forever? Can I bear the pain of it?

But I can't let go. Something in me holds on, in the encroaching dizziness and nausea and fog. I never thought it would hold on so tight.

I can barely hold the telephone, but I dial, as the numbers jump and spin before my eyes.

"Is this the hospital? Dr. Sternfeld's office?"

"Dr. Sternfeld?" I whisper. My voice comes froglike, my tongue is thick. "I want to speak to Dr. Sternfeld."

"Who shall I say is calling, please?"

"Janet. Janet Moss."

Clicks. Silence. His voice.

"Janet?"

JANET

Suddenly, I don't want to answer. I didn't want to call him. I am angry. Why did it have to happen this way?

"Janet?"

"I just took fifty Doriden, Dr. Sternfeld." Why did I call him?

"Where are you, Janet?" His voice is calm.

"I'm not going to tell you," I answer. "I called to say good-bye."

"You called to tell me where you are." He is stern, not angry. Why should he want to save me? Could he give me something—a pink pill, a purple one, one that could make my life bearable, ease my pain?

My voice is failing; I can barely keep my eyes open.

"Janet. Tell me where you are." Inside myself I can hear crying. A little girl is crying.

I don't want to tell him. I do want to tell him. The receiver is slipping from my hand. If I tell him, it will be for nothing. Nothing. Why can't I be strong? Why can't I just end it—strong?

"Janet."

"Don't be mad at me." I am whispering. Will he punish me for taking the pills? That is my biggest fear.

Next to the blackness which is coming—fast—faster.

"I'm not mad. I want to help you." His voice, as it filters through my sleepy fog, is tinged with panic.

"The Biarritz," I whisper.

Crash, as the phone falls to the floor.

A blackness more dire than sleep.

Light, muted and shimmering, seemed to surround me as I opened my eyes. Pearl white, the swaying gossamer walls and the high-peaked ceiling above. Was I underwater? Could this be heaven?

I could see shadows moving beyond the white gauzy squares that defined my space. My head seemed filled with the same flickering pale light that surrounded me. I was lying down on a bed. But where?

As I tensed my muscles to sit, I felt bands tighten across my chest and legs. I couldn't get up. Right to left, I turned my head. Nothing but white gauze curtains, squaring off my place. A jar, hung upside down above my bed, seemed to be dripping a clear liquid through a narrow tube, downward, into—into MY ARM.

"Where am I?" I tried to scream. "Help."

But no sound came from my lips. Nothing but a rush of air, as my mouth shaped the noiseless words.

"Help." I tried again, louder.

A Suicide Attempt and Monroe Park, Again

No sound. No response from the moving shadows outside my square.

Something had happened to me; I couldn't speak. I was alive, it seemed, although I couldn't remember anything beyond swallowing the Doriden in the bathroom of my hotel room. Where was I, how had I gotten there? And why, dear Lord, couldn't I make any sound come from my throat?

Had God punished me for trying to take my life?

"That's ridiculous," I said silently to myself.

Then why couldn't I speak?

"How will I ever get out of here? No one will find me. I'll rot away on this stark white bed. They won't know I'm here until the stench of my body, as it rots in its muteness, makes them stop and look."

Without realizing it, I had moved my right hand to my throat. Horrified, sick, my fingers touched something—a hole, surrounded by a hard metallic substance, in my throat. There was a hole in my throat and I couldn't feel it! Accidentally, while fingering the thing in my throat, I covered the hole. I had been talking to myself. Suddenly, there was sound. If I covered the hole so the air didn't escape, I could form distinguishable words!

"Help! Help!" I screamed, and though the words came raspy and muddled, at least I could talk. In an instant, two white-coated figures appeared, nurses, followed quickly by a doctor I didn't know.

I was in Hampshire Hospital, they explained. Intensive Care Unit. An ambulance had taken me from the Biarritz Hotel after I called Dr. Sternfeld.

"I don't remember calling Dr. Sternfeld," I said.

"I'm sure you won't remember a lot of things, dear. You've been in a coma. You were a very sick girl."

"And this," I tried to say, forgetting to cover the hole in my throat, but pointing to it.

"Doriden is a very dangerous drug," the doctor continued. "We pumped your stomach, but there were complications. You couldn't breathe, you had pneumonia. We did a tracheotomy."

"Like Elizabeth Taylor," I croaked the joke.

"Dr. Stinson says your scar won't even show. It'll be better than hers," a nurse crooned, as Dr. Stinson, who looked more like a Princeton football tackle than a surgeon, stood and beamed.

"We'll take the tube out in a couple of days," a smiling nurse added. "And you'll be as good as new."

As good as new. But that wasn't very much to look forward to.

I pointed to the tube that was dripping into my left hand.

"An I.V.," I was told. "When you were in the coma, you couldn't eat, and we had to keep up your strength. So we've been feeding you intravenously. That can stop soon."

When the curtains parted and Dr. Sternfeld appeared, a two-day growth of beard shadowing his chin, his clothes crumpled, and his eyes pink, I was suddenly overcome with remorse.

How could I do this to him? And to my parents? Where were they?

Remorse. And the sickeningly vivid perception in the depth of my loneliness and my stomach of a failed suicide attempt.

What now?

Dr. Sternfeld sat on the edge of my bed and took my hand in his. I had nothing, I was starting from scratch.

"You almost didn't make it, Janet," he said.

"I'm very sorry I did," I wanted to whisper. "Are you mad at me?" I asked.

"No. Just glad you're alive."

"Please don't be mad at me," I pleaded, holding my thumb over the hole in my throat in order to produce recognizable sounds.

"We have a lot of work to do when you get out, Janet," Dr. Sternfeld said. "But we won't be able to go on like this, living in constant fear that you are going to cut your wrists or take pills."

It wasn't clear what he was implying, though I heard an undertone of—I can only call it threat—in his words. I ignored it; my powerlessness was too immense to contemplate.

"Then you won't stop treating me now?" That had been my greatest fear.

"I won't leave you, Janet." I was crying, while Dr. Sternfeld sat, holding my hand. I thought he might cry too.

"Someone's here to see you, Janet," he said, rising.

"Who?" I asked.

"I'm sure you'll be surprised." He pushed aside the curtain, motioned with his left hand, held a passage space open for my visitor, and disappeared.

The young man stood self-consciously near the foot of my bed. His hair was dark and long. He had a heavy drooping mustache, tortoiseshell glasses. Dressed in brown tweeds. His hands showed his nervousness, as he twined and untwined his fingers—long, slender, delicate fingers, with a fine silky pattern of hair on each hand.

"My God," I thought, a rush of recognition flooding me. "It's Matthew."

A Suicide Attempt and Monroe Park, Again

But I didn't know the face. He was so changed. It had been how long? Five years?

"Hello, Janet." The voice was strange, too. He sat down on the chair to the left of my pillow. I had to strain, turning my head, to see him.

I didn't know what to say to this man, my brother. I had loved him more than any living being, though only God could explain why. At best, he had ignored me; at worst, he had used me and left me frightened and scarred from that first experience with man-power. Yet I adored him, forgave him everything, mourned his loss in my dreams and my fantasies and my everyday when he disappeared from my life. Why had he left me? I knew it had nothing to do with me, personally; that leaving was, rather, Matthew's way of solving his insoluble conflict with my father.

Dr. Sternfeld had told my parents that Matthew felt he must cut off *all* contact with his family in order to survive himself. They hadn't been able to accept it, that final break, and the years had accumulated more unanswered letters and uncashed birthday and anniversary checks than most hearts could bear.

If he could only have kept Matthew in therapy with him a few months longer, Dr. Sternfeld told my parents, he could have gotten him to make a more human, realistic choice for his life. They believed him; the failure was Matthew's.

I was staring at him. How the hell did he get to Hampshire Hospital? How did he know I was sick?

"It's good to see you," I said, but, forgetting to cover my hole, no words came out, just a rush of air.

"It's good to see you." This time the sound came.

"How do you feel?" Matthew asked. His long fine fingers were clutching the seat of his chair.

"Oh, just great," I answered. "Except for the fact that I'm being fed through tubes attached to my arms and I'm strapped down and I have a pipe in my trachea and I can't talk, I'm fine. How did you know I was here?"

"Dad called me. He said you were very sick."

"I've been very sick for years now," I wanted to scream at him. "And you never came."

"I guess I was," I said limply.

"Have you been having a bad time, Janet?" Matthew asked. He still looked past me, concentrating his flickering brown eyes on an invisible point near the foot of my bed.

"Yeah. You might say that."

"Are you seeing Jake Sternfeld?" he asked.

"Yes."

"You're lucky. He's a good man."

"Yes, I know," I said, pondering for a forbidden instant the picture of the two of us—one scared rat of a man who was so frightened of himself, his past, and his father, that he was going to spend his life in hiding; one mental patient, diagnosed schizophrenic, failed suicide, who was headed for a future as a complete emotional invalid. Not very good advertisements for Jacob Sternfeld. I closed my mind to the heresies.

"I'm sure he'll help you."

We talked a few minutes, exchanging inanities, trivialities of social intercourse. Sometimes I forgot to cover the hole in my tube in my throat and the voiceless words rushed forth unnoticed.

"How's Sara?"

"Fine."

"That's good. Say hello to her for me, Matthew, please." I wanted desperately to say "I love you, please come home, I miss you"; so desperately that the want was like acid, eating a hole in my stomach.

"Sure. I will." Stop. "I have to go now, Janet. The doctor said not to stay too long."

"Go? Oh. Of course. Go."

He stood up, his brown eyes tired, vacillating, almost caught.

"Thanks for coming to see me, Matthew."

"I hope you feel better soon."

"Bye."

"Yeah. Bye."

He disappeared through the white curtain that was walls and door of my room. We never touched.

I stayed at Hampshire Hospital for three weeks, until my tracheotomy healed, all vital organs were functioning satisfactorily, I was eating acceptably, and Dr. Sternfeld and the hospital doctors were convinced I was no longer imminently suicidal. Then I went home.

Dr. Sternfeld went on his vacation in July, leaving me shriveled in fear that I wouldn't survive his absence. He berated me for that fear, scolded me for my growing dependence on him, gave me a month's supply of tranquilizers, sleeping pills, Darvon, and muscle relaxants, and left his day-by-day itinerary with me—more, he said petulantly, than he would do even for his wife. I bathed in the somewhat mystifying light of his favor, warmed by his concern and devotion, puzzled by his anger at my dependence.

Before he left, though, he warned me of a change to come in our relationship. Starting that day, if I wanted him to put his arm around me I would have to ask him. The time of using a symbol for my helplessness and need, an extended cigarette, was over. I would have to assert myself, *ask* for what I wanted.

"I can't do it," I thought to myself, panicky that he might withdraw his protective arm forever. It would be too humiliating to ask him to care for me, love me, comfort me. Why did I have to ask anyway? If he really cared for me, he would come of his own accord when I needed him. He wouldn't wait to be asked. And if he didn't really care for me, well, then, he shouldn't put his arm around me at all.

We had gone over these questions many times in my sessions. Did he put his arm around me, give me the few sustaining exquisite moments of total snuggling, weeping protection, as therapy? Was it only as my doctor that he had, for months, answered the mute symbolic offer of a cigarette and come and let me cry in his arms? Did he truly care for me, about me? These were the most vital concerns of my life; he must have known that, known how completely I was centered on his moods and whims and wisdom; known it even as he rationed himself to me, made a carrot of his love, thrust his itinerary in my hand, and berated me for the pathological laziness and resistance to treatment that made me cling to him like a life raft. I would have a month to consider if I could lower myself enough to beg for him; a month to hide my anger that he should use my helplessness, and not acknowledge his part in my growing dependence.

"What if I can't—ask you?" I asked clumsily.

"Then you will do without my arm around you." He seemed to me at that moment indescribably smug and insulated.

"But that's not fair," I cried.

"Janet," he spoke softly. "Do you trust me? Do I have to prove that I care for you?"

"I don't know," I cried.

"Would you like me to put my arm around you now? This will be the last time I ask, you know."

I was a pool of powerlessness, limp with needing him.

"Yes," I said, covering my eyes with my arms for the utter shame of it all. "Yes."

JANET

The next few months were a total misery of desolation and anxiety. I felt helpless and trapped, terrified by my dependence on Dr. Sternfeld and my parents, more and more certain in the dusty drugged corners of my brain and body that I was an alien in the world, waiting, almost wanting, in a pathetic, ironic way, to regain my true identity—mental patient. The pretense of trying to pass on the outside was excruciating. Tensions with my parents built.

One evening, in the Hotel Sumner, where I was staying with Maggie, my old friend from Oceanville, in what turned out to be an abortive attempt to gain independence, I walked into the shower, turned on the water, and began to cut my wrists.

I don't know why I did it. Only that living in a rundown Greenwich Village hotel with a drugged friend, cut off from the world moving fast outside my window, was relentless agony. My life had become unbearable and wrist-cutting had become the only way I could act on my life to affect it.

It was strange that this act, picked randomly at a time of despair almost two years before, had become, during my months of hospitalization, in a sense, *me*. My symptom. My statement. I had adopted it permanently at Oceanville. And now, I couldn't shed it.

I was relieved, almost glad, when I entered Monroe Park Hospital that fall. This time, Dr. Sternfeld didn't need to do much convincing. For all its horrors, the safety of that place called a hospital tantalized me, seduced me into again being a mental patient. I was becoming institutionalized, slowly, without realizing it. I could survive only in a hospital.

I went to the fourth floor instead of the seventh. There patients wore clothing, the dayroom door was not locked, and the more bizarre symptoms of our madness were less evident. But the heavy door leading to freedom was still sealed, the windows thickly screened, the toilets without locks. And the pervasive, deadening belief that we, the incarcerated ones, were somehow less than human, hung over us like fog in a Louisiana swamp, unmistakable in the arrogant condescension of the glass-boothed staff.

But I was used to it; in fact, I barely noticed the attitude; or if I did, I accepted it as my due. After all, wasn't I sick? Wasn't sick a synonym for bad? Didn't I deserve to be treated this way?

And when Dr. Sternfeld told me he wanted to give me shock treatments, I consented, easily. Why not?

Twenty. I had twenty shock treatments. The memory of them is a blur of pain and confusion; a total misery of the spirit.

And when they were done, and the curtains of flapping confusion straightened again in my brain, it was as if nothing had happened. Only the memory remained. And would, I found, forever.

November 22, 1963. The sounds from the radio in the nurses' station spilled into the corridors. I was standing at the pay phone, preparing to make a call when I heard the announcement.

"The President has been shot." And a moment later, "President Kennedy is dead."

For the first, and perhaps the last time, the halls of Monroe Park grew silent. For a moment, as the disbelief and horror of it all sifted through our separate auras of pain, we became part of the "real" world, related to the outside. Every person on the fourth floor, that terrible moment, was stilled by the news. We looked at each other; for a too short while we forgot our pains and symptoms, sharing, with tears and holding the grief all the world was feeling. We were alive, part of the human race again.

And then it was gone, as the nurses reminded us that it was medication time.

It had all been illusion, I thought, that shared humanity we had experienced, that glorious second, engendered by tragedy, when I thought, "Perhaps I'm not crazy." Later that evening, occasional references to the assassination floated in the ward air. But the moment had passed, a moment of suspended unreal time for us. We each resumed our poses, our symptoms, our hallucinations, and our mental patient lives. That was, after all, the "real" us.

Dr. Sternfeld went on a late-autumn vacation, leaving me to the flurried occasional care of Dr. Lessing, the frenetic humanoid who administered shock treatments.

I had been at Monroe Park for three months, made friends, and become more deeply enwebbed in the hospital world and obsessed with my symptoms and derangements than I could have anticipated. In my mind I had no articulated doubts that I was sick. My major task—and only source of hope, I thought—was to disentangle the distorted threads of experience and perception in my brain, with Dr. Sternfeld's help. If I became angry at him, of course it was because I was sick. And when, my face pressed to the screen of my fourth-floor window, I watched the passing world of people bundled against the cold receding farther from my grasp, I wanted to kill (or die), it was, of course, my sickness speaking. The irrational me.

(Do you realize, I ask myself now, that I believed that nonsense, that psychiatric drivel, manufactured by this industry that deals in suffering? I believed it, yes, as only a desperate outcast can believe, with mad passion that would brook no questions. No one could ever, then, in years to come, accuse my tormentors of "coercion" in treating me. My good Lord who watches over *esprits fous*—where were you all those years?)

Dr. Sternfeld returned, suntanned and ebullient. I wanted to feel glad that he had gone island-hopping in the Caribbean for two weeks. I didn't like myself for begrudging him his few weeks of rest. Childish possessiveness, he called it; a little girl's petulant anger that she could not totally own her daddy.

"No," a voice inside me said. "Don't let him con you. He did leave you; you have every right to be angry."

But he was back, and the rush of gladness I felt when he came to see me obscured the iceberg of rage that was beginning to surface. My guardian was back; I could be released. It was mid-December. I returned home. Again.

My parents came to the hospital to take me home. They waited uncomfortably, while I kissed my new friends good-bye and thanked the nurses for all their attentions.

"Good-bye safe world of locked doors and sickness," I whispered into my scarf as the elevator descended. "I will be back. I know it. This is my real home now."

We drove to Brooklyn in silence, my parents solicitous, leaving me, for once, to the privacy of my thoughts.

Chanukah. Christmas. New Year's. On January fifth I would be twenty-one.

"Last year around this time," I thought, "I was being discharged from Oceanville. To start a new life." A laugh that was a chunk of bitterness escaped from my lips. My parents looked at me, fear in their eyes, drew deep breaths, and looked away again.

What had happened in this first year of my so-called new life? We moved through the cold gray streets, passing winter-wizened people huddled against the wind. They seemed a different species; we were no longer related. They were the healthy ones; I was one of the outcast sick.

"Someday maybe I'll be well, too," I thought. "Someday I'll join them." It was this promise that sustained me, not Dr. Sternfeld, although he was, in a sense, part of the promise. He held the key to the door that would someday open to admit me to the regions of complete serenity, calm, joy, fulfillment—the Land of Mental Health. No demons dwelt there. Suicidal thought withered before maturity. There were no words for rage, frustration, despair, and pain.

A Suicide Attempt and Monroe Park, Again

I let my mind roam for awhile in those sun-warmed undulating fields. That was what I was striving for: to enter the golden realms of the Everyday Well-Adjusted Normal Mentally Healthy Soul. "And what," I wondered, "have I ever done that I should be banished from this land?"

As we drove over the Brooklyn Bridge and I lightly touched the scars on my wrists, I listened, for the millionth time in my life, to the high whine of the car wheels on the ridged metal floor. It seemed to be singing of my own desperate pain, reminding me, with its insistent stridency, that I was different: I didn't belong; I never would. Mine was the world of mental hospitals, pills, doctors, shock treatments, and suicide attempts. I would live forever in the country of despair.

But Dr. Sternfeld said no, I had a chance, there was a core of "health" in me; I would get "well."

Well was functioning, going to school, working, getting married, having children, never wanting to die.

"I will never get well," I said, just barely out loud. Lately I had had a feeling that someone, a young girl, could hear me, although I couldn't see her, or even prove she was there.

Yet, some part of me believed Dr. Sternfeld. Believed him because he was strong, kind, concerned, forceful, eloquent, a man, and a psychiatrist. He had to know something I didn't know, I repeated endlessly to myself. From his vast knowledge and training he had to know I was curable. It was, as he so often said, only a question of finding the right treatment, the right combination of drugs.

Not for an instant did I entertain the idea that he was hit-or-missing around with my body chemistry, my brain, my mind, my freedom, and my life. He wouldn't do that. He was a professional.

But as we sped along I reviewed my first year of treatment with Dr. Sternfeld.

As soon as I was out of Oceanville, I recalled, before I even began therapy with him, he had started me on drugs. I couldn't even remember now what that first drug had been. There had been so many others during the ensuing months. Was it eight, maybe ten different tranquilizers he had tried? Not to mention the sleeping pills and muscle relaxants and amphetamines. I had not, I realized with a start, been without some kind of drug during the entire year, except for the times I was taking shock treatments.

Oh, yes. Shock treatments. Twenty-six in one year. I shuddered as I recalled the treatments, the terrible encompassing helplessness and fear as I was wheeled into the shock room, the euphoria as the sodium pentothal flowed into my veins, the dreadful headaches, and perhaps worst of all, the foggy confusions and loss of memory that lingered long after the headaches were gone. And then, as soon as the fog in my brain cleared, I had begun to feel the same way I had before the treatments.

Then why had he given them to me? Why had I taken them? I didn't know and I didn't want to think about it. But I continued my assessment of the year. In a mental hospital twice—a total of six months in Monroe Park, the gilded cage.

Wrist-cutting. Too many times to count.

One major suicide attempt, and a month in Hampshire Hospital.

"Why?" I thought for the hundredth time since that day in June. "Why?" I said silently, wonder mixed again with remorse and outrage. "Why, when oblivion was almost within reach, had I called Dr. Sternfeld and blown the whole thing?"

I had no answer. Just as I had no answer to the nagging shifting questions I asked myself each night before I fell over the edge of darkness into sleep. "Why do I stay with him? Why do I go into the hospital each time? Why do I take the pills and the shock treatments? Why? Why?"

"Because I love him. I believe in him. I need him. Dammit. Besides him, I have nothing."

But something was very wrong. I was worse off now than a year ago, before I started seeing him. I knew that. "He's helping me," I wanted to scream, to quiet my own questions. "He cares about me; he's a good doctor."

The car stopped. We were home. Another year was beginning.

"Mother," I said as she gave me my sleeping pills that evening, "I want to ask you something. Please."

She wavered, an anxious shadow flickering across her eyes. Then she sat beside me on my bed.

"Do you think I'm ever going to get well?" I asked.

"Dr. Sternfeld says he is very optimistic," my mother answered evasively.

"But what about you? What do you think?" I asked again.

"I have faith in you, Jan."

"But do you think I'm going to get well?" I was talking too loudly, too insistently. My mother was frightened; I frightened her, I realized.

"Yes," she answered slowly, collecting herself. "I know you are going to get well. Dr. Sternfeld is going to make you well."

Suddenly I wanted my mother to hold me, to tell me it was all going to be all right. The nightmare would end. I would wake up, sound and whole.

"I'm sorry," I was crying into her nightgown. "I'm sorry about everything."

But she was tired, and long ago the doors had shut on her springs of feeling. She had shut them so she could survive. She couldn't hold me, I knew it, and long after the door closed behind her, I cried into my pillow.

I was twenty-one. A grown woman. And I was crying because I wanted my mother. But it felt good to be in my own bed after four months of Monroe Park, and I barely noticed the squid, as he crouched in his corner of the room.

"Tomorrow I'll see Dr. Sternfeld," I said, as I slipped into a drugged sleep.

The tomorrows came, went, came and went. My days flowed indistinguishable, one into another, defined and bounded by the rituals and effects of constant drug-taking and my visits to Dr. Sternfeld.

Mary was a senior at Ellis.

Dr. Sternfeld's mood was solemn.

"I've come to a decision, Janet," he said one day after I had settled myself on the edge of the brown leather couch with my ashtray and my cup of water on the small table near my knees. Usually, I had to get up at least once during the session to refill the tiny two-ounce paper cup. Without the water I couldn't speak; my mouth and tongue were too dry from the Thorazine. Another ultimatum was coming; I could sense it.

"I cannot treat you anymore," Dr. Sternfeld began, "if every time you feel depressed or upset you cut your wrists. Each time you indulge yourself in this kind of self-destructive activity, we must interrupt therapy to take care of you, physically."

In my head, a distant mechanism of recognition had been activated. Maybe that was a purpose of wrist-cutting, I thought furtively. To interrupt therapy. Wasn't that the purpose of it the first time, with Dr. Berman? True, only someone like me, helpless, pained, self-hating, would choose this bloody stopgap technique. But there it was. Along with a question: Why should I want to interrupt therapy with Dr. Sternfeld? I loved Dr. Sternfeld. He was going to save me. I couldn't answer that question, and even the tentative posing of it made my heart beat with anxiety. I buried the thoughts and questions that were bombarding my mind.

"That wastes my time and yours," Dr. Sternfeld continued. "Besides, it's too dangerous. One of these days you may really kill yourself. It's time you tried to control yourself."

The questioning perceptions of the moment before had disappeared as if they had never existed. Panicked, I could think of only one thing.

"What if I can't control myself?" I cried.

"Then I'll have to stop seeing you," he answered.

The prospect of a world without Dr. Sternfeld was inconceivable.

"But I can't." I was whimpering. Pathetic and shameless, I felt sick. But Dr. Sternfeld seemed to be encouraging my display of self-pity and pridelessness. He sat back, almost smiling.

"I am making a contract with you," he said after a pause. "As long as you do not cut your wrists, I will treat you. If you make even a small attempt, a scratch, you will have to find another doctor."

Live for him. That's what he was saying. He knew, I thought, with the rationally functioning part of my brain, how centrally important he was to me, and he was playing on it.

"How can I live if I can't cut my wrists?" That strange coded question rotated in my head. What would I do with the seething mass of destruction and turmoil that grew inside me, inchoate and agonizing, and turned, finally, into slashes on my arm?

"But that's not fair," I whined. "You don't really care about *me* at all. If you did, you wouldn't play these games with me."

"I am trying to protect you, Janet," Dr. Sternfeld answered. "And I am trying to give us uninterrupted time for therapy. You were in the hospital almost six months last year, do you know that?"

What hope was there for me? Where did the tears come from, the endless tears?

"I don't think I can do it," I said. "I'm too obsessed with the cutting."

"You can. You'll have to. Just think, 'This is no longer an option for me. It is not a possibility.' If you allow yourself to think about it, to plan it, if you carry razor blades, you will probably do it sometime. You must quit—cold."

"It's easy for you to say." I was finally feeling some of the anger inside me.

"And another thing, Janet," Dr. Sternfeld added. "No more sunglasses."

I felt dizzy, falling from the second blow. He was taking away my props all at once, knowing I would do what he said, out of a helpless dependence that had become my life's strongest motivation.

"Why?" I screamed. "Why are you doing this to me?"

A Suicide Attempt and Monroe Park, Again

"It is time that you took some steps toward becoming an independent person. The longer you depend on these external symptoms of yours, the harder it will be to shed them."

"I can't. I'm too scared." I was crying.

Dr. Sternfeld watched me from his deep armchair comfort.

He spoke about independence, yet he cultivated my slavering dependence like a rare flower, kicked me, and waited for the thanks.

"The hour is almost up, Janet," Dr. Sternfeld said. "How have you been feeling with the new dosage?"

"My hands keep shaking," I said. "And my dancing legs; it's awful."

"I'll give you some more Kemadrin for that," Dr. Sternfeld said. "But do you feel any better now that we've increased?"

"No," I said. "I think I need more. Could you raise it just a hundred milligrams?"

"I don't know. We'll see." The subject was closed for the day.

Talk about dependence. In the year since I had begun taking them, the drugs had given me nothing but problems. The large doses of Thorazine forced my anxiety deeper and deeper inside, surrounding it with a cocoon of groggy heaviness. I could always feel it, though, my real self, fluttering around in its Thorazine cage. I had grown terribly frightened of what would happen if my sickness, faintly heard, were to be released, to explode with all its pent-up savagery. I hated the drugs, but I needed them. And Dr. Sternfeld, with his endless permutations of possible combinations and dosages, was the architect of my fear, my belief, and my only source of temporary surcease.

I stopped cutting my wrists, I took off my sunglasses, and I survived.

For a month or two, embroiled as I was in the constant battle not to think about cutting my wrists, I did feel better, invigorated even. The winter seemed not so cold. And, as I expressed my gratitude to Dr. Sternfeld, his former warmth returned. I was pleasing him. He had been angry with me, I knew, although he denied it when I spoke of it, attributing that idea to a projection of my own feelings of shame and guilt.

Whatever I felt, it was never right, it seemed. It was always a product of my "sickness."

I saw Dr. Sternfeld at least three times a week. A self-described eclectic, his therapies were wide and various: He prescribed Darvon for my menstrual cramps, oversaw posture exercises to eliminate tension and create a new body image for me, vetoed or okayed my perpetual diets, screened my friends, suggested busywork activities, judged my parental conflicts, monitored my hemoglobin and my bowel movements, raised or lowered my inevitable drugs. In short, he took over my life.

"You're very lucky, Janet," my mother would say morosely, "that Jake cares so much about you. He loves you. Remember that."

I never had a response for these spontaneous defenses of Dr. Sternfeld. Each time a hard chunk, angry and acid, would rise in my throat. I would swallow it down, protectively. Why, I wondered, did I react so? I loved Dr. Sternfeld.

The pervasive message I received from my parents, again and again, was that I should be grateful to Dr. Sternfeld for his devotion in spite of my wrist-cutting and suicide attempts. Even Dr. Sternfeld, in moments of pique, let me know that it was only his patience and love that kept him with me.

I never, in the face of these exhortations to gratitude, mentioned the nagging, barely articulated question that existed always, like a flickering shadow in the corners of my mind: We were paying him thirty-five dollars for each forty-five minutes of his so-called devotion, weren't we? Could that really be called devotion?

"Not such extraordinary martyrdom, after all," I thought but never dared to say. And in the day-to-day pain of trying to exist on the outside, I thought only of my sessions, built my plans around the precise hours, and took the words of kindness and reprobation that fell from Dr. Sternfeld's lips as authentic jewels, his unique gift to me.

As the days wore on and I survived, groggy and dull in my Thorazine trance, I would hear no criticism of him from anyone, not even myself.

Franklin Central Hospital

The drugs and my weakness took their toll. "I can't go on," I finally said to Dr. Sternfeld. "I can't make it on the outside. I know I'm going to cut my wrists. I try not to think about it, but I can't help it. I want to go to the hospital. That's where I belong. Send me to a hospital for the rest of my life."

I hadn't meant to say all that, and, listening to myself, I heard the melodrama in my voice, the self-pity, the veiled accusations and threats, as well as the real despair and hopelessness. Dr. Sternfeld's mouth had hardened slightly. He leaned forward.

"I don't think you know what you're saying, Janet," he said quietly.

"I do. I do. I can't even read a book anymore. My mind is disintegrating. I could never concentrate enough to go back to school. Everyone I meet knows something's wrong with me. I'm an outcast."

"I know you are suffering," Dr. Sternfeld said. "And I feel great sympathy for your pain. But you haven't given yourself a chance; that's why I wanted you to have this pause, this respite from the fear of wrist-cutting."

"But it's no good," I interrupted.

"In spite of your pain, you are very spoiled, Janet," Dr. Sternfeld said. "You still see yourself as deserving special treatment from the world, and you are angry that you don't get it. I don't think you know what a *real* hospital is like."

A shiver ran up my spine.

"You're used to Oceanville and Monroe Park," Dr. Sternfeld said disdainfully. They are palaces compared to a real hospital. I am quite sure you wouldn't like to be in a hospital for the rest of your life."

"No, I wouldn't like it. But at least I'd belong there. And how can you accuse me of feeling special—you're the one who treats me special; you told me so." Suddenly, as the quiet fell like an avalanche on my head, I was afraid.

"I am very tired of jumping in panic every time you have a fleeting suicidal feeling," Dr. Sternfeld said. "You have us all, your parents, me, your friends, dancing to the tune of your depression. That is power. And I'm sure you know it."

"That's not fair," I cried. "I don't mean to manipulate you. Or my parents. I can't help what I feel. Please don't be angry with me," I begged.

"I know it has been hard for you, Janet," Dr. Sternfeld said. "But you can get well. I have great faith in the drugs, if we can only find the right combination, the right one. And I have faith in you, too. You're strong. We need to do so much more talking, so much more opening up."

"I'm so scared, Dr. Sternfeld," I whispered, not daring to look up. The wracking shaking tears were coming again, as they had so often in the months since I left Monroe Park. "I'm so afraid I'm going to fall apart. I'm going to disintegrate into pieces on the floor and no one will be able to put me back together again." That was a recent belief I had developed: The feelings in my body were so intense they would cause me to break into a million drillion jigsaw pieces on the floor, if I let myself go and cried.

"Why don't you cry?" Dr. Sternfeld said. "Go ahead and cry. See what happens."

"Would you come and sit next to me, please?" I asked him in a whisper.

Wordlessly, Dr. Sternfeld rose. In a moment he was sitting beside me on the hard couch, his large body warming and holding me, strong, protective, so dear.

"I'm here, Janet," he said. "Go ahead. Cry."

"I'm afraid. I'm so afraid," I whispered.

We had been through this scene many times. Yet each time it was as real as though it had never been suffered before.

"You won't fall apart," he said. "But you have to realize that yourself."

The funnel of pain that had concentrated in my body exploded. Was I falling into a billion pieces? I heard the howl, the wail that was my anguish, as it fled my mouth. I was crying, deep sounds escaping my harrowed body. Small, small I was, so scared of the feelings buried and powerful inside me. Would I ever be well? Dr. Sternfeld held me, steady, loving, as I cried until no sounds, just hulking sobs of silence filled his arms; until I was too tired to even breathe. I hadn't fallen apart.

How would I ever thank this man for his holding me?

How, in the face of this favor, would I ever express anything but gratitude?

How could I ever leave?

"I've been doing some thinking, Janet," Dr. Sternfeld said several weeks later. I had been feeling steadily more suicidal and had asked him again to put me in the hospital. I wasn't even sure that I really wanted to be hospitalized forever. It seemed the only way.

"There is one thing we haven't tried yet. It has its disadvantages, but if there's a possibility it might get you out of this . . ."

"What?" I asked. I almost didn't care.

"Insulin shock," Dr. Sternfeld said.

"What?" I almost shouted.

"Insulin shock," Dr. Sternfeld repeated.

"No," I said. "No. I don't want it."

"There has been some startling success in cases like yours," Dr. Sternfeld said.

"No. I don't want anymore shock treatments."

"This is completely different from electric shock," Dr. Sternfeld said. "You would get injections of insulin, in increasing doses, until the desired effect was achieved. Insulin coma."

"My God!" I said.

"It is not painful," he continued, "but it is a long process, involving up to forty injections. The results are often more dramatic and long-lasting than electric shock, but, because of the time involved, most places have stopped giving the treatments."

"I don't want them," I said.

"Franklin Central Hospital gives them."

"No," I said again, visions of the snake pit rising before my eyes.

"You wanted to go to a hospital," Dr. Sternfeld countered.

"Not a state hospital," I shuddered.

"You can't stay in Monroe Park forever. It's too expensive," Dr. Sternfeld said. "And besides, if I sent you to a hospital now, it wouldn't be to a country club like Monroe Park. If you want a hospital, you'll get the real thing this time. You can see what it's *really* like to be a patient. See if you want *that* for the rest of your life."

Was I imagining the cruelty and anger of his words? Was the message of punishment I was receiving so clearly really there? It couldn't be. Not Dr. Sternfeld.

"He wants to teach me a lesson," I thought, horrified. "Teach the spoiled little girl what a *real* mental hospital is like. He thinks I've had it too good. After all, weren't Monroe Park and Oceanville just vacations from responsibility? A country club, he called it. My God. It's not possible!"

"I will not force you to take the treatments," Dr. Sternfeld continued easily, as if his interlude of vindictive moralizing had never occurred. "I will not force you to do anything. Think about it. Think about being good to yourself, for a change."

"No, no, it's all wrong," I said, facing the icy winter day with my stunned horror. I wouldn't go to a state hospital, not voluntarily, never. And I wouldn't take insulin shock; I had a mental picture of rows of comatose women and men, each lying on a bare, stained mattress in a fortress that was called a hospital, the whole scene dominated by bald and white-haired psychiatrists, all taking notes. It might not be totally accurate, but it wasn't far from the truth either. That I knew.

The weeks went by; Dr. Sternfeld continued his steady pressure to convince me to take the treatments; my options were nil, the circle closed. I felt myself waver. More than anything, I did not want him to abandon me.

"I think we should give it a try, Janet. We cannot let any door pass unopened."

We. We. Whose body was going into shock, anyway?

"I'll be able to see you as often as now. We can continue therapy with no interruption and you can have the safety and protection of the hospital."

Safety. Protection. Only someone who had never been inside could use those words so glibly. It made me furious, but I didn't know it. Didn't know that the black knots in my chest were anger toward Dr. Sternfeld and his arrogant plans for my life. I was afraid to be angry with him, so I pushed myself so far from the feeling that I sensed only the intensity, not meaning.

"What are you afraid of, Janet?" he asked again and again.

"The treatments."

"I have told you there is nothing to be afraid of." Subject closed.

"I am afraid of going into the hospital. A state hospital."

"You will be a voluntary patient. I will see you often. There is nothing to be afraid of."

My mind swept back to Oceanville and Monroe Park and the voluntary patients I had known who had been committed. What would my chances be at a state hospital when I wanted to leave and Dr. Sternfeld didn't want to let me go?

Nothing to be afraid of: locked doors, powerlessness, ridicule, humiliation, and barred windows. Did he have any idea what it was like to be caged? To have no privacy? No rights? No freedom? No credibility? No matches? No keys? Did he even care? Yes, maybe, but weren't these minor considerations, after all, compared to the *therapeutic* benefits of the hospital experience?

Bullshit.

"I think you are afraid of finally facing yourself and getting well," Dr. Sternfeld said.

Resistance. One of the deadly sins.

Finally, Dr. Sternfeld began to threaten. Not in gross words, but the message was clear. If I did not go to Franklin Central, voluntarily, where he could have me locked up and "safe" and still treat me in his spare moments, he would have to stop seeing me.

I consented, partly out of fear and partly out of a blindness in me that believed his hype about getting well, and a state hospital and insulin being the answer. I wanted to die. I wanted to get well. And, in spite of his obscured motives, I believe Dr. Sternfeld wanted me to get well, too. The fact that with each successive hospitalization he was further condemning me to a life as a mental patient probably did not occur to him. Neither did the idea that maybe I was not sick at all, and that my perceptions and hallucinations and fears and despairs were not symptoms but my valid expressions of outrage at the indignities I was undergoing, my coded way of saying "I am lost and afraid." Not sick. I think he cared that I was suffering, in a sense, and wished to alleviate that suffering. He was not an unkind man. But he was incapable of perceiving that using his influence on me, vulnerable and dependent as I obviously was, to convince me to voluntarily allow myself to be locked up, drugged, shocked, and otherwise abused, in order that he might "help" me—to tout a hospital as a refuge and haven, rather than as the institution of degradation and ritual punishment that it is—was unforgivable and demonstrated that his loyalty was to the precepts of the American Psychiatric Association, to the profession, not to the fragility and suffering of his patients.

If it had been, I realize now, he would have let me writhe in pain on the streets, rather than admit me to Franklin Central Hospital. But to do that would have been an admission that he and his fraternity of helping professionals did not possess all of the answers.

Two weeks before I was scheduled to be admitted to Franklin Central, Dr. Sternfeld discovered that the hospital had discontinued its Insulin Shock Unit.

"Will you still go?" he asked.

"Yes," I answered, worn down from the weeks of trying not to submit. "Why not?"

On a Tuesday, early in April, my parents moved to a new apartment and I moved to Franklin Central Hospital. I stayed there for eleven months.

JANET

When my parents walked me through the heavy iron gates, up to the door of the admissions building, I felt certain they would never see me again. My mother, grasping my arm with tight arthritic fingers, looked a hundred and twenty. My father, his face a lined paper mask, was gray, almost not there. None of us, as we huddled together in the brown faded lobby, really believed it was happening.

"Jake said— " my mother began hoarsely; but she couldn't continue, the words hanging, a mocking specter of faith, in the stale dirty air of the noisy lobby. I held on to them both, one with each hand, and stared hard at the candy machines that stood like sentinels against the far wall. As we crossed the grounds of the hospital, a woman screamed; looking up, several feet to the left of the path, I saw her, on the top floor of a mammoth brick building, shrieking and screeching, waving her toothpick arms through the iron bars, pressing her thin blotched face to the bars, as if by pressure and wanting she could force the world to take her back. Her screams echoed through the April air, but the slow gray men and women in their drab ill-fitting cotton clothes who walked vaguely in twos across the scruffy grass, hadn't even blinked. Transfixed, I watched as two attendants yanked her out of sight, listened as her screech of anguish ended in a howl of pain.

"Dr. Sternfeld is sending me here to get well," I repeated to myself. This is a hospital. I am sick and I am going to get well here. "Lord," I prayed silently, as the fear and nausea in my throat rose, threatening to choke me, "please don't let that woman be me. Please." Staring at the candy machines, I couldn't forget her, couldn't convince myself it was all a long and unendurable nightmare, couldn't understand why I was there, why Dr. Sternfeld had sent me there, why I had come, why, why, and why.

I felt myself slipping away from this grim world, closing it out, letting the waves of brown wash over me as I made myself safe in the dark place of no-feeling that was always waiting for me, in an unknown spot, deep, deep inside my body, near where I was born. I knew, without saying the words, that my only hope for retaining my sanity was to retreat to my dark place. But I was afraid, as I had been at Oceanville, that I might never be able to find my way into the air again.

A name was called; it belonged to the body I was trapped in. I answered, but the voice was not mine. Looking through my tears at my parents, as I had looked longingly through rain-washed windows at the forbidden wet world outside when I was a child, I saw them, distorted, unattainable, unclear, receding and receding, Gatsby's light. The extended interview of Monroe Park and Oceanville,

Franklin Central Hospital

the pleasant admissions lady, present to soothe the conscience-stricken committing relatives, the coffee machine—these amenities didn't exist here. They were part of an easier past. This was the real thing. And, in the bare, inexplicable, undeniable facts of the grounds and waiting room of Franklin Central Hospital, was a meager wisp of a hint of what was to come. I think we all remembered for an instant, the day, four years earlier, when the three of us had sat together in another waiting room, at Ellis College. Then there had been a future, a chance, a hope. But at the first hint of trouble, we had abandoned ourselves and our dreams to the discretion of professional helpers, psychiatrists. This was the end of that trip. It was with wonder almost that each of us, separately, surveyed the scene; there were no words; there was no way, in the midst of such pain, to call a halt to the whole thing. We had come too far. Dr. Sternfeld had been crowned king; he was ruling by divine right.

The name Moss was called, my suitcase and pocketbook were abruptly taken away, my parents filled out the necessary forms. I signed where required. The door to a long dark corridor was opened, and through the sheet of tears in my eyes, I watched my parents turn away, my father holding my mother as she broke down in silent sobs. "At least you can go home," I whispered. The door closed and locked behind me.

"Okay, move it along. And I want quiet." Mrs. Boyle's commands trumpeted through the poorly lit hallway. It was dinnertime. Sally had defecated on the floor and the two patients assigned to clean it up had dawdled. We were late and Mrs. Boyle was angry. She ran her ward like a military prison camp and was proud of her discipline, proud that her ward was always on time, proud that we were the show ward of the hospital, receiving visiting inspectors and high-ups in the mental health world. Now she was angry and everyone was afraid. You could never tell what Mrs. Boyle might do when she was angry. A few days earlier she had locked Hester in seclusion for eighteen hours and not given her any food. Once, I heard, she kept medicine from an epileptic patient, who went into convulsions and almost died. No one wanted to be in Mrs. Boyle's bad graces.

"Move it," I heard again. We walked two by two, our ward joined by the sad vacant women from west ward, a silent straggling group, up the filthy dark stairwell to the dining room. As usual, the stench was overpowering and my stomach lurched in a nauseous spasm. I covered my mouth and turned toward the wall.

"Lord," I prayed, thinking of Mrs. Boyle. "Please don't let me puke."

"You okay?" Hester whispered, edging her way forward to stand next to me.

I nodded yes, my hand still covering my mouth.

"What kind of slop are we getting tonight?" she wondered aloud.

"Creamed sheep shit!" Dena said.

"What the hell's going on down there?"

"Nothing. Nothing, Mrs. Boyle."

"Keep it quiet!"

I wanted a cigarette, but we weren't allowed to smoke on the stairs. Or in the dining room. Or anywhere except the tiny locked room at the far end of the corridor on the ward. I wanted a smoke so badly I might even have risked it, if I could have gotten a light. But the patients weren't allowed to carry matches. And even in the smoker Mrs. Boyle wouldn't always give you a match.

Waiting. Why did we always come early just to wait for the kitchen staff to open the door? I looked from face to face, from body to frowsy body. Angry, vague, dull, unfocused, sad, pained, wasted. Young, old, in-between. The double line of women seemed endless. I had been in the hospital only a month and I felt perfectly at home among these women; we were all outcasts, all unacceptables. I remembered, with a momentary twinge, my first session with Dr. Sternfeld a week after my admission.

"How are you doing, Janet?" he asked as we sat down, a large desk between us in the only conference room on the ward.

"I'm not staying here," I said. "How could you have sent me to such a place?"

"What do you mean, Janet? This is the best ward in the entire hospital."

"It's awful. Awful. I don't belong here. I want to leave."

"Are you too good for this hospital, too good for these patients?"

"No, that's not it." How could I make him understand? "They made me take off my clothes and stand naked in this room with five doctors. They made me stand there and they took away my clothes and talked about me as if I wasn't there. It was horrible. I was so humiliated I thought I'd die." Dr. Sternfeld was impassive.

"They made me shower in a huge room with no shower curtains, just a drain in the middle of the floor, while they watched me and they made me move my bowels in these toilets with no doors and no seats and there's always shit on the floor and no toilet paper. And they locked up my clothes and they took my books and they put me in a dormitory with twelve women who moaned and cried all night.

They wouldn't give me anything to help me sleep and I had to wear a white gown that didn't tie."

Dr. Sternfeld's face had turned to stone.

"Are you listening to me?" I screamed.

He didn't answer, only sat, a buddha, above it all. I couldn't stop the rush of words.

"They took me down to the basement. Two attendants took me through these snaky corridors to a tiny room where an old man sat. They took my fingerprints. The old man took pictures. Mug shots. They treated me like a criminal. And they wouldn't let me get my Tampax from the locker and I bled all over the floor and nobody cared, nobody cared." I was sobbing, anger, incomprehension, and misery mixed.

"Janet," Dr. Sternfeld began precisely, with the superb patience you use to speak to a simple-minded adult. Or a precocious but stubborn child. "What you describe are nothing more than normal admission and orientation procedures. They are not pleasant, I grant you, but neither are they unendurable. Everyone in this hospital has gone through similar experiences. They survived. And they didn't have private doctors to complain to, either. You're not so fragile or so different. I've been telling you that for a long time."

Dr. Sternfeld could make the word "fragile" into an accusation, the sin, perhaps, of pride in my own uniqueness, a symptom of my illness, a cause for shame.

"I don't belong here," I said. I felt myself clawing on a steep polished wall, my claws unable to pierce the surface. I remembered a cat I once knew named Raucous who had been declawed but who still tried heroically to climb trees. He would take a leap four feet up the trunk and cry and struggle to maintain a grip as he slid pathetically to the ground. Stupid and ridiculous we had called him.

"I don't belong here. I want to leave," I repeated. Dr. Sternfeld seemed not to hear.

The sense of powerlessness that I had experienced at Oceanville and at Monroe Park was so acute at Franklin Central that I was in a constant state of panic. The small freedoms I had always taken for granted—smoking a cigarette where and when I pleased, choosing my bedtime, showering in privacy, taking a walk—these were all gone. "Why?" I kept asking myself. And why were there bars on my bedroom window? Of all the indignities of institutional life, from sleeping linenless on rubber-sheeted beds to taking supervised showers to eating in silence with looney-spoons (no knives or forks were allowed), the worst was having bars on my window.

"You promised you would stay a month." Dr. Sternfeld finally spoke, resurrecting an unwilling concession I had made under fire.

"I can't stand it. I'm going crazy here," I said, my voice shrill with fear. Surely he could see he had been mistaken in sending me to Franklin Central, I thought. But a remembrance of Dr. Sternfeld's punitive "I'm going to show you what a *real* hospital is like" lapped at my consciousness. Surely he must have known how truly degrading it would be for me, I thought. I shut away the persistent knowledge that he himself worked in a similar institution.

"A month is not a very long time," Dr. Sternfeld said. His voice came hollow, through a tunnel that extended from my head to the world outside.

"Maybe not for you," I tried to say. But no sounds came. I was too afraid to accuse him.

Waiting, waiting for the doors to open to the dining room. My hair, wet from its afternoon washing, lay cold on my back. I sometimes thought that my long hair was the only thing that distinguished me from the rest of the patients. Mostly the women had short hair, cut bluntly and shapelessly across the forehead and neck by attendants so that in an eerie way, young and old, blond, brown, and gray, all the women looked related. A special tribe. My hair reached to my waist and, since my admission to the hospital, had become more precious than ever before. I kept it impeccably clean, washing it three or four times a day, whenever I could, in a further effort, I suppose, to distinguish myself from the other women, and from the dirt and odors that permeated the hospital, overcoming even the foul disinfectant we were forced to use on the floors and walls.

"Why are you washing your hair so often?" Dr. Sternfeld asked when he read my chart.

"I want it to be clean," I said. How could he ask such a stupid question?

"It can't get dirty in an hour," he said.

"You don't know," I answered.

"I don't think this compulsive hairwashing is a good thing, Janet. I want you to cut down to once a day."

"It's not compulsive," I said. "I just want to be clean."

"You want to be special," he accused. "You want to be different."

"And you want me to be a filthy vegetable, like the others," I screamed.

"No," he said. "I want you to admit that you are sick, like the other patients. Until you realize that, you won't get better."

The words floated past me. What did they mean, anyway, these silly words like "sick" and "well," "hospital," "patient"? I was in prison; I knew that. So did everyone else. Why did he continue with his medical farce?

"I'm not hurting anyone by washing my hair," I said.

"Only yourself," he answered.

I had, at all costs, to protect my hair. Inspiration came.

"But until I realize that myself," I answered, watching his eyes, "it won't do any good to force me to stop." He nodded, thinking over what I was saying.

"Remember," I said, "you always said you could take away the symptoms—like the wrist-cutting—but the sickness would remain?"

"Yes, I remember," he said.

"Please, don't make me stop washing my hair."

I had won, but I didn't know at what cost. I never knew how Dr. Sternfeld would show his anger; and I was still afraid for my hair.

Still waiting, the restlessness and impatience for food undulating through our ranks, the tension of silence growing fierce.

"Janet," I heard. A small thick voice coming from the stairs below.

"Janet Moss."

"My God," I thought. "Someone has recognized me."

"Janet, I'm here."

I turned away, praying the voice would go away, praying Mrs. Boyle would punish its owner for speaking.

"Janet Moss."

In an instant of exquisite timing the heavy doors opened and we poured, uncontainable, into the steamy dining room. I let myself be carried by the swell of women struggling to be first on the food line. A strange gray light filtered into the dining room through the dirty encrusted barred windows and, moving through the columns of dust motes, I felt almost disembodied. I hadn't moved far, only a few feet into the room. I stood against the left-hand stone wall, my stomach heaving from the smells, watching, trying, as I had for a month, to comprehend.

The room was tremendous. Two rows of twenty long wooden tables with attached benches, each seating at least fifteen people, were nailed, row upon row, into the floor. Mrs. Boyle stood on a high ledge near the windows, her arms across her chest, whistle in her mouth, surveying the scene. Two other attendants stood at strategic spots in the room. Once we were all inside, Mrs. Heller, Mrs. Boyle's lieutenant, locked the door.

As usual, I let myself be moved along by the hungry group. I took the spoon and metal plate that were provided, allowed the patient behind the steam table to put the creamy mass that was dinner on it, and, trying to breathe only through my mouth, took a seat at a table. I couldn't eat. Whatever that smelly gelatinous mess was, I knew I couldn't eat it. And knew, too, I would have to find a way of giving it to someone else without Mrs. Boyle seeing. I would probably be hungry then, eat candy bars after dinner, feel guilty and upset, eat more, and embark on another cycle of eating sweets. In a month of ice cream and candy indulgence I had gained ten pounds and was still gaining.

I sat, my face a mass of pimples, my body heavy and unwieldy. A grotesque, like all the others.

"Janet." I turned my head as someone sat down on the bench next to me.

"Remember me?" she asked. It was the voice on the stairs.

"Remember me?" she asked again.

I looked at her face. It was fat, yet the soft flesh, as it hung flaccid from her bones, gave her a hollow look. Her eyes were milky blue, like a newborn baby's, her hair very sparse. In her cotton state dress she looked like a thousand other women I had seen in the hospital. Tired, beaten, obscure.

"No," I said. "I don't know you."

"Yes you do. I'm Mrs. Freed. Jimmy's mother." She tried to smile but instead she giggled.

"Jimmy. Yes, of course, I remember you, Mrs. Freed." But I didn't. Not at all. Jimmy Freed was an old friend from my camp days whom I hadn't seen in several years. But could this wreck of a tittering woman be his mother? I was horrified.

"You didn't recognize me for a minute?" she said. "I look different, right?"

My God, she had been a slim straight young woman with a fine taut face and brilliant eyes.

"A little," I said. "What are you doing here?"

"Trying to get out." It was a pat hospital joke.

"I mean," I stuttered, "who—?"

"Put me in?" She finished my question. "John. Mr. Freed. Jimmy's father." Her face had hardened into a mask of hatred. "I wouldn't give him a divorce. He wants to marry this young girl. Oh, Janet, for years he's been bringing home these young girls; he's been driving me crazy."

I remembered Jimmy speaking of his father's affairs and his mother's suffering.

"So when I wouldn't give him his divorce he began threatening me. I became hysterical. He had me committed; he said I attacked him with a knife. It was a lie. Oh, my God, what have I done to deserve this?"

Mrs. Freed was leaning over the table, her heavy arms wrapped around her head, rocking back and forth, moaning low.

"He got his divorce. Now he's trying to have me declared incompetent, too," she said. "He'll take my money, my house, my life."

"I want quiet in this room," Mrs. Boyle's voice trumpeted forth. "You sound like animals with all your sounds. I try to be nice, let you talk a little, and what do I get? A racket, that's what. Well, we're going back to silent meals. Starting now. I don't want to hear *a sound*."

Human voices stilled, we ate, each of us furtive and alone, to the rattle and clank of metal on metal. Parading out in mute double file at the end of the meal, we relinquished our plates and spoons to the attendant at the door, allowed ourselves to be searched for possible concealed food or utensils, and shuffled our way down the stairwell and back to the ward. Jimmy's mother went with her group and I didn't see her again for many months. I learned she had been transferred to a closed ward on one of the upper floors. In fact, I thought I saw her once, pressing her face to the bars to get some air, crying of her anguish to the deaf patients below.

I tried to adjust to life on the ward. I made friends. I went to Bingo. I typed for the Community Bulletin. I tried to be pleasant and do my work, cheerfully scrubbing the hall and toilets each morning. I tried not to alienate Mrs. Boyle. I submerged my anger and prayed that someday the squid would annihilate her. I took my pills, I didn't complain. I kept my room clean; I didn't bother the staff with silly requests. I was a good mental patient.

And bit by bit my mind went limp.

"It is enough to drive a sane woman mad," I said to my friend Hester. She and her husband, both heroin addicts, had held up a liquor store, using a gun to frighten the owner. Her husband was in jail and Hester was serving her sentence at Franklin Central, a psychiatric prison. Don was getting out in eight years; Hester had no idea when, or if, she would ever be released. But the judge had been kind to her, he said, in not sending her to prison.

"It really does get to you, kid," she said.

"But I must have been crazy to begin with. I must have, Hester, I must have. Why else would I be here?"

JANET

"I am going to give you shock treatments, Janet," Dr. Sternfeld announced on one of his weekly visits.

"No," I said, standing up and backing away toward the door.

"I think they are worth a try. Anything that might get you out of this depression, take your mind off your suicidal feelings, is worth a try."

"How can I feel anything *but* suicidal in here?" I wanted to say. But the dangerous words would not form. I couldn't accuse Dr. Sternfeld of torturing me.

"No, please," I begged, knowing I would give in to his will, as I always had, not wanting again to have my brain burnt.

"Let's give you another week," he relented. "See if you feel better."

"I want to feel better," I said suddenly. "I try, but nothing seems to work. I'm so afraid all the time. And then there is always that doubt that you have forgotten me and that you don't really care."

"If I didn't care, would I be here now?" he asked, kindly, soothing, benevolent, wise, as always. A hug, a pat, a moment of warmth. He was gone.

Six days later, at five-thirty in the morning, they came to get me.

"Moss." It was my name, barked into the quiet, still-dark morning.

"Get up, Moss. Come with me." I didn't know the white-coated man who stood by my bed. Nor the man whose bulk filled the doorway, shutting out the hall light. Big Mary, my roommate, stirred, creaked her bed, and continued her Vesuvian snoring. Here, in my room at the end of the hall, I was all alone. Whatever they wanted, they were staff, and I knew better than to resist. Still, I didn't move, playing for time.

"Get up, Moss," he said. "You deaf or something?"

"No. No." I pushed the covers away and sat up.

"Then come on. I don't have all day."

The tall attendant took my right arm, squeezed it with his large hand, and jerked me to my feet.

"I'm coming," I said, frightened, hurt. "Please let me get my robe and slippers." It was chilly in the early May morning, and the stone floor, with its patches of thin linoleum, was icy.

"Forget it, sister. Move."

Feeling ghostlike, fear squeezing my heart till I thought, like a child-clutched balloon, it would burst, I let the two large men with their heavy key rings jangling from their belts, move me harshly through the cold morning corridors.

"Please. Where are you taking me?" I asked, though in my intestines and my brain I knew. Polite. It was most essential to be polite.

"Shock," the tall man said, laughing. Hearty. "Where do you think?"

Polite, panic nipping at my mind, I said, "There must be some mistake. I'm not scheduled for shock. My doctor hasn't ordered shock treatments for me, I'm sure."

"Listen to Miss Fancy, man," the shorter heavy attendant spoke. "Her doctor. She thinks she's got a private doctor, in this dump. That's something, huh?"

They laughed, secure in this camaraderie of power, safe in the knowledge that I was insane.

Up three dark flights, through the dank corridors we moved, my bare feet aching from the cold, my body flopping against one, then the other of the men. This was a part of the hospital I had never seen. Where were we going? Moving again, the walls, men, and my body elided into a brown tunnel, washed in urine. Like sulphurous fumes from a twentieth century Inferno, the smell of urine rose higher, filming the nostrils that lived on my face.

"Piss, piss," I heard myself scream. "The whole world is made of piss. Don't kill me."

The room was small, a square of topaz light in the deranged darkness.

I had walked in, "Don't kill me" falling from my mouth. I had walked in and I had seen it, faced it, the machine. In Monroe Park, they had wheeled me in, backwards. I had never seen the torture machine.

"No. No. No. Please."

"We only want to help you, Miss . . . er . . . Moss."

"Get her up here."

"No. No." I am moaning. "No," as the heavy leather straps confine my body. I can only look up, praying for the pentothal that will float my fears away. The pentothal.

"Give me the I.V. now," I beg. The machine stands guarding me. If my arms were not tied down I could touch it, that is how close its devil force stands, waiting for my sleep.

"Please put me out," I cry. They are all around me, these white-coated men. Why? Why? I feel cold suddenly, wet cold on my temples.

"Dear Lord, they are putting the jelly on."

"The better to burn you with, my dear." Who is that? Mellow-

JANET

Voice, Queen of the Forest. She haunts my room and has followed me, standing in the corner, her hair a filigree of laughters, watching as they punish a disobedient snail.

It is cold, this sticky vile jelly. Cold on my head. The cold before the fire.

"Where is my I.V.?"

Laughter. Male. "Shut up, Moss, or I'll plug your mouth."

Men. There is one at my feet, one behind, another to the right of the hard stretcher where I am chained. I can look only into the fierce white light that shines, an eye of pain, from the ceiling. Ice on my temples. They are pressing the sides of my head together, cold irons, pressing my brain.

"Electrodes on," I hear.

"Dear God, no."

"This will help you, Miss Moss. Don't be afraid. You won't feel a thing. Everybody ready? Voltage set? Go!"

I open my mouth and the scream surrounds me. My body a lurch and a scream of pain. I am impaled on a pain. A firecracker, pain and lights, burning, screaming, my bones and my flesh. I am on fire. Shorter than a second. The fragments of a bomb sear my body. Blue-white lights, fiercer than God, going through me, my body, poor body, a contortion, a convulsion of ripping, searing. Pain incarnate. Branded. I cannot comprehend. Burning, burning, my fingers and toes, my limbs rigid with pain, stretched longer than the night. Shooting, shooting again, my body is charred. No breath. Hiroshima. The living dead.

"I didn't want to frighten you," Dr. Sternfeld answered the same afternoon. "That's why I didn't tell you exactly when the treatments would begin."

"They didn't give me any anesthesia." I spoke slowly, the words bringing the memory of my burning too clear. "How could you do that to me?" The immediacy of the terror and the pain, lingering in my aching body, killed the caution that usually shrouded my words.

"I wasn't aware that they didn't use an anesthetic," Dr. Sternfeld said. Did I sense a hesitation, a film over his gray-blue eyes? He continued, more confident as he gathered speed and ease. "But it doesn't *really* matter, Janet," he said. "You can't feel the treatments. Even with no anesthetic."

"How do *you* know?" I screamed, control gone.

"It is physiologically impossible to feel the treatments, Janet," Dr. Sternfeld continued.

"But I felt it. I did. And it was awful." (How dare he presume to know?)

"I'm sure you didn't, Janet. Your anxiety and the aftereffects of the treatment may be contributing to that idea."

"I *did feel* it. I felt the shock as it went into my head. It shot through my body, lightning."

Dr. Sternfeld was calm, unruffled, direct. "Janet, I am telling you that you could not have felt the treatment. Before the electric shock reached the part of your brain that perceives pain, you were unconscious. The physiological processes of your brain insure that, even without an anesthetic, you will not feel the treatment. Would we give them to you if that wasn't true?"

"I felt it."

"Do you think I'm lying to you?"

"I don't know." Even that concession was a risk for me to say. Suddenly, I was afraid he would not come back; he would leave me to molder in Franklin Central Hospital, a cabbage, permanently electrically charged, rotting, with Mrs. Freed, on the top floor.

"I wouldn't lie to you, Janet."

"But I felt the treatment."

"You are mistaken. You will see, when you have the next one."

"No, please. Don't make me go through it again."

"You said you wanted to get better. We must try everything."

"Don't give me another, Dr. Sternfeld. Please."

"I'll be away for a while in Washington, at a conference. I'll call when I get back, Janet."

He put his arm around me, embraced me, and held me warm. He didn't even make me offer him a cigarette.

That night I dreamed I was being electrocuted. Again I felt the white-hot shocks screech through my body and I woke up screaming.

"Why Janet, what is the matter with you?"

"They're trying to kill me, Miss Jones. They're trying to kill me."

In the ghost light of the dayroom I sat with Miss Jones, the night attendant, and cried.

"You been havin' bad dreams again, girl?" she asked.

"My doctor says I can't feel the treatments," I sobbed, "and I know I can. He won't stop them. I'm going to be burned alive." I covered my face with my arms, doubled myself into a ball in the torn plastic chair and wept.

"You gotta pray, girl. I been tellin' you, you gotta pray."

JANET

Miss Jones was a fervent Seventh-Day Adventist. She saw us all as sinners, locked up in Franklin Central as punishment for our transgressions.

"Never mind your doctor. You gotta embrace Jesus. Take Him into your heart if you want to be saved." I closed my eyes, remembering Mrs. Petra and the many nights we had sat together in the dayroom at Oceanville, drinking warm milk. Miss Jones was going on.

"Now you go back to your room and pray that Jesus will forgive you. Then you won't have no more treatments and no more doctors and you'll go out in the world and teach the Gospel to other sinners."

"Could I have another pill, Miss Jones, please?"

"I'm not supposed to, you know, but, well—"

She gave me two Seconals and I slept, finally, drugged to oblivion.

Two days later, they took me again. And three times more the following week.

Dr. Sternfeld was in Washington. No one cared that I woke up each night, screaming in hysteria of my incineration.

"You must be a bad sinner, Janet," Miss Jones said, " 'cause the devil is raging in you."

"They're trying to electrocute me," I screamed. But no one listened and even the Seconals couldn't put me to sleep.

During my waking hours the brown pee-smelling halls were filled with horrors. I sat in my room watching a cat perched, sullen, on the rusting fence outside the barred windows. It seemed that "things" were chasing me all the time. I ran, but ended up, always, cornered in the rat hole. My room.

My mind had begun to disintegrate, finally. And, running through the halls to escape the laughing man or the telephone monster, I would find pieces of myself, stuck, with a cold white jelly, on the damp brown walls.

"I am afraid you have left me forever," I wrote to Dr. Sternfeld, "and will not return. I am afraid that you have left so that They might kill me undisturbed."

Sick with remorse, I tried to apologize for the bad, bad thoughts that lived in my bombed-out brain.

I know that's the sick part of me that wrote that, but now it doesn't feel as though there is any healthy part of me. I'm sorry for imposing on you with these letters, but somehow I feel that letters are less of an imposition than telephone calls. I know you will come.

Franklin Central Hospital

I know you care. But why these doubts? I am traveling far. Will I ever return? My words and those of others have a hollow quality. Try to follow me to the shining shifting agony. But I cannot stay still; I must move away from the menace. He laughs and laughs. Who is this man? Can I ask you for help again? These tears of blackness come, I am covered with mud, terror stalks, and I can only cry. Far above the tide the bird song arranges itself and he laughs, cruelly, while the sun shines with cold brilliance and indifference. I know I'm not supposed to want you to be a father and to love me. Please don't go away. If my trust dissolves, there is nothing left. And I am afraid of that too—nothing left.

I wondered when they would be over, these ritual burnings. The pain, I would never survive the searing pain.

"Paranoid delusions," they wrote on my chart. "She thinks there is a conspiracy to kill her by electrocution."

Again and again they took me to the square, lighted room and, increasing the voltage, sent the juice to the center of me where poetry once stirred.

Dr. Sternfeld returned, saw me a moment in my dark bare room and stopped the treatments. He never mentioned them again and neither did I.

It was full spring, Thea and Ken were married, Mary was preparing to graduate from Ellis, and I was trying to see if I could walk from my room to face the world without starting to scream again.

In August a trailer truck crushed a blue Volkswagen on a wide interstate highway in Colorado and Larry was killed. Dr. Sternfeld came to tell me about it.

"I don't believe you," I said.

"It's true, Janet. He's dead."

Dr. Sternfeld looked as if he would cry, but his voice barely neared my grief. The beautiful young soldier I had called Larry. I had told everyone in the hospital that the silver friendship ring I wore, a double band with two hands clasped, a gift from my friend Laura, was really an engagement ring from him. Among the ragged of Franklin Central, anything as substantial as a promise of marriage was an impressive link to the outside, status.

"When is the funeral?" I asked Dr. Sternfeld.

"I don't think you should go; I'll go," he answered.

"I won't fall apart, I promise. Please let me go. I want to. I loved him."

"I'll go for you. Everyone will understand."

"Understand what?"

"That you're too sick to come. You're in the hospital. I'll pay your respects."

My own loss was too profound to really touch. It was a hole somewhere deep in a cavern in my heart. If I could go to Larry's funeral I would reaffirm my own humanness. (Did they think we couldn't mourn?)

True, I hadn't seen Larry in many months. But he did write to me, at least once a week. Perhaps he wrote only from pity, perhaps his devotion had been what you show to a senile parent in a nursing home—duty. But we had loved each other once, and he had shared my first anguished realizations that I was in trouble, splitting from the body he wanted to take.

"I can go. I'll be all right," I said again.

"No, Janet. Please trust me. It's better this way."

Dr. Sternfeld went to the funeral and increased my medication. I wrote a poem about the beautiful young soldier, and dreamed of Larry's young body crushed beneath a truck.

Madelon and Anthony, two old high school friends, were to be married August twentieth. The week before the wedding Dr. Sternfeld gave me a special pass to go with my mother to buy a new dress.

"It's good to see you getting back to yourself, taking an interest in clothes again," he said.

It was a fine dress we bought and it even concealed some of the fat that had accumulated on my once-thin body in the time I had been at Franklin Central. I weighed more than I had ever weighed in my life. My face was a mass of irritated pimples, which nothing could hide.

"I'm afraid to go, Hester. Everyone's going to be watching to see if I'm really crazy. I know I'll start to cry and embarrass Maddy and Anthony."

"They don't expect you to act weird or they wouldn't have invited you."

"But what if I take a knife and cut my wrists?" I was panicky, building myself up to a full scale anxiety attack.

"Just go," Hester said. "And enjoy yourself. You'll be okay. And nobody'll even notice your skin."

"I can't. But I want to go so badly."

"Then go."

"I'm going to call Dr. Sternfeld. Maybe he'll come and see me."

"You're lucky enough to have a pass," Hester said. She hadn't been out of the hospital in nearly a year. "Go."

"I'll call him. He is still at the hospital. I hope he won't be mad."

I took a dime from the two dollars I received each week from petty cash and, my breath short and pressure building in my chest, I waited in the lobby for a free phone. Ten minutes later I was back in the dayroom, the anxiety gone, replaced by tears.

"He said I shouldn't have called him," I cried to Hester. "And he couldn't come either. He said I should have handled it by myself."

"But he said you should call him if you feel really anxious, didn't he?" Hester asked.

"Yes. But I never know what he considers *really* anxious. I just wanted to talk to him to straighten out some of the things in my head. It's so scary, going outside."

"I know it is." Hester was sympathetic.

"So he took my pass away. The bastard."

"No," Hester said, incensed. "Why?"

" 'Cause he said if I was so upset that I couldn't handle my feelings I obviously couldn't go to the wedding."

"Maddy and Anthony will understand, kid," Hester said.

"I know. But that's not the point. I don't want people to always 'understand.' 'Oh, we can't expect anything more from Janet, she's *sick,* you know.' I wanted to go to the wedding; I could have gone. I only asked him for a few minutes of his precious time and he gets so goddamned mad and takes my pass away. It's not fair."

Two days later I swallowed my misery and asked to be allowed to go with the group from the ward on their weekly trip to the movies.

"Moss, your doctor says you're still too upset. Wait till next week," Mrs. Boyle reported back.

So he was even afraid to let me out in the street in a group, watched by attendants. Or maybe, he was still mad that I had called him.

"I promise I won't run away," I told Dr. Sternfeld when I saw him later in the week.

"Why do you want to go?"

"I just want to get off the ward and off the grounds."

"I thought you didn't like the idea of going out in a supervised group like that. You said it was demeaning."

I buried my anger and lied. "I don't mind now. The important thing is that I'll get out with people and see a movie."

"I thought you didn't like those people. You felt quite superior to them at one time."

"Well I don't now. We're all in the same boat." We all have to beg for our freedom, I wanted to say. "Please, I'll be good."

"Maybe next time." That was a final answer.

I did eventually get permission to go to the movies, and each Thursday our sad group, seven or eight female patients and two aides, dressed in street clothes instead of uniforms, walked the few blocks to the movie theater. We walked double file, stopping on each corner to be counted, like kindergarteners. Must make sure that no one strays or runs away. The loonies from Franklin Central out for an airing. I watched the faces of the people we passed, saw the shrinking and the repulsed recognition as we moved down the street, a sluggish shorn group.

"You shouldn't feel self-conscious," Dr. Sternfeld said. "Nobody knows you're from the hospital."

Of course not. We were just an average everyday group of women in our cotton state dresses and unmatched shoes, walking double file with our buddies, having our admission paid for us and our tickets counted by our keepers. Your ordinary bridge group taking in a show.

The final indignity for me, though, was that I never saw an entire movie. I was taking so much Mellaril that I always fell asleep after a half hour of the film.

The laughing man continued to follow me around. He stood and chortled while I scrubbed the floors and walls of the bathroom each day. He stayed with me while I sat, useless and groggy, in occupational therapy, trying to decide if I should knit a scarf or make a potholder. He drowned out the records in music appreciation and his grim peals echoed through my ward during the night.

"Repetitive monstrosities, arbitrary, harassing and mangling my brain and my heart," I wrote in my notebook.

Dr. Sternfeld, please come tonight. The bugs, I can't tell which are real and which I have made up. The squid comes back again and again to lurk and sit complacent and evil. I try not to depend solely on you, to find, as you say, new sources of strength in my surroundings. But the floors are brown and someone is yelling, "Josie, Josie, whatsamatter, where are you, go to hell, you friggin' whore." I try to care about myself. Away, high above the trees and concrete, a lone jay sings, flutters fruitless wings and pardons us, please pardon us, our transgressions. You aren't coming and the world, fragile and intense, collapses.

"They aren't true hallucinations," Dr. Sternfeld said. It was fall and I had begun visiting Dr. Sternfeld. I never knew when he would call to say he had time to see me, so each day I hung around outside the small locked room that served as a nurses' station, waiting for the phone to ring that would mean I was free, for an hour.

"But I hear them, I see them."

"Yes, but you know they're not real."

"I'm going psychotic. I know it."

"No, Janet. You're not psychotic."

"What am I then? At Monroe Park they diagnosed me as a chronic schizophrenic. I know, I read my chart one day when the nurse wasn't looking."

"It doesn't matter what they diagnosed you as. I know you and you are not psychotic."

"But the hallucinations." They were terrifyingly real to me: monsters of varying description, animals from *The Peaceable Kingdom* come alive, the laughing man and mellow-voice girl. I saw them, I heard them, and while I knew, in a sense, that they were my own creations and that no one else perceived them, I continued to be frightened at the strangeness of my mind.

"Maybe we should call them visions," Dr. Sternfeld said. "Really, they are your unconscious thoughts, feelings, and fears made concrete and projected outward for you to see and hear."

Simple. A film of my mind. Nothing to it. Just sit back, relax, and enjoy the show, Janet.

"They're getting worse," I said. "More vivid. Sometimes I can't even think for all the racket and pictures in my head. Maybe you can increase my medication; that might help."

This was a familiar scene. I would ask for more drugs, not that they ever did anything but further confuse me, alienate me from my real feelings and from other people, and produce dreadful physical side effects. Dr. Sternfeld would hesitate, hold out a possibility of a huge increase, retreat from his position, tease, consider, and usually finally relent, a bit. "Well, maybe another hundred milligrams a day." Always, ostensibly, within a carefully thought out therapeutic regimen.

As long as I had known him he had believed my ultimate salvation would come through drugs. Shock treatments and hospitalizations were just interim measures, emergency techniques. Never mind that they didn't "work" either. We all—he, my parents, I—got the illusion that the Great Man was straining to his utmost to cure me. And I, ever naive, pained, and vulnerable, criminally dependent, had gotten hooked.

"You cannot become addicted to Thorazine," Dr. Sternfeld said.

JANET

"These drugs are completely harmless," Dr. Sternfeld. "Your body never acquires resistance to these tranquilizers," Dr. Sternfeld.

Bullshit! He was the great experimenter with chemotherapy. And my body was a perfect test tube. I didn't think this way at the time, though, knowing only that I wanted more and more and more, believing that the drug-induced fog in my mind, my shaking hands, and fuzzy words were really me, a product of my "sickness," when really, they were a product of Thorazine, the Evil Pacifier, Friend of the Keepers.

I found every excuse for needing more drugs. I couldn't sleep. I was anxious. I was hallucinating. I was nauseated. I was suicidal.

"Please, Dr. Sternfeld, can you increase my medication now, just a little bit?"

"I don't know. I was thinking of decreasing and starting on something new."

Sheer panic of me facing me, naked.

"I need something now; I feel as though I'm going crazy. Please help me."

"Get down on the floor."

"I don't understand."

"Get down on your hands and knees."

"Why?"

"If you really want it so badly, you can beg for it."

"I don't understand." I am beginning to be afraid, the tears are coming.

"Beg me for it. That's the only way I'll give it to you."

He is joking, I think. I don't know why he is torturing me like this, but he doesn't mean it.

"The hour is almost up, Janet. It's time to go back to the hospital."

"Please, I need something."

"Then beg for it."

Down on my hands and knees on the rug, my face buried in the dust. Can I go any lower? "Why are you doing this to me?"

"I want you to see how you lower yourself to get what you want."

This is therapy, this groveling humiliation? No. Something is very wrong. He is smiling, almost.

"I will call the ward and order an increase."

I cannot see through the tears that are drowning me.

What can I say of my mother and father?
For almost ten months they visited me faithfully. Twice a week

they came to the ward, carrying their colored passes and a carton of cigarettes, no matches, and we sat, locked in a small smoky room for an hour and a half. Each time they came I saw my world anew, through their silent, suffering eyes.

"Do you remember Jimmy Freed, Mom?"

"Yes, I remember him. From camp."

"Well, his mother's here. On another ward."

"Good heavens, why?"

"Jimmy's father wanted to get rid of her, so he had her locked up."

"She must be sick if she's here, Janet."

"No. Just strange. And he wanted to get married again."

They looked around, saw the dirt, smelled the urine, heard the spurts of laughter and occasional echoes of screams, disembodied sounds from behind locked doors. They saw the misery, the degradation, my own suffering and despair and they couldn't say a word. Just suffer themselves with their own sense of guilt. I could hear them in my mind.

"Why did we put her here, Ben?"

"Jake said it was the only thing left to try."

"But she's not getting better. She's worse."

"She's sick. Jake said she needs a hospital. We have to believe him, Helen. Would he steer us wrong?"

"But it's so awful for her."

"It must be for the best, Helen. Jake says so."

"I'm coming home for the weekend. Dr. Sternfeld is giving me a pass."

I saw fear in their eyes. Would I act crazy and embarrass them? Would I try to cut my wrists?

"That's wonderful, darling. We're so glad."

But they weren't. They were afraid.

"You don't have to worry. I'll be a good little girl. I won't embarrass you and I won't tell anyone I'm in the hospital."

"Janet!"

"No, it's okay. I understand."

I am not a member of your world anymore. I am an alien. You are afraid of me. I am a mental patient. Mental patients do strange things. Your daughter was buried, years ago. And you are afraid of this creature-girl who laughs at the wrong times, cannot hold a coherent conversation, cries, shakes her hands, and thinks only of death.

JANET

Is it a wonder, with what they have done to me, that you are afraid?

I am afraid, too. But somehow, we go on.

When I returned from the weekend my father brought me inside while my mother waited in the car.

"I'm sorry," she said, turning away. "I can't go in."

"But I'm the one who has to stay here," I wanted to scream. "You're so delicate you can't stand it for a minute, but you can stand to send me in for a lifetime. What about me? This is my home."

Still, she couldn't come in.

In March 1965, I was called to appear before the staff. Six men sat at a long table in a dreary brown room. I knew only one of them, Dr. Bonner. The interrogation lasted seven minutes.

"Your name?"

"Janet Moss." I shuffled my feet.

"Ward?"

"Admissions, One."

"How long have you been a patient here?"

"Eleven months, sir."

"Why did you first come to the hospital?"

They know all the answers already, never looking up, rustling their papers, me, in front of them as Dr. Bonner asks the questions.

"I was very sick," I say. "I was suicidal, I didn't want to live."

"And now?"

"Now, I want to live, sir. I am not sick anymore."

"Did you come voluntarily?"

"Oh, yes, sir. My doctor, Dr. Jacob Sternfeld, wanted me to come. So I came."

"Have you been taking any medication?"

"Yes, sir. Mellaril. Librium. Compazine. Doriden."

"Are you still taking medication?"

"Yes, sir."

"Did you have any other therapy in the hospital?"

"Yes, sir." I am choking on the words, a wave of rage and remembered pain launched in my throat. "I had shock treatments."

"Did they help you?"

Goddamn them, the bastards, the whole tale is written in the papers they hold and arrange, peruse, and rustle, while I speak.

"Yes, sir. I feel much better now."

Franklin Central Hospital

I remember Hester's advice: Whatever you do, don't antagonize them. Be grateful, be humble, thank them for their help.

"You feel you are ready to return home?"

"Yes, I do, sir."

"No more suicidal thoughts?"

"No. No. I'll never think that way again. I am well now."

"You will continue treatment with Dr. Sternfeld?"

"Yes, of course."

"You may go back to the ward now, Miss Moss. You will hear our decision this afternoon."

I am numb, I am white with anxiety and fury. Did I shuffle enough? Will they let me go?

At two o'clock that afternoon the verdict was in. Although there had been some disagreement about my readiness to leave, Dr. Sternfeld's strong recommendation had turned the tide in my favor. I was to be released from Franklin Central Hospital and return home to live with my parents, with the provision that I continue my medication and my intensive psychotherapy. Spring, 1965.

"Good-bye," I said to friends and fellow sufferers.

Good-bye barred windows, silent mealtimes, begging for matches, coffee made with warm tap water.

Good-bye Rhoda, Cindy, Lorraine. I hope your children remember you. Yes, Betty, you will go home someday.

"Hey, kid. Take it easy. I'll see ya." Hester.

"Sure."

We embrace, hugging, crying, knowing we won't see each other and that if we did, it would be awkward and strange, an insult to the closeness that had made our lives bearable inside. If we had met anywhere else we would never have been friends. Inside, through common pain and compassion, we touched. Without the hospital, we would have nothing but memories, yearnings, and separateness.

"Let me know what happens with you. And Don's appeal," I say, knowing she probably will write, that I probably will answer, and that the letters probably will peter out gradually, until I am a shadow in her memory, she a play of light in mine. I know, I have been through these beautiful-dreadful intense hospital friendships before. No doubt I will experience them again.

The heavy iron gates close behind me. I am a prisoner again.

Outside.

1965–1966

Often during the year following Franklin Central, I wondered which prison was worse: the outside or the mental hospital. Often, it didn't much matter, as the two blurred into one vast life locked in an agony of frustration and impossibility. Twice during the following year I was a prisoner in Monroe Park, yielding to Dr. Sternfeld's arguments that I needed the "rest." Of course, our wrist-cutting contract was still in effect, and I would have done anything, anything, rather than lose him. He held his threatened departure over me like a whip, and, inevitably, I bowed to it.

More shock treatments. More drugs—my mind was fogged.

Our sessions continued, three, four times a week. I cut my hair to prove to my parents I was no longer depressed or insane, and I mourned my lost waves like a broken dream. I vacillated between the belief that I was completely insane and my heretical, doubting question, "Am I really sick at all?" Dr. Sternfeld never let up in his crusade to make me face myself, interpret my symptoms, and find the meaning of my guilt. Every incident, relationship, and flurried feeling was further evidence to support his growing conviction that a great part of me wanted to be sick and that I would go to any length to avoid being well and facing adult responsibilities.

My sickness was a way of competing with Sara for Matthew's attention and love. My so-called frigidity and sexual fears were designed to keep me a child, still my brother's lover. My helplessness was assumed to get people to take care of me—my brother, my parents, the hospital. My wrist-cutting, originally designed to prove to Dr. Berman how sick and in need of help I was, had become a lingering problem, a way to punish myself for my feelings of sinfulness and guilt. These were his theories.

"You are sicker than you have any right to be," Dr. Sternfeld said again and again, increased my medication, smiled, and raised his prices. I let him twirl me around in his office while I screamed from the visions that attacked my brain.

"You must learn to face the anxiety that produces your hallucinations," he said. Twirl, twirl, and the room and my body spin and the monsters and sea-devils, bloody and cackling, are eating my guts.

I let him sit next to me on the couch, hold my arms and run his fingers over the white scars on my wrists, while I screamed that the touching sent vibrations of tingling pain through my arms and the cutting was almost happening again before my eyes.

"The scars are old now," he said. "You shouldn't feel anything when I touch them."

I close my eyes in an exquisite shiver of weaving remembrance and nauseated pain.

I lay on the couch at his request and fantasized living with him on a Greek island, described our idyllic life together, and when the fantasy ended in my suicide, I apologized.

"Weren't you happy?" he asked.

"Yes, very."

"Then why the suicide? Why does the future always include your death?"

"I don't know," I mumble. "I'll never escape."

He hammered away at me, demanding that I talk, grope, expose my pain, stripping me one by one of my symptoms—my sunglasses, my wrist-cutting, my dream of becoming a poet. It was the spring of 1966 and I stood before him and the world, my despair banished to the deepest caverns of my core, calm, huddled small and tightly gripped, my exterior smooth and malleable. In short, acceptable.

"Isn't it wonderful what Jake is doing for Janet?" my mother and father asked each other, wondering deep within themselves if this pale, thin, drugged and lifeless creature could really be their child.

"He is so devoted," they told their friends. "She can call him anytime. He's even seen her on Sundays. And he takes an interest in everything she does, not just in her sessions. 'Whatever works,' that's what he says."

I loved him. I would do anything for him. He had saved my life.

Everyone concurred; my "cure" was a miracle. The chaos of my mind, the wild slavering animal of my craziness, was finally chained inside me, jumping to Dr. Sternfeld's commands, tamed before his disciplined care. Without him, I would go mad. With him, I entered a period of calm. And who can say why. The years of hospitalization had worn at my spirit. I had accepted myself, finally, as a marked one, ordinary clay, a mental patient. Dr. Sternfeld had been trying to get me to know that about myself for years. No more wild statements of screaming despair in the night, no more bloody cries, futile, alive. No more "episodes." I think, perhaps more than anything else, I was tired. Passive, quieter. I would seek the so-called normal life; I would try to function.

I don't think I ever made the conscious decision to stop exposing my pain in symptoms that always landed me in hospitals and to start trying to pass as a noncrazy. It was a gradual process, a giving way, almost a giving up—a sapping of spirit.

I didn't expect very much from my life. Perhaps a temporary clerical job, to be followed, I knew, by more hospitals, more shock treatments. A continuous, eternal shuttle between prisons. It would end in suicide, eventually, because there was no other way out for me. That was my secret; I kept it safe. I was still the sniveling snail from another planet, but now I was quiet, unobtrusive in my differentness. No longer an embarrassment to anybody, I held myself carefully, tenuously, together. And I tried, oh, I tried so hard, to make it in the "well" world.

It was my sessions with Dr. Sternfeld that tested my true strength.

"I want you to stand in the corner," he says, "and turn your face to the wall. You're a bad girl."

"No," I cry, some vestige of self-respect rising angrily from me.

"I want you to go and stand in that corner," he repeats. "Or I will stop treating you."

"This must be a game," I think to myself. "A devilish game. What meaning can it have?"

"Why? Why do you want me to stand in the corner?"

"Don't you know, Janet?" he asks.

"No, I don't. Why are you doing this to me?"

"Stand in the corner or I will stop treating you," he repeats.

"I won't cry," I vow. "Good Lord, will he really do it? Really send me out alone on the streets?" I am torn, cracked by wanting him, by knowing I couldn't go to the degradation of the corner, by suffering humiliation enough in my hesitation.

"I should say no, just no, and mean it," I cry.

"Then say it," he orders.

"I can't. I am afraid. Why are you torturing me?" I am shaking with fear and incomprehension. I think to myself, "I am a sniveling snail and he knows it."

"Well?" His voice is tensed and high.

"I can't." My body is strung with indecision across his couch. I will snap with the tension.

"All right," he says softly.

"All right what?" I whisper.

"It's okay, Janet." In an instant he is sitting beside me and I am shaking with tears in his arms.

"Why?" I ask, crying.

His face is grave as he holds me. "I wanted to show you how you would lower yourself to get me to take care of you. I wanted you to face your need for dependence."

"Mon dieu," a voice whispers in my head. "The man is crazy."

I am helpless with tears.

"I am going to rape you and you will cooperate," he says another day. "Or else I will stop treating you."

We go through the scene again. I cannot walk out. I cannot say yes. He tortures and plays me, tickling my anguish.

"Please, please," I beg. "Stop torturing me like this." And I am afraid, too, for my body, as he holds me and comforts me.

"You must face your twisted neurotic needs," he says.

We are partners in crime, I suppose. After all, I never said no to his "therapies."

June 1966. Still trying to pass for normal, seeking escape as I always was, cultivating my calm so that only Dr. Sternfeld shared my secret life of turmoil, and so even I had begun to suspect that perhaps I might succeed in the play of the outside, I practiced the typing and shorthand I had studied the summer after my freshman year of college, and got a job as a secretary in a real estate office in Manhattan.

Carter, Grayson and Hendricks was the *real world,* and I had finally made it. My ability to function there was the first tangible proof to my parents and Dr. Sternfeld that the "miraculous cure" was not a mirage. I was "well."

Each day I traveled on the steaming crowded subway to Forty-second Street, walked the five blocks to the staid building, rode the elevator to the eighth floor and joined the covey of "girls" who were the backbone of Carter, Grayson and Hendricks. There were ten of us, each assigned hierarchically to one of the staid men who were the company. Of all the secretaries I was the lowest, since I worked for the least important man, a careless, aging, stupid person who had not progressed from his position as second vice-president in twenty years. He wrote few letters and the bulk of my work was typing leases and bringing his coffee and doughnuts twice a day. It was not demanding work, just boring and enraging.

The most difficult part of my job was establishing a relationship with the other secretaries. I was the lowest and the newest. It was necessary to show respect for them in direct relation to the position of their bosses. Be one of the girls, yet not be too eager or too fast. Laugh at the right jokes, but not too loud. Keep up, but not too far. Tell of my boyfriends, but not brag. And most important for me, the fact of my life that dominated my waking hours at the office and my dreams at night: don't let them find out the truth. Don't let them know I am a mental patient.

"Oh yes, I went to college for awhile. Couldn't stand it. I quit."

"Where'd ya go?"

"Brooklyn College."

"Oh yeah? Did ya know Arlene Sanders? She went there a year."

"I— I don't think so."

"Oh yeah? Too bad. She quit to get married. Had twins, I hear."

I tried to keep up with the chatter of the other secretaries, join casually in the gossip, share their enthusiasm for clothes and their bosses. But if I had ever had that easy way of being part of the group, I had lost it, forgotten it, in the years of hospital living.

I mustn't feel superior. That was what Dr. Sternfeld always said. What did I have to feel superior about? They were the normal ones pursuing normal goals—man, marriage, security. I was the inferior one, the alien. The task of concealing that fact, of making up a new past for myself to camouflage the real one was harrowing.

"I'll never pass," I thought. "I will not make it in this world."

The separateness I felt was excruciating. My yearning to belong again (if I ever had) to this society where people "functioned" was pathetic. I knew I could never fully belong to this constellation of flunkies, that I would never really make it as a servile, smiling, genial, stoical secretary. But I would try. Always try. Until my deep hidden self could not bear the tension of deception any longer. And I would crack. Just like at Ellis.

"Janet, take this letter."

"Where are those leases?"

"You're a cutie. When'd we hire you?"

"Coffee! Over here."

"Yessir. Yessir. Yessir."

I thought I would go mad, smiled as I sat importantly behind my IBM Executive typewriter, asked Dr. Sternfeld for more medicine for my anxiety, discussed my fear of becoming a functioning adult, and prayed that I would pass for normal.

After my first week (no longer did my parents have to lie about my whereabouts) I spent the night at Thea's and Ken's apartment on 115th Street. Thea was the only hospital friend I had remained close with. We had known each other since the old days at Monroe Park, and I had seen her emerging stronger as the years went by, although Ken still did dole out her medicine to her and watch for the reemergence of her symptoms.

I was lying on their bed, staring out the narrow window, across a courtyard at the brick wall of the building next door. Suddenly there were lights, neon lights flashing on and off. Pink and green neon lights, a sign on the wall. It said SMOOCH. Flashing on and off. In spite of myself I started to laugh.

"Thea," I called. "Ken. Quick. Come here."

They came, tumbling over one another and the books and clothes on the floor, running from the tiny kitchen-living room.

"What is it, Janet?" Ken asked.

"Is anything wrong?" Thea was concerned.

"No." I couldn't stop laughing. I pointed out the window. "Look at that sign."

Four eyes turned toward the wall.

"What sign, Janet? I don't see any sign," said Ken.

"Oh lordy, you're hallucinating again."

"But it's there. I see it."

"What does it say, Janet? It must be awfully funny."

I was still laughing. "It says SMOOCH. Would you believe it? SMOOCH. In pink and green neon."

They started to laugh, too, and soon the three of us were hysterical on the floor.

"You know something," Thea said as we lay giggling and out of breath, "you're the only person I know whose subconscious has a sense of humor."

And we were off again, spasms of laughter shaking us until we hurt.

Later, after dinner, we sat in the candlelight of the shadowy bedroom and I looked through the window at the drab brick wall.

"It was so vivid, Thea. I thought it was real. That's why I called you in. To see it."

She nodded.

"The people I work with would never understand what happened. They'd be scared of me."

"It's the same with me, at school," Thea said. "I try not to say anything unusual. Just be drab and ordinary."

"I guess we're really sick, then. Because they're the normal ones." I felt as if I was talking to myself, to my many selves and the creatures who inhabited my world, often more real than the people I worked with or saw on the street.

"No," Thea said. "We're the visionaries, the creators. We won't settle for the ordinary. Something in us won't let us compromise. We just can't make ourselves fit into the spots that were set out for us. And we can't cut ourselves off from our feelings."

"Dr. Sternfeld says that's not true. If I say those things to him, he says it's a way of avoiding facing my sickness. And my responsibilities."

"But we *are* different, you know," Thea said quietly. "And I think we always will be. It doesn't mean we're sick. Maybe they're really afraid of us, how crazy we seem to them, how different we are. Sometimes I think it makes them see something in themselves they want to bury, their own craziness; then, they can call us sick, separate themselves from us, and feel a whole lot safer."

"But you go to Rheingold and you take his drugs." It didn't make sense.

"I know I do. 'Cause sometimes what I'm feeling and seeing scares me, too. And sometimes I believe I really am schizophrenic, like they say. And then, I want to get cured and I go to Rheingold and he gives me more therapy and more drugs to cure me and I feel better, sort of. Knowing that I'm going to be cured. But then, I know I'm just different and that I'll never be normal. And if I keep on trying to be normal I'll be miserable the rest of my life. But you're right, I do keep on going to my shrink. Because what I feel is very, very scary sometimes."

"And he makes it seem as if it's not really you, but your sickness, right?" I asked.

"Yeah, right."

"You know, Sternfeld does the same thing. Thea. It's not fair how much we have to suffer, though."

"But you did see SMOOCH and all sorts of other things and they never will."

"And I cry and I'm scared and most of the time I'd give that up to be like them, normal, and go to work and get married and have kids. And be a little content."

"It didn't work when you went to school. It probably won't work now, this secretary job. You have to be you. You can't be a slave or follow anyone's plan. You're special. I don't care what Sternfeld says."

"I fucked up at school because I got sick." The ears of my mind had clicked closed to Thea's pleading. I spoke grimly. "And if I fuck up again it'll be because I get sick again."

"Do you really believe that?"

"Yes. I don't know. Please, Thea, don't make it harder for me. Something close to a normal life is almost within my grasp. Don't make me blow it to pieces. Please."

Two weeks later my old friend Ina called. We had known each

other since our freshman year in high school, and although we did not see each other very frequently, we still felt close.

"How goes it?" she asked.

"It goes," I said. "I'm still working. That's something, I guess."

"You sound like you need a rest. Want to come up and spend the weekend with Stephen and me? We rented a little cabin in the woods in upstate New York. A friend of Stephen's is coming, too. A guy. Paul Gotkin. You'll like him. What do you say?"

"Are you trying to fix me up with him, Ina?"

"No. Really."

In the years I had been hospitalized all of my friends, at one time or another, had tried to get me dates.

"I don't think so, Ina. I couldn't hack it. I'm too tense."

"Oh come on, Janet. It'll just be us and this guy, Paul. You won't have to act with him. It'll do you good to get away from the city."

I hesitated, wanting to go, afraid and anxious. "I'll ask Dr. Sternfeld when I see him Wednesday night," I said. "And I'll let you know."

"Of course, go," Dr. Sternfeld said. "It will be good for you."

"I'm sort of afraid of meeting this Paul person. You know, I always think people will feel sorry for me, and think I'm strange, or hate me."

"It hasn't happened at work, has it?"

"No, but I act at work. I'm another person. The real me is invisible at work."

"But I see the real you," he said.

"I wonder. I wonder if I'm not really completely invisible, a product of everyone's imagination, even yours."

"That's fantastical thinking again, Janet. You're indulging yourself."

"I guess so."

"I want you to go this weekend." He smiled, rose, and put his arm around my shoulder. "We've come a long way, Janet. Let's not stop now. Call it doctor's orders, but I want you to go spend the weekend with your friends."

We both smiled. I was young, he protected me, and nestling in against his warming body I felt safe and loved.

"Everything's going to be all right," I thought. "I have heaven."

"Until heaven changes his mind," a voice in my head intruded unexpectedly. "Then you're stranded again. Dying and scared."

"You shut up," I muttered.

"What did you say?" Dr. Sternfeld asked.

"Nothing," I answered. "Just the words of a new poem I wrote."

"Now have a good time. And I'll see you Monday."

We embraced and I moved through the heavy oak doors into the foyer where my father waited to drive me home. I was still afraid to travel alone at night.

"Okay, Ina," I spoke into the phone. "I'll be coming up. Dr. Sternfeld said it was all right."

"Great. We'll pick you up at your house on Saturday. About ten-thirty. Okay?"

"Sure. I'll be ready."

What would happen? How would it end, this life I was living, this charade of normality? What did they all see when they looked at me?

"It has to end in pain, I know it. But dear Lord, won't you let something good happen to me, for a change?"

I packed a small valise with a bathing suit, shorts, jeans, a dress, underwear, a toothbrush, and my bottles of medicine, asked my mother for my sleeping pills, and, sticking my tongue out at the squid stationed across the room, fell asleep in a moment.

Paul

PART 2

Meeting

"*Schmuck,*" *I said to myself.* "Don't just lie there. Do something."

I lay motionless in the pitch darkness of my summer cabin. In her own bed, at right angles to mine, Janet rustled and turned.

"She's not asleep," I thought. "Go ahead and say something. Anything at all."

I fought to keep my breathing even. I wondered how I could lie like this, only a few inches from her bed, without making some kind of play for her.

That I didn't want to say anything to her, that I didn't find her very attractive, that I knew her emotions to be erratic, all slipped away from me. I was obsessed by an image of my own manhood. A lifetime of social pressures and adolescent boasts and mating tensions taunted me.

I kicked my feet in frustration. I was sharing the rent of this isolated cabin with Stephen and Ina so that I could be alone periodically, so that I could escape the pressure of the city, the feeling that I had to look good or be charming. Now, because they had invited their friend Janet for the weekend, I felt hounded again by social obligation.

"You fool," I berated myself. "This is too good an opportunity to pass up. Will you say something, at least?"

"Are you sleeping?" Janet suddenly asked.

I disentangled myself from the sheets and sat on the edge of her bed. I leaned down and awkwardly kissed her, a passionless kiss of obligation. She sat up and faced me. In the dim light of the room I could barely make out her features.

"I thought you were sleeping," she said. "You were so quiet."

"No. I wasn't sleeping."

I kissed her again, but this time she pushed me away.

"No," she said.

"What?"

"No. I'm afraid."

"Afraid?" I was startled. "Of what?"

She buried her head in her arms.

"O my God," I thought. "What am I getting myself into?"

"What are you afraid of?" I asked, again.

"I don't know," she said. She turned away from me. "I'm sorry. I'm really sorry."

"Look," I said. "I don't want to hurt you. Let's just sit and talk. That's all. What are you sorry about? What are you frightened about?"

She lifted her head but she continued to look away from me. The nighttime summer insects kept up their endless chirping, buzzing din. I glanced at the door to Stephen and Ina's bedroom. They had been sleeping for a couple of hours and I envied them.

"I'm sorry I bothered you," she said. "You must think I'm terrible."

"I don't think you're terrible."

She studied me carefully. "I wanted you to kiss me," she said. "I was lying awake thinking, 'What can I say to him? How can I make him kiss me?' "

"Why?"

"I like you. I liked you the first moment I saw you."

Her combination of directness and innocence appealed to me. I was later to call her Miranda, after the heroine of *The Tempest*. She seemed to have been living apart from the world for a long time and to have only recently returned to it.

"I like you too," I said. But I wasn't totally honest. She hadn't really attracted me when I met her earlier in the day.

"What are you frightened about?" I asked again.

"About everything. I wanted you to like me. I wanted you to hold me. But I don't even know what to say or do."

"There's nothing special to do."

She made a face. "You don't understand. I haven't been able to feel anything for anyone in a long time. I get all awkward and frightened, as if I can't say anything right."

"But there is no right way."

She turned away from me again. "You don't understand at all," she repeated.

I held her against my chest, but she stiffened in my grasp. She sounded odd to me. I was taken aback and I was a little frightened of her as well.

"Did Stephen tell you anything about me?" she asked.

"He said you were his favorite of Ina's friends."

"Did he tell you about my problems?"

"A little bit. Not much."

She looked down at her wrists.

"He said you'd been in and out of mental hospitals," I told her.

Meeting

"He said it was very sad because he doesn't know anyone who tries harder than you."

"As if that means anything," she said.

"I don't know anything about it."

"No. I guess not." She leaned against me. "I don't really want to talk about it. It's dominated my life for so long."

"But it's over now?" I asked.

"I'm not in the hospital. Whatever that means."

She gripped my arm tightly. "What I wanted to say to you was that I wanted you to like me very badly. I wanted you to like me so much that I got all tied up and flustered and scared that you wouldn't like me. And then I didn't know where to go from there."

"And what I tried to say," I explained, "was that you didn't have to try so hard."

I kissed her again and held her tightly against me. I looked over her shoulder, out the window, into the night. Fatigued, confused, I was off-balance, unsure of my feelings.

Her lips against mine, her body pressed against me, she seemed insubstantial; I felt as if I were grasping a ghost. I suppose I wanted to be loved by her. Yet, because I mistrusted the stability of her emotions, because basically I mistrusted her, I fought off a sudden passion and carefully held myself away from her.

At dawn we went for a walk. The cabin was built on the bank of a small private lake and we circled the water, making our way through the woods. Although the sun was newly risen, it had a scorching, heavy look that precedes a steamy day. The morning grass felt fresh against our bare feet. We stopped at the base of a boulder and I lifted her onto it, climbing after her. Through the trees we could see the glassy water, the lily pads, and the reeds.

"Stephen and Ina will be surprised if we're not in the cabin when they wake up," she said.

"I suppose they will be," I answered.

She reached for my hand. "I didn't expect anything like this to happen when I decided to come up with them this weekend."

"I guess I didn't either," I said. "If I thought anything romantic would happen I wouldn't have come up."

"Why?"

"Because I didn't want to be involved with anyone this summer. Because I rented this cabin so that I could be by myself."

"Are you sorry you came up then?"

I thought for a moment. "No," I said. "I'm really not."

"It's strange how life is," she said. "Just the night before, I came out here to this lake at about three o'clock in the morning and I lay on the grass and I just wanted to die. I thought that there was never going to be anything good in my life and I asked God to let me die, to please let me die."

I stared at her as she spoke. In a shapeless dress, her body looked painfully thin, almost boyish. Her face was childish, her nose too long. But I hadn't been lying when I told her I was pleased that I had met her. Perhaps it was her innocence and vulnerability that attracted me to her. I had made a commitment to her when I listened so sympathetically through the night and I wasn't even sure that I wanted to back out of the commitment.

Yet as I listened to her words I felt a terrible wave of fear and I could only think, "What the hell have I gotten myself into?"

The hit song of the summer of 1966 was "Strangers in the Night." A great big hit, it played everywhere. During those long, erratic summer days it played over and over again, Frank Sinatra's soppy homage to chance meeting, unexpected love, and romance at first sight.

During those months the news reports were menacing: the bombing of Vietnam; seething, raging, burning ghettoes; dropping out; campus unrest. The Beatles were in full flower, hippies were coming into style, the New York Mets were still losing, and assorted superstars were rising and falling with dazzlingly decadent speed.

As for me, I felt I was going nowhere. A recent moment of despair—a girl I liked refused to go out with me—had dragged up a bitter sense of loneliness, spiraling me into a month-long period of depression. I was twenty-four years old and I felt suddenly burnt out, suffering from a sense of weariness and alienation I did not understand.

We had undoubtedly been looking for someone, Janet and I. Despite our uncertain feelings, we took a sudden and intense pleasure in each other's company. We saw each other or phoned each other constantly after our meeting, filling our time together with small talk, laughter, and discovery.

We came from similar backgrounds. We had grown up only a mile or so apart. Although her father was an educator and mine a businessman, they both belonged to a loosely knit, upper middle class, Brooklyn elite and their friends overlapped. While Janet had gone to one white, middle class high school, I had gone to another. And while she had frequented one neighborhood movie theater or had hung out on one main street or had gone to dances at one synagogue, I had done the same things at other places.

If the details of our childhood were different, the essential experiences were the same; and on a superficial level, we knew each other well.

Or so we thought at first.

In her own way, Janet was a legend. Months after meeting her I would run into people who knew of her. A high school golden girl, she was one of those unattainable adolescents who seem to slide through the horrors of growing up, one of those superstars who seem always at the center of people's thoughts when they trot out their frail, demented memories of their school years. A long time before, I had secretly hungered after a girl like Janet, but I had known that I was too much of a *nebbish* ever to get her.

A curious incident occurred a week after we met. In the late afternoon I phoned Janet at work.

"Will I see you tonight?" I asked. We had seen each other every night.

"No. I can't make it," she said.

"Oh. Why?"

She hesitated. "I'm busy tonight. I have a date. Sort of."

"A what?"

"Well it's not exactly a date. Someone called my father to ask for a job. And I got to talking to him and he asked me to meet him for a drink after work."

"I thought we had—I thought we made a commitment to each other."

"We have," she said. "If I meet him for a drink, it doesn't have anything to do with our commitment."

I thought about what she said. "How would you feel if I went out with someone else?"

"I'm not really going out with him. I'm just meeting him for a drink."

"But why?"

"Because I want to. Because I told him I would."

"And you wouldn't mind if I went out with someone else?"

Her voice was cool. "That would be up to you."

"You don't see anything wrong with meeting him?"

"I certainly don't. I don't see why you're making such a fuss about it."

I slammed the receiver down. I paced back and forth across my office. In my mind I was making some kind of perverse symbolic stand, balancing my needs and desires against what I saw as my self-respect. I saw her meeting with this man as a struggle between us. Until that moment I had not realized how deeply I had committed myself to Janet or how much I wanted our relationship to work.

The telephone rang.

Janet's tone of voice was carefully sweet. "I think we were disconnected."

"No. We weren't disconnected."

"You hung up on me?"

I didn't answer. She knew I had hung up the telephone. I let the silence hang in the air.

"I thought about what you were saying," she finally said. "Look. I don't want to upset you. I don't really want to go out with him. I don't really want to see anyone but you. I don't even know how I got involved with him."

"Do you understand why I got so angry?"

"I guess so. I don't know. I didn't think meeting him was so very important. I just couldn't say no."

I wasn't certain myself why I had gotten so angry. My bitterness had gone beyond reason or thought, spilling out of years of rage and mistrust.

"It was important to me," I said.

"I know it was. That's why I finally said to myself, 'What the hell are you doing? You don't really want to see anyone but Paul.' "

We met later, as we had done all of that week, at a Brooklyn subway station. She had seen the man after work and cancelled her date with him. We walked down Church Avenue, past the bargain stores, discount drug stores, and fashion outlets into a bar.

"I was crying after you hung up on me," Janet said.

"I'm sorry. I was very angry."

"No. It wasn't even your fault. I was more upset with myself."

"Why did you agree to go out with him?"

"I told you. I couldn't help it. I couldn't say no."

"Why couldn't you?"

She stared at me. "Oh, look," she said. "He called to ask me out when I was having dinner. I couldn't refuse him when my parents were listening to me. I felt as if I should say yes."

"I don't understand."

"I know. It doesn't make any sense. You don't know what my mother is like, though, when I don't do what she expects me to do. I get silent accusations from her or pitiful sighs."

She made a bitter face. She squeezed the stem of her cocktail glass in her fist.

"But it's not her fault either. I suppose I would have done the same thing even if they hadn't been listening. I couldn't help myself.

That's what really frightened me. I was doing just what I used to do."

"I don't understand that either," I said.

"You didn't know me in the past," Janet said. "I used to put on a special face. I used to be sweet and charming and full of enthusiasm."

"So?"

"It wasn't really me. It was a false face."

I stared at her. The feelings behind her words were intense but I didn't understand them.

"We all put on false faces," I said.

"But mine almost killed me."

Later, we sat in my car, in front of her parents' house. The martini had gone to my head and I felt light-headed and fuzzy-minded.

"It's been an upsetting day," she said.

"I guess it has been," I answered. I was still holding myself away from her. I watched her light a cigarette. In the flash of the matchstick I could see that she was frowning. She wore a black cotton summer dress. Her arms were bare.

"Are you still angry at me?" she asked.

"I guess I am."

"I told you that I didn't think it was very important whether I met him or not."

"I know you don't think it's important. That's one of the things that makes me angry."

"I also told you why I agreed to go out with him. That I couldn't help it. How much it frightened me that I couldn't help it."

"And I don't really understand what you mean."

She stared at me. Across the street, I could see the lights of her house. Her parents didn't like me. On this quiet, residential street, their lights shone down like a reproach.

"You don't understand," she said. "You don't understand that I almost killed myself because I didn't know who I was. I've had no life for myself because I've always done everything everyone wanted me to do."

She spoke with a passion that startled me. Her manner was usually tentative, as if she had no real confidence in her words. Her tentativeness, her shakiness, her diffidence, were signs of her long unhappy years. Her pain pushed her anger and hurtfulness inward and gave her an air of soft vulnerability which I found moving and terribly sad.

"I don't want anything from you," I said.

"I know you don't. That's what makes you so different."

"But I'm not different."

"I don't know. I never felt comfortable with anyone before. I used to think that I could never be with anyone without talking, that I had to fill up all the silences with words."

I shook my head in confusion.

"And I certainly never thought that I could love anyone. I thought love, marriage, that was for other people, not for me."

I couldn't tell her that a month before, when a girl had refused to go out with me, I had lain on my parents' living room couch and, with an absurd loneliness and self-pity, I had been suddenly certain that no one would ever love me.

I held her against me instead of talking and she began to cry softly into my chest.

"It must have been terrible for you," I said.

"You don't know," she said. "You really don't know."

I suppose I didn't know. But I thought I did. I could only see her unhappiness and pain in my own frame of reference.

As I lay in bed that evening I thought about the day. I thought about Janet's pain and my own pain and about my surprisingly explosive anger. The events of the summer were forming a pattern: my extended depression, my overriding sense of meaninglessness, my terrible loneliness.

I didn't know why I wanted Janet as badly as I did. Whatever the mysteries of romance, I would not have, with any reason or thought, chosen her for physical reasons. And yet, whatever the logic, she haunted me.

Past midnight, as I tossed in bed, the telephone rang.

"Did I wake you up?" Janet asked.

"No. I wasn't sleeping."

There was silence.

"I just called to tell you that I was sorry about today," she said.

"That wasn't necessary."

"And that I love you."

I waited a moment before I answered.

"I love you too," I said.

There was another long silence. I felt suddenly foolish, as if I wanted to take back my words. But I couldn't take them back. I had meant them.

"What are we going to do?" she asked.

"What do you want to do?"

"I don't know. I want to see you all the time."

"We could move in together," I said.

"Dr. Sternfeld wants me to get my own apartment before I move in with someone else. He doesn't want me to go from one dependency situation to another."

"That makes sense."

"Yeah. I guess so." Her voice was suddenly tentative.

"Paul?"

"What?"

"I'm scared of living with you. Before I met you I wasn't sleeping through the night. I used to see terrible things, the image of a squid in the corner of my room."

Oddly enough I responded only to her fear, letting her words slip out of my mind.

"I get frightened too," I said. "It's not easy to suddenly plan to live with someone."

"Do you think we'll stay together?"

"Of course we will."

"No. We won't," she said.

"What do you mean?"

"We won't. I know we won't. I know we won't last together more than a month."

Despite Janet's pessimism about our long-range plans, we followed Dr. Sternfeld's recommendation and at the beginning of August moved into separate apartments.

Janet's month-long sublet, a cramped, one-bedroom apartment, rose two stories above Eighth Street, the glossiest, most commercial street in Greenwich Village. The apartment was narrow and airless, with a kitchen that folded out of the wall, and a dining room that took over half the living room.

We lay in bed one evening, on two halves of a trundle bed that rolled apart when we made the slightest move, listening to the souped-up cars roaring down the street and the loud voices of tourists and hustlers as they passed our window.

"This is ridiculous," I said irritably. "Let's move into one apartment."

"After a month," Janet insisted. "If everything works out."

"What do you mean, if everything works out? If things don't work out, what are you going to do? You can't stay here past August anyway."

"Then I'll go someplace else."

"You could always go someplace else if we lived in one apartment."

The splendid logic of my argument stopped her for a moment.

"It's the principle of the thing," she finally said. "The idea that I have a place of my own."

"That's ridiculous."

"It's not ridiculous. Everybody needs a room of their own."

I reached for her but the bed began to roll apart and I started to dangle between the two halves. She put her hand on my chest, pushing me down, but I grabbed her arm and we fell together, in the midst of clumps of dust, crumbs of food, bobbie pins, dressmaker pins, and old, discarded underwear.

"The woman who rented me this place is not much of a housekeeper," Janet said.

"I don't know. At least she puts everything into one pile."

She tried to rise, but I held her down against my chest.

"Let me up," she said.

"Why should I?"

She pushed hard against me, her fingers digging into my flesh.

"I said let me up," she repeated, her voice rising.

"I'm trying to, Janet." In the narrow space between the beds, she floundered against me like a person struggling not to drown, and finally I had to wrap my arms around her and lift us both onto the bed.

"I don't like to be held down," she said, panting.

"I don't like to be held down, either. But there's no reason to get hysterical about it. I was only kidding."

She stared at me oddly. As we had struggled together I had seen an explosiveness in her eyes that had startled and frightened me, that I could not easily forget.

"I'm sorry," she said. "It just frightens me to be trapped like that."

"That's okay. I'm sorry too. It was a silly joke."

"I'm really sorry I made such a fuss."

"I said it was okay, Janet."

We sat facing each other on the bed.

"Paul?" she suddenly said.

"What?"

"Let's move into one apartment together. It's crazy shifting back and forth like this."

"But what about the principle you were just talking about? What about Dr. Sternfeld's idea of dependency?"

She hesitated. "I don't care what he says. Fuck the principle. Fuck the whole damn thing."

Living Together

At the end of the summer, we moved into an airy, high-ceilinged apartment in the Park Slope–Prospect Park section of Brooklyn. A cheerful, colorless lesbian couple lived below us in the basement apartment. Above us, Miss Snow lived with her dozen cats, her roomful of antiques, and the terrible odor of mustiness, animal excrement, and despair. The front apartment was occupied by Bunny, her constantly yapping dog, and her floating cast of multinational, interracial boyfriends. And on the top floor, slick-looking Howie Marks, who studied accounting and was engaged to a beautiful girl from Bay Ridge, smoked so much marijuana that a permanent little cloud seemed to hover above the house, as if we were all possessed.

The house itself, built of battleship-gray stone, was a hundred years old. A false parapet served as a front landing. Three floors of bay windows bulged from its side, making it look like a small medieval castle. It had been a mansion, one of the buildings that overlooked or bordered Prospect Park. In another, more leisurely age this area was called the Gold Coast of Brooklyn, but like most of New York City it had seen better days.

Our apartment was a rambling, spacious, one-bedroom unit with stained-glass windows, a wood-burning fireplace, twelve-foot ceilings, and scroll work on the doors and moldings. We furnished it sparsely with hand-me-downs. As we lay cramped together in our single bed at night, we thought ourselves immensely fortunate, as if the filigree details along the ceiling above our heads mirrored the sudden richness of our life together.

One afternoon I drove Janet to Dr. Sternfeld's office, double parking in front of his fine, spacious house. We sat in the car talking, waiting for her session to begin. It was the start of September and a late-summer heat wave had just broken, giving the air an unexpected chill.

"Why don't you come in and meet Dr. Sternfeld?" Janet said.

"No. I don't think so," I answered. "Maybe some other time."

This was a queer reluctance on my part but I chose not to analyze it. In my eyes there was a strange bond between Janet and Dr.

Sternfeld. Something uncommonly intimate, an eerie closeness that I didn't then understand.

"Oh, come on," she said. "He wants to meet you."

My first impression of Dr. Sternfeld was confused by contradictions in his appearance. He wore his dark hair long, just below the nape of his neck, and he had a bristling pasha mustache so that from the shoulders up he looked dashing and sharp. But he was dressed in pleated pants, a starched colorless sport shirt, and an old man's type of sandal, all of which made him seem unfocused to me, as if he didn't know who he was.

The sliding door to his office was open and he sat at his desk, leafing through papers, his feet propped up on a leather footrest. When he saw us he rose and came forward, his hand outstretched.

"I'm Dr. Sternfeld."

"This is Paul," Janet said.

"I'm not surprised. I didn't think it was anyone else."

We shook hands. His handshake was properly firm.

"I've heard a lot about you," he said.

"I've heard a lot about you too," I said.

We went into his office. Janet balanced herself on the edge of a leather couch. I sank into a leather armchair that was tilted so far backward, my feet couldn't touch the floor. The room was spacious, cluttered with bric-a-brac, Chinese artwork, and statuettes.

"I just wanted to tell both of you," he said, "how pleased I am. From what Janet tells me, I think she's very fortunate."

I thanked him. I was watching his hands rather than his eyes. They lay folded in his lap like soldiers at arms. His voice was warm and pleasant. He spoke slowly, with a studied indifference, as if he chose every word carefully, for style as well as effect.

"I assume Janet holds no secrets from you," he said. "That she's told you everything about herself. I can assure you that she's well now, or at least that there's a qualitative difference in her state of mind, if you know what I mean."

I nodded as if I did.

"Good," he continued. "Now that you've both got me here, is there anything you'd like to ask me? Anything you'd like to know? Just fire away."

"I can't really imagine what Janet was like," I said. "It's impossible for me to picture her."

"It was awful," Janet said. "You can't have any idea just how awful it was."

"There were times," Dr. Sternfeld said, "when she was more

trouble than six patients. When I would have traded her in for a dozen other patients."

He leaned back in his chair, folded his hands about his head, and laughed at his last thought.

"There were times," he continued, "when I felt that I was the only link to life that Janet had. When she would come in here and be absolutely nothing and I would hold on to her and literally pump life back into her system."

We were all silent. I looked over at Janet. Her nose wrinkled as if she were about to cry.

"It must have been terrible," I said. I didn't know what else to say. I felt embarrassed, as if I had stumbled upon wellsprings of emotion that had nothing to do with me. We were talking about a Janet I could only vaguely imagine, another Janet, like a character in a book.

"It was just awful," she said. "If it wasn't for Dr. Sternfeld, I wouldn't be alive now. Or if I was alive, I'd be locked up some place."

"There was a time," Dr. Sternfeld said, "when she wanted to be hospitalized for the rest of her life, which was something we had to fight against. Which was something we couldn't allow."

I shook my head, a meaningless gesture. I shifted my position in the chair, but my legs continued to dangle helplessly. I looked from Janet to Dr. Sternfeld and back again.

"What made the difference?" I asked. "I mean, what suddenly made such a change in Janet?"

Dr. Sternfeld leaned forward in his chair.

"I could give you a lot of psychiatric language and some educated guesses, but I don't see any point in doing that. Let's say everything came together; all the work we had been doing over the past five years, all the talks we had. She was sicker than she had any right to be, and when she got well, it was unexpectedly sudden. Call it a miracle if you'd like. But I wasn't surprised. I wasn't surprised about it at all."

I looked at him. "And you expect her to stay well?" I blurted out. I hadn't meant to ask the question so crudely. I turned toward Janet, but she hadn't taken her eyes off Dr. Sternfeld.

"Let me put it this way," he said slowly. "I don't expect her ever to be the way she was before. She still has problems and maybe we'll try to work some of them out. But as sick as she was? I don't think so."

We all looked at each other.

"It was a tough road," he continued. "There were things I did for Janet that I wouldn't even do for my wife. Like giving her my vacation itinerary or letting her call me at all hours of the night. But it's over now."

He stretched his arms over his head.

"Do you have any more questions? I hadn't intended to talk about all these things."

"Was I really worth a dozen other patients?" Janet asked.

"At least one dozen. Maybe two or three."

In the waiting room, I leafed through a pile of *Time* magazines. I read about Elizabeth Taylor and Richard Burton, about Linda Bird Johnson's romance with George Hamilton, about the Vietnam war and finally, I put down all the magazines and stared across the hallway at the heavy wooden door to Dr. Sternfeld's office. A radio was perched on the molding above my head. Mood music drowned out the sound of voices. But in between the commercials I thought I heard Janet speak. I thought she was crying.

I had a sudden chilling fantasy that Dr. Sternfeld was telling her that she shouldn't see me anymore.

"He's a nice enough fellow," he was saying in my fantasy, "but I don't think he's the right person for you. I think you should play the field anyway. Not stick with one person. Wait a while. Don't make any snap judgments. See who else you'll meet. You'll make a wiser decision."

"But I love Paul," Janet said.

"You only think you love Paul. He's the first man you've met since you've been well. Don't you think you ought to play the field more before you make any definite decision?"

I shook my head to clear away my thoughts.

I looked down at my hands. I had rolled last week's *Time* magazine into a thin cylinder and without thinking I was rhythmically tapping it against my thigh. From another part of the house I could hear thudding footsteps and from just outside the window I could hear little girls playing.

"You are a silly, insecure, frightened bastard," I berated myself. And yet I couldn't shake my fantasy out of my head.

I suppose I had been frightened by Dr. Sternfeld or at least I had felt threatened by him. In his relationship with Janet there was a hint of control and power over her. I didn't for a moment believe that he would ever try to stop Janet from being with me. But I thought he could. And when the door to his office creaked, shook, and finally sprung open, I was almost surprised to see that Janet was smiling at me.

"He likes you a lot," she said as we drove home. "He thinks you're even nicer than I described you as being."

I smiled politely. I hadn't thought I was particularly impressive.

"He's not angry at us then? For moving in together?"

"Why should he be angry at us?"

"You were afraid that he would be." I was put off by her surprise.

She fiddled with the door handle. "I didn't really think he'd be angry at us. He was only concerned that I should always know that I had my own place to go back to."

We drove in silence. We circled a traffic island where a bustling skating rink once stood. I had taken my first date there, gliding across the crowded ice. I was fourteen and I had never been more frightened in my life.

I looked at Janet. For a moment I couldn't bridge the gap between then and now. She was unfamiliar to me; it was as if I couldn't remember which girlfriend I was driving where.

"What's wrong?" Janet asked.

I smiled. "Nothing really. I couldn't remember who you were."

"Am I that memorable?"

"I'm not joking. Did you ever have the feeling that you momentarily weren't certain where you were?"

"Are you kidding? You're asking me? I specialized in dissociative reactions."

"I forgot," I said. Her face was set in a tight-lipped, ironic smile, but beneath her smile she was deadly serious.

I realized that I didn't really know her at all. We had lived together for three weeks and I was falling deeper and deeper in love with her. But we were in a transitory stage between the first bellow of romance and the gradual intimacy of being able to see into each other's minds. She was as blank to me as a statue. And as I drove, I was suddenly frightened because I couldn't possibly guess what she was thinking.

"I didn't mean to attack Dr. Sternfeld," I said. "You had said he might be angry if we moved in together."

"I didn't say he'd be angry. You must have misunderstood me."

"Anyway, I'm glad I finally met him. He's a charming man."

"He's very important to me. I don't know how I could ever really thank him for what he did for me. He saved my life."

"I know that," I said. I could respond to the depth of her feeling for him. My own feelings were less certain. But I held them inside me and I reached for her hand.

"What I don't understand," I said, "was that there must have been a turning point. There must have been a moment when you knew you had passed through the worst of your suffering."

"There was a turning point," she said. "There was the time Dr. Sternfeld finally laid down the law to me. He said, 'No more wrist-cutting; no more suicidal thoughts.' Otherwise he wouldn't treat me. I remember going home on the bus and feeling trapped—feeling enraged and devastated and betrayed, and at the same time, feeling helpless because I needed him so much and didn't know what to do."

She fumbled with a cigarette, lit it, and stared out the side window, so that when she spoke again I had to strain to hear her.

"But it worked," she said. "His threat must have touched something inside me, because after that afternoon, I was no longer as obsessed with death and I began to get well."

"When did this happen?" I asked.

"I don't know. A long time ago."

I stopped at a traffic light and stared at her. There was a vapidness in her eyes now that made me feel far away from her and it frightened me. Or perhaps her words frightened me. I was startled by the matter-of-factness of her story.

"It must be strange for you now," I said.

"Of course it's strange for me. Everything's strange. Six months ago I was in a hospital. And now . . ."

She let her words dribble away but I knew what she wanted to say. As I looked at her I was struck again by the vacant distance in her eyes.

She was truly special. She was capable of wild bursts of energy, of moments of overwhelming allure and charm. She used her attractiveness well; it must have been difficult for her not to use it. She had charmed everyone throughout her life—her parents, her friends, Dr. Sternfeld, even me. But I hungered now for what was behind her vacant eyes.

There were special things, frightening things tucked away inside her eyes and I felt all the more isolated from her, even jealous perhaps, for not being allowed to see them. Because I loved her and because I thought I would spend the rest of my life with her, I was frightened by this isolation.

"Are you worried about getting sick again?" I asked.

The light changed and a car in back of me began to beep its horn. I continued to look at her.

"No, I'm not worried," she said. But I knew her well enough to see, by the tightness of her mouth and the tilt of her head, that she wasn't telling me the truth.

In the evening we made love. Afterward we lay side by side, naked on the bed. I stroked the inside of her thigh. She placed her hand on my knee and began to run her fingers up my leg.

From the front apartment we could hear the noise of Bunny's party, the muffled, booming rock-and-roll beat, the drone of indistinguishable voices. Above us, Miss Snow thumped back and forth across her apartment. The bedroom had no overhead light. Our bedside lamp left part of the room in shadows so that the corners of the far wall were lost in darkness. Janet's hand brushed across my thigh and then her grip tightened and her fingers dug into my flesh.

"What's wrong?" I asked.

"I can't touch you."

"You can't touch me where?"

"I can't touch your penis."

"You could just before."

"I know. But I can't now."

"Then don't."

"But I want to."

I laughed. "Then do it."

"It's not as simple as that."

"I know it's not." I looked down at my penis. It hung limply between my legs, looking, in comparison to her anxiety, strangely featureless and harmless.

"Look, Janet," I said. "It's only so much skin. It's just another part of my body, no different from my arm or leg."

She reached for me but her hand hovered in the air. The muscles of her face tightened.

"Janet. It's really not so important. It's not worth making a thing about."

Her fingers brushed across my belly and finally her hand closed around my penis. She held me tightly with cold, bloodless fingers, as if she had grabbed hold of a challenge that had nothing to do with me. And then her grip loosened and for a moment she fondled me. She pulled her hand away, took a deep breath, and lay back on the bed. I stared up at the ceiling, at a filigree detail on the molding, a thin, lacy circle that wound round and round like a child's puzzle.

"I'm sorry," she said.

"About what?"

"About—about this."

"It happens, Janet. I told you. It's really not so important. It's only a momentary thing."

"It is important," she said bitterly. "I get very frightened. I'm afraid I'll close myself off like I used to do. I spent years talking to Dr. Sternfeld about sex. Session after session after session . . ."

"Oh, hell," I interrupted. I turned on to my side and propped myself up on my elbow. "You can't hold on to my prick and you're ready to turn it into a big psychiatric thing."

"It is a big thing. I reach for you and get this awful wave of revulsion and anxiety."

"Maybe I'm revolting."

"Ha. Ha. Ha."

As she glared straight ahead, I studied her profile. In two months she had changed physically. Her muscles had relaxed and her face had taken on an open, vibrant look. In her parents' living room, there was a photograph of Janet at twenty, her nose thrust forward, her lips pinched together; she looked fearsomely virginal, like the most dried-up spinster.

She had taken to sex with a startling passion, though, with a freshness and lack of self-consciousness that I found rare and beautiful. She carried her body loosely, as if she were newly born, and I found it difficult to see her problem now as more than momentary, an adjustment to finally coming physically alive.

"Maybe I'm too overpowering and appealing," I said.

"That's not funny either." But her own anger was lessening.

"What kind of sexual things did you talk about with Dr. Sternfeld?" I asked.

"We talked about everything. How I wouldn't let myself feel anything. How I was out of contact with my own body."

"What do you talk about now? How does he feel about you turning into such a sexual creature?"

She looked at me strangely.

"He said he wasn't surprised at all. He said that he always knew that anyone who fought so hard against sex had very strong passions. He knew that once I let myself go I would practically explode."

I began to laugh.

"What's so funny?" she said.

I reached across and grabbed her shoulder.

"Sometimes you confuse me, Janet. I don't know whether to pity you or envy you."

"What does that mean?"

"I don't even know," I said.

Later that evening she asked me if I planned to marry her.

"I thought you were sleeping," I said. It was nearly midnight. I had been reading for a half hour.

"I wasn't. I was lying here and thinking."

"I haven't really thought about marriage, Janet."

"I don't really care about it for myself. But my mother keeps bothering me."

"She wants to know if my intentions are honorable?" I asked.

"No. That's not it. She just keeps asking me if our relationship is going anywhere."

I stroked her hair. She was lying on her back, looking up at me.

"I don't know what 'going anywhere' means," I said. "I think we get along really well. We love each other. I suppose if we want to we'll get married."

"It isn't so important to me. If it wasn't for my mother I wouldn't even think about it. But she keeps bugging me. What's going to happen? When is it going to happen?"

I lay my book on the bedside table.

"I suppose if we want to we can get married during the winter," I said. For some reason, the winter seemed years away.

Janet rolled onto her side and closed her eyes. I continued to stroke her head. With her eyes closed, with her hair sprawled across her face, she looked so childlike, so helpless and vulnerable, that I had to fight off a sudden moment of sadness. I felt extremely tender toward her.

Bunny's party had ended a long time ago, but the music droned on. Miss Snow continued her vigil, thumping across her apartment.

"You're very strange," Janet said. She didn't open her eyes. "I hardly ever know what's going on in your head."

"I was thinking the same thing about you," I said.

"About me? I babble about everything that comes into my head. Every silly, trivial, boring thought comes right out of me."

"Maybe," I said.

"You," she continued, "you're a regular moody Harry. You never say anything you think."

"Perhaps I don't think anything."

"Bullshit. I'm sure you're thinking all kinds of deep thoughts. But you won't ever let me in on them."

"Perhaps I won't let myself in on them."

"See," Janet said. "That's the kind of thing you say which sounds deep and philosophical, as if it means something important. But it's just a way of covering up how you really feel."

She sat up in bed.

"But I'll open you up. You'll see." She began to tickle me. "In another year you won't recognize yourself. I'm a regular can opener."

PAUL

I wrestled her down on the bed but she pushed me away and sat upright again.

"How about December twenty-fifth?" she said.

"What about it?"

"It's Christmas Day. How about that as a day to get married?"

"Oh, hell," I said.

"What's wrong with it? I think it's a classy day to be married."

I pushed her down, holding her by her shoulder.

"I love you incredibly much," I said. "But I'm too young to be married."

The idea of marriage remained on Janet's mind. One evening, when I returned home late from a night out with a friend, she was waiting up for me. We sat in the living room and I drank a beer and told her about my day.

"Are we going to end up fighting and bickering?" she asked. "Like all married people seem to do?"

"I don't think so," I said, and smiled. "We're not going to fight at all."

"I used to think," she said, "that there was something wrong with people who fought with each other. I used to see my parents do ugly, subtle things to each other and think that if this was marriage I wanted no part of it."

"You come from a daintier family than mine. My parents' fights couldn't be called subtle."

"I always thought that if life was filled with the type of ugliness, hate, and pain I sometimes saw, it just wasn't worth living."

"If you keep talking like that," I said, "you're going to lose your Miranda image."

She kissed me, pressing her body tightly against mine.

"I told Dr. Sternfeld about what happened the other day," she said. "How I couldn't touch you."

"Oh, yeah."

"He said he wasn't surprised at all. I always had that kind of sexual trouble. He reminded me that he used to have me lie on his couch and try to picture a penis in my mind, try to imagine handling it or fondling it."

I looked at her quizzically.

"For what reason?" I asked.

"He wanted me to come face to face with my sexual feelings. He used to have me imagine other things. Like living on a desert island with him. Having sex with him."

I shook my head. "It sounds weird," I said.

"It's not weird. I couldn't feel anything at all then. He was the only person in the world I had any feeling for. And even still, when I imagined living on a desert island with him, I ended up imagining that I killed myself."

I had a sudden funny thought.

"How big a penis did he want you to imagine?" I asked.

"What do you mean?"

"I just had the thought of you lying on the couch imagining a giant penis. Like a zeppelin."

"Or a Goodyear blimp," she said.

I put my arm around her and pulled her toward me.

"And I told Dr. Sternfeld about our planning to get married," she said. "He thought it was a good idea."

"Who cares what he thinks?" I said.

"I don't understand."

"I mean who the hell is he? What is he, God? Omnipresent. Does he have to pass on our marriage? Fuck Dr. Sternfeld."

Marriage

On Christmas afternoon, 1966, in the midst of a blizzard, we were married at an elegant hotel on Manhattan's Central Park South. Janet wore a white brocade dress, white silk shoes, and a silly little white pancake hat. I wore a black mohair suit.

The rabbi who married us had unkempt black hair, startlingly black eyes, and a blue-black beard. Because he didn't "want to marry strangers," we met a week before the ceremony in his spotlessly clean study and discussed adolescence, civil rights, the mayor of New York City, and the existence of God.

Our marriage was a private ceremony, performed in a cluttered, airless hotel room.

At home, later that evening, I asked Janet whether she thought being married would change our relationship.

"I don't see why it should," she said. "It only gives us a piece of paper. That's all."

"Your father can come into our apartment now," I said. "He doesn't have to sit outside in the car and beep his horn. Our parents don't have to feel that we're living in sin."

"That has to do with them, not with us. I don't see how being married could really change our life."

"No, I don't see how either," I said. "I don't see how it can make us different at all."

And yet it did make us different. I swear it did.

Looking back at that first year of our marriage, I have trouble figuring out why or even how our life changed. We suddenly found ourselves drifting from moment to moment, without a sense of where we were going or what we were doing.

Our days settled snugly into a routine. We rose together at seven, shared a hurried cup of instant coffee, and went our separate ways, to work. We phoned each other at least twice a day, spent quiet weekday evenings at home, and on the weekends we slept late, cleaned the house, squabbled over who would do the laundry, and entertained ourselves.

One morning, while Janet teased her hair and put on makeup, I began bellowing about having no clean socks to wear. She was always in disgustingly good humor in the morning, bustling about the house with maddening efficiency and cheer. As I screamed about hating to wear dirty underwear, I saw her face begin to freeze. She sank down into our hard little sofa and held her head in her hands.

"Do you think I'm superwoman?" she said. "Do you think I can do just everything? Do you think I can work all day and cook dinner at night and keep the house clean and take responsibility for your laundry too? Well, I'm not superwoman. I'm not."

I laughed because she spoke cutely, as if she meant her words to be a joke. But I couldn't miss the seriousness in her voice and all morning I brooded about what she said.

At lunchtime I phoned to apologize for yelling at her. I asked her why she had never complained to me before about all the work she was doing.

"Well, I'm scared of you," she said.

"Scared of me? Me?"

"Well, I am. I'm afraid of displeasing you."

I was startled. "I don't want you to be frightened of me, Janet," I said. "At least I don't think I do."

There was such a long, heavy silence that I finally said, "Are you there, Janet?"

"Yeah, I'm here. I guess you don't want me to be scared of you. I've just had a lot of years of being frightened of people."

"But you don't have to be frightened of me."

"No. I guess I don't," she said.

Soon after we were married, Janet switched jobs, changing from a low-paid secretary in a mid-Manhattan real estate office to a low-paid secretary in an organization that designed college-level social-work education courses.

Although the atmosphere was more exciting, the work was similarly dismal, and she took pride in her stick-to-itiveness rather than in her skills, in her ability to work hard, to accomplish painstaking tasks, and to accept drudgery. Yet, after awhile, that sense of pride began to fade.

We didn't need the money. Her salary paid for her weekly visits to Dr. Sternfeld plus some extra that we banked. But she continued to drag herself to work out of a strange, unquestioned need, until she could no longer stand doing so.

"Why am I doing it?" she said to me one afternoon. "Why am I working at some job I can't stand when I don't even have to?"

PAUL

We were sitting in a Fifth Avenue bar. At five-thirty it was filled to capacity. The room had a raucous, driving ambiance; it was as if the patrons were having difficulty calming themselves down.

"I don't know," I said, feeling like a straight man. "Why are you doing it?"

"That's what I'm asking you. It's a serious question."

A gray-haired, whiskered waiter elbowed his way through the crowd around the bar and planted himself against our small table. We ordered two martinis. We had not been to a bar nor drunk martinis since that first month we had been together.

"I even know why," Janet said. "I'm still trying to prove that I'm well. But I don't have to prove anything anymore, do I? I am well."

"What would you like to do, Janet?"

"I don't know. I'd like to go back to school, I think."

"Then why don't you?"

I understood the complexity of what she was saying. I had done enough things in my life to prove something—to prove I was tough or brave or smart—to understand the obsessiveness of her drive to prove herself normal. But I also understood the futility. She couldn't make herself into something she wasn't; she was one thing, or she wasn't; trying to prove herself normal only made her feel unreal.

I fingered my collar as I listened to her speak. I wore a tie and jacket only to meet her in Manhattan. I didn't usually wear them to work.

"Are you happy with what you do?" she asked.

"I'm reasonably happy."

"Working in your father's business?"

"I said I'm reasonably happy. I don't love it all the time. But I have a good salary and independence."

"Then why do I have to love what I do?"

"You don't have to love it," I said. "Why are you arguing with me? I'm not the one who brought up the subject."

"I'm just trying to figure out why I feel as if I should continue to work. Why I feel quitting is some kind of cop-out. I don't know why anyone does what they don't want to do. I spent so many years being different from everyone else, not being able to do anything. Now I can function. And so what?"

I swallowed down most of my drink.

"I mean I don't feel anything has any purpose," she continued. "What's the point of doing anything?"

"A million dollar question," I said. "I can't give you an answer."

I could have told her that this was a question I had asked myself throughout my adolescence. But I didn't feel like telling her.

Marriage

Perhaps I should have asked her why she was first posing the question to herself.

"Why don't you do something you really want to do?" I finally said.

"Maybe I will go back to school," she said unenthusiastically. "Maybe I'll think about it."

I looked around the room. People came and people went and the same modish, gaudy atmosphere prevailed.

"It's a shitty, draggy world," she suddenly said.

"That's something of an overstatement," I said.

"Well that's the way I feel now."

We grew considerably closer that year. We had moments of incredible ecstasy and joy. Often we'd lie in bed at night, laughing at some silly joke, unable to go to sleep. We thought ourselves immensely fortunate; we were unquestionably well suited for each other and we were very much in love.

On Valentine's Day Janet bought me a pair of red flannel pajamas, made me a heart out of red construction paper, and wrote me a poem about her being a witch. I bought her a wooden Flexible Flyer sled. We trotted out together into the newly fallen snow. Just inside Prospect Park we slipped and tumbled down a little hill while padded, roly-poly children glided around us.

During the winter I often waited outside the subway station for Janet to come back from work. I sat in our white car, surrounded by a faded real estate office, a Spanish grocery store, a dingy luncheonette, and a laundromat. She came up the stairs, her orange tweed coat buttoned to her neck, the beige angora hat we bought on our honeymoon pulled over her ears, her cheeks flushed from the rush-hour crowd. I loved her more than I had ever imagined I could love anyone. And I knew that we were both very young.

And still, the closer we grew together, the more tightly the rest of our life seemed to bind around us.

In the spring of 1967, we ate dinner at Janet's parents' apartment. With the dishes stacked neatly in the sink, we sat around the kitchen table, finishing our coffee. Janet told her parents that she had decided to return to college and a strange, awkward silence hung over all of us.

"What does Dr. Sternfeld think about your going to school?" Janet's mother asked.

"He thinks it's okay," Janet said. "We haven't talked about it much. It has its dangers. But he's sure I can handle them."

"What kind of dangers?" Janet's father asked.

PAUL

I looked from one of my in-laws to the other. My mother-in-law was leaning forward, her elbows resting on the table, her chin resting on her hands. My father-in-law slumped backward in his chair.

"I've always had trouble in school," Janet said.

"You've always done quite well," her mother replied.

"I mean psychological trouble. I have complicated feelings toward school that I haven't worked out yet."

I walked across the kitchen and poured myself another cup of coffee from an electric percolator. A half-dozen *Time* magazines were neatly stacked on a nearby counter. I leafed through the top copy.

"Anybody else want coffee?" I asked.

"Do you think you ought to wait before you quit your job?" Janet's father asked.

"I'm not quitting just this minute," Janet said archly. "I gave two weeks notice. And then I'm taking a couple of courses in summer school."

"Does anyone want coffee?" I repeated.

"Do you think you ought to cut yourself off," Janet's father asked, "without having anything to do?"

"She's not cutting herself off," Janet's mother said. "Didn't you hear her? It's almost time to start summer school."

"I'll have another cup of coffee," Janet said.

When Janet went into the bathroom, I sat at the table again and faced my in-laws. They had not liked me at first; they had disapproved of me or they had been frightened of me. Their early dislike had left a scar on all of us, making our present relationship cool and awkward. At best, I was not at all what they wanted for a son-in-law. The more obvious they made their disappointment, the more perverse, sullen, and irreverent I became.

"Do you think it's a good idea for Janet to quit her job just now?" her father whispered to me.

"I don't see why not," I said.

"What does Jake Sternfeld say about it?"

"I don't know. I don't really talk to him."

They studied me coolly. I fiddled with my coffee cup.

"Janet will be okay," I said. "Going to school is what she wants to do. I don't see why you're so worried."

"We've had a lot of practice being worried," Janet's mother said.

"I know that," I said sympathetically. "I can understand it."

"We're used to worrying every time she makes any kind of a change in her life. It's difficult to stop."

Marriage

I nodded automatically. I did sympathize with them. Although I could not really understand their worry, I could empathize with their obvious confusion and pain.

"You don't know what it was like," Janet's mother said. "Always wondering what was going on in her head. She'd lie inside in her room and we'd sit out here and wonder, 'Is she thinking about cutting her wrists? Is she thinking about suicide?' "

"You don't have to worry now," I said.

"It's not easy just to turn off fear and worry, dear."

The bathroom door creaked and Janet walked into the kitchen, looking tense and tired.

"We were just talking about Tony and Emily Taylor," Janet's mother said. "Do you remember we all spent the summer together in 1949? Do you remember how much they loved you?"

In our car, going home later that evening, Janet was enraged. I took a sharp right turn at the Coney Island Avenue circle and went into the park. This was the long way home, but at night the overhanging, shadowy trees and surrounding meadows gave us an illusion of traveling through the country.

"I feel like I'm watched every time I go into their house," Janet said angrily. "I can't say anything without my mother's eyes boring into my face."

"You are watched," I said. "It's not your imagination."

"I can't stand it. How would you like to have someone constantly looking at you? What are they studying me for? Signs of what? Anxiety? Suicide?"

"It's hard for your parents to forget the past," I said.

"Tough. It's hard for me to forget it also. But I try."

I wheeled the car through the park. The roadway had been designed a long time ago, with curves and bumps in order to keep horses and wagons from racing too fast. I took a curve with too much speed and the tires screeched against the cement.

"I want to get out of here," Janet said.

"What do you mean?"

"I want to get away from everyone. From my parents. From your parents."

"Where do you want to go?"

"I don't know where I want to go."

"You can't run away from problems," I said.

"My brother ran away."

"Do you think your brother's happy?"

"I don't know whether he's happy or not. At least he's free."

"Do you really think he's free?"

"Whether he's free or not, he's away. And that's freedom of sorts."

On impulse I passed our exit by. The road was circular; in ten minutes we would reach it again.

"I just know," Janet continued, "that I worked at a boring, dismal job all year long and I heard everyone tell me how special it was that I could do the same tedious things that hundreds of thousands of other women could do too."

"What would you rather do?"

"I don't know what I'd rather do. But I don't like the way we've been living either."

"How would you rather live?"

"I don't know how," she screamed. "What do you want from me?"

"I don't want anything from you. I'm trying to understand what you're saying."

Her eyes were flashing angrily.

"I'll tell you what I'm saying. I'm saying that I'm tired of pretending that I'm something I'm not. I was sick once and I'm sick now and I'll be sick until I'm a wrinkled, gray-haired old lady tottering in to see Dr. Sternfeld, if I live that long, which I probably won't."

She was breathing hard. I was confused and a little frightened.

"You're not sick," I said.

"What am I, cured? Miraculously cured?" she said.

"That's what I'm told," I said.

"Well you can't believe everything you're told."

"What the hell brought this on, anyway?" I said. "You're not sick now. And you won't be sick again."

"Then why am I so unhappy?"

"I get unhappy sometimes, too. Since when is being unhappy a sickness?"

She began to cry.

"Since when is unhappiness a sickness?" I repeated.

She heaved a deep sigh and lay her head on my shoulder. My fingers dug into the steering wheel.

"I can't stand this tension," she finally said. "I can't stand the feeling that my parents are always watching me, waiting for me to prove that I'm finally normal and acceptable, that I'm not going to slide off into sickness again."

"It's not even their fault," I said. "Sometimes we fake things. We pretend to be what we're not. And they sense that something's wrong with us."

Marriage

She looked at me uncomprehendingly. I eased my foot off the gas pedal and coasted around a sharp curve.

Her parents were critics who disliked something and then intellectualized the reasons for their feelings later. They held an unclear vision of us in their heads, only the sense that something was wrong with us, that we didn't quite match up to what they expected or wanted. But they were hardly different from most parents; certainly no different from my own.

"Why do you keep calling yourself sick?" I asked Janet.

"What am I supposed to call myself? Pixilated?"

I lay in bed later, unable to sleep. The evening had shaken me up. Next to me, Janet snored lightly. I touched her back and she stirred, whipped up her head and then threw it back on the bed. I stroked her hair, leaning on my elbow and staring off into our dark, cluttered living room.

Her outburst had upset and frightened me. I couldn't make much sense out of it then. It was only a long time later, after many dreary, desperate nights, that I was able to understand what her anger and emotion were all about.

I've often told myself that if we had been able to make it through that first year of marriage, our life might have turned out differently. What we had been trying to do that year was to hammer out a life that was conventional, acceptable, and yet exclusively our own, that pleased our parents and yet ultimately pleased ourselves. I don't know what compromise we would have made with our aspirations, our visions, and our dreams, or whether our life would have been any worse than it is now. But we couldn't compromise at all. That was the point. Janet had experienced too much and had suffered too much to compromise any part of herself. I could have made peace with what we felt was expected of us. But she could not settle for anything less than living her life the way she wanted to live it. Her struggle for personal fulfillment was literally a matter of life and death. Although she did not yet know it, the consequence of dishonesty, deceit, and compromise was severe.

In May, Janet stumbled upon an old razor blade that she had hidden a long time before in the pocket of a forgotten pair of jeans. Holding the blade in its red sheath, she demonstrated how she used to cut her wrists. For some reason, I expected her strokes to be tentative and dainty but they were not. Instead, they were as carefully controlled, as meticulously concentrated as Janet's small, painstaking handwriting.

Until that moment I had never perceived the depth of her feelings. I had seen her startling capacity for joy, of course, but I had never guessed at the explosively dark forces inside of her. I was suddenly brought closer to something more terrifying than I really cared to see, something I would unfortunately see again.

"How could you do it to yourself?" I asked.

"It made me feel good," she said nonchalantly.

"While you were doing it?"

"No, afterward. But strangely enough, as bad as the pain was, it never felt real. It never felt like my own arm."

"I thought you'd be more tentative," I said.

"It's not easy to cut yourself," she answered. "It takes real strength, concentration, and skill. Especially if you want to cut into a vein, to kill yourself. Take it from me. I was an expert."

Her voice was bland and toneless.

"Did you ever see your face when you cut your wrists?" I asked.

"Why?"

"Just your little demonstration was terrifying to see. You looked ice cold and unreal, as if you were possessed."

She stared at me blankly.

"I can understand a lot of things," I said. "Pain. Despair. Not wanting to live anymore. But I can't understand why anyone would want to cut themselves up."

"There's nothing to understand. It felt good."

But I knew she wasn't telling me the truth. She was playing a role with me, purposely being cool and perverse.

I don't think either of us understood ourselves very well, understood the drives and impulses bubbling inside ourselves. In Janet's case, the result of this lack of understanding was catastrophic.

Breakdown

Janet's breakdown came during the summer of 1967, although the signs of it must have been present for a much longer time. And yet where is the line between stress or pressure and breaking down? When do tears become signs of helplessness and desperation, or fear and worry become anxiety? There was no traumatic moment to pinpoint that summer, no glaring symptom, no episode to push her over the so-called edge of sanity.

From one point of view, she had never really shaken off all the scars of her years of misery. Despite all the talk of miracles and cures she was no different this year than she had been the year before. Her problems were the same. Love, the giving and taking of love, had held her together for a time. It would have been nicer if love had been able to hold her together for a longer time. But love was certainly no substitute for strength, confidence, and awareness.

She slid into her misery and pain as smoothly as she had slid into her fine spirits and even now, it is still not apparent why, or even how, it happened.

We rented a small cabin for the summer, just outside a village called Arlington Falls, only sixty-five miles north of New York City. We used the cabin only on weekends, until my two-week vacation at the end of August. For most of the summer Janet attended summer school.

On a Saturday afternoon in the middle of July, Janet sat crosslegged in the grass outside our front door, writing in a spiral notebook. Standing in the doorway, I looked past her, across the long sloping meadow, to the dense woods that surrounded the property. Off to one side, hidden by a rolling hill, I could just about make out the white and red-edged house which belonged to the Blooms, the strange hermitlike people who owned the land.

I came up quietly behind Janet, but she heard my footsteps and lay back on the grass, squinting up at me.

"What are you writing?" I asked.

"A letter to my brother. I want to tell him what's happened to me in the ten years since I've seen him."

PAUL

"How I survived my nervous breakdown?" I said. "My life in a looney bin?"

She didn't find me funny.

"I just want to tell him about you," she said. "About how happy I am now. How much I still love him."

For talking about happiness, she seemed uncommonly grim.

"Can I read it?" I asked.

"Sure, I'd like you to. But after I finish it; I'm not even sure I want to send it."

She left the notebook lying on the grass. It stayed there throughout the night so that the next morning when I picked it up again, the pages were wet with dew and much of the ink had smudged and run. I wanted to talk about her letter that same afternoon, but it was much later, in the middle of the night, that we finally had the opportunity to discuss it.

I had woken up out of a deep sleep with a frightened start. I lay quietly on my back listening to my own deep breathing. Overhead, I heard a scratching and scurrying noise, the sound an animal makes as it skitters across the roof.

"Are you awake?" Janet asked.

"What are you doing up?"

"I was listening to the animal."

For a while we lay silently.

"Should I finish the letter to my brother?" she asked.

"Have you been lying here thinking about it?"

"My mind is racing with all kinds of thoughts. I was thinking about my past. I can't even remember when my brother left. I can remember the whole awful year when he fought constantly with my parents. But not when he decided he wanted no more part of them."

"Is it so important to remember?"

"He was the most important person in my life. I worshipped him. I would have done anything he asked me to do."

"Then I suppose you should write to him. You have nothing to lose."

"I'm very frightened, though."

There was a thud overhead and the furious scratching of two animals chasing each other across the roof.

"The call of the wild," I said.

"So it seems."

"We should go to sleep," I said.

"I won't sleep tonight."

"What do you mean?"

"I'm too keyed up."

Breakdown

"You'll sleep."

In a few minutes Janet was dozing. I couldn't fall back to sleep. I buzzed with a dull, restless anxiety. I felt like a child again, frightened of whatever demons lay in the darkness of my mind. Something I had seen in Janet was upsetting me. A premonition perhaps, a glimpse of something coming apart inside her. I knew that something was soon to go wrong, and yet I didn't know how I knew. I translated my instincts into nightmarish infantile fear and I couldn't trust it.

As I tossed in bed, Janet suddenly woke up.

"See, I told you I wouldn't go to sleep," she said.

"You were sleeping."

"Oh."

"Did you ever have nightmares as a child?" I asked. "Did you ever have to sleep with a light on?"

"I wasn't allowed nightmares," she mumbled. "My parents wouldn't admit I had them."

"What do you mean?"

"Ask me in the morning." Her voice trailed off and I could tell by her breathing that she was again asleep. I lay awake for awhile and then I fell asleep myself.

In the bright glare of the morning I forgot to ask her about nightmares and I forgot about my own middle-of-the-night fears.

She did finish writing the letter to her brother, although she struggled with the words for a few weeks. It was a gracious, loving letter that told him about her marriage, her years of pain, her new feeling of life, and how much she loved him and wanted to see him.

"Do you think he'll answer me?" We were sitting on the front steps of our Brooklyn house.

"I hope he does," I said.

The sun was bright. It was a sultry, muggy day.

"Then I should mail it?"

"That's up to you."

"No it's not."

"Who is it up to?"

She was silent for a moment.

"I showed the letter to Dr. Sternfeld before I gave it to you. I asked him whether I should mail it."

"What did he say?"

"He said it was up to me."

"That's what I said also. And he knows better than I do."

"The hell he does," she said haughtily. But then she laughed. She saw Dr. Sternfeld on a steady, once-a-week schedule. Although they had practically discontinued therapy—he saw no reason to dig into feelings or problems that caused her no real pain—they couldn't leave each other. At thirty-five dollars a shot, they discussed questions of day-to-day living on a friendly, halfhearted level as if they were still tangled together by the ferocious intimacy of the past, unable or unwilling to give up their relationship.

"Are you angry because I showed him the letter before you?" she asked. "You're not jealous of my psychiatrist, are you?"

"Why should I be?" I said. "I've replaced him in your affections haven't I?"

At the end of August we went to Arlington Falls for our two-week vacation. Our first week was quiet and uneventful. We slept late, read, sunbathed, waded in a nearby stream, and threw together haphazard easy meals. But we were stiff with each other, like newlyweds. I kept wanting to ask Janet what was wrong with her, what she was thinking, but somehow I couldn't.

We were marking time that week, waiting for something, good or bad, to happen. And something did happen.

One afternoon we were talking to Mr. Bloom. He was a middle-aged man with pasty skin, soft features, and wisps of hair that curled on the top of his bald head like corkscrews. He had been a music teacher in New York City and his fidgety arms were always moving as if he was forever trying to lead recalcitrant youngsters in a version of "Bless This House."

Like most people, he took a liking to Janet. When he offered to show us his homemade collection of stuffed lifelike animals, we felt we couldn't refuse. We followed him into a small cramped studio attached to the side of his colonial house. He snapped on an overhead light, waved his restless arms at a long dusty table, and stepped back with pride.

On the table, placed neatly in a row, were a series of posed animals: a squirrel climbing a piece of driftwood, an owl perched on a shellacked branch, a red fox frozen in flight. The appearance of tension in their muscles, the pull of their tendons, clashed with the aura of lifelessness that was so apparent in their beady marble eyes. Janet, standing next to me, noticeably stiffened.

"It must be difficult to make them," Janet said conversationally. I looked at her strangely.

"There are tricks to it," Mr. Bloom answered. "Like anything else. Chemicals to treat the fur. The aim is to make them look as lifelike as possible."

Breakdown

He held the squirrel out to us.

"This is my favorite," he said. "The amount of work I put into it is fantastic. The more hours you spend the more artless and simple it looks."

I reached out my hand to hold the animal but I hesitated. The squirrel was heavier than I expected; its fur was brittle and hard. I found it ghastly, a vision of death rather than life.

"How long have you been doing this?" I asked.

He smiled sadly. "Ever since I was a kid. I've always loved animals. As I've always loved life."

"You love life?" Janet blurted out.

"Look at this," he said. He took the squirrel out of my hands and settled it into its place on the table. He rubbed his restless hands together.

"You have to look at the details. The illusion of motion. The straining muscles." He shook his head sadly. "I dare say, you have to love life."

In our cabin, a short time later, Janet grimaced.

"I'm going to have nightmares tonight."

"I know what you mean."

"I'm not kidding. I used to hallucinate things like that."

She shuddered and added angrily, "Look at what he does. And they called me crazy."

"What does being crazy have to do with what he does?"

"It's a sick thing to do to animals."

She went to the bathroom. I could hear her rattling the medicine bottles. Because the summer had been oddly disquieting for her, she was taking two Libriums as a regular dosage and was allowed two more if she needed them. This was already her second of the day.

In the evening we went to the movies. The movie theater was a modern glass and white stone building in the middle of a tawdry little shopping center. The movie was *Bonnie and Clyde*.

On this Saturday evening the theater was packed. We sat in the second row, almost on top of the screen. I slipped my arm around Janet's back and she wriggled closer to me. But her muscles were tight and just touching her made me tense and frightened.

I couldn't concentrate on the screen. My mind was racing with memories of the past few months, filled with images of Janet's moodiness and with thoughts of my own unshakeable dread. In the flickering gloom the Barrow gang was plundering its way through grim, Depression America, but from my angle of view all I could see was the slant of Warren Beatty's handsome jaw and the slope of

PAUL

Faye Dunaway's elegant nostrils. I moved in and out of a mindless reverie until I was suddenly startled by the ferocity of the film's violence.

On the screen, Gene Hackman had been shot in the head. As he clawed at his face, blood pouring through his fingers and leaking down his arm, I looked at Janet. I couldn't understand at first why the blankness of her face so terrified me. There was something eerie and familiar in the petrified cast of her muscles. She wore the same frightful death-mask expression as Mr. Bloom's stuffed animals.

"Are you all right?" I asked.

She began to cry hysterically and I pulled her from her seat and half dragged her outside.

Sitting in our car, Janet continued to cry.

"I can't stand it," she sobbed.

"I don't understand."

"I feel like I'm nothing. I feel like I'm just shit. I can't pretend anymore."

"Pretend what?"

"I can't pretend that I'm anything more than a piece of shit. I can't pretend that I'll ever make it in this world because I won't. I can't."

Her words tumbled out in a fearsome torrent of anger and bitterness. There was no check or limit on her emotions. I just wanted to calm her down and finally she let me hold her and soothe her.

In the cabin, we sat at the kitchen table.

"Are you okay now?" I asked.

She nodded wearily. "I'm still shaken up. But I feel a little bit better."

"What happened?"

"Welcome to a full-scale anxiety attack," she said sarcastically. "I was sitting in the theater and all I could think of were those damn stuffed animals. And then with all the blood in that movie, it suddenly seemed as if it was my own blood. I saw waves of blood flooding all over me."

She shuddered and I automatically stood up and walked over to her. She held up her hand to stop me.

"Don't pity me," she said angrily. "I can't stand people pitying me."

"I don't pity you, Janet. Pity has nothing to do with the way I feel about you."

She looked at me with mistrust.

"I understand something about unhappiness and about pressure,"

I continued. "I sympathize with you. It's been a difficult summer."

She shook her head. "That's not why I feel as bad as I do."

"Then why?"

"I don't know why. Because I'm not a person. That's why. I'm a nothing."

"That's not true," I said.

She turned away from me looking into the darkness of the living room. Helplessly, I stared at her profile.

"Should I take another Librium?" she asked.

"Sure. Why not?"

"I already took the two extra I'm allowed. You think it's okay to take another?"

"I think you should if you need it."

"That's the way I feel also. I'm going to be very sleepy because I just took a pill, before we went to the movies."

"Take it, Janet," I said. "If it's going to make you feel better."

I watched her move away, to the bathroom. In her billowing chemise dress she looked huddled together, childlike and vulnerable. She was gone a long time and I began to worry, thinking about pill bottles and razor blades. But I sat where I was. I wasn't going to look after her.

When she returned to the kitchen she seemed more like herself. She had washed her face and combed her hair. Her eyes were still swollen from crying.

"Should I call Dr. Sternfeld?" she asked me. "Should I tell him what just happened?"

"I don't know," I said. "You know better than I do."

She ran her fingers through her short hair.

"On one hand I think I should call him," she said. "That he should know about this anxiety attack. But I also think it would be better if I got through this episode without him."

"Would you feel better calling him?"

"I don't know what he could do for me," she said.

I walked to the sink for a glass of water. The tap groaned and sputtered like a man's last breath.

"Would he mind if you called him?" I asked.

"He wouldn't exactly mind. He might think though that I should handle things myself."

"What do you think?"

"I think I should do it myself." She flattened her hair against her forehead and then ruffled it up again. "I think I should deal with myself without his help."

"I think so also," I said. I was affected by what I thought to be courage on her part. "You're a different person than you used to be. I'm sure you can handle yourself better than you used to."

She shrugged and then yawned. Her eyes were hooded and cloudy.

"You look drained," I said.

"I am," she answered. "I suppose I should get myself into bed. Sleep it off, so to speak."

She stood up.

"You'll be okay," I said.

"I know I will," she said, without any conviction. "After a good night's sleep."

I was awake long after she had fallen into her deep drugged sleep. I lay in bed next to her, with a paperback in my hands. But the book was a prop; I couldn't read it.

I thought about Janet, trying to make sense out of her recent outbursts of emotion. Even in my own worst despair I always knew that I could touch my own unhappiness and pain, that I had control of it and knew its boundaries and limits. Janet's explosive outbursts had a depth and quality that went beyond anything I had ever seen.

Her emotions were naked and limitless. Watching them spill out of her was terrifying, like peeking into some dark secret corner. What was most frightening was that they emerged suddenly, out of no place in particular and disappeared just as unexpectedly, elusive and inexplicable. I didn't think then of Janet as being mad or sick. I watched her pain and suffering and simply wondered what was going on inside her.

During the next week we adjusted to tension and pressure as best we could. Janet's decision not to call Dr. Sternfeld seemed to bring us closer together. We felt as if we were working toward a common end to get through a period of pain and despair by ourselves. And yet beneath everything we did was an undercurrent of terror that came out as explosively and unexpectedly as Janet's tears.

One day, after we had been wading in the stream that ran through the woods in back of our house, she suddenly began to cry. I held her against me until she stopped.

"I almost forgot how bad I felt," she said.

"I don't understand how you feel."

"It's difficult to explain. It's like a dull empty pain somewhere deep inside me, where I can't touch it. It's always with me. When I forget about it, like I did a few minutes ago, it comes back to me suddenly. And I can't keep myself from crying."

We wandered through the edge of the woods until we came to a large boulder that reminded us of the one we had sat on last summer when we had first met.

"Do you remember that first morning?" I asked.

"Of course I remember it. It was the happiest moment of my life. It was like something out of the movies. I had already fallen so in love with you that I could hear strings and bells and somebody singing 'Love Is A Many Splendored Thing.' "

"I wasn't sure how I felt about you."

"I knew that," she said sadly.

"But I grew to care for you very much."

She suddenly turned away. "I don't see how you could."

"Because I know you now."

"No, you don't know me. You don't know what's inside of me."

"Yes I do, Janet."

She faced me again and I held her in my arms.

"I don't know why I can't be one of those women who remain pretty when they cry," she said. "Instead of having swollen eyes and a red nose."

We returned to Brooklyn in the evening. I lugged the suitcases into the bedroom and laid them on the thick tweed carpeting.

"I want to call Dr. Sternfeld," Janet said.

"Do you want to be alone?" I asked.

She nodded and I ambled into the living room, closing the flimsy louvered doors behind me. I sat on our hard orange couch and listened to the murmur of Janet's voice and her occasional sniffles and sobs. When she came out of the bedroom, her eyes were swollen from crying.

"He wants me to see him first thing tomorrow morning," she said. Her voice was cold and toneless. Her face had lost its color.

"What did he say?"

"He said I should have called him earlier."

"Why?" I asked. I was startled. All my convictions about courage were dissolving. I felt embarrassed and upset, as if I, too, had made a mistake.

"He doesn't want me to play doctor," she said evenly. "And he doesn't want me to be a hero. He was very angry because I didn't call him when I first got the anxiety attack. He said that he's the doctor. He's the one who should determine what I should do."

We stood on either end of the couch, separated by squares of tweed carpeting.

"How do you feel now?" I asked.

"Just awful. How am I supposed to feel?"

"Does he want you to do anything special?"

"He increased my medication. He wants me to double up to make sure I'll get a good night's sleep."

I nodded thoughtlessly. "Was he really mad?"

"He was angry," she said. "He didn't want me to let an anxiety attack build up into . . ."

Her voice trailed away.

"Into what?" I pressed her.

She ignored me, pushing past me to get to the bathroom.

I went into the hallway for the mail. Stuffed between bills, envelopes of coupons, sales brochures, and supermarket newspapers, were two postcards from Brooklyn College. Janet had received A's in both her courses.

Shock Treatments

"*I want—*" Janet started to say.

I lowered my newspaper. It was a Sunday morning in early October and we were just finishing breakfast.

"I've been thinking about it for a couple of days," she said.

"What are you talking about?" I asked, annoyed that she had interrupted my reading.

"I want shock treatments," she said.

"Shock treatments?"

"I've been thinking about it. I don't want to go through all those years of torture and agony again. If shock treatments can lift me out of this episode of anxiety, then . . ."

She spread her hands out helplessly.

"I thought you hated them," I said.

"I do hate them. And I'm deathly afraid."

"Then why in hell would you want to go through it again?"

"Because I don't know what else to do. I don't know whether I'm going to have them or not. I'm only going to ask Dr. Sternfeld what he thinks."

"I just don't see how you can say you want shock treatments," I said.

She stared at me coldly.

"Because I don't think you understand how truly awful I've been feeling."

Sitting in Dr. Sternfeld's office a few days later he said the same thing to me. He leaned forward in his swivel chair, fixed me with a penetrating stare, and said very solemnly, "I don't know if you understand how awful Janet's been feeling since the end of the summer."

"I think I understand," I said. "I live with her, after all."

"In here, I mean," he said, making a waving motion over his head. "Not on the surface. But how she feels in her head. Where it counts."

Dr. Sternfeld had recently trimmed his hair but he had kept his bristly mustache so that he now looked bookish, tweedy, and kindly, a classic psychiatrist, like Howard Da Silva in *David and Lisa*.

"I only know what I see on the surface," I said. "And that's awful enough. All the pain and tears."

"Yes, but there's a process going on inside her brain," Dr. Sternfeld said. "What you see is only the tip of the iceberg. Only the surface behavior and not the assumptions behind it. The trick is to reach inside her." He made a dipping motion with his hand. "And shake up her way of thinking. Joggle her old patterns of dealing with the world before they settle in."

Janet shifted her weight. We were sitting side by side, both of us perched on the edge of his couch. I had just been invited into the office. For the past half hour I had sat in the waiting room, hearing, between the breaks in the easy listening music, the muffled sound of Janet's gasps and sobs.

"I don't like to use something as extreme as shock treatments," Dr. Sternfeld continued. "I hope you know that. It was Janet who suggested it to me and I'm afraid I have to go along with her thinking. We're hoping that the treatments will lift her out of this episode. We can do it the slow way of course, through psychoanalysis. But those anxiety attacks are draining her of all her resources and confidence. She feels depressed and worthless, unable to function, unable to deal with her feelings. I'd like to load her up and see if we can lift her out of this state of mind, if you know what I mean."

I nodded as if I did know what he meant, a habit of mine. But I didn't understand what he was talking about. In a state of tension and confusion myself, I felt as if his barrage of words was bouncing off my brain.

"Why did all this happen?" I asked him.

"Why did she get sick again?" He swiveled back and forth. "I don't really know."

We stared blankly at each other. He sucked in his lips and rubbed his chin.

"I can give you theories, of course," he said. "That's all we have in my business. The letter to her brother certainly was a big contributing factor. But unfortunately we have no traumatic event to pin this episode on. I think I once told you that I didn't expect her to get sick again. But knowing Janet as I do through the years I'm not really surprised it happened."

Janet began to cry and I put my arm around her, holding her tightly against me.

Shock Treatments

"The only question now," Dr. Sternfeld continued, "is how long this episode is going to last. I don't like to make predictions, as Janet knows, but I don't think it will go on too long. You can't ever take away the resources she's built up over this past year."

Janet took a tissue out of her purse and began dabbing at her eyes. Dr. Sternfeld fumbled with the pocket of his white shirt.

"Do you have a cigarette?" he asked me. "I've been grubbing from Janet all session long."

I handed him a cigarette and he held out his hand for a match. He lit the cigarette, dragged deeply, and leaned back in his chair.

"But I wanted to talk to you about shock treatments," he said to me. "Do you know anything about them?"

I shook my head.

"I didn't think you did," he said. "I'm certain that the thought of Janet having treatments frightens you. But I wanted to assure you that there isn't the slightest danger involved."

"I've heard stories about brain damage," I said.

He shook his head. "I'm very conservative, as Janet can tell you. I've given her many, many treatments over the years. If there was even the slightest possibility of brain damage I wouldn't have risked it."

"What I don't like," I said, "is the idea of running an electric current through Janet's body."

"Interestingly enough it's not the surge of electricity that has any effect on her, but the convulsions caused by the electric shock. Electroshock therapy was discovered accidentally, while working with epileptics. But I understand what worries you. I can only assure you that the amount of electricity used is quite small."

"How does it work?" I asked.

"The treatments?" He smiled. "Nobody really knows. We have theories . . ." He shrugged. "But I don't think anyone can tell you with any certainty how anything really works on the brain."

"You said there are no side effects."

"I didn't say no side effects. I said no danger. She'll come out of each treatment with a terrible headache. And more seriously, she'll suffer a certain amount of memory loss."

"What kind of memory loss?" I asked, suddenly concerned.

He chuckled. "You'll find it more disquieting than serious. It's only a short-term memory loss with no real pattern to it. Every person is different. She might forget your name for a short while or forget when you were married or what movie you both saw the night before. And yet she might remember every detail of a dinner you ate two months ago." He laughed. "It's all perfectly normal. The farther she gets from each treatment, the more this memory loss begins to fade."

He looked at his watch.

"We only have a few minutes remaining," he said, "and I'd like to work out the details of the shock treatments. As I told Janet, I would only give them to her as an outpatient and, fortunately, Monroe Park, which has her records, also has such outpatient facilities."

We decided on the date of the first treatment, made arrangements for a Dr. Lessing to administer them, and talked about how many treatments she would need.

"I see only twelve, or at the absolute most, sixteen treatments," Dr. Sternfeld said. "After that they'd lose their effectiveness. Either they're going to bounce her out of this state of mind quickly or they won't work at all."

Janet began to cry and he put his arm around her, pulling her shoulder against his chest. There was an odd primness to the way he held her, like the rigid embrace of a prostitute, mechanical, businesslike, yet charged with the uncontrollable mystery of a profoundly fervent act. From stories Janet had told me I knew that his gesture had great meaning and significance but I couldn't guess at that meaning by looking at him.

Without thinking, I edged myself away from Dr. Sternfeld and Janet, sliding through the open office door into the hallway. From the second floor I could hear the muted sound of a family squabble.

"I never thought I'd need treatments again," Janet said.

"That's always been one of your problems," Dr. Sternfeld answered. "You block out the possibility of something bad happening so it comes as a devastating shock to you. I've warned you about your vulnerability. You know how to be sick, after all."

"But you also told me I wouldn't get sick again," she said peevishly.

For a moment I had a fleeting glimpse of weariness and distress in Dr. Sternfeld's eyes. For a moment his shell seemed to fall away, and beyond the clutter of his pomposity and style, I saw wounds and terrors and immense sadness. But I made a conscious effort to ignore what I saw. We were marching my wife off to the vagaries of an electroshock machine. I very badly wanted to believe in his infallibility.

"I didn't promise you that you wouldn't get sick again," he said to Janet, "or that you wouldn't ever need help. I only told you what I thought. I'm sorry that you have to go through all this pain." He looked up a flight of wooden stairs, into the darkness of his second-floor landing. Upstairs a little girl was wailing. "But I'm not surprised that you're having so much trouble. We have a lot of serious problems to work out in the future."

Janet and I walked outside into a bright, crisp fall afternoon. A blustery wind blew brown and red leaves off the trees; the leaves swirled around us like frail living creatures. We lingered at the door to our car.

"You were strangely quiet," I said to Janet.

A white ice cream truck roared past us, a relic of another season.

"I didn't have anything to say. I was all talked out by the time you came into the office. I didn't want to talk about shock treatments anymore."

"Are you changing your mind about wanting them?"

"Why should I change my mind?"

"People do change their minds," I said.

"Don't you want me to have them?"

"It's not my business, is it? But they frighten me."

"They frighten me also. And I'm the one having them."

"That's true," I said blandly.

"And they probably won't even do any good."

"What do you mean?"

"I mean they never worked in the past. I see no reason why they should work now."

"Then why did you ask Dr. Sternfeld for them?"

"I must have been crazy," she said.

"What kind of answer is that? I certainly don't want you to have them."

"Well, I'm the crazy one. What's your excuse?"

She opened the car door and started to slide into the passenger seat.

"That's not fair, Janet," I said. "You're the one who knows what she's doing. I don't know anything."

She looked up at me expressionlessly.

"Maybe you don't know," she said. "But it's a hell of a thing to depend on what a crazy person knows."

I started to argue with her, but changed my mind. I walked around the car and seated myself behind the wheel.

"You're just nervous," I said.

"That's a weak-kneed way of putting it."

"Scared shitless?" I offered.

She smiled. "You would be scared also."

"I told you, I am frightened."

"But you don't even know what to be frightened about," she said.

"That's true."

"Then why are you arguing with me?"

"I'm not arguing with you."

"You're telling me I shouldn't be frightened."

I started the motor.

"I'm not telling you anything of the sort," I said. "Do you think I'm Dr. Sternfeld? If you don't want shock treatments you shouldn't have them."

"It's too late now."

"It's never too late."

Her eyes clouded and the muscles around her mouth tensed. She started to say something and then stopped herself. Her lips were tightened together as if she was holding in some raging storm of bitterness and anger. Finally she just shook her head and said, "Oh, fuck it."

I inherited Oscar Lessing, the shock-treatment doctor, from my father-in-law.

"Any intern can press the button," Dr. Sternfeld had told me. "You can just as well use whoever Monroe Park has on call. But the first time Janet had shock treatments her father felt that he wanted someone prominent. And he had heard good things about Dr. Lessing, so he was our man."

At thirty dollars per electric charge (not to mention twenty-two-fifty for the use of the hospital room), we signed him on.

As I followed Lessing down the corridors of Monroe Park, his elegant gray suit flapping like hung laundry, his elbows churning and twisting, ragged sheets of paper fluttering beneath his arm, I had to resist the impulse to laugh at him. He could have come out of Dickens, a few comic characteristics bound together into a human being. But like the best of Dickens, he was essentially not funny at all.

I didn't actually meet Dr. Lessing until the middle of November, one month after Janet started treatments. He found me in the waiting room on the second floor of Monroe Park, introduced himself, gestured toward an exit door and took off down a long corridor. I hurried after him.

"It's hard to find an unoccupied conference room," he said over his shoulder. He spoke stiffly.

"Too many doctors?" I offered.

"Too many patients," he said.

We settled into a cramped, windowless office. He dumped a

shabby folder of papers onto a desk top and lowered himself into a swivel chair. I pulled up a straight-back chair across from him.

"I have her file right here," he said, scattering the papers with his long bony fingers. He held up a tattered piece of paper triumphantly. "She has had seven treatments, no?"

"Seven treatments," I repeated.

"I have to confer with Dr. Sternfeld, of course. I think she'll need more. We had planned on at least sixteen, no?"

"I thought we had planned on a minimum of only twelve," I said.

He seemed disturbed by my statement. He studied his sheet of paper thoughtfully. An old coffee stain was spread over the paper like an ink-blot test.

"Is that my wife's record?" I asked.

"This is part of her record." He swooped through more papers. "I have her past history here somewhere, too."

All the time we talked his head was bobbing up and down like a stork.

"I will confer with Dr. Sternfeld later this afternoon," he said. "After only seven treatments I'm afraid we can't judge how many more she'll need."

"She seems very out of touch with things," I said.

"Very confused, no? That's normal."

"It's more than confused," I said. "Out of things. Almost in her own world."

He looked at me uncomprehendingly. His thin face was pained, like a man who well understood suffering. But God knows whose suffering he comprehended. I didn't think it was Janet's or my own.

"She should be confused and forgetful," he said. "That is quite normal."

He intimidated me. Or perhaps this frightening world of electro-shock treatments intimidated me. I felt alienated from the room, an unreal husband talking to an unreal doctor about his unreal wife.

He began to gather up his papers, stuffing them sloppily into his file folder.

"I suppose I ought to ask you how my wife is doing," I said.

"Your wife is doing quite well," he answered. "It is much too early to tell how successful we are. I will talk to Dr. Sternfeld later and perhaps he can give you more information."

He stood up and held out his bony hand. His papers, jammed beneath his other arm, fluttered precariously.

"It is unfortunate I have another conference," he said, slipping past me, out the door. "We will talk again."

I hurried back to the waiting room. I was afraid that Janet would be frightened if she came up from the basement treatment room and found me gone.

The waiting area of the outpatient clinic shared its space with the men's medical ward. Separated from the ward by only a partition of metal chairs, I could watch shuffling old men in hospital gowns and bedroom slippers and young men in brightly colored bathrobes pacing across their section of the large square room or lounging in worn easy chairs. In my own uncertain, unstable world they were reassuringly constant, always in the same place doing the same thing, and I began to look forward to seeing them. But not once during all the months I came to Monroe Park, did any of them ever look back at me. They smoked their cigarettes, chatted together and read their newspapers within a goldfish bowl but, rather pitifully, they insisted on pretending that the bowl didn't exist at all.

This divided room, half in the hospital, half out, mirrored my own divided mind. I waited two mornings a week in this second-floor half-world feeling as if I had entered some bleak, outreaching terminal sphere. I was both in the middle of life, working, socializing, and I was out of it, sucked into an atmosphere of isolation, sickness, and grief.

So, when I finished my conference with Dr. Lessing, and hustled back into the waiting room, I felt a buzzing anxiety in my stomach as if I no longer had any safe solid ground on which to stand.

Janet had not yet come upstairs. Only a few people sat in the waiting room's rows of metal chairs—a boozy, middle aged, red-haired woman, a young nun, and a bald-headed man who was sleeping with his mouth open. I considered these people, these transient shock-treatment patients and their families and friends to be seedy and unfortunate. With blind, self-protective snobbery, I thought of Janet as special, somehow outside their circle.

I walked over to a large coffee urn, pressed the spigot and filled up a styrofoam container with murky, undrinkable liquid. I took a back row seat, gazing across the room at the inpatients.

I was reading *Tender Is the Night*, about the expatriate psychiatrist and his complicated, ambiguous, sacrificial marriage to one of his patients. Although I loved Fitzgerald, particularly the abstract romanticism of *The Great Gatsby*, I had never read this novel. Nor had I then known how much of it was based on Fitzgerald's relationship with Zelda, his own wife. I found the book disturbing; I suppose I identified with it. It was not until many years later that I actually finished it.

I picked up the book now, but before I could open the pages, Janet came upstairs. She shuffled in from the elevator, part of a group of wobbly, disheveled women. A young aide led the group to the desk so that they could be signed out. I met her at the front of the room.

"Do you want a container of coffee?" I asked.

She shook her head. Her hair was matted against the sides of her skull; the bosom of her blue paisley dress was stained with saliva; on her temples were remnants of the gray, pasty conducting cream and deep scratches that were caused by the abrasiveness of the metal electrodes.

"I'd like some aspirins," she said to me. "I have a splitting headache."

"What's our license plate number?" I asked. This was a private joke between us, a regular test of her memory.

She smiled, "5241KD."

Riding down in the elevator I asked her if she wanted to stop for breakfast.

"I want to go home and I want to go to sleep," she said. "Can't I just have a couple of aspirins?"

"When we get home," I answered. She was not allowed any medication until two hours after the treatment.

At the lobby's glass exit door I held her by her arm and buttoned up her tweed coat. Through the door we watched people pass, bundled up in their heavy clothing. The weather was ferocious, frigid, with a raging wind.

"Where's the car?" she asked.

"On the corner."

We walked huddled together against the wind. I held her tightly, feeling only the padding of her heavy coat.

When Janet and I reached the car she passed it by and began to turn the corner. I pulled her back.

"Is that our car?" she asked.

"That's it," I said.

She flashed me a foggy, idiot's smile.

That same inscrutable smile remained on her face for most of our ride home. She stared straight ahead, off in her own dreamy world. As we drove across the Brooklyn Bridge she started to say something, but a blank quizzical expression came across her features, as if she had suddenly forgotten what she wanted to tell me.

"What is it, Janet?" I asked.

She continued to gaze out the front window.

"I don't remember," she said.

"Janet," I said, after a few moments of silence.

PAUL

"What?"

"What did you want to say?"

She ignored my question.

"Janet," I repeated.

"What?"

"You wanted to say something."

"Did I?"

"You did."

She wrinkled up her brow.

"Oh. I was going to tell you about Dr. Lessing."

"What about Dr. Lessing?" I asked after more silence. "You were telling me about Dr. Lessing."

"Was I?"

"Janet. For God's sake what's wrong with you?"

She finally looked at me, crinkling up her nose.

"There's nothing wrong."

"You're goddamn far away," I said.

I looked across at Janet. I wasn't really surprised at her foggy state of mind. This was her regular reaction to a shock treatment. The first month of treatments had followed a pattern, her Monday treatment melting into her Wednesday treatment, the fuzziness of her Wednesday treatment slowly fading away until, by the weekend, the first vague throb of anxiety began fluttering in her belly.

Her fogginess, although giving us both some peace, was creeping under my skin. In the bizarre erratic mental illness world that I had just entered I was most frightened of losing contact with Janet, of having her withdraw from me. While I knew I should have let her alone, I couldn't help pushing her.

"How do you feel?" I asked. We were a few minutes from home.

"I feel fine," she said, sounding surprised at my question.

She gave me her silly smile and I was suddenly angry.

"For God's sake, Janet. Will you come back to me?"

She furrowed her brow quizzically.

"What do you mean?"

"It's like being married to a zombie," I said.

"What do you mean?" she repeated.

"My God, Janet," I exploded, yelling at her. "I can't take any more of this. I can't stand your withdrawals and your idiotic fog."

My outburst was childish and hysterical and I was embarrassed by it as soon as I started talking. But I couldn't help doing it. Tension, frustration, and anger had overcome me. I was surprised to see the depth and intensity of my feelings.

I interrupted myself, letting my tension hang in the air.

"I feel all right," Janet said, still looking at me in puzzlement.

"I know you do, sweetheart," I said wearily. "I know you do."

At home she collapsed fully clothed on the bed and fell right asleep. I removed her shoes, rearranged her pillows, and stroked her head, feeling the old, brittle traces of conducting paste that had blended into her hair.

I walked into the kitchen and telephoned Dr. Sternfeld. The slow unanswered ringing emphasized my feeling of isolation and aloneness. Time had stopped dead for me while I cared for this child version of my wife.

Finally, he picked up the phone.

"I just spoke to Dr. Lessing," he said. "I was going to call you and Janet tonight."

"I spoke to Dr. Lessing this afternoon," I said.

"I know. He told me."

"What's going on?" I asked.

He hesitated. "We've decided to let a week go by before we give her any more treatments."

"Why?"

"Well, we'd like to test their effectiveness. It's difficult to judge how successful they are until they wear off a bit."

He was silent. He didn't usually volunteer information. The quality of his answers usually depended on the quality of my questions. But he spoke so carefully that sometimes I thought he was manipulating me. In his halting tone of voice he always made me feel as if he was holding something back from me, as if he knew something I didn't and shouldn't know myself.

"How does it look so far?" I asked.

"It's too early to tell. She seems in less pain. But I suspect that once the effects of the treatments disappear she'll be in trouble again."

"So she'll need more?"

"I think I told you that I'd be surprised if she has less than sixteen treatments."

"She seems very disoriented," I said. "Very out of things."

"I don't know what you mean."

"I mean she's more than confused. Really off in her own world."

"A little disorientation is normal," he said. "An unfortunate result of the treatments."

"No, I mean almost totally unresponsive. Feeling no pain."

He was quiet for a moment.

"I still don't know what you mean. Your description doesn't sound familiar to me."

"It's like living with a zombie," I said.

He sighed. "I sympathize with what you're going through. I'm sure it's not easy for you."

"Are the treatments going to work?"

"I don't know the answer to that question, Paul. They've had limited success in the past. They used to just make her more anxious. Although she's depressed and pessimistic, she's not really in a classical depression. But she asked me for them. And I thought they were worth a try."

"But you don't know if they'll work?"

"I'm always optimistic," he said wearily. "I always have hope."

At the end of December, a few days before Christmas, I was eating lunch with my father in a large downtown Brooklyn restaurant. We were regulars and sat in the back of the crowded room, separated from the noisy shoppers by a plastic partition and a little railing.

"Shock treatments are serious business," my father was telling me. "They're nothing to take lightly."

We had been talking about Janet's series of treatments. She had been given her sixteenth and last two weeks earlier.

"I know they're nothing to take lightly," I said tartly. "I'm practically an expert on not taking them lightly."

"Your Uncle Fred was given shock treatments many years ago, after he attempted suicide. And Sid Teller when he was in a deep depression."

"And they worked?"

"They never had any trouble after that as far as I know. Sid Teller is still a miserable son of a bitch of course."

"And Uncle Fred is only half a person," I said. "Only person I know with a zero personality."

"You can't make someone into something they're not. Can you?"

"You certainly can't," I said.

We munched on our hamburgers and french fries.

"Do you want a cup of coffee?" my father asked.

I nodded and he gestured toward our waitress, holding up two fingers.

"How is Janet doing?" he asked.

"Okay, I guess. She's still pretty fogged up but the worst fuzziness is beginning to wear off."

"Will she need any more treatments?"

Shock Treatments

"Not if I can help it," I said. "I can't stand what they do to her. But Dr. Sternfeld isn't really sure that these will work. He's considering another twelve."

"I don't understand how he can give her more of something that's proven a failure."

"Things don't always work as fast as you'd like them to work," I said, sucked into a lifelong, temperamental father-son argument. "You have no patience."

"I'm an impatient man," he said.

"I know. That's what I just said."

The waitress cleared away our dishes and left two lukewarm cups of coffee.

"There was something I wanted to talk to you about," he said. "Will you continue to drive Janet to her shock treatments?"

"Why shouldn't I?"

"This is our busy season you know and my partners might have objections to you taking days off."

"Half-days," I interrupted. "And I take work home."

"I know you do. I have no objections. But do you think it's fair to other people to take advantage of your position?"

"Look Dad," I said, swallowing down my anger, "it's only a temporary situation. I don't want her to go by herself. The more support Janet gets, the faster she'll come out of this state of mind."

"This is all up to you," my father said. "You're your own man." But he spoke dubiously, as if he wasn't sure I was.

In my office, later, I sat at my dilapidated desk and shuffled papers aimlessly. The electronics firm that had previously rented this floor had used my office as a storeroom. Heavy, frosted windows, exposed pipes, and a wardrobe closet led me to call this room the dungeon.

I was arranging merchandise orders from twelve hundred Woolworth stores into numerical rotation when Lillian, the bookkeeper, buzzed me on the intercom.

"Your wife," she sang in her most melodious voice, "on line one."

I picked up the telephone.

"Am I disturbing you?" Janet asked.

"No you're not," I said.

"Are you sure?"

"Of course I'm sure."

"I am disturbing you."

"No, you're not, Janet. I told you, you weren't."

I cradled the phone in my ear and picked up a stack of orders.

"How are you?" I asked.

PAUL

She dissolved into tears. I felt my stomach tighten in an old, familiar manner.

"What's wrong, Janet?" I asked, trying to keep my voice even.

"I can't take it anymore," she sobbed. "I'm going out of my mind. The same old thing again. I'm never going to feel any better."

"Take it easy, honey. Just take it easy," I said, trying to calm her down.

Her pain, her waves of anxiety and inexplicable fear, were mixed with panic, desperation, helplessness, and a terrible pessimism that made her believe that this pain would never cease. I tried to reach through her suffering, telling her that I empathized and sympathized with her feelings. But as I talked to her she wore me down and I had to fight off my own feelings of panic and helplessness.

"Do you want me to come home early?" I finally asked.

"No, I don't," she said, making an effort to pull herself together. "I don't know what to do. I feel just like I did before I had the shock treatments."

My father's partner Sam came into the office to pick up his coat from the wardrobe closet, giving me a dirty look as he slid by me. Seeing me on the telephone made him nervous. I was taking money out of his pocket, bread out of his mouth.

"I don't think your feeling necessarily means that the same thing is happening again," I said to Janet. I was walking a line, trying to keep my language bland and yet be of help to her. Behind me, in the wardrobe, hangers were rattling like a marimba band.

"What do you think it means?" Janet said sarcastically. "That I'm getting better?"

"Everybody has their bad days," I answered. The rumbling in the pit of my stomach told me that I didn't believe my words.

There was a loud crash behind me. I turned to see Sam standing in a pile of hangers, coats, and shoes. He waved a pudgy finger at me.

"Pick up the clothing, will you?" he said, bounding out the door. "When you're finished."

"Don't be mad at me," Janet said.

"Why should I be mad at you?"

"I don't know. You won't ever leave me, will you?"

"Of course not, honey," I said. "I love you."

"I know you do. I just get silly and panicky."

"Why don't you go out for a walk?" I offered. I was drained of emotion. "I'll talk to you later. It must be depressing to be alone in the house."

"Yeah. I'll take a walk," she said. "It is depressing."

I walked wearily down a short corridor into the factory. Bright dusty light streamed through the casement windows giving the long, rectangular loft an almost golden ambiance. Discarded patterns, cartons of finished brims and crowns, rolls of piqué and bits and pieces of lace and ribbon were carelessly strewn across the wooden floor. Middle-aged Puerto Rican women, the backbone of the garment industry, sat in a precise L-shaped pattern, each woman hunched over her thundering sewing machine.

I turned the corner of the loft into the shipping department area. My father was careening about, balancing a pyramid of boxes in his arm. My cousin Harvey was blocking an endless line of bonnets. My Uncle George, my father's oldest brother, was screaming unintelligibly at one of the shipping clerks.

I walked into the bathroom, leaned my back against the clothes lockers, and closed my eyes.

My father followed me into the bathroom.

"I was thinking," he said. "Why don't you and Janet take a vacation? Go to Florida maybe."

"How can I take a vacation?" I asked. "How can I take off the time?"

"You both need a vacation, don't you?"

"I guess we do."

"Then what are you worried about? You'll take a week off, that's all. I was thinking: It will do more for Janet than all those damn psychiatrists and shock treatments put together."

We did go on vacation, but not before Janet was given another series of twelve shock treatments. The theory behind this new series was different from the theory behind her previous series.

"I want to really load Janet up this time," Dr. Sternfeld explained to both of us, a few days after Janet's panicky phone call. "Dr. Lessing and I agree that perhaps we spaced the last series too far apart."

"When will she start?" I asked.

Dr. Sternfeld coughed apologetically.

"After the holidays, I'm afraid. This is an awkward time. Christmas and New Year's coming up."

The weeks passed. On Christmas Eve, our first anniversary, Janet prepared an elaborate meal, a mock celebration with candles, our fanciest china, and champagne. After dinner, lying in bed, she buried her head in my chest and she cried bitterly, for all her lost years, for all the torment and sadness she knew was coming. Although I held her tightly and kept talking, I could think of no adequate words to comfort her.

PAUL

We were living in isolation. I suppose the pressures on us, our frustration, our helplessness, could have pulled us apart from each other. But they didn't. They made us closer. Our infrequent moments of peace and joy were ecstatic and they reminded us of what we struggled for. They almost sustained us.

On January third, Janet started a new series of treatments. Three times a week for the first two weeks, two times a week after that, I drove her to Dr. Lessing's private office, a nondescript suite of rooms on the top floor of a luxurious apartment building.

At the end of January he ushered me into one of the inner rooms.

"I have good news," he said, sweeping his arm toward a leather armchair. The room was warm and comfortable, with soft blue carpeting, a shiny mahogany desk, and a wall of bookshelves. "We will give her only twelve shock treatments."

"I thought that was settled before we started," I said.

"That's right." He nodded in his storklike fashion. He drummed his long fingers on the same shabby overflowing folder of papers that he had carried at Monroe Park.

"How do you find her?" he asked.

"Very fogged up," I answered, ready to go into a long description. "Incredibly distracted, confused, and—"

"But not in pain," he interrupted. "No?"

"She's feeling no pain at all. If she stubs her toe she just smiles her stupid smile."

"That's good," he said, continuing to nod. He opened his file folder, rippled abstractly through the papers, and sighed philosophically. "I've handled Jane's case for many years—"

"Janet."

"Janet's case," he said. "I don't know how many times I've treated her."

"Very many times," I told him.

"What?"

"I said many times."

A disturbing sense of unreality was again coming over me. I felt as if I was part of a stage set, indulging in prepared patter. The blue office, the muted desk and bookshelves, all called forth a calm cool medical atmosphere. But I no longer believed this illusion. The conferences and consultations were, to my mind, a bit of razzle-dazzle. There was nothing scientific about what they were doing to Janet. It was the grossest form of guesswork.

As I watched Dr. Lessing rustle his papers and wave his arms I was suddenly very angry, perhaps most angry at my own part in this masquerade.

"I thought the treatments never worked on her," I said.

"They've worked," he answered. "Sometimes you can't always see it, no?" He smiled and held out both his hands in a cuplike gesture. "Sometimes what you see on the surface has nothing to do with what's underneath."

"I don't understand," I said.

He laughed. "It's complicated, no?"

"I mean I don't understand what you're saying."

"It's a technical matter. Electroshock therapy works best on deep depression, paranoid-schizophrenic states and even certain extreme forms of neurosis. I don't think we've tapped all the ways to help people, though." He shook his head. "So much suffering in the world. So many unfortunate people. And we have only inadequacy."

"What does this have to do with Janet?" I asked.

He shrugged, a weary, burdensome gesture.

"It's sad," he said. "It is very sad."

I went outside, buttoning my coat against the wintry weather. But I couldn't stop shivering. I entered an expensive-looking luncheonette and sat at the empty formica counter.

"Give me a cup of coffee," I said to the heavy set, rainbow-haired waitress.

"Just that?" she asked.

I nodded.

"Have something with it?"

"I don't want anything with it."

"I'll have to charge you the minimum."

"What's the minimum?"

"Fifty cents."

I stood up to leave but I felt suddenly silly about being so frugal. I was paying Dr. Lessing $840, Monroe Park $280, an anesthesiologist $120, and Dr. Sternfeld an average of $200 a month. I lowered myself onto the stool again and gestured for the coffee.

I was still shivering while I drank it. My hands shook and the cup rattled against the saucer. I fumbled for a cigarette.

I thought of Dr. Lessing and how his manner had chilled me. I was to discover, years later, that Dr. Lessing advocated psychosurgery, believing in the healing power of slicing out a portion of a person's brain. I wasn't really surprised. In my eyes he was a ghoul and should have been working in some dim laboratory with Lon Chaney dragging in a fresh supply of bodies.

Driving into Brooklyn later, I asked Janet to tell me our license plate number.

PAUL

"5241KD," she said.

"That's right," I said. "Always right."

She stared dreamily out the window.

"How the hell could you let yourself be treated by a ghoul like Dr. Lessing?" I suddenly asked.

She looked at me blankly, as if she didn't understand my words. In the blandness of her expression I saw a question that probably wasn't even there: How could *I* let her be treated by him?

"I don't know," I said out loud.

"What?"

"Nothing, I'm starting to talk to myself."

Four days after the last shock treatment we rushed off to Miami Beach, almost as if we were afraid to allow the effect of the treatments to wear away. Dr. Sternfeld handed me a package of ten Doridens, told me to be extremely careful about doling them out to Janet, and guaranteed both of us that we would have an extraordinary time. He was wrong. We didn't have a bad time but we didn't have a good time either. Our vacation was as blank, as disjointed, as full of nothingness as Janet's state of mind.

The weather was mild, the streets crammed with tourists, and the hotels in competition with each other for levels of opulence and garishness.

We tried our best to enjoy ourselves. Somewhere in their collection of memorabilia, our parents probably still have a picture postcard we sent them, a photograph of Janet and me climbing on a boat for a tour of Miami Bay. No doubt the postcard sustained them for a time and made them happy. Over the next few years they would have precious little to be happy about.

"How much longer can you take it?" my father asked a few weeks after we returned from Florida. We were eating lunch.

"What do you mean?" I asked.

"Just what I said. How long can you live with Janet the way you've been living? Never knowing what's going to happen next."

"I don't think that's a fair question," I said. "This is a temporary time."

He looked away from me, at a long line of people waiting to be seated. "I mean if all the psychiatry in the world doesn't work on her. And all those damn shock treatments. If all the love and attention she gets doesn't work. And a lovely vacation . . ."

"I still don't think you're being fair, Dad. I keep telling you that things don't always work as well or as fast as you'd like them to."

"I'm talking about you, though. How much can you stand? Can you take another year like this one?"

"I can't answer a question like that."

"Two years? Humor me."

"Why do you always have to anticipate things?"

"Three years?"

"It won't last that long."

"How do you know? Suppose she's like this the rest of her life?"

"She won't be."

"Suppose she is. How do you know she won't be? Because her psychiatrist says it's only temporary? What does he know?"

"I know it also," I said. "Because I live with her. Because I know her."

"Okay. Let's suppose it's only temporary. What's your breaking point? Five years?"

"I don't know, Dad."

"Ten years?"

"Okay," I said, finally worn down by his stubbornness. "Let's say five years. I don't know. Let's say I can only take it for five years."

"That's all I wanted to know. I'm only asking a question."

I knew, though, that he was asking more than a simple question. He was expressing his own frustration and pain, asking me, the architect of his misery, what he could do about his feelings. I didn't know what to tell him. I didn't know what to do with my own feelings. I watched his hands as they fumbled with his pipe. They were my own hands, long thin fingers and tapered palms.

"I just don't like to see you sacrifice your life for Janet," my father said. "Like a magnificent obsession."

"She's not my magnificent obsession," I said. "I still lead my own life."

"You can't put your full efforts into your work. Can you? You don't see your friends."

"I see my friends," I said. "But I don't pretend my life is normal."

"That's all I'm saying. I just want you to understand that you're not leading a normal life."

Despite my argument with my father I knew he was right about something: I had chosen to give up a part of my life for Janet. To a certain extent I had no choice. She was like a great actress making sweeping, larger-than-life, commanding gestures. But beyond these gestures was real pain and I responded to that pain because I loved her and because I couldn't ever judge the depth and profundity of her misery and despair.

Back in my office, I received a message that Janet had phoned. When she heard my voice she started to cry hysterically. I calmed her down.

"Please don't be mad at me," she said.

"I'm not mad at you, Janet," I said. "I love you."

"I started hallucinating. That's why I got so frightened."

"Hallucinating?"

She started to cry again.

"Like I used to," she said. "That's what frightens me. I'm falling apart."

"You're not falling apart," I said. "I'm sure it's nothing."

"It's not nothing. I saw a man laughing at me. I don't think that's nothing."

"I just mean that you're frightened and upset," I said. "When you're unsettled you can think almost anything."

But I didn't believe my own words. I was frightened and upset myself. My perception of Janet was again muddled, spinning out of control.

Monroe Park I

The hallucinations were difficult for me to take. They didn't so much frighten me as they demoralized me. I found Janet's inner world of laughing men, animals, menacing knives, and shadowy, ill-defined figures surprisingly easy to accept. But the implications of the hallucinations upset me: she was getting worse.

"They're not hallucinations, you know," she told me. "Dr. Sternfeld always said they weren't hallucinations."

"What are they? Pictures on your eyeballs?"

"No," she said, ignoring my sarcasm. "Technically, they're visions, because even though I actually see them, I don't accept their reality."

Despite my sarcasm, I was pleased about the new word. I was getting adept at catching hold of vague distinctions and small consolations. But I was still at least half a skeptic.

"I don't understand," I said, "the line between seeing the visions and believing them to be real."

We were parked in front of Dr. Sternfeld's house, waiting for her session to begin. A March wind was pushing chilly air and I kept the motor running and the heater on high. On the radio the Beatles were singing one of their old hits, about wanting to hold someone's hand.

Janet lit a cigarette, inhaled deeply, and started coughing. I slapped her on the back.

"It's difficult to explain about the visions," she finally said. "Sometimes they're so real I can talk to them. Or reach out to touch them. And yet I can stop myself from believing in them. I can say, 'Hold on, Janet. You know they're just visions.'"

"What do they do?" I asked. "Do they float past your eyes like balloons?"

"No," she said. "According to Dr. Sternfeld, they're projections from my subconscious that mysteriously break through into my conscious mind like dream images. Even when I'm not aware of them, I always have the creepy feeling that something is with me. It's damn frightening. It makes me think I'm going mad."

"How can you be frightened of going mad? You've been there and back. I thought what's unknown is most frightening."

PAUL

"That's where I'm going," she said, sweeping her hand in an expansive melodramatic gesture. "Deep into nothingness and the unknown. Do you think it's easy? Shot full of electricity without anything coming from it. Medicated up to my eyeballs. And all I see stretching ahead is more dismal years. I can't function. I can't do anything for you. I can't do anything for myself. And most of the time the laughing man is with me, laughing at me for daring to think I could be a normal human being."

"At least you're never lonely," I said.

"Ha. Ha."

She opened the car door and started to slide out. I held her arm, leaned toward her, and kissed her on the lips. Her lips were ice cold and bloodless.

After she left, I circled the block and passed by a group of young women who were gently rocking their baby carriages. A trio of old men gossiped nearby, and a little girl, elegantly dressed in a fire-red pants suit, turned circles on the sidewalk.

I finally had to admit to myself that my life had completely passed out of my control. I had been holding myself together by believing that I understood what was happening inside Janet's head. I had tried to identify her pain, her alienation, her despair with my own feelings. But I couldn't identify with her anymore.

We were becoming separated by a flurry of eccentricities, diagnostic phrases, psychoactive drugs, and ugly, terrifying drives and compulsions. And I was finally becoming a true believer. When Dr. Sternfeld made the point that Janet was ill—like someone with tuberculosis or diabetes was ill—I nodded in agreement. The concept of sickness made her behavior and emotions explicable and controllable, placing the horror and torment that was inside of her in someone else's hands.

The only things I knew about "mental illness" I had picked up from books, movies, or television. I had long ago been horrified by Olivia de Havilland's plight in *The Snake Pit* and moved by Joanne Woodward's cure in *The Three Faces of Eve*. I had been touched by the romantic melancholy of *David and Lisa* and stimulated by the insights in *I Never Promised You a Rose Garden* and *The Fifty-Minute Hour*. But the world of the mad had always come across to me as dark and exotic, somewhat terrifying, like a five-page spread in *National Geographic* on some primitive buried tribe.

If I was confused about Janet's state of mind, I was also confused about my own feelings; I couldn't even guess at where I was going. Janet, on the other hand, knew where she was going. That evening, as we lay together in bed, she told me that she expected to be in the hospital soon.

"Why do you say that?" I asked. The muffled boom of Bunny's record player came through the walls; Miss Snow's endless thumping came down through the ceiling.

"I don't have any choice," she said.

"Of course you have choices, Janet."

"That's what Dr. Sternfeld says." She balanced her head on her upraised arm and looked at me. I was lying on my back. "He says that I have plenty of options. But I don't believe him."

"I thought you hated the hospital," I said. "You keep telling me how much you dread and fear it. And now you say you're going to end up there."

"I just know I will."

"How do you know?"

"Because the same pattern is going on that's been going on for years. The drugs. The anxiety attacks. Every time I'm under stress, I want to cut my wrists. It always ended up in the same way, the hospital."

"This time you're different," I said.

"What makes me different? That I'm a married woman? That I have more responsibilities I can't meet? I'm still the same blob of nothing I always was. Where else am I going to go?"

"You always say pessimistic things. Like ending up in a hospital."

"This time it's true."

I rolled on my side and faced her. Miss Snow had suddenly stopped pacing and the silence above our heads was ghostly.

"Maybe it is true," I said. "I don't know."

"I do know," she said.

"Well I don't know. You always say pessimistic things."

"This time I mean it."

"Okay. You mean it."

She opened her mouth to say something else, but I clamped my hand over it. She pushed me away. I reached over and started tickling her.

"Oh, go to sleep," she said.

This time her pessimism was accurate. We were on a road that led only one way. Despite thousands of milligrams of tranquilizers and antidepressants, despite sessions three days a week with Dr. Sternfeld, she was moving further and further into her own world of hopelessness and pain.

PAUL

Finally, in the early fall, she saw herself as being at the limit of her strength, without inner resources or hope, with only one option left to her—death.

One day in September Dr. Sternfeld invited me into his office. I was sitting in the waiting room, trying to read six-month-old copies of *Life*, *Time*, and *Today's Health*. The sliding door to his office sprang open and he poked his head out of the doorway, motioning to me. His face was noticeably rigid and tense.

"It's no good," he said, even before I entered the room. "I think we've gone as far as we can go. We really don't have any choice any more."

"You want her in the hospital?" I asked, trying to keep my voice calm.

He looked across at Janet who was perched on the edge of his couch.

"I think the risk factor is too great now," he said. "You know she's been feeling suicidal for weeks. I don't like the hospital. I think hospitalization is a demoralizing experience. But given the overwhelming intensity of her feelings, we have no other option."

"When do you want her in?" I asked.

"I just called Monroe Park," he said softly. "They can take her tonight. I think that's the best idea. I don't see any point to stalling."

"Am I going to the fourth floor?" Janet asked.

"I can't guarantee which floor they'll put you on," Dr. Sternfeld answered. "The important thing is to get in tonight. You can always get yourself transferred afterward."

"I don't want the seventh floor," she said.

Dr. Sternfeld sighed. He was standing by his desk absently playing with one of those clear plastic paperweights that, when shaken, shower a flutter of artificial snow. I was still standing in the doorway.

"I told Janet that I want her to be assertive," he said to me. "And I want you to help her. As long as she's in the hospital, I want her to use it. If she wants anything, she'll have to rely on the resources of the hospital."

"You'll still come to visit me?" Janet asked.

"Of course I'll visit you. But I want you to use everything the hospital has to offer."

"How long will she be there?" I asked.

He sighed again. "I don't know. Let's let that go for a while. I told Janet that she's in for a minimum of three weeks. My own guess is that if all goes well, she'll be out in six weeks. But in the meantime, I want her to be safe from her feelings, to have the security of knowing that whatever happens she won't be able to get out."

I looked at Janet. Her face was distorted with pain. We had been living together for two years and I thought we knew each other well. But my eyes, as I watched her face, were blind.

"I think this is the best thing to do," she said to me. "I can't go on living the way I've been living." I nodded.

"I'm sorry, Paul," she said. "I'm really sorry."

"Don't be sorry," I said. "You have nothing to be sorry about."

"You both better go," Dr. Sternfeld said. "The sooner you get to Monroe Park the better it is."

He put his arm around Janet, embracing her in his stiff awkward manner. He held her for a long time and she cried against his shoulder. He looked over the top of her head at me.

"It's not the end of the world, Paul," he said. "I know it feels like the end of the world. But everything always turns out for the best."

I had always thought of myself as poker-faced. I didn't know that my emotions showed.

At our apartment a few minutes later, Janet packed a small overnight bag. She was taking only a few items with her: a couple of nightgowns, a handmade woolen sweater, a red bathrobe, her sandals, a change of underwear, her blue paisley dress.

"This is the first time I'm not taking my e. e. cummings book with me," she said.

"Do you want it? You can bring it."

"No. Maybe you'll bring it to me later."

I walked into the living room because I knew I was going to start crying. Tears ran down my face, tears for the dull emptiness inside me, for this whole dead year, for more pain and emotion than I could possibly express. And for other, deeper things that were still locked away inside my head.

Janet came after me. I turned my face away from her.

"Don't cry," she said, trying to hold back her own tears. "Don't you cry."

"I'm supposed to make you feel better," I said. "Not the other way around."

I drove very slowly to the hospital. At one intersection a trailer-truck had sideswiped a Volkswagen and both drivers were outside their vehicles, shaking their fists at each other.

"I never thought I'd be going into the hospital again," Janet said.

"You told me a few months ago that you thought you would."

"I mean right after I got well. Then I thought I was through with the whole damned business of drugs and being locked up."

PAUL

"I guess some things weren't meant to be," I said stupidly.

"No. It wasn't meant to be," she repeated.

Monroe Park presented its familiarly cheerful, plastic facade to us. I parked in front, in one of the spaces reserved for doctors.

The receptionist, in her glass-enclosed cubicle, nodded to us as we entered the lobby. A group of nurses brushed past us, on their way out for coffee. We sat on a wooden bench outside the admitting office waiting for the admitting doctor to come downstairs. The hospital was exceptionally quiet. The only sound was the clickety-clack of a typewriter.

The property clerk approached us. She stopped short when she saw Janet.

"I know you," she said. "Don't I? No. Wait. Don't tell me. I know your name."

She was a brisk little woman with a pinched face, dyed blonde hair, and a gasping, breathless way of talking. She snapped her fingers.

"Susan."

"No," Janet said.

"Don't tell me."

"Janet," I said.

"You told me. Well that's okay. I never forget a face at least. How long has it been? Two years?"

"Three years," Janet said.

"I shouldn't say I'm happy to see you," she laughed. "Still, I'm always glad to see a familiar face. It makes the world cozier, if you know what I mean."

The admitting doctor, a thin, sleepy-looking young man, appeared. He moved Janet toward a small office, held the door open for her and slammed it shut after she walked in. I went into the admitting office.

The secretary was filling out Janet's admitting forms. She typed mechanically. She had done the same thing thousands of times. Through all the miseries of admission, the crying, the screaming, the pleading, she had processed all her forms.

Yet, there was something reassuring to me in her single-minded attention to detail and red tape. She was steady and constant, a sign of stability. No matter how shattered I felt my world to be, the boring business of living was still going on.

"Do you have Blue Cross/Blue Shield?" she asked me, "or Major Medical?"

I nodded. "All of them."

Monroe Park I

"We're not a member hospital." She smiled coyly. She was an unattractive young woman in her late twenties. A blob of red hair, balanced on her heavy face, jiggled as she spoke. "You won't get anything from Blue Cross unless she's going to the medical floor anyway. As for Major Medical, you'll have to arrange to get paid directly."

I read a mimeographed sheet of paper entitled Rules for Visitors. Visiting hours were Tuesday and Thursday evenings 6:30 to 9:00 and Sunday, 1:30 to 4:00. No incoming phone calls were allowed. Newly admitted patients couldn't call out for twenty-four hours.

"Why can't new patients call out sooner?" I asked the secretary.

"We used to let them call out right away," she said. "We're always changing our policy. It's more therapeutic this way. Makes it easier for them to adjust."

Janet came into the admitting office, looking weary and drained. She leaned against me.

"What floor am I going to?" she asked.

"The fourth," the secretary said, her hair wagging up and down.

"A semiprivate room?"

"I think you're in a dormitory room."

"I want a semiprivate room," Janet said, her voice rising.

"Look, Janet," the secretary said impatiently. "There's nothing I can do tonight. You came in on very short notice. Try the nurses tomorrow. Maybe we can get you transferred then."

Janet signed a standard form, committing herself for thirty days. The form had a clause which called for a review of her "state of health" after that thirty-day period ended. The hospital had the right to hold her another thirty days or to transfer her to a state hospital. For at least sixty days, the question of her freedom was in the hands of Monroe Park.

I signed a form giving the hospital the right to use any type of treatment they thought best. I signed another piece of paper waiving the hospital of all responsibility in case of accident or death. I handed the secretary a check for $912 and watched her study the signature.

Janet and I went outside and sat on the bench again, waiting for an aide to accompany her to the fourth-floor locked ward.

"How was the interview?" I asked her.

"Like always," she said. "The same kind of shithead who's always interviewed me. He wouldn't even look at me. 'Do you hear voices? Do they tell you to hurt yourself?' He looked more frightened of me than I was of him."

PAUL

Her words fell away and we sat in silence. The secretary was no longer typing. We could hear the scraping sound of a telephone dial and then the soft murmur of her voice.

Neither of us knew what to say. The sadness of our parting was so profound, the open-endedness of our separation so overwhelming that I suppose we both were numb. It was impossible, for me at least, to assess our future. I had no vision of what was going to happen to Janet. Or myself.

"I'm going to miss not sleeping next to you," Janet suddenly said. "It's been two years since I've slept alone."

"I'll miss you," I said.

"How can you miss me? My complaining and nagging?"

"I'm used to it," I said. "It's hard to manage without it."

"I didn't want to go to the hospital," she said. "I don't want to go now."

"It's a little late."

"I know it is. I just didn't know what else to do."

"I didn't want you to go," I said. "I can stand a lot of things. The hospital really gets to me, though. It makes me feel so isolated from you."

"I know it does. I'm sorry."

"It's not a question of being sorry. It's not your fault."

"I feel it is my fault. I feel the whole miserable wasted year is my fault."

"It's no one's fault," I said. But even as I spoke the words, I didn't know if I believed them.

"Do me a favor?" she said.

"Sure."

"Don't sleep in the apartment tonight. It's very lonely by yourself."

"What's the difference?" I asked.

"It's not a good night to be alone."

"Maybe I'll sleep at my parents' apartment."

"I wish you would."

An aide strolled by us, disappeared into the admitting office, and reappeared again with a neat file folder of papers. He waited, standing a discreet distance from our bench.

Janet gripped my hands and kissed me on the lips.

"Please take care of yourself," she said.

"I will, Janet. But more important, you take care of yourself."

I watched her walk down a long corridor to the elevators. In her loose, swaying chemise dress she looked fragile and girlish. She moved with quick, shuffling steps, her shoulders hunched forward and her head bowed. Her arms swung back and forth with a sharp, jerky precision like a mechanical instrument. She didn't look back at me.

I watched until she disappeared around the curve of the corridor, waiting until I heard the elevator click shut behind her. I didn't want to take the chance of seeing her again. I had already built up all my walls and defenses, and I didn't want to risk having them crumble apart.

As I walked down the corridor, the property clerk bustled after me. The lights were dim in the lobby and a janitor was sweeping up the day's-end collection of bits of paper and cigarette butts. The receptionist leaned her head against the glass of her cubicle, her eyes closed.

I called my parents from a phone booth in the lobby. My mother's voice broke when I told her where I was.

"I suppose it's not surprising," she said wearily. "Everybody's been talking about the hospital for months."

"It's not surprising," I responded. "It still shakes me up. I don't know what's going to happen next."

"What are you going to do tonight?"

"If you don't mind, I'll sleep at your house."

"Do you want me to fix you something to eat? You probably haven't eaten all evening."

"I'm not really hungry," I said.

"You should eat something. It's important to keep up your strength."

"If there's any time not to be a Jewish mother," I interrupted, "this is the time."

"Do you want me to call Janet's parents?"

"No, I'll call them myself when I get to your house."

In the morning I was considerably more relaxed and clear-headed. I sat at a glass table in my parents' sunny little kitchen and with surprising relish, finished off the huge breakfast my mother prepared for me. I had slept nearly twelve hours, until noon. The thoughts that had so disturbed me the night before had taken on a different cast this morning. My helplessness, my loss of control, now seemed almost a relief to me, as if a burden and responsibility had been lifted off my shoulders.

I was still drinking my coffee when the telephone rang. My mother lifted the receiver.

"Hi, dear," she said, surprise in her voice. "How are you? I'm glad. Yes, Paul's right here. Yes, I'll put him right on."

PAUL

"I thought you couldn't call out for twenty-four hours," I said to Janet.

"I'm not supposed to." Her voice was tentative and weak. "A nurse is letting me make a quick call."

"How are you?"

"Just lonely," she said.

"Why? What's wrong?"

"I don't know. It's silly. I just feel out of place here. Everybody knows each other. I feel like I'll never belong here."

"You make it sound like high school," I said.

"It is. Sort of. I walk into the dayroom and everybody's in little groups, talking to each other. I feel so clumsy and shy."

"It's hard to adjust," I said. "Like any new place."

"I suppose you're right. But you know me. I think that I'll never feel at home here."

"But you will."

"I know I will. I can't talk much longer now. I really called to tell you two things. That I was assertive like Dr. Sternfeld told me to be and I got my room changed. And that I love you."

"I love you too," I said mechanically.

"I missed you so much last night," she said. "I feel so frightened and lonely and helpless. I can't wait until I see you on Thursday."

I hesitated before I answered her. A familiar clot of anxiety was forming in my stomach. I looked into the living room where my mother was watering her wall-to-wall, windowsill-long stretch of plants.

"I can't wait until I see you too," I finally said.

My mother was staring out the living-room window when I got off the telephone. I stood next to her and looked out the window myself. Across the street, on the terrace of a long flat apartment building, a round little man in a sweatsuit was doing slow laborious push-ups.

"How is Janet?" my mother asked.

"She's okay," I said. "She's having trouble adjusting to the hospital."

My mother, a good-looking woman with pale blond hair and soft features, nodded noncommittally and resumed watering her plants. It was difficult to wrestle true feelings from her. From generation to generation, her family passed on the ability to shut trouble out of their world. My grandmother and my mother and my uncles and aunt could easily slide into a rose-colored fantasy world where all people were beautiful and nothing was ever cruel or wrong.

Perhaps because I, too, shared that same ability, it was suddenly important for me to know how my mother felt about Janet's hospitalization.

"I suppose everything's for the best," my mother said. "Perhaps now she can straighten herself out."

"Maybe she can," I said. "Although I lose heart sometimes."

"You mustn't lose heart. Who else does Janet have?"

"That's just the point," I answered. "When Dr. Sternfeld goes away for a few weeks, I feel totally at a loss, as if I can't handle everything myself."

"It's not easy."

"You're damn right it's not easy. I don't know what to expect anymore. I don't even know if I want any more of it."

I hadn't meant to blurt out my feelings. My rage was unexpected and uncontrollable, and I was sorry as soon as I started to talk. My mother held her watering can in front of her, looked at me, and then peered out the window again.

"Do you see that woman crossing the street?" she said, pointing to a red-haired woman with a beehive hair comb. "She's a kept woman. Every Wednesday and Friday at five o'clock a black limousine pulls up in front of the house. Like clockwork."

I remember saying something melodramatic to myself as I waited Thursday evening for Monroe Park's visiting hours to begin: "This is it" or "Here I go." I also remember that even then, as I sat in the cool crowded lobby, I detailed in my mind different ways of describing the experience of visiting the locked ward of a mental hospital. I suppose now that I wanted to distance myself from this experience, to see myself as an observer rather than as an intimately involved participant. I didn't know what to expect when I went upstairs. I smoked a cigarette, swiveled in my plastic chair, and tried to hide, even from myself, the full intensity of my anticipation and fear.

A young woman pushed a wooden desk into the middle of the lobby and people jostled each other, trying to be first in line. We were supposed to tell her the patient's name and to receive in return, a visitor's pass. I was afraid that I might stutter badly, as I do when I'm very nervous. But I didn't have any trouble.

On the fourth floor, we were jammed into a tiny hallway waiting for someone to unlock the door to the ward. The two elevators creaked up and down, throwing more people into the unbearably crowded space. An adolescent boy examined us through a small window at the top of the door, peering at us with vacant, unblinking eyes.

PAUL

"Who is he?" a man behind me asked. "Anyone know him?"

The boy was nudged out of the way by a frumpy, middle-aged woman's face and someone stuck an elbow into my neck waving at her.

"Whadda they waiting for?" a man asked. "It's past six-thirty."

"Just try to ask them for extra time when nine o'clock comes," someone else said.

I craned my neck, trying to look through the window into the ward. All I could see were faces.

"Let us in already," somebody at the front said, banging on the door.

An aide appeared at the window and held up two fingers.

"It's unconscionable to let us wait like this," a man at the back of the room said. "They shouldn't have let us come upstairs."

"Sometimes we have to wait until they finish giving out the medication," another voice said.

Finally, the door sprang open and we stampeded in.

Janet was standing in front of the nurses' station. Embracing her, feeling her familiar shape against me, filled me with terrible sadness and I shrunk back—ever so perceptibly, I thought—away from her.

"You don't look bad at all," I said.

"How did you expect me to look? Like the Madwoman of Chaillot?"

The mob of visitors and patients, bunched together at the door, was slowly breaking up into little clots and dissolving down a long pale-yellow corridor, into the dayroom.

To the right of the entrance, in their glass enclosed booth, two starched white nurses scribbled in their notebooks. A male nurse lounged against the opposite wall and a slender horse-faced woman, hands on her hips, surveyed us with distant vapid eyes.

"Do you want to see my room?" Janet asked, pointing past the nurses' station to another hallway.

Her room was clean, neat, and agreeably spartan, like a well-kept, low-budget motel. There were a set of lockers at one end of the room, two wooden dressers, and harlequin prints on the walls. I sat on Janet's bed, bouncing on her concrete mattress.

"So this is what a mental hospital looks like," I said.

"How did you expect it to look?"

"I'm not sure," I said. "Less pleasant, I suppose. Less bland. More exciting. Less like a normal hospital."

She reached behind her and tapped on the window.

"There's heavy wire mesh behind the glass," she said. "To keep people from hurtling out, which I sometimes think about doing."

Monroe Park I

"Then it's safe here?" I said.

"If you want to call it that."

An aide appeared in the doorway and coughed apologetically.

"We'll have to leave," Janet said to me. "A new policy. No visitors in the rooms."

The dayroom—a hodgepodge of milling people, ping-pong tables, blaring television, old sofas, formica tables, and straight-back chairs—rattled with an unbelievable din. A young boy brushed against us, shrunk back, and then slithered around us.

"What's wrong with him?" I asked.

"Nothing. No one ever comes to visit him. That's all."

The library, a small cubicle off the dayroom, was empty. We shut the door behind us, closing off most of the noise.

"Alone at last," I said.

Janet smiled weakly.

"Do you feel any more comfortable about being here?" I asked.

"Somewhat," she said. "I'm sorry that I called you the other day. I just felt so out of place here."

We were sitting next to each other on a stiff little couch. Across from us, in a low bookcase, were a few rows of hand-me-down books: Reader's Digest condensations, Booth Tarkington's *Penrod*, *Anthony Adverse*.

Janet started to cry. I put my arm around her, feeling nervous and awkward, as if I could only make meaningless gestures to her.

"I put on lipstick and I washed my hair," she said.

"Just for me?" I asked.

"Not for the hospital staff."

"Why do you knock the hospital?" I said. "You wanted to come here, after all. You must think it's going to do you some good."

"I don't know what it's going to do for me. I just had to go some place."

"But why knock something that might help you?"

"Because it's a damn humiliating experience." Her voice rose as she spoke, but she looked guilty, as if she wanted to take her words back.

"I'm sorry," she said. "I just feel so depressed. And useless."

"I know it's depressing being here," I said.

"Dr. Sternfeld said that he's thinking of giving me shock treatments. Did I tell you that?"

"You told me about it before you went in."

"I see these damn animals all over the place. Childlike animals, like the creatures in *The Peaceable Kingdom*."

"You make it sound almost pastoral."

PAUL

"It's not. I see this laughing shadowy man also, who tells me to cut my wrists. And I would if I could. I don't even care what happens to me anymore."

The door swung open and an aide poked her head into the room.

"I didn't know anyone was in here," she said. "Keep the door open. It's not supposed to be closed."

We walked into the dayroom, played a game of ping-pong, and sat at a table, drinking coffee. I was pleased at how quickly our time together passed. I had been afraid that my visit would seem endless, that we would be strangers without anything to say to each other. The noise and ruckus of the dayroom seemed always to connect us, breaking through her symptoms, complaints, and petty hospital difficulties.

This first evening, before I left, Janet handed me a letter she had written to me her first night in the hospital.

"It's mushy and sentimental," she warned me. And then as she embraced me she said, "I don't know what I'd do without you. I would have nothing at all to live for."

Her words chilled me. As I rode down in the elevator, I held her letter away from me. I couldn't read it then. Years later when I found it again among my papers, I tried to look at it. But I couldn't. It brought back too painful a moment.

"The important thing," Dr. Sternfeld said to me, ten days after my first visit with Janet, "is not to treat her as if she's special. She has a talent for getting people to take care of her. Even in the hospital. It's done her nothing but harm."

I sat in a leather armchair in his office, looking across his round head at a Cambodian stone rubbing on the wall.

"Janet can be childish, selfish, demanding, and manipulative," he went on. "As long as she gets any benefit from being helpless and sick, she's going to go right on being sick."

I shifted in my chair.

"What help does she get from the hospital?" I asked.

"She's safe," he said. "She can fall apart and someone will always take care of her. But I want her to pay a price for this safety. I want her to be assertive, to make her own way in this imperfect world, like the rest of us."

"I thought you put her into the hospital because of her suicidal feelings?"

"That's the immediate reason. The top of the bowl. But don't forget that they're not just suicidal feelings. They're her signals to me, her way of forcing me to put her into the hospital. She can't allow herself to do something for herself. She can't say, 'I need help and safety.' She has to demonstrate her desperation."

"But you take the suicidal feelings seriously?"

"Of course I do. I take all suicidal statements seriously. Particularly in Janet's case. She's compulsively honest, the actress who believes her act. She used to threaten to cut her wrists if I didn't do something she wanted me to do. I'd say, 'Go ahead and do it.' And she would."

His chair squeaked as he leaned back in it. He laughed humorlessly at the memory.

"I never had much room to maneuver with her," he added. "I had to walk some very narrow lines."

"She was hard to handle," I said.

"She was impossible," he said slowly. "But I was all she had. I was the only thing that stood between life and death for her."

Although there was no anger in his voice, only weariness, I affixed my own anger to his words. I wanted to see Janet as childish and manipulative. Anger clarified and simplified my jumbled emotions.

I had arranged this special Saturday afternoon session. As a rule, Dr. Sternfeld didn't like to discuss his patients behind their backs. But in special cases, like during hospitalization, he made exceptions. I was extremely grateful. I hungered for information.

I stared out the window at the gray empty street and tried to phrase a question that had haunted me since Janet first entered the hospital. I felt a sudden warm kinship with Dr. Sternfeld, as if we shared a common and difficult burden.

"You must have a lot of questions to ask me," he said. "I'd rather answer your questions than just talk randomly. I don't want to give you information you don't want to hear."

"I suppose I should ask you what's wrong with Janet," I said.

"That's much too broad a question," he responded. "I couldn't answer it if I wanted to. If you ask me why she broke down in the first place, that's easy to explain. The perfect all-American supergirl with the all-American super-boyfriend, going away from home for the first time, to a superschool that was chosen by her parents.

"But why her sickness lingers?" he said. "Or why her symptoms are more extreme than they have any right being?"

He shook his head in puzzlement.

"Does her condition have a name?" I asked.

He laughed. "I'll tell you what I always told Janet's parents. If I give you a name you'll run right for a medical dictionary and probably misinterpret everything you read."

PAUL

"Janet overheard the hospital diagnosing her as schizophrenic," I said.

"She's not schizophrenic," he said sharply. "Or at least not in my judgment. There's a subtle and difficult distinction to make. She achieves an orgasm during intercourse which schizophrenics are not supposed to do, and she is capable of sustaining lasting relationships."

Sometime later, when Dr. Sternfeld's secretary mistakenly mailed me a completed Blue Cross form, I discovered his official diagnosis for Janet. She was labeled an "affecto-schizoid reaction," someone who only acted like a "schizophrenic," someone who quacked like a duck, waddled like a duck, but wasn't a duck.

Even if Dr. Sternfeld had told me his label for her this Saturday afternoon, I wouldn't have known how to consider it. Despite my momentary sense of camaraderie with him, I was overwhelmed and intimidated by the legions of scientific material that loomed behind his words. He was leading me along, after all, picking and choosing what I could stand to hear, as if the terrible mysteries of the mind were best hidden from a layman like me.

Near the end of the session, I stumbled through the question that I had earlier tried to phrase: Was Janet going to withdraw from me?

He looked at me in surprise.

"I don't know what you mean," he said.

"I mean, is she going to lose contact with reality, disappear into her own world?"

He smiled and stretched his arms slowly over his head.

"If this is any consolation," he said, "she's hit rock bottom. She's as sick as she's ever been. I doubt very much that she'll get any sicker. I know that the visions and the suicidal feelings are disturbing symptoms, but you have to remember that they're only symptoms, manifestations of her distorted state of mind, of her overriding sense of worthlessness and sinfulness."

"Sinfulness?" I said, surprised.

"Another part of the puzzle," he said, with a tight smile. "What sin of thought or deed makes her want to punish herself?"

He tapped a cigarette, leaned back in his chair, and balanced the cigarette above his eyes. I watched him idly roll the thin cylinder between his fingers. Finally, he stuck it unlit between his lips.

"I'm trying to cut down," he explained, "by not lighting them."

"Has it worked?"

"Not really. I cut down more successfully by grubbing from my patients."

"I know he ordered it," Janet said. "I get it every day."

"I don't have it written down."

"Why don't you call him?"

"We did call him. He's not in his office."

"Then call him at home."

"Let's wait until tomorrow. We'll call him then."

"But I want it now."

"Don't raise your voice, Janet."

I waited a short distance from the nurses' station, leaning against the pale-yellow wall. Some of the late visitors threw quick furtive glances at Janet as they straggled onto the ward. A tiny gray-haired old woman in an oversized cotton dress planted herself in the middle of the hallway watching the scene with undisguised amusement.

"I said I want it now," Janet repeated.

"And I said we'll wait for tomorrow, Janet."

"Can I at least have a shot of Sodium Amytal?"

"You don't need a shot, Janet."

"I do need it. I'm telling you that I need it."

"And I'm telling you to keep your voice down."

Involuntarily, I edged away from the nurses' station. I was embarrassed by Janet's yelling; there was a nakedness to her rage that seemed to me different from anything I had ever heard. It was a limitless, unchecked, unsocialized explosion of feeling. She was volatile, a time bomb; her lack of restraint was why she was in the hospital. Or so I thought at the moment.

"Can I or can I not have a shot?" Janet fumed.

"I'm telling you for the last time that you can't."

"I want it."

"You're flirting with the seventh floor," the nurse said with icy fury. "If you don't grab hold of yourself, I'm going to put you in the Unit."

"I don't care what you do to me. I just want what's been ordered for me."

As Janet's voice continued to rise, the little gray-haired woman backed away from her. She bustled toward me, a precise little person.

"I don't belong here," she said. "I'm just a visitor."

"That's nice."

She studied me slyly.

"But you see, I came up to the wrong floor and now I can't get out because the doors are locked."

"I can't open them," I said. "I'm just a visitor myself."

"These people belong here," she said, pointing to Janet and the nurse. "Not me."

Janet turned abruptly from the nurses' station and stormed into her room. I followed her.

"They won't give me my medicine," she said to me. "They lost my fucking order."

"I heard," I said.

"Can you imagine it? They do nothing all day but sit in their glass cage writing about us in their little books. And they can't even keep a fucking order straight."

"What are you going to do?"

"What can I do? If I make too much of a fuss, they'll send me to the seventh floor."

"They can't send you there without Dr. Sternfeld's permission," I said.

"They can do anything they want to do." She looked at me as if she had noticed me for the first time. "Would you do me a favor and call Dr. Sternfeld? Tell him that I have to see him."

"I don't know, Janet."

"Oh, please, Paul. Please do it for me."

Before I could answer her, an aide appeared at the door.

"Mrs. Higgins wants to see you at the nurses' station, Janet," she said.

"What does she want now?"

"I dunno. I think she wants to give you a shot."

I looked up in surprise. I was leaning on the washbasin.

"Now she wants to give me a shot," Janet said.

"She says that you're very agitated."

The injection put Janet right to sleep. She had described the first sensations of Sodium Amytal entering her system as if it were wave after wave of something mellow and sweet, "a mixture of honey and scotch."

Dr. Sternfeld had ordered Amytal Sodium on an as-needed basis when she was being given shock treatments and could not have a steady dosage of tranquilizers. He had emphasized that she would have to assert herself by asking for the injections.

Whether or not he had designed these injections as a test of aggressiveness, they had blossomed into a complicated problem. Janet was constantly balancing her desire for relief from anxiety against judgment of how terribly she suffered. She had to second-guess how Dr. Sternfeld would judge her pain (was she in enough need or copping out?), convince the nurses that she was really suffering, and finally make peace with her own sense of cowardliness and shame.

I stared at her now, through the open door of her room. She was lying fully clothed on her bed, wearing the same rumpled paisley dress she had put on when I drove her to the hospital. One arm was curled over her pillow, the fingers outstretched as if straining for something just beyond her reach. Her other arm was hammered rigidly against her side. I couldn't see her face.

I kept looking at her, trying to pull my thoughts together, wondering what I was doing in such a terrible place. Finally an aide came over to tell me that I couldn't stand in the hallway, that I would have to wait in the dayroom for Janet to wake up.

I took the elevator to the lobby instead and paid my bill.

The cashier, a pale young woman with a longish nose, luxurious brown hair, and dark liquid eyes, always flashed me a dazzling smile when I handed her my semimonthly thousand-dollar check. I fantasized that her smile was especially for me.

"When do you get off from work?" I pretended I would ask her. "How about a cup of coffee?"

I knew, though, that I could never ask her out. Even if I could lay aside my guilt, I wouldn't want the tension of another woman's company. But it made me feel good to fantasize; it made me feel masculine and part of the world.

When I went back upstairs, Janet was just waking up. I sat on the foot of her bed while she rubbed her eyes and ran her fingers through her hair. A new head nurse had been assigned to the ward and there was now a flexible policy toward visitors in the rooms.

"I'm sorry," Janet said to me. "I was so wrapped up in myself that I hardly even knew you were here."

"That's okay," I said.

She leaned against me and tried to clear her head.

"Would you call Dr. Sternfeld like I asked you to?"

"I don't know, Janet. I'll see what I can do."

Before I left that evening, as we hugged at the door, an aide jangled her keys, leaned toward us, and said, "Two lovebirds." I waited until the heavy door closed behind me and then I mumbled, "Fuck you" under my breath. I didn't feel at all like a lovebird.

I was suddenly very angry. Alone in the elevator, I banged on the wall, the hollow metallic clang, the dull senseless pain in my palm, symbolizing my futility and stupidity. It was easy for me to see why I was angry at Janet, at her helplessness, at her demands. But I felt my anger went beyond her and I couldn't see where it lay.

PAUL

Driving back home, along an almost empty highway, I concentrated on the road. I drove this route twice a day now. Dr. Sternfeld had recently surprised me by giving me an open pass, and every evening I pulled together my strength and energy and fought rush-hour traffic, dragging myself to Monroe Park. I couldn't say that I really minded the traveling or that I minded the daily strain of visiting Janet. I had nothing better to do with my time anyway. But the atmosphere of the hospital was getting me down. The seedy aura of helplessness and misery hit me as soon as I entered the ward. I had long ago lost my initial sense of strangeness and fearfulness. I now felt myself an intruder, slipping in and out of this special little world where I had no real place.

I thought back to Janet's earlier explosion of anger and why I had been so embarrassed by it. I realized that it was not her excessive rage that had so discomfitted me. As I witnessed the scene, I had been embarrassed by my own inappropriateness, as if I were a child, listening through my bedroom wall to my parents fighting or making love. Janet's outright panic and childish unsocialized rage made as much sense within the context of the hospital as the nurses' icy superiority. They fed off each other: the helpers and the helped, the keepers and the kept, the watchers and the watched. They needed each other. Outside the hospital the world was chaotic and ragged, but inside there was order, shape, rules, and meanings.

Monroe Park was a "good hospital." I never saw or heard of any outright brutality. But with its glass booths, its charts, its passes, its jangling keys, and its locked doors, it was a closed-in world of petty rules, invasions of privacy, arbitrary excesses of power, and shrunken spirit. And it made me sick.

But why was I so angry about it?

Later, I lay fully clothed on my bed, blew smoke up at the ceiling, and thought about my need for Janet. Her need for me was easy to understand. I was her only connection to the outside world, her comfort, and security. But my own needs were woven with slender and more intricate threads.

I suppose, in a strange irrational way, I was jealous of the hospital, jealous of the simplicity of its need for Janet, jealous of my own lack of place. In my own way, I needed her to be "sick" also. I had no simple focus for all my feelings toward her, no way to separate my fear, guilt, frustration, and anger from my love for her.

I very badly wanted to have a wife, home, and family, but I had to struggle to keep up the illusion that I would ever have them. Everyday Janet asked me if she would ever feel better, and I always gave her the same answer, that she would wake up one morning and all the pain would have disappeared. But I had no more faith in the future than she did. I was neither optimistic nor pessimistic. I went through the motions, trying not to think about what was going to happen next.

I fell asleep with a lit cigarette between my fingers and woke up a few minutes later, a gaping hole in my shirt and the odor of burning cotton in my nostrils. I stubbed out the cigarette, rolled over on my side, switched off the bedside lamp, and thought, before I fell asleep again, that I could have burned the house down. I didn't even care.

In the morning I phoned Dr. Sternfeld.

"I'm just calling you because Janet asked me to," I said.

"I already told her I would see her in a few days."

"She's very upset."

"That's too damn bad," he said sharply. "She'll have to learn to live with it."

I was taken aback, but I felt a vicarious buzz of excitement in my stomach. It was more than tempting to be angry at Janet. But another thought came into my head.

"Are you doing this on purpose?" I asked.

"What do you mean?" the doctor asked.

"Maybe I credit you with too much manipulation. Are you trying to focus her anxiety? Trying to teach her something?"

"I promised her that I would see her soon," he said stiffly. "I always fulfill my obligations."

"What's going to happen?"

"She's very disturbed, as you can see."

"I mean in the future."

"I don't know, Paul. I really don't know."

She got better. Or more precisely, her symptoms retreated deeper inside her. Even at best, the hallucinations were frequent companions, old familiar faces, popping up unexpectedly like out-of-town relatives. Under stress, the suicidal thoughts or the desire to cut her wrists still seemed to her to be reasonable options. And she still tended to fall apart under the slightest pressure. But the surface roughness smoothed away, and if she wasn't quite at peace with herself, she was at least calmer, and more in control of her fears and angers.

She didn't know what made her feel better and I certainly didn't know either. The incident with the medication seemed to be a turning point, as if her explosion of feeling had loosened some knot inside her. I told her later that I had been shaken by the intensity of her anger, but she shrugged it off as if my perception meant nothing at all.

When Dr. Sternfeld finally visited her, a few days after my telephone conversation with him, she settled into a smoother, less stormy state of mind. A week after that, she simply woke up in the morning feeling, as I had so carelessly predicted, different from the way she had felt the night before.

In the beginning of November, Dr. Sternfeld tried an experiment; he gave her a pass to come home for the weekend.

I arrived at the hospital early on Saturday morning, but the nurses insisted that Janet attend her regular weekly group therapy session, and I had to wait in the dayroom. Gail, her roommate, offered to prepare me toast and instant coffee.

"It's been a long time since anyone made me breakfast," I said when she carried a paper plate and cup to our speckled formica table.

"It's been a long time since I've made breakfast for anyone," she answered. "I was never much of a housewife, either."

"It looks fine. Just great."

Bright morning sunshine poured through a wall-length row of windows, but the overhead lights were lit anyway, casting shadows on the clean linoleum floor. Across the dayroom, the continuously running television set was broadcasting a garbled Saturday morning cartoon. Behind us, a thin young boy was randomly stroking pool balls across a scarred pool table. Two male aides played ping-pong nearby and four middle-aged women gossiped over their paper cups of coffee.

I chewed on cold buttered toast and stared across at Gail. There were sharp bitter lines around her mouth and a moistness in her clear blue eyes which spoke of a paradox in her nature, an incredible toughness, and yet a vulnerability. She was confined to Monroe Park in an experimental methadone program. For many years, she had been an addict and a high-priced, high-class whore.

During the month they had roomed together, she and Janet grew increasingly close. But there was an odd strain between them. They were both obsessive charmers, precocious little girls, locked in an eerie sexual competition.

"Are you nervous about taking Janet home?" Gail asked me.

"Do I seem nervous?"

"I thought you might be."

"I suppose I am a little frightened," I said. "As terrible as it is coming here every night, at least I'm used to it. I'm afraid that we may have forgotten how to relate to each other."

"I doubt it. You both seem like you relate beautifully. My old man and I had that kind of relationship, while it lasted."

I knew that her husband, a black artist, had committed suicide many years before. I didn't know what to say about him, so I filled an awkward silence by downing the rest of my coffee.

At the door to the dayroom, people were lining up for morning O.T. They formed a straggly line, young boys and girls in jeans, middle-aged women in slacks and cotton dresses, a smattering of old people. Most of the old men and women sat on the worn couches that were strung along the sides of the room, idly talking or staring into space.

"Are you going up to O.T., Gail?" an aide asked.

"Not this morning. I'm not in the mood to make ashtrays."

The aide studied us suspiciously, but shrugged her shoulders and turned away.

Gail fumbled with her coffee cup. Her thin hands were shaking. I didn't know if I made her nervous.

"My life just fell apart after my husband died," she said. "I lived the next couple of years in a haze, not caring what I did or what would happen to me. I never had to work street corners, thank God. And at least I never had to buy shit from any of those grubby pushers."

"When did your husband die?" I asked.

"A long time ago," she said dreamily. She slowly lifted a cigarette to her lips, but her face grew hard as she lit it.

"You mean, why am I still living in the past?"

"I didn't say that, Gail."

"I'm saying it. I've been told before that I'm using my husband's death to justify the mess I made out of my life."

"You can't believe everything you're told," I said meaninglessly.

She looked away from me towards the line of people stumbling out of the elevators.

"Look at this place," she said bitterly. "This is my last chance. If I screw up this methadone program, I'll never make it anywhere."

"I have a friend who believes in last chances," I said. "He drives himself to a point of total collapse on the theory that then he'll be forced to do something constructive with his life. But there's always more than one chance. It's a romantic view of life to think there's only one chance."

"I wouldn't call myself romantic," she said. "I just know that I'll never get another chance."

PAUL

We were still drinking coffee and talking when Janet came out of her group therapy session. She entered the dayroom, looked around for me, and caught my eye.

"What's going on here?" she said, as she sat down at our table.

"We're arranging a tryst," I said. "Midnight at the nurses' station."

I realized suddenly that my joke was tactless and I was momentarily embarrassed.

"Don't worry," Gail said. "No money changed hands."

The weekend with Janet, as I suppose I could have predicted, was a disaster. The morning sun disappeared behind a bank of clouds and the sky grew as solemn and gray as our expectations for the future. Our apartment, which had once appeared so bright and cheerful, now seemed cluttered and claustrophobic. The continuous rumble of Bunny's phonograph formed a jarring counterpoint to our dismal mood.

We took a short walk through the park and ate an awkward disjointed dinner in a local Italian restaurant. In the evening, we lay in bed watching television. Janet pressed her thin body close to me.

"Don't be angry with me," she said.

"Why should I be angry?" I asked, surprised.

"I can't make love with you."

"I didn't even ask you," I said, keeping my voice light.

"I know you haven't. But it must be on your mind."

"Actually, I wasn't even thinking about it. I'm just happy to have you home."

"I want to make love. I really do."

"Then why can't you?"

"I don't know. I just can't pull my feelings together."

"We have plenty of time," I said unemotionally, the conversation eerily reminiscent of our first weeks together.

"I can't do anything at all," she said. "There are so many things. The house is such a mess."

"Are you criticizing my housework? I cleaned it especially for your homecoming."

"No. I mean all the things that are piled up. The mending to do. The laundry. The closets to be cleaned out."

"That's not why you came home."

"I guess not."

Before she fell into her heavy drugged sleep, she whispered to me, "You know, we should have just kept living together. We should never have gotten married."

"That's true," I said.

"I mean it, Paul. I'm not kidding."

"I'm not kidding either."

I tried to watch an early Peter Sellers comedy, but I couldn't concentrate on the screen. I picked up an anthology of the best science fiction stories of the year, but my mind kept wandering off in all directions. Finally, I shut off the television, switched off the light, and climbed beneath the covers, lying close to Janet. When I threw my arm across her shoulders, she murmured unintelligibly, kicked, and pushed me away. Her nightgown had risen above her hips.

Exhausted, with a familiar knot of fear in my stomach, I soon fell fast asleep.

In the morning, when she phoned Dr. Sternfeld to tell him about the previous night's anxiety, he ordered her back to the hospital.

I drove back slowly. As depressed as we both were about the failure of the weekend, I suppose we were relieved as well. Whatever pressure we had both felt, pressure to be at ease or to be ecstatic, we had been overwhelmed by it. For the first time all weekend, as we circled through the stark, glistening park, we were comfortable with each other.

"I told Dr. Sternfeld about your theory on the hospitalization," Janet said.

"What theory?" I asked.

"Your idea that my misery and pain and anxiety were a process that I had to go through and get out of my system. That the month of shock treatments just dulled my senses and stalled the process. That being without drugs allowed me to reach the depth of my pain and allowed me to pull myself up. By myself."

"What did he say?"

"He said it was possible. But there was no way of knowing what would have happened if I didn't have the shock treatments."

I nodded. I had no real faith or confidence in my theory. But I thought that to go around a problem only washed away people's strength and alienated them from their feelings.

"He said that he thought starting me on Thorazine lifted me out of this episode," Janet continued.

"Thorazine?" I said.

"That's what he said."

I edged the car carefully through a series of sharp winding curves. Through the bare trees we could see a kaleidoscope of Sunday activity: kids throwing footballs across the meadows, a pickup softball game, dogs scurrying after each other, men and women strolling down the paved walkways. A bicycle wobbled in front of me, and a heavy-set man in a sweatsuit frantically pedaled until I finally grew impatient, swerving away from him.

I parked and we walked hand in hand to the hospital.

"I'm sorry the weekend didn't work out better," Janet said.

"I'm sorry also."

"I don't really want to go back to the hospital."

"And you don't want to go home yet. That's quite a problem."

We lingered in front of the entrance to Monroe Park, shifting from one leg to the other to keep warm. A group of aides came bounding out the door, waving to us like old friends.

"Why do you stay with me?" Janet suddenly asked.

"What do you mean?"

"I saw you with Gail yesterday, and I was jealous. She's everything I'm not. Tall and beautiful. Everyone in the hospital thinks she's more appealing than I am."

"That's silly, Janet. Are you in a race with her? Look at the mess she made out of her life anyway."

"I know that's true. But I can't help feeling inferior to her. You take away my sickness, and I have nothing left anymore. I have no identity. Nothing."

I fastened the top button of my coat and lifted my collar against the cold. For some reason, neither of us wanted to go inside.

"I stay with you because I care for you deeply," I said, although I didn't know whether I was telling the whole truth.

She turned away from me and pressed her palm on the glass door. She was wearing her bulky orange tweed coat and the white mohair hat we had bought on our honeymoon in Greece.

"Most of the time I just want to die," she said. "I feel that I have nothing to live for."

I fought down a mixture of fear and revulsion.

"How about living for us?" I said evenly.

She looked into my face, her gray eyes hooded and dull.

"Sometimes I really don't think I know you," she said quickly. "Sometimes I don't think you understand me."

Despite the failure of the weekend, despite her generally low spirits, it became apparent that Janet would soon be leaving the hospital. She was only marking time now; the "compulsive" suicidal thoughts that had prompted Dr. Sternfeld to lock her away had been worn away by time, the dullness of her days, lack of temptation, drugs, and the shifts and flows of her emotions.

In the middle of November, a few weeks before her own release,

Monroe Park I

Janet's friend Angie flung herself into her room to say good-bye. Angie was a heavy, big-boned woman with a boisterous warmth, a suffocating sentimentality, and a tendency to drop suddenly into a wooden, shell-like depression. She had been Janet's first and closest hospital friend.

"I wanted to make sure to say good-bye to your wonderful husband also," she said, slipping her head in my direction.

"Why wonderful?" I asked. I was awkwardly balanced on the edge of Janet's bed.

"Because you haul yourself up here almost every night. You come and go like nothing in the world ever bothers you. It's a pleasure to see you, the way you come bouncing in here."

"I can't help bouncing," I said. "I walk on my toes. It was the style when I grew up."

Out in the hallway, Peggy, a new nineteen-year-old patient, was wailing and moaning, going through her nightly confrontation with the nurses. Every evening she whined for her mother, so fitfully and so childishly that her performance crossed the border of anguish and became annoying, embarrassing, and too much to handle; the hospital joke.

"Are you taking a vacation?" Janet asked, ignoring the ruckus just outside the door. "Like your doctor advised you to do?"

Angie was suddenly serious.

"I don't think so, Janet. I want to see my son."

"That's why you should go away for at least a few days," Janet said. "Why go right back to the same situation that brought you in here?"

"I can't help it," Angie said. "After all these months separated, he really needs me now."

Angie's youngest son had been born with his urinary system reversed, his genitals inverted, his bladder fastened to the outside of his groin. He was highly susceptible to disease and was continually in the hospital, a constant strain on his parents.

"You need a perspective," Janet said. "If you get too deeply involved again, you'll just tie yourself up in knots. And end up back here."

Angie threw her head back; her coarse black hair cascaded over her forehead.

"You tell me what I should do. Take more pills? How can I not get involved?"

Foster, an aide, appeared in the doorway.

"What is this, a meeting?" he said good-naturedly. "What's going on here?"

"My husband's picking me up in a few minutes," Angie said. "I'm just saying good-bye to my good friend Janet and to her wonderful husband."

"I don't want you back here now," Foster said. "I don't want to see your ugly face again."

Peggy's moans grew unnaturally shrill and Foster stuck his head out the door to watch her. I brushed past him and stood in the hallway by his side. She was crumpled up in a solid little ball, her fists beating on the floor. A pencil-thin nurse with a startlingly beautiful face stood rigidly over her.

"Get up off the floor, Peggy. I want you off the floor."

A collection of patients had gathered near the nurses' station, watching the performance with open amusement. A group of aides came running in from the dayroom.

"I said off the floor," the nurse repeated. "I'll give you five seconds to stop acting like an infant. Otherwise you're going right up to the seventh floor."

Peggy looked up coyly.

"I want my mother. I want my mother. I want my mother."

Two aides hauled her to her feet and propelled her to the door.

"I'm giving you your last chance," the nurse said. "Do you want to go upstairs?"

Peggy kicked at the nurse but missed, her foot thudding against the yellow wall. An aide unfastened the lock, and they heaved her outside toward the elevators.

"Lots of action," I said to Foster. "How come you didn't do anything?"

"Shit, man. I usually hide in the bathroom when there's trouble. You should see this place on Sunday after the visitors leave. It's like a zoo. All this pent-up energy when they've had nothing to do all weekend."

I walked back into Janet's room. Janet was sitting on her bed crying. Angie held her head against her bosom.

"What's the matter?" I asked. "What happened?"

"I think she's sorry to see me leave," Angie said.

Janet disentangled herself from Angie's grip and wiped her tears away with her forearm.

"I don't know why I suddenly started crying," she said. "I just think that I'll never get out of this place."

"Of course you will," Angie said. "You'll be out very soon. Every day you get better and better."

Janet shook her head. "I just can't see myself ever leaving here."

Monroe Park I

"She's frightened of going home," I said. "You can understand that."

I certainly understood her feelings. After all these months, I was frightened of having her home.

Angie threw her heavy arm around Janet's shoulders.

"But you will be leaving soon," she repeated. "In a few months we'll be having lunch together."

Janet smiled. "I guess I know that we will," she said. "I really look forward to it."

They never did have that lunch, though. After her release, Janet thought of Angie often and considered phoning her, but she never did. Whatever had tied them together, whatever had cut through age, class, and lifestyle, had disappeared, as wistfully as a summer romance, once they left the hospital.

At the end of November, Dr. Sternfeld set an official release date. On December second, after almost three months of hospitalization, I arrived early in the afternoon to bring Janet home.

I rode the creaking elevator up to the fourth floor. I ran my fingers over the metal wall, almost expecting to find the spot I had pounded a few months earlier. There was no mark, of course. All I was fondling was the hard blue-green paint.

Janet had already emptied her locker and chest of drawers. She was removing postcards from the wall over her bed. Her father, a nostalgia buff, had sent her an almost daily series of turn-of-the-century postcards and valentines. Although she hadn't wanted anyone but me to visit her, she appreciated receiving mail. It was a link to the outside world.

She carefully peeled off the Klee poster I had bought her and she packed away the cardboard drawing that she and Gail had once draped over the little window on the door to their room. The drawing had lasted only a few hours. A nurse had berated them and torn it down.

Finally, good-byes and release procedures completed, we stood by the front door waiting for Foster to let us out. He jangled his keys importantly and said to Janet, "Don't come back now. I don't want to see your ugly face again."

"I've heard that routine already," I said. "A few weeks ago."

"I don't have any new routines, man. I'm too weary to think of anything new to say."

We stepped outside the door of the hospital, into the bright sunshine. I put my arm around Janet's shoulders. The air was clear and crisp, a tantalizing remembrance of fall.

"How does it feel?" I asked. "Finally being out?"

"Scary," she answered. "I'm just not used to it. I look around me. I see all these people walking, the cars whizzing by. I feel out of place, as if I no longer belong out here."

"It will probably take a few days to readjust," I said.

We stopped for breakfast on Eighth Street in Manhattan, down the block from the little apartment where we had first lived together in the summer of 1965. The Village was changing, growing more and more commercial. An old brick building that had once stood next to Janet's sublet had been torn down and a new high-rise was soaring up in its place. Fast-food stores had replaced the old luncheonettes, and fancy men's shops, bargain record stores, and tawdry souvenir stores had replaced the more neighborly shops.

We sat in a booth, picked at our cold waffles, and swallowed down our lukewarm coffee.

"I scrubbed the apartment," I said to Janet.

"You didn't have to do that."

"I wanted to. I wanted to give you a clean start."

"Very funny," she said. "That's really a terrible pun."

We fumbled with our food in silence. I watched her face. It was blank and strangely unfamiliar. She stared moodily into space.

"It must have been awful for you," she said. "All the months I was in the hospital."

"It was only awful sometimes," I said, choosing my words carefully. "After a while I got used to the screwed-up way we were living. After you began to feel better a lot of the strain came off me."

"It was terrible for me, also," she said. "I missed you so much."

I was surprised at how quickly a wall was breaking down inside me. I had been nervous and defensive about her homecoming. I had spent a rare sleepless night tossing and turning, thinking about our relationship.

"Do you think I'm starting to take care of you, Janet?" I asked. "I mean, is our relationship getting hopelessly warped and out of joint?"

She thought about what I said.

"I always asked Dr. Sternfeld how you could still possibly love me," she said. "I've been such a mess. He said that people don't love each other for any particular reason. People love each other only because they love each other. That's always been a difficult concept for me to accept."

What Dr. Sternfeld said was true, of course. Lots of people sustain tragedy in their marriage, major illnesses, great personal frustrations, economic upheavals. What made us different, though, was the complex, overwhelming division between us, the division between the "sick" and the "well," the "normal" and the "abnormal," the "sane" and the "insane." We were on different sides of a bleak mysterious chasm that we could only vaguely comprehend. The ground between us had been labeled and defined by somebody else.

"Do you think we can hold on to what's real and solid between us?" I asked.

"Turn over a new leaf?"

"You have a talent for these quaint phrases," I said.

She laughed. "It's not even a question of turning over a new leaf either. I think that we've generally managed to sustain a healthy relationship."

"At least you can't say that you hold any secrets from me."

"But I do," she said, her face turning serious again. "You don't really know me."

"How can you say that? It's not every man whose wife parades her unconscious in front of him."

"You don't really know all the terrible things inside of me."

"The feeling of sinfulness that Dr. Sternfeld talks about?"

"The famous mysterious feeling of sinfulness. The basis for my need to punish myself."

We finished our coffee, pushed away our plates of half-eaten waffles and sat back in our booth, smoking cigarettes.

"How much did all these months cost?" Janet asked.

"Five thousand eight hundred eighty-one dollars for the hospital, four hundred fifty dollars for Dr. Lessing, and a thousand dollars for Dr. Sternfeld."

"How can we afford it?"

"We can't. Not on two hundred dollars a week. Every month is a new financial challenge for me."

As I stood up to leave, Janet reached across the table and gripped my hand with such painful fierceness that I involuntarily winced. She quickly loosened her hold, almost as if she was embarrassed by her sudden passion.

"Maybe I'm just lighthearted about leaving the hospital," she said. "But I feel better than I've felt in months. I know I'm going to be okay, Paul. I know we're going to make it through together."

I felt almost lighthearted myself. I was surprised at how suddenly my spirits had risen once we left the hospital.

"I love you so much," Janet said, tears misting her eyes.

PAUL

"I love you, too," I said, feeling happy and peaceful for the first time in months. "But don't cry, for Chrissake. I've had my fill of tears."

She smiled. "I won't cry. You'll see. I won't ever cry again."

Monroe Park II

Four months later, March 2, 1969, I brought Janet back to Monroe Park.

We had moved. Our old brownstone apartment had been filled with too many terrible memories for Janet, memories of bleak wasted days, dying dreams, and great pain. None of the windows faced the front street. They overlooked a scruffy little garden, a weathered brick wall, and the rear of a faded tenement. The inner direction of the windows had begun to mirror Janet's own feelings of isolation and to symbolize her growing sense of separation from the rest of the world.

So we tried something new. We sacrificed a stylish neighborhood for a larger brighter apartment, and in the beginning of February, we moved deeper into Brooklyn, to the bottom floor of a brick two-family row house in a quiet middle-class neighborhood a few blocks north of Sheepshead Bay. The apartment was spacious. A huge kitchen-dining room slashed through the width of the apartment, separating a square front living room from two airy rear bedrooms.

I have always thought that the strain of moving precipitated Janet's second hospitalization. She was unable to control her energies, incapable of pacing herself. While I grumbled and cursed over the packing and unpacking of the thousands of little items we had accumulated over our two and a half years of marriage, she went briskly and cheerfully through her banal little tasks. She collapsed soon after, into a month-long state of anxiety and jumbled irrational despair.

In the beginning of March, Dr. Sternfeld granted her an emergency Sunday evening appointment. Just when I expected her to return home, she phoned to tell me that he was holding her an extra forty-five minutes.

I paced across our new apartment, trying to make myself believe that this extended session was a good sign, that she had sunk to her lowest darkest level and was now grappling with her bottom-line fears and naked obsessions. Despite her constant anxiety, I thought she was growing stronger. Her hallucinations were clearer and more explicable, hooded shadowy figures that she called the elders and that Dr. Sternfeld said were projections of her "overactive superego," her rigid puritanical conscience.

Over the last few months, we had grown closer. Our life, although painful and open-ended, had, at least for me, achieved a day-to-day intimacy, shape, and focus.

I saw our car snake into the driveway and I watched Janet drag herself up the front steps. When I saw her face in the hard indoor light, I knew that something was wrong. She sat down heavily at the dining-room table. I leaned against our refrigerator, against the handle which had to be pulled twice before the door finally clicked shut.

"Dr. Sternfeld wants me in the hospital," she said.

"When?"

"Now. This evening."

"I don't want you to go."

"I don't want to go either, Paul. I don't really have any other choice."

"No, I mean it," I said. "I'm not just going through the motions."

Her face was taut, the muscles around her eyes strained into tight round bulges. She was wearing blue jeans and a pale yellow, high school sweater, all of which made her look unbearably young, like a lost child.

"I damn well mean it," I repeated. "I don't want you to go in."

"Shh. Keep your voice down."

Panic that had been building up for a long time came flooding out of me, and I indulged myself, placing no check on my emotions. This was not my finest or bravest hour, and it was only a long time later that Janet finally allowed herself to become angry about it. But I had to make a stand against my life which was again pulling away from me, to retain, however fragile and momentary my retention, a power over my existence. I had to test her also, to see if the bonds of our love were stronger than her pain. It was a pathetic performance, but perhaps I knew even then that when she entered the hospital again, something was going to die inside of me.

I cried and she stood next to me, cradling my head against her small heaving breasts. She spoke with such calm and rationality that I was taken aback and later, when I thought about this moment, I was embarrassed as well.

"What kind of life is this for you, Paul?" she asked. "You come home from work, and I'm so wound up from the dreariness of my day, from shopping with my mother or just sitting here, that all my terror and unhappiness come pouring out of me almost the second you walk through the door. I can't even help it. I don't even feel safe enough to let out my tears and rages until I see you."

I felt her swallow. I looked up into the sudden stoicism of her eyes.

"You drink down a glass of scotch to unwind," she continued. "We go out for dinner because I'm too upset even to cook. We watch television and I fall asleep in the middle of a show because I can't keep my eyes open. What kind of life is it for either of us? I don't know what to do. Maybe if I go into the hospital I can straighten myself out and at least be a wife again."

She made perfect sense, of course. But I couldn't listen to her words. The anger and depression that I had repressed for so long had taken hold of me and even if I could have pushed them away, I felt no desire to do so.

Finally she disappeared into the bedroom, closed the door firmly behind her, and phoned Dr. Sternfeld. When she came out a few minutes later, she could only muster a tight smile.

"I'm not going into the hospital tonight."

"What did he say?"

"He said it was against his best advice. But I think he understood how you felt. He wants me to call him in the morning."

She was framed in the doorway to the bedroom. The harsh back light cast shadows over her frail figure, making her look one-dimensional, like a projection. Three generations of Kramers, our landlord's family, were clambering about upstairs. The door to the second bedroom was open, piles of books and records strewn about like the remnants of a catastrophe.

I sat down at the table, laying my head in my hands. It had been only a hollow victory for me; I felt no peace and no real elation. But it had been a rite I was forced to perform. Even months later, when I was ashamed of my indulgence, I knew that I had done the correct thing. To have acted against what I felt would have been as dreadful as struggling against a natural force, as battling against a wind or beating against a storm.

Later that evening, though, when I prepared her next day's ration of medication, I began to question the wisdom of what I had done.

For almost a year now I had been hiding her jars of medicine, doling out a daily supply of pills. Originally, Dr. Sternfeld wanted to avoid temptation for Janet, and although I hated acting as nursemaid, I had at least thought my status would be temporary, only as long as this "momentary painful episode." Later, I swallowed down my revulsion, as I swallowed down other horrible parts of my life, not knowing what else to do.

PAUL

During the times Janet felt relatively good, I hid the bottles carelessly; but now under the pressure of her "suicidal compulsions" I was again taking special care. I filled her clear plastic vial with the fifteen hundred milligrams of Thorazine that were prescribed for her anxiety, with the Kemadrin that relaxed the cramped muscles the Thorazine caused, with the Compazine for her constantly nauseous stomach, and with the Prolixin, a "psychic energizer," for her depression.

I replaced the Thorazine and Prolixin in their hiding spots, high on the top shelf of the closet, beneath a clutter of old sweaters, mufflers, photograph albums, Monopoly and Scrabble sets. They rattled against other half-filled bottles of pills that were scattered behind our discarded clothing like old memories—Tofranil, Mellaril, Librium, Valium.

I eased the less dangerous Kemadrin and Compazine beneath my papers on the bottom of my bedside table, recounted the pills, dropped them back into their vial, and snapped down the white plastic cap.

I swung open the bedroom door and walked into the bathroom. Janet was leaning over the sink, holding up her forearms so that they were reflected in the medicine cabinet mirror.

"Do you remember when I once demonstrated how I went about cutting my wrists?" she asked.

"I remember."

"How you had asked me how I could do it to myself? How I could feel such revulsion for my body? How I could stand the blood and the pain?"

I nodded.

"I couldn't really answer you then. I was too far removed from the desire. But I want to cut my wrists so badly now that I can hardly control myself. It's like a passion, almost sensual throbbing in every cell of my body. The tension builds up so unbearably that it seems the only way to release it."

"What tension?" I asked.

"The tension of being myself."

On the tile floor of the bathroom, next to the toilet bowl, a thick crumpled wad of toilet paper nestled against the wall. I pointed to it.

"I can always tell when I'm preoccupied," she said. "When I start missing the bowl. My mother's two biggest complaints about me when I was living with her were that I didn't put the cap back on the toothpaste, and I sometimes threw toilet paper on the floor."

"How can you miss the bowl?"

"It's not easy," she answered, almost managing a laugh. I just fling it out between my legs. And sometimes I miss."

After she fell asleep that night, I switched off the television, paced the length of our new apartment, and finally settled on our hard orange living-room couch, staring out the front window into the street. The sidewalks were empty, the night still.

I looked at my watch. It was only eleven o'clock.

I had always been an introspective person, I thought. I had spent a great amount of time in my head. Exceptionally shy as a child, I had only burst out of my shell in late adolescence, when I discovered a talent for humor, an ability to find funny, nonconsequential things to say. I had always thought that I knew a lot about the human mind. But Janet's pain and obsession were mysteries to me. I felt now that I would never be able to sink into her mind, that I would never really know her.

I realized that I was frightened of her, as afraid of her passions and distorted feelings as I had been frightened as a child of the pitch-black night. Or was I only reading my fears into her? In some ways, I thought, all people are unnaturally frightened of madness (laymen, psychiatrists, even the mad themselves), as if we all sense a common irretrievable loss and mystery in the deepest darkest levels of our mind. I had flirted a number of times, in my greatest despair, with the idea of suicide. But I knew, even then, that I could never possibly harm myself. I knew that I had no real choice in the matter. I was stuck, sometimes unhappily and sometimes senselessly, in this not always pleasant world. Janet was a threat to me, a threat to the careless security of my being, a ghostly reflection of my own non-control and vulnerability.

I knew that I couldn't stay with her if she harmed herself. We lived together, after all, in a fragile unspoken balance of trust. I couldn't have stood the pain of seeing her hurt or the final sorrow of accepting a betrayal of our openness and trust.

I wanted now to stay awake all night. A terrible vision flooded over me, a picture of waking up in the morning to find her cut and bleeding or even dead. But I couldn't keep my eyes open. Anxiety worked like a sleeping pill for me.

I sat, propped up in bed, smoking a cigarette, trying to keep myself awake. Next to me, Janet stirred in her sleep and I leaned toward her, kissing her warm cheek, running my fingers down her back. But she might as well have not been there. I felt as alone as if she had already gone into the hospital. And this feeling of aloneness, even more than my earlier thoughts, made me decide to take her to the hospital.

PAUL

"I'm glad you decided to take her to Monroe Park," Dr. Sternfeld said to me when I phoned him the next morning. "I was going to call you anyway, Paul, and tell you that it didn't pay to keep her out anymore. The risks are too great. I can no longer predict what she'll do."

"I guess it doesn't pay," I said.

His voice sounded mechanical and far away, like a computer.

"I'll call ahead and tell them you're coming. They're undoubtedly prepared for her. They expected her last night."

The admitting procedure was reassuringly familiar. Another dull-eyed resident interviewed Janet and the same blobby red-haired woman blandly typed out the correct admitting forms. Later, we sat on the bench outside the office, clutching our sheets of papers, waiting for an aide to bring her upstairs.

Foster and a group of aides walked by. He did a double take when he saw Janet and came back toward us.

"Lookee here," he said. "It's Janet. Come to join us again?"

"Hiya Janet," another smiling aide said. "Coming back to the fourth floor?"

"That's what they tell me," she answered.

There had been only one hitch in the admitting ceremony. Janet had refused to sign a paper waiving her right to determine treatment.

"My doctor isn't going to give me shock treatments," she said. "He promised I wasn't going to have them."

"These are standard forms, Janet," the admitting clerk said. "They're designed to protect us from any damages. Nothing more."

"I don't want to sign anything that gives you the right to give me shock treatments," Janet insisted.

"Unless you sign all these forms, I can't admit you."

The clerk pushed a fluff of red hair away from her eyes. We stood in silence, in a stalemate.

"Look. If your doctor says he won't give you treatments, then I'm sure he won't," the clerk said. Her eyes suddenly dazzled, with an inspiration. "Anyway, your husband has to approve them before we can give them."

Janet turned to me. "Is that true, Paul?"

"I suppose it is true."

"And you won't sign anything, will you?"

In truth I didn't even know what I had signed. I hadn't even looked. I assumed, as in the last hospitalization, that I had already waived my rights to determine treatment as well. But I felt I had no choice but to lie.

"I won't sign anything," I said.

"See now," the clerk said triumphantly. "Just sign these papers, Janet, and we can bring you upstairs."

Now as we sat on the bench, Janet gripped my hand and said, "You won't let me have shock treatments, Paul. Promise me you won't."

"Of course I won't," I said. "I hate them as much as you do. You're so fogged up from them you don't even know what you're like. You act like a zombie."

"I'm just so afraid of somebody making a mistake. Or of Dr. Sternfeld springing them on me unexpectedly."

The fourth floor aide appeared and Janet hugged and kissed me good-bye.

"I'll call you as soon as I can," she said. "Where should I call you?"

"Try me at home," I answered. "If I'm not there, try me at my parents' house. You can always catch me during the day at work."

She kissed me again and then rose from the bench, staring down at me. The aide stepped behind her, nudging her elbow.

"Is there something wrong, Paul?" she asked. "You seem distant and cold."

"I'm just tired," I said. "And all drained."

"Please take care of yourself. I need you so much."

But I had lied about my coldness also. As I watched her again disappear around the curve of the hallway, I felt absolutely nothing, only a familiar anxiety, as if I had been tranquilized myself.

"I'm not surprised that this happened," Dr. Sternfeld told me later that evening. I had phoned him from my parents' apartment. "I know I predicted after she got out of the hospital the last time that she would never have to go in again. That she had paid her final dues. But I can't say that I'm really surprised. She's been heading for this for a long time."

"I thought she was making good progress," I said. "Growing stronger, grappling with more essential material."

"But it doesn't seem to make any difference," he interrupted. "You can see that. This isn't a very good sign. She comes out of the hospital and four months later she's back in again." He hesitated. "It's a signal that we're doing something wrong."

I suffered through a few moments of dead air. He was waiting for me to phrase a question. But I couldn't think of anything intelligent to say. His style, his posture of doubt and vulnerability, had blurred my own feelings toward him. When Janet was feeling good, I saw him as a successful psychiatrist. When she was hospitalized, I saw him as a failure.

"What's going to happen next?" I asked, that same question I had asked so many times before.

"I can't really tell you, Paul. We'll just have to wait and see. There was a time when she wanted to spend the rest of her life in the hospital. I fought against it, of course. I couldn't let it happen."

His words, combining with my own lack of emotion, startled me.

"You mean she could be hospitalized for the rest of her life?"

"I didn't say that," he said carefully. "I don't really know, of course. It's always a possibility."

A dead spot in my heart was growing outward, sweeping over all my senses.

"Sometimes I feel as if I've reached the limit of what I can take," I said.

He sighed. "I do understand how you feel. The only thing I can tell you is that if you ever decide to leave her, the best time to do it is when she's in the hospital. When she's safe, best able to struggle through her feelings without hurting herself. If I was going to leave her, I'd do it when she was in the hospital."

I felt for a strange moment as if we were in a race. I thought that if Dr. Sternfeld abandoned her, I would never be able to leave.

"Are you thinking of leaving her?" I asked.

"I didn't say that either. If I can reach her, I know that I can help her; but whether or not she lets me reach her is another question."

I hung up the telephone and stumbled into my parents' bedroom. They were lying on their bed, watching television.

"Were you just talking to Dr. Sternfeld?" my mother asked.

"He says that Janet might conceivably be hospitalized for the rest of her life."

My father climbed out of bed and turned off the sound. They were watching a basketball game. Little men were silently scampering across the screen, throwing a tiny rubber ball at a little hoop of wire.

"We always knew this could happen," my father said. "Maybe it's just as well it finally happened now, instead of years from now."

His face showed a mix of emotions, relief, no doubt, and yet sadness for me and for Janet as well. Our parents had received little pleasure from us these past few years.

"I got the feeling that Dr. Sternfeld wants to be rid of her," I said.

"Of course he wants to get rid of her," my father said. "Isn't it obvious that the man failed? He doesn't know what to do for her anymore."

"He always said she was more trouble than any six of his other patients," I said.

"Of course she is. She's an albatross around his neck."

"Are you going to tell Janet's parents?" my mother asked.

"I'm going to tell them that they have to do more to support her. I can't bear the whole financial burden anymore. Otherwise she'll have to go into a state hospital."

"She's been in a state hospital before?" my mother asked.

"She spent a year in Franklin Central," I said. "According to Dr. Sternfeld, it did her more good than harm."

I took a Miltown that evening and fell into a slow, languorous stupor. I lay in bed in my parents' den, feeling my brain whirlpool away from me. I couldn't pull any emotion out of my dulled senses, and all of a sudden I wanted to. In my half-sleep, I could only see Janet slipping forever away from me. Dr. Sternfeld's ambiguity had given my imagination space to maneuver and, in my panic and dullness, I had willingly written my own script.

I woke up the next morning convinced that Janet would be hospitalized for life. I wasn't certain even then how much of this idea I had taken from my conversation with Dr. Sternfeld and how much I had simply willed myself into believing. The implications had certainly been in Dr. Sternfeld's words, but I had gladly switched his ambiguity into black and white certainty.

Later that evening I told my group therapy session that Janet was "hopelessly ill," that she would never again be "normal" or "well." I had started therapy a few years earlier with Dr. Goldstein, a middle-aged Queens psychiatrist who had an unfashionable crewcut and a bitter tongue that put me off and yet in a strange way appealed to me. The strain of living with Janet had gotten to me and, child of my time, I had looked outside of myself for help.

The members of my group were stunned at my revelation. They gaped at me with barely concealed pity and sympathy, nobody knowing what to say.

Exchanges of emotion were not normally a part of our session. Dr. Goldstein ran a tight, dispassionate ship. He believed that people used their personal miseries to cover up deep distorted patterns of behavior; if they didn't quite manufacture their own problems, they were more than willing to wallow in them, to create treacherously elaborate smokescreens in order to cover up that most painful and elusive truth, the reality of their own nature.

So six people that I had grown to know well over my three years of therapy sat in a semicircle of leather-backed armchairs, in a gloomy, awkward silence. Gloria dabbed at her eyes with a crumpled tissue; Daniel coughed in embarrassment; Bonny shuffled her feet like the petulant babyish young woman she so often was; and Phil stared morosely into space.

Finally, Dr. Goldstein cleared his throat and said, "It's much more painful to live with someone who's permanently institutionalized than it is to have them dead. It's a constant burden. Much harder to adjust to, to make peace with."

After the session ended, I lingered at the door, waiting for everybody to leave. It was the beginning of March, and we were prepaying our bills, fifty dollars for four (or five) weekly ninety-minute sessions.

"I hope you'll be coming regularly now," Dr. Goldstein said when I handed him my check. My Tuesday evening sessions conflicted with hospital visiting hours, and during Janet's last hospitalization I had chosen to visit her instead.

"I suppose I can ask her doctor to give me a visiting pass for another night," I said.

"I wish you would. You're under a lot of strain now. I think we can be of some help to you."

He shifted in his chair, rearranging his legs with his hands. He suffered from a serious hip ailment; every six months he entered the hospital to have calcium deposits scraped from his hip bones. He had a brusque sarcastic manner that always made me feel uncomfortable in his presence, and always separated me from him. In my three years of therapy, I had grown to respect his mind, but I had never felt any great affection for him.

"I know how painful it is to live with your wife," he said. "These are frightening symptoms. They frighten me."

"The hospital diagnoses her as schizophrenic," I responded. "But her doctor always says that the diagnosis is inaccurate. She only appears to be schizophrenic. She's capable of having an orgasm and she's capable of sustaining lasting relationships."

He nodded distractedly.

"You know that she wasn't sick when I married her," I continued, suddenly wanting to prove my own good sense. "She was fine. She had what her doctor called a 'complete miraculous cure.'"

He looked at me queerly.

"Then what are you talking about? Why are you handing us this pile of shit? If she got well once, she can get well again."

His words surprised me; what he said was true, of course. But his statement threatened my rarely achieved, carefully constructed certainty, and I simply shrugged away his questions. I started to leave his office, but I hesitated at the door and turned back toward him. He was reaching for a pad of bright yellow, legal-size paper.

"You take notes after we leave," I said.

He laughed. "I've been doing my job for thirty years. I know what to do."

I stepped back into the room. He was a frequent traveler to exotic faraway places, and he decorated his office with tribal masks, outlandish statues, and primitive drawings.

"In the past few months, I feel I've made a breakthrough," I said. "When I first came here, I looked upon therapy almost as if it was some kind of religion, as if it were going to give me absolute peace and happiness."

"What I try to tell you people," he said, "is that I can't really change your life. Gloria still expects me to find her a boyfriend. Daniel expects me to fix up his marriage, get him a job, make him blissfully happy. I can't do it. At the bottom of everything, you people are still only left with yourselves."

"That's hard to accept," I said.

"Of course it is. But I'm only telling you something you really know already. All the fluff of life, the drive for money or success or even happiness, is just a kind of razzle-dazzle, a way for people to hide the truth from themselves. Your wife's in the hospital. I know it's very painful. But on the other hand, so what? Whether she lives or dies, you're still stuck with whoever you are."

He picked up a pencil and then rolled it back on his desk.

"I couldn't treat anyone like your wife. If she can't stand living in the world, let her go into the hospital."

"It's a terrible place."

"Then let her not go into the hospital," he said irritably. "I can't perform magic. At best, I can only help you people catch a glimpse into yourselves."

Coming out of Dr. Goldstein's office I stopped to look up at the sky. A rolling, gray-black wave of clouds dominated the sky, wiping out everything but a misty half-moon and a few sparse flickering stars. I climbed into my car and drove to my in-laws' apartment. They had offered to take me out to dinner.

We ate a quiet awkward meal in an expensive, fashionable Italian restaurant. The restaurant, a small narrow room, had all the trappings of stylized upward-moving pretension, round red-clothed tables, a fancy wooden wine rack, and a wall-length mural of Mount Vesuvius in endless eruption. We silently picked at our food, trying hard to find a common plane of sociability. Janet's "illness" which held us all together also pushed us apart. We had never really grown together. We were still frozen in the first moments of my courtship; I was still that unknown young man who had taken their daughter away.

"Have you spoken to Janet yet?" my mother-in-law asked.

My mother-in-law ate her food mechanically, with a slow ladylike primness. There was little resemblance between Janet and her mother. Although they were both small, their faces were shaped differently. Their manners were radically dissimilar. Janet laughed too loud and often spoke with a bluntness that made her mother wince.

"Janet phoned me this afternoon," I said. "As usual, she's having trouble adjusting to the hospital."

My father-in-law fidgeted all through dinner, jumping up constantly to make phone calls.

"He just can't sit still now," my mother-in-law said. "Actually it's just as well that the school system is in such turmoil. It keeps his mind off Janet, if you understand what I mean. But everybody wants to talk to him. He has a talent for charming people. I guess you'd call it charisma. Janet has it also."

"I guess she does," I said.

"She does. Everybody has always loved her. Even now, I meet people who knew her as a child. They tell me how much they loved her."

I couldn't look at my mother-in-law. There was something pathetic in what she was telling me. But I suppose I could even understand her attitude. She couldn't bear seeing her daughter as she was now. She had nothing to hold on to but the memory of a person. And even that memory called forth only a shell.

As we drove back to my in-laws' house to pick up my car, I sat in the back seat staring at the outline of their heads. I couldn't bring myself to tell them what I had wanted to say all evening, that I had virtually concluded that their daughter was hopelessly ill. Finally, I simply asked them for money.

The automobile was filled with the heavy tense silence which always appeared whenever I asked them for money. I was infuriated. I was only asking them for financial help, after all. Not a piece of their flesh.

"How much do you want?" my mother-in-law asked.

"A thousand," I said.

"Helen will take it out of our savings account tomorrow morning," my father-in-law said. "She'll mail it to you. Is that okay?"

"That's okay."

Monroe Park II

I gazed out the side window. We were driving
neighborhood of squat brick houses like the neighborho
Janet and I were now living. As we shot past the houses, I c
bright living-room lights and the occasional flicker of a tele
set. A long-haired young girl was walking a dog. A group of y
boys were gossiping in front of a garishly lit pizza place.

My anger was already disappearing into my cold unemotionality.
But the coldness was disappearing also, being replaced by a terrible
sadness, a sadness for my in-laws as well as for myself.

I had read many books about how parents had psychologically
damaged their children. My own therapy taught me the theories of
early childhood conflicts, double messages, and inflexible upbring-
ings. I didn't doubt the truth of these theories. But, as I rode in this
silent car, I thought that the mysteries and complexities of a family
were really too much for the dryness and pseudoscience of books
and theories to handle.

What had Janet's parents done to her? They were quite ordinary,
good, loving, honest people. In the best way they could, they had
loved her. They had enjoyed her, brought her surprise presents
when she was sick, taken her traveling with them. She had slid
easily and spontaneously into loving me, after all, and she had to
learn how to love from someone. Other people had survived terrible
childhoods—broken homes, beatings, a total absence of love—so
what had her parents really done?

They were undoubtedly rigid people. Like others, they believed in
original sin, the concept that children had to be controlled, molded,
and shaped into goodness and respectability. They had found it
difficult to accept anything outside their own visions and concepts.
But where did their responsibilities end? It wasn't their fault that
Janet had chosen to close off her angers and fears to them. She had
appeared to be perfect. Could they possibly know that perfection
was much more dangerous than raggedness, hostility, or failure?

Neither Janet nor her brother had really ever challenged them.
They had both given up fighting for themselves a long, long time
ago, and they had never offered an elegant luxury to their parents,
the opportunity to grow and change.

Janet's parents had done everything they could for her. They had
spared no expense, wrecking their own lives trying to save her.
They had listened to what everybody said, and had done exactly
what everybody told them to do. And they were still trapped by her,
as trapped by their dreams and frustrated hungers as they had been
trapped by their guilts and obligations. And they thought I was
trapped as well.

I realized that their earlier silence was not a reluctance to help me, but an embarrassment at my inability to fulfill my financial obligations. They didn't know me yet. They couldn't possibly know that I would never stay with Janet solely out of obligation. I had always been able to cut and run. Perhaps Janet, torn by an inability to back away from principle or duty, had seen in me the same quality I was suddenly seeing in myself, the freedom to give up and fail.

I felt free. The realization that I wasn't going to stay with her out of obligation opened up my emotions and cleared my perspective, reminding me of who I was.

My father-in-law pulled behind my car, breaking my train of thought.

"Do you want to come upstairs for a cup of coffee?" he asked.

"I'm exhausted," I said. "I think I'll just go home."

"Have you spoken to Jake Sternfeld recently?" he asked.

"Just last night."

"He won't really talk to me anymore. He told me to get all my information from you."

"You can understand his feeling," I said. "He doesn't want to get involved with too many people. Just talking to me is enough trouble."

"But we feel so isolated now," my mother-in-law said. "At least in the past we knew what was going on."

"There's nothing good to tell anyway. It's not a good sign that Janet's hospitalized again."

She sighed, the same deep sorrowful sigh as her daughter.

"Don't you get down, Paul," she said. "You mustn't let yourself get down."

"I always fulfill my obligations," I said, making my own private joke.

"Does Jake think she'll come out of this episode soon?" my father-in-law asked.

"He says that if he can reach her he can help her."

"At least Jake Sternfeld is taking care of her," my mother-in-law said. "He really loves her."

"I suppose he does, after all these years," I said. "In his own way, I suppose he does love her."

Soon after I arrived home, Janet phoned me.

"Where were you?" she asked. "I've been calling you all evening."

"I had dinner with your parents."

"How was it?"

"Nice. Your father charmed the waiter and your mother told me how many people love you."

"Oh, shit."

"How are you?"

"I'm okay, I guess. I'm very drugged. They just gave me a shot of Thorazine which hurts like hell. It's intramuscular."

"You feel better, at least?"

"I feel all drugged. I can still feel my anxiety fluttering around deep inside me. The reason I was trying to call you was that I got into a stupid argument with one of the aides. He asked me why I was crying, and I told him I was afraid of going totally crazy. He says that nobody goes crazy anymore with all the drugs and sophisticated treatments. I got all upset, and they probably wrote it up in their little books. Now they won't even let me go up to occupational therapy tomorrow."

"You're not going to spend the rest of your life in hospitals, are you, Janet?" I suddenly asked.

"What are you talking about? Where'd you get that idea?"

"I don't know. It's been rattling around in my head for the past couple of days."

"I hate it here, Paul. I always have. As much as I'm pulled toward the safety of the hospital and toward being taken care of, I can't stand myself for wanting it. I feel so separated from the world. Like some pathetic caged animal. And I miss you so much I can hardly bear the loneliness."

"I miss you too, Janet," I said. "I feel as if I haven't had you for a very long time."

When I hung up I realized I had panicked. My conclusions about Janet were exaggerated and distorted. Perhaps Dr. Sternfeld had panicked as well. I drew my conclusions from my telephone conversation with him, after all. Or perhaps my distortions came solely out of my own head, a justification for Dr. Sternfeld's care in talking to me, a justification for the general reluctance of psychiatrists to talk to the relatives of their patients. Yet in hindsight, I had taken my cues from his attitude as well as his words. Buried beneath his calm phrases, I sensed a terrible weariness and an uncontrolled aura of rage. Perhaps finally, as my father had said, Janet was truly an albatross around his neck. Out of some strange need or pride or duty or even love, he was as trapped as the rest of us; he couldn't let her go.

She grew stronger. Ultimately, her fifty-nine days of hospitalization proved to be a profound and revolutionary experience for her, not because of the hospital itself, but because of someone she met there: a sixteen-year-old boy by the name of Michael Clifton Christopher.

"I really wanted you to meet Mike," she said on my first visiting day. We were seated at a table in the dayroom. "He's still out on a pass with his mother. Maybe he'll be back before you go home."

"I'd like to meet him also," I said.

"He's just great. You'll love him. I told you how he forced the nurses to let me participate in the sensory relaxation exercises. They didn't want me to participate at first. They were still disturbed about my argument with the aide."

She had told me about Mike. He had wheedled and nudged the staff, had fought through Janet's natural reluctance and general despair, and had finally dragged her into this special recreational activity. The occupational and recreational therapists, the lowest rung on the therapeutic ladder, were drawn from those young people who were then called hippies. They brought some of the fashions of the counterculture to the hospital—long hair, love beads, and an Esalen-type sensory encounter project.

"It was the most profoundly moving experience of my life," Janet explained. "Four people held me and bounced me gently in the air and touched me. At first I closed myself off, but then I relaxed and I felt wave after wave of pure sensation, as if I were experiencing my body for the first time."

Despite a drugged, hooded dullness in her eyes, she spoke with an animation that startled me. Caught between the infectiousness of her excitement and my own confusion and unhappiness, I mentally stepped back from her, making myself somewhat distant and cool. It seemed suddenly unfair to me that she should be having such a good time.

"You seem in remarkably good spirits," I said.

"Don't let it fool you," she answered. "I just had a good day. Most of the time I can't stop myself from crying. And I wouldn't trust me near a razor blade."

A thin young woman wormed her way through a nearby knot of patients and relatives, and seated herself at our table. She made a nervous waving gesture with her hand and smiled at us. She was ordinary looking, neither overly attractive nor overly unattractive, with thick curly hair, small cat eyes, and a sharp narrow nose. She was dressed severely, in a well-cut, black wool suit.

"I assume this is your husband," she said to Janet. "I've already met your doctor. And now, I just wanted to come over and meet your husband."

"Was Dr. Sternfeld here already?" I asked Janet.

"I forgot to tell you. He dropped by this afternoon. He said he was heading uptown and just wanted to come in for a moment."

"He seems like he's a remarkable man," the thin young woman commented amiably. "He took a couple of us aside and told us how he wanted us to treat Janet. He said that she has a talent for getting people to feel sorry for her. So he wants us to make sure we treat her like a full-fledged adult."

"I guess I should introduce you," Janet said stiffly. "This is my husband Paul. Sue Rule."

"The Sue you told me about on the telephone?" I asked.

"No. No. That's Sue Mahoney, a patient. This is another Sue. She's staff."

"Where's your uniform?" I asked. "What do you do? Change clothes before you go home?"

"We have a new policy now," Sue Rule explained. "None of the staff wears uniforms anymore."

"On the theory that the patients won't be able to tell you apart from them?" I said.

"Oh, no. Not really. Unfortunately, we have so much work to do, so many notes to write up that we don't have much of an opportunity to mingle with the patients. It's too bad, really. But I think our street clothes make us seem friendlier. It's important symbolically. Don't you think so, Janet?"

Janet made a horrid face.

"Anyway," Sue Rule continued, "I did want to meet you. I've taken a personal interest in Janet, as you can see. I think that despite her first . . . uh . . . unfortunate outburst, we can all pull together and turn this hospitalization into a rewarding experience."

Janet leaned back and rolled her eyes up into her head.

"Anyway," Sue Rule continued, "I do have to run now. I'm really pleased to meet you."

She leaped up, shook my hand briskly, and disappeared, working her way back through the crowd.

"Have you ever met such a shithead?" Janet said.

"You certainly have a talent for short graphic descriptions," I responded. "She just wants to help you."

"Oh, yeah," Janet groaned. "What should I do? Go down on my knees and be grateful? What should I call her? Sister Mercy of the Healers?"

A voice on the loudspeaker made the second call for the end of visiting hours and, almost simultaneously, an aide came over to shoo me outside. I swallowed my anger. I had never quite adjusted to the standing-in-line, filling-out-forms rules of life, but I was old enough to accept them.

I lingered at the door to the ward.

"You're in much better shape than I expected," I told Janet.

"Did you really expect me to spend the rest of my life in the hospital?" she asked. "That's a strange idea."

"I have a lot of strange ideas," I said nonsensically. "I manufacture them."

We embraced and kissed. Before I went off to the elevators, she said, "I'm sorry you didn't get a chance to meet Mike. He's very important to me."

Walking out the front entrance, I brushed past Mike, although I didn't know who he was at the time. His face held my attention, and I turned in the doorway to look at him. He was quite tall, well over six feet, with a smooth adolescent complexion and a soft, downy peach-fuzz beard. But close up, his face was oddly pitted and lined, and his eyes were old, as if he had skipped through a lot of years. After I knew him, I used to say he was sixteen going on eighty. He was one of those burned-out children who had done everything, gone everywhere, tasted everything, shot everything into his system. I don't want to romanticize him. In many ways, he was only a tortured, mixed-up child. But he was fiercely talented—in less than an hour he once sculpted a beautiful statue of a sorrowful crying woman that still lies in our living room—and he was very sweet.

His hospital stay was only a temporary stop on a long self-destructive trip. Whatever he felt or suffered, he was a child who experienced his passions far too deeply. He was in a race with himself, to see if he grew into his feelings before he destroyed himself.

Janet loved Mike, as deeply and as purely as she had ever loved me. During the first month of her hospitalization, they spent an enormous amount of time together, secluding themselves in a corner of the occupational therapy room or trying to find privacy in each other's rooms. She loved him, I suppose, because he saw clearly into her, past her overlay of anxiety, self-pity, and sadness. And he loved her because she simply loved him in return. Besides knowing me, her relationship with Mike was the single most profound experience of those first years that I lived with her. As loving me had changed her, this one short moment of loving him changed her as well.

They loved each other solely as friends do, although the hospital read more insidious motives into their relationship. They found relief from their own pain in the comfort and love they gave each other. Once, Janet told me, Mike broke down and cried in front of her. He had never before let anyone touch him as deeply as Janet had. They were inseparable.

In the middle of March, Janet phoned me at work, hysterical. The weather was unseasonably warm, and I was dressed in jeans and a T-shirt, luxuriating in the sweat and effort of my labor. When the intercom buzzed twice—my personal signal—I knew that Janet was on the telephone. I was annoyed. She was always breaking my concentration, never letting me lose myself in my work.

When I lifted the receiver, she was crying. I had to cup my hand over my ear to hear her, blocking out the rumblings of the machinery.

"What's wrong?" I asked. "What's the matter?"

"I just got into a fight with Sue Rule. You remember her? The nurse you met a few weeks ago."

"I remember Sue Rule."

"She caught me crying in the hallway, and she told me that she and the other nurses have been discussing me. They think I'm agitated because of my relationship with Mike. They think we're spending much too much time together."

"Did you tell her to buzz off?"

"How can I tell her to buzz off? This is a lunatic asylum here. You never know what anyone's going to do to you."

I shook my head, trying to get myself to concentrate on Janet's problem. A few feet away from me, a worker was leaning against a long table, blocking a child's hat on a steam dye.

"What's really wrong, then, Janet?" I asked again.

"She said—" Janet started to cry again, and I said nothing, waiting for her to stop. She blew her nose into the receiver, the sound irritating my eardrum. "She said that she thinks that I have all kinds of repressed sexual feelings toward Mike. That I'm unhappy because of my unfulfilled sexual feelings toward him."

"Repressed sexual feelings? My God."

"I told her that I'm twelve years older than he is. That I'm almost old enough to be his mother. She got very serious and said, 'You've heard of an Oedipus complex, haven't you?' "

I couldn't help laughing, loudly.

"Oedipus complex?" I said, still chuckling at the thought. "What did she have? One year of psychology and she thinks she knows all about the human mind."

"Maybe it's funny to you. But they don't want us to spend any more time together. They won't let us go into each other's rooms."

"I'm sorry for laughing, Janet. But it's just so ludicrous. Oedipus complex? It's the funniest thing I've heard in a long time."

"Then you don't think she's right?"

"Of course I don't. Anyway, she has the whole thing wrong. Oedipus had the sexual desire for his mother, not the other way around. And I know you. Repressed sexual feelings? That's not your problem."

"Sue Rule is going to write it down in her little book. It's going to become a permanent part of my record."

"It's ridiculous. No one's going to take it seriously."

"I'm telling you it's going to become part of my hospital record."

"Have it your own way. I'm not going to argue with you. So what? Let it be in your record."

Soon after this episode with Sue Rule, Mike was released from the hospital. Unchecked and unconfined, he continued on his boundless self-destructive plunge. We heard from him infrequently. He enrolled in a heroin maintenance program in England, spent a few months in a fancy French asylum, entered an Indian ashram. In the spring of the following year, he returned to Monroe Park where he died, a victim of some mysterious mixture of prescribed or unprescribed drugs.

I took off from work and Janet and I went to his funeral. His new doctor, one of the superstars of psychiatry, the man who had almost single-handedly created the concept of drug therapy, ambled solemnly through the elegant, Upper East Side chapel, a familiar, shadowy presence. After a short, emotionless service, Janet wandered out alone into the street. I followed her. Although she tried for a long time to make peace with the sadness of the short, passionate, wasted life of someone she had deeply loved, she couldn't ever do it. Neither she nor Monroe Park was going to forget him.

Janet continued to suffer. During the first six weeks of her hospitalization, through March and into April, she was almost always in pain. I was used to her suffering by now. Separated from her by the hospital I was at least thankful that I no longer had to bear the full weight of her complaints. I began to see her pain as part of what Dr. Sternfeld called an "episode," a momentary crisis of exaggerated and distorted emotion. And I knew that someday, this episode would pass.

I visited her, took her out for dinner on passes, drove her to see Dr. Sternfeld, and one weekend, even arranged a semiholiday in a stylish Manhattan hotel. But nothing I did for her made her feel better. Her pain was unreasonable and mysterious; it seemed almost to be grafted on to her, unconnected to her thoughts or will. After a while, I grew impatient; my strength and tolerance were rapidly diminishing.

"Can't you do anything at all?" I asked Dr. Sternfeld one day on the telephone. "It just goes on and on."

"I understand your impatience," he said. "Sometimes I even share the impatience myself, although, of course, I wouldn't allow myself to listen to it. I don't know what to do for her anymore. I've just about run out of ideas. I can't give her shock treatments, for instance."

"She's deathly afraid of shock treatments," I interrupted. "Everytime the aides gather people to go to the shock room, she practically has an anxiety attack."

"I know she's frightened," he said. "That's why I wouldn't even consider them. I remember that when I gave her shock treatments in Franklin Central Hospital she got so anxious anticipating them that I finally had to stop."

"How about vitamin pills?" I asked. Recently, I had watched a television program where a psychiatrist had called vitamin therapy, "the brightest hope for those crippled by mental illness."

"You mean mega-vitamin therapy," Dr. Sternfeld answered. "Massive dosages of B complex? Two men here in New York make fantastic claims about them. And you probably know that Linus Pauling recently came out in support of their claims. But I've read a lot about this subject and so far nobody has ever duplicated their findings. For the time being, I remain skeptical."

"You don't have any miracle drug up your sleeve, then?"

He chuckled. "I'm afraid I don't. I've tried just about every pill on the market on Janet, and they don't really work. They lessen anxiety, of course. But they don't work as well on her as they do on other people. At their best, they should actually change her behavior, if you know what I mean."

I didn't know what he meant, but I let his statement pass. I found it hard to believe that those candy-colored, pill-shaped chemicals could really change behavior.

"I have been toying with an experimental idea," he continued. "I was discussing Janet's case with a colleague of mine at a psychiatric conference. He suggested trying lithium carbonate."

"I thought lithium was used only on manic-depressives."

"Normally, it is. But nobody really knows how it works. We think it interrupts a cycle. Maybe Janet is just suffering through a long drawn out cycle. I don't really know; nothing I do seems to help her.

I've always believed that one of the ten thousand enzymes in her cells was somehow unbalanced. But we don't know enough about enzymes for me to check it out."

We endured one of our familiar telephone silences. I did have a question I wanted to ask him, but I wasn't certain how I should phrase it.

"I don't want to be insulting," I finally said, "but maybe Janet should see another doctor."

"No. No. I'm not insulted at all. I considered the idea many times myself. But you have to understand that she's been so attached to me that if I had suggested it, she would have misinterpreted me. She would have thought that I wanted to abandon her."

"Maybe she can use a fresh approach," I said. "Someone who isn't so personally involved with her."

"I wouldn't say I'm personally involved with her," he said stiffly. "But you might broach the idea with her."

"I don't know if she'll listen to me either," I said. "But I might as well try. I don't know what else to do. She's pathetic to see. She feels like an absolute nothing."

"If it's any consolation, at least we don't have to worry about a suicide attempt when she feels the way she does now. Suicide is an assertive act. Only when she feels stronger and a little more sure of herself, do we have to worry."

"Then the trick is to keep her feeling like nothing," I said, making another of my silly jokes.

"The trick is to reach her," he said quite seriously. "To dip down inside her head and turn her aggressiveness outward, instead of toward herself."

"You wouldn't hazard a guess about the future?" I asked.

"I think you might as well face a painful fact, Paul: She might always be the way she is now, in and out of hospitals, always faced with some crisis."

His words didn't particularly affect me. The television program which had featured the vitamin pill psychiatrist had also included a panel of "ex-mental patients," members of an organization called Schizophrenics Anonymous. Another psychiatrist had spoken about the need for schizophrenics to understand the nature of their illness, to understand that they would be crippled for the rest of their days and would never be able to lead normal lives. I had admired the heroic stoicism of the ex-patients, as I had been saddened by their inhuman lifelessness and their pathetic lack of expectation. In my own unhappiness, I had thought that I, like them, must learn to adjust to the realities of mental illness. I couldn't expect much from life either. If Janet could learn to live with her suffering, we might at least have a chance to build a life together.

"I think I can live with anything that happens," I said. "I spent a couple of days killing Janet off, but now I've made a certain peace with reality."

"I don't understand what you mean."

"I misinterpreted something you once said to me. I thought that you told me that she'd be hospitalized for life."

"I never said that, Paul."

"I know you didn't. I told you that I misinterpreted you."

"And I'm not predicting that she'll stay the way she is now. If she got well once, she can always get well again. I'm only saying that I wouldn't be surprised if she never got any better."

I didn't have the heart to ask Janet about changing doctors. She clung to Dr. Sternfeld as tenaciously as a child who doesn't want his parents to go out for the evening. And, in my own way, I clung to him also.

Eventually, she was well enough to leave the hospital. After $4,095.20 worth of pills, bowling trips, and confinement, I brought her home. We didn't celebrate her homecoming; we felt no great joy, no elation, no hope. We expected, at best, to endure the coming years. Neither of us knew what was in store for us.

In the summer of 1969, on a three-week vacation in Shelter Island, we almost managed to forget our troubles. For a few weeks, we were almost able to crank out a semblance of hope, briefly, to see the possibility of turning our life around.

We rented a small, isolated summer cottage and settled happily into it, doing practically nothing with our time. One evening, after making love, we lay side by side on the old creaky bed.

"We should really do this more often," Janet said.

"Do what? Make love?"

"What do you think I'm talking about? Cutting wood?"

Exhausted from too much sun, in a languorous state of mind, I lay on my back, watching the chit flies gather over our bedside lamp.

"The trouble is," I said, "that you're usually too preoccupied with your pain. And if you're not, I'm exhausted from working all day."

"Married people don't screw anyway," Janet said. "That's another reason why we should never have gotten married."

"You can't help being married in that sense. Living together as long as we have would have made us married already."

PAUL

These first summer days had been remarkably peaceful, reminding us of the first ecstatic months we had lived together. Despite our pain, despite the pulls and pressures on us, we were still remarkably well suited for each other. We liked the same things and thought the same way.

"I want a baby," Janet suddenly said.

"So you want a baby."

"I mean that; I want to conceive one now. Right this moment."

She raised herself on her elbow, studying my face for some sign of emotion. Usually we discussed having children at odd, inappropriate times, like when she was hospitalized or most unhappy, as if simply talking about a brighter future could wipe away our darkest moments of hopelessness and despair. She had wanted a baby for a long time. But I knew that she thought she would never have one.

"What do you want me to say?" I asked. "Don't douche. Maybe that will do it."

She made a disgusted face. "You know I'm taking birth control pills. I'd have to stop them before we could even try. Usually, when I tell someone that I want a baby, they look at me as if I'm even crazier than I am. I feel like some kind of leper, like I'll pass on some terrible disease."

"I don't feel that way, Janet."

"I told Dr. Sternfeld recently about how badly I want a baby. He asked me what I wanted to prove."

"Do you want to prove something?"

"I don't know. I suppose that's part of it. Wanting to prove that I'm normal, a real woman. Dr. Sternfeld told me that he understands my desire. That in my mind, a baby offers me unqualified, unguarded love. But he said that this is obviously not the time to consider having one. As long as I'm under his care, he expects me to ask his permission before I do anything."

I rolled on my side to face her, squinting because I had been staring into the bedside lamp and was momentarily blinded. Talking about babies had opened up a sore nerve in me. I suppose I wanted a baby also. I had no reason to believe that Janet would survive her torment. Somewhat sentimentally, I thought that a baby would serve as a remembrance of her, a remembrance of our good times together and of our love. But I didn't want to think about children now.

"Suppose you get to feel better," I asked, "what do you want to do? I always assume that we generally want the same things in life. But what do you want to do with yourself, personally?"

She wrinkled her brow. "I hardly ever think about what I want to do anymore. At one time in my life, I thought that I wanted to be a great poet. Or at least teach in college. But now I'd just like to lead a simple normal life. Have children, take care of my home, cook for you."

"That's not very ambitious," I said.

"I'm not very ambitious anymore. If I can just come out of this, I'll settle for the most normal life I can achieve."

"I'd like to think that we learned something from all our pain," I said. "I know that I've learned a lot of things from you."

"Have you really? I always think that I'm just a drain on you. That I drag you down with me."

"I'd be lying if I said that you didn't often make me terribly unhappy. But I sometimes think about what our life would have been like if you hadn't had such trouble. I would have gone dumbly off to work and come back to you all preoccupied, worrying about money or about making it. Now I'm just thankful for a good day. I go to sleep at night thankful for achieving some satisfaction or having some fun. Thankful that we still love each other."

I watched her eyes mist over. I hadn't meant to sound sentimental.

"That's a nice thing to say," she said. "Whether you mean it or not."

"Of course I mean it," I said, suddenly angry. "I wouldn't say it if I didn't mean it. Anyway, all this talk about babies. We can't have one without sex."

"That's what I've been trying to tell you." She pressed her body against mine.

"Whatever that sinfulness Dr. Sternfeld always talks about is," I said, "at least it's not sex."

"But it is. I had shut off my sexual feelings for so long. I had that revulsion about Larry pawing me."

"I thought Dr. Sternfeld always said that you exaggerated the importance of those incidents with Larry."

"I exaggerated its psychological importance. He always said that he wasn't surprised at how quickly I had taken to sex. He knew that it was all locked up in me, ready to explode."

"So your sinfulness goes beyond sex," I said. "Passion itself. All those feelings wrapped up inside you, turned against yourself."

"What makes you so smart?"

"Suffering," I said half-joking.

"No," she answered, quite seriously. "You just have a big mouth."

We continued this same conversation the next afternoon. We

PAUL

woke up at ten, ate a leisurely breakfast, packed two sandwiches in a paper bag, and drove across the island to the deserted beach we always frequented. The day was clear and warm. Lying next to each other on a blanket on the sand, we closed our eyes and fell into a dull dreamy stupor.

"I still want to know what you'd like to do with yourself," I said, my eyelids shutting out the brightness of the sun. "I wasn't satisfied with your answer last night."

She stood up and padded across the sand, into the water. This was August and the sand crabs had come into shallower water. A dozen or so crabs were washed up on the beach, looking unnatural and misshapen against the clean white sand like a collection of petty thoughts.

When I joined Janet in the water, she was lazily floating on her back. Across the bay, I could barely make out the town of Greenport. I could see the outline of a little harbor, the shimmer of pleasure boats rolling in the bright water. Janet was wearing a bikini. Although she was quite thin, she had always been obsessed with her weight, afraid that people would think her fat. Now, alone on the deserted beach, she felt suddenly free; she didn't care what she wore.

"This is real freedom for me," she said as we dried off again in the sun. "Having no one around like this. When I used to travel on the subway, I thought everybody was staring at me. I've always based my life on what other people thought of me."

"That's almost a genetic defect," I said. "It seems to run in the family."

"I suppose it does."

We lay silently on our blanket. Finally she leaned toward me and said, "What you asked me before? Whether I have any big dreams for myself? I don't really have any dreams left. I wasn't kidding when I said I only want a simple ordinary life."

But I knew something about her that she didn't know about herself. She was an aggressive, ambitious, intelligent young woman, and I doubted that she would ever really be satisfied with herself. She had always been pulled in two directions, toward achievement and toward simplicity. She had never truly dealt with anything real in life, with questions of personal satisfaction or the problems of meaningfulness. She had always switched from one stereotype of a person to another, and had always been treated as such—as a perfect child, a perfect student, a mental patient. Whatever she felt, she experienced it far too deeply, and she had never found a suitable place for her passions, either as a woman or a human being. Despite

Monroe Park II

Dr. Sternfeld's talk of illness, of self-destructive compulsions and distorted perceptions, I knew that she was bursting with the substance of humanity, with frustrations, drives, and a controlled, catastrophic rage. She just wasn't yet willing to see herself as a human being.

"It's so comfortable and peaceful here," she said. "I wish we didn't have to go home again."

"We could always move to a place like this," I said. "Do you think you could do it?"

"I don't know. On one hand I want to get out of Brooklyn so badly. I just don't know if I can afford to leave Dr. Sternfeld right now."

"Maybe you could do what Dr. Sternfeld told you to do last summer. Take Shelter Island back with you."

"Don't laugh," she said. "Maybe I can fool you. Maybe I can do it."

But we both knew as we lolled on this quiet beach that she couldn't.

A few days after we returned to Brooklyn, she was back into a typical pattern of upswings and treacherous emotional plummets. Renting this new apartment had been a mistake in judgment. Our neighbors were rigidly upward-striving; they had come out of working-class backgrounds and were relentlessly pushing themselves into the middle class. The neighborhood women's pursuit of status, their Tupperware parties, bowling tournaments, and shopping trips threatened Janet. They were friendly enough people, but they seemed part of a world Janet could never really enter. Their single-minded pursuit of the American Dream made her feel odd and different, as if they could never accept or tolerate her eccentricities, as if she would never achieve a normal life.

We adjusted to our erratic life. We moved through September, noting with satisfaction that we had passed the anniversary of her first hospitalization without incident. We celebrated our third wedding anniversary, weathered a midwinter crisis, and came into early spring with our senses dulled, without any conception of the future. Janet was bored and restless. She phoned me at work constantly. She didn't know what to do with her days.

"Why don't you do something constructive with your time?" I asked her one afternoon, trying to divide my attention between her demands and the paper work that was piled up on my desk. "Why don't you read a book or go to a museum?"

"You know I'm so fogged up that I can't concentrate on a book.

And everytime I get involved in something and almost lose myself, I get another anxiety attack and have to stop what I'm doing."

"This is terrible, though. When you spend all your time thinking about yourself, it saps your strength and demoralizes you. Why don't you ask Dr. Sternfeld if he has any ideas about what you can do with yourself?"

"He says my day-to-day business is my concern. He's only interested in changing what goes on in my head."

"That's true," I said, thinking of Dr. Goldstein's similar attitude. "He is a psychiatrist, after all."

"Yeah. But since when did he ever stop short of running my life. Only when he doesn't know what to do with me."

Despite Dr. Sternfeld's momentary discouragement during Janet's second hospitalization, he had not run out of ideas. He experimented with a "psychic-energizer" called Prolixin, planning to raise the dosage to an almost "unheard-of level." The dosage was to be so high that we arranged to purchase the drug wholesale, but before we could follow through on our arrangement, the experiment failed. As he increased the dosage, Janet became increasingly anxious, so he stopped.

He tried other combinations of drugs, but he always came back to the aspirin of tranquilizers, Thorazine. In March 1970, we suffered a trauma that should have changed our thinking about drug therapy, but senselessly, it hardly even affected us.

Janet had been feeling relatively good for a few weeks. Remembering the pleasures of sensory activities, she had involved herself in a daily program of exercises. While she was doing her evening exercises in the den, I lay on our bed, watching the eleven-o'clock news. The news was typically unpleasant: our war still raged endlessly in Vietnam; our college campuses were in turmoil; all kinds of "experts" were predicting there would be a long, hot, chaotic summer.

While I watched I heard a loud, disquieting thud. I ran into the den and saw Janet writhing on the floor, her mouth gaping open, her limbs kicking spasmodically, her eyes rolling back into her head.

I had learned to expect and accept almost anything in life. I was no longer amazed at what happened. If someone had told me that Janet was suddenly possessed by the devil, I would have shaken my head sadly and said, "Okay, what can we do for her now? What kind of pills do you suggest? What kind of treatment?" But I was frightened. She didn't respond when I called out her name. I bent down to touch her, and she kicked her legs upward, brushing indifferently against my outstretched hand. The pupils of her eyes had disappeared into her head. I thought she was dying.

I ran into the kitchen to phone Dr. Sternfeld, but in my panic, I couldn't find our address book. I dialed 911, the emergency police number.

"Should we send oxygen?" The voice on the other end of the phone asked, after I had given him my name, address, and a short, garbled description of Janet's condition. I had always wondered how I would react in a crisis, and I was pleased to discover that I had kept at least a part of my mind clear.

"Oxygen?" I said irritably. "I don't know. How should I know?"

"Listen to me carefully," the voice insisted. "Just keep calm. We're sending out a car right away. We just have to know whether to bring anything special."

"I told you I don't know. Send everything. What's the difference?"

I pulled the long phone cord across the kitchen so I could peek into our den. Janet was still involved in her grotesque, spasmodic dance. It made me somewhat ill to look at her. I dialed information and got the phone number of Dr. Sternfeld's office.

"This is Dr. Sternfeld speaking," the familiar, calm, clear voice proclaimed.

"Dr. Sternfeld. Thank God," I said.

"I am presently not in my office," the voice continued. "This is a recording of my voice. When the buzzer sounds, you will have fifteen seconds to leave me a message. Please speak clearly and distinctly into the receiver."

Suddenly afraid that I wouldn't have enough time to say everything I wanted to say, I recited a confused, panicky description of Janet's condition. In searching for an accurate descriptive phrase, I hit upon the word convulsions. For the first time, I realized that I had witnessed a physical episode, not some strange new manifestation of her mental condition.

Just as I hung up the phone, the doorbell rang and when I opened the door, two burly, overweight policemen burst into our apartment.

"We've got an oxygen tank in our vehicle," the taller of the two said.

"I don't think we'll need it," I said, trying to put on my coolest manner.

In the shadowy row of brick houses across the street, I could see that window curtains were parting and that faces were peering out at me. A small crowd was gathering down the block, attracted by the police car's flashing beacon.

PAUL

Janet was oddly quiet. She was no longer writhing. Eyes closed, lying on her back on the floor, she looked peaceful, as if enjoying a long, satisfying sleep.

"She looks awfully quiet to me," the taller policeman said. "Is she still breathing?"

"I think so," I said stupidly. "Her chest is heaving up and down."

The other policeman was studying our kitchen.

"This is certainly a nice place you have here," he said. "How much does it cost you?"

"Two twenty-five a month. What the hell's the difference?"

The phone rang and I picked up the receiver.

"Paul? This is Dr. Sternfeld."

"I'm surprised you understood my message," I said. "I was afraid I was unintelligible."

"Well, just calm down and tell me exactly what happened."

"I don't know what to say. I think she had some kind of fit; some kind of convulsions."

He was silent for a moment. I pulled the cord across the kitchen again. Janet had opened her eyes and was raising herself on her elbow.

"Convulsions," he repeated thoughtfully. "You know that I'm giving her two thousand milligrams of Thorazine a day. An enormous dosage. I'm afraid that convulsions are sometimes an unfortunate side effect."

"Thanks for telling me now."

"I don't believe in telling you about possibilities. Why should you have to worry about what might happen?"

I was in no mood to wrestle with medical philosophy. My panic had just about disappeared. I wanted to see how Janet was feeling.

"I think she's getting up now, anyway," I said. "It was an awful experience."

"You had never seen convulsions before, had you? They are frightening. I want to assure you that they're quite harmless. They look much worse than they are. The biggest danger is that a person might hurt themselves when they fall. Or swallow their tongue and suffocate."

One of the policemen was helping Janet to her feet. She looked sleepy-eyed and unsteady.

"How about brain damage?" I asked.

"Not in Janet's case. Convulsions are caused by oxygen momentarily shut off from the brain. But for such a short time? I don't think so. You should have her checked by a doctor though, for broken bones or internal bleeding."

"Don't you want to see her tonight?"

"You want me to come over now?"

I was in no mood to be polite either.

"Of course I do. That's what I've been saying."

"Well, it's late." He hesitated. "Okay. Certainly. If it will make you feel better. I'll hop in my car and be over in ten minutes."

Janet had risen from the floor, had brushed past the two policemen and had disappeared into the bathroom.

"Are you okay, Janet?" I asked through the closed door.

"I'm all right. What happened to me?"

"Has this ever happened before?" the taller policeman asked.

"Not convulsions. She's had a history of mental problems."

I knew that I said the wrong thing as soon as I opened my mouth. They exchanged sly knowing glances.

"We really should bring her over to the hospital," the shorter one said.

"I was just speaking to her psychiatrist on the phone," I said. "He's coming over to look at her. That should be adequate."

The taller policeman put his forefinger on the side of his nose and screwed up his face.

"I suppose that will do. We'll have to write up a report, though."

He copied down our name, address, and a short description of what happened. I ushered them to the front door.

"All in a night's work," the shorter policeman said.

"We'll still have five heart attacks and a couple of stabbings before the evening ends," the other one said.

"This is really a nice place," the short one said to me. "You say you pay $225."

"I wouldn't care if it were $25 a month," the tall one said. "If I had to hock my right arm, I wouldn't live in this city."

"Don't you want to be where the action is?" the short one asked.

"Fuck the action. I want to know when I go home that my wife is still in one piece."

They were laughing when I hustled them out the door.

"What happened to me?" Janet asked when I came back into the kitchen. "I don't remember anything."

I hugged her, holding her tightly against me.

"You went through convulsions. According to Dr. Sternfeld, it was a result of the Thorazine."

"I just remember going into the den. The next thing I knew, I was lying on the floor, those two monstrous policemen standing over me."

PAUL

"You look groggy. Why don't you sit down? Dr. Sternfeld will be here soon."

"He's coming here, now? That's great. I'll just boil some water for tea."

A few minutes later, the doorbell rang again and I jumped up from the table to let Dr. Sternfeld in.

"I parked at the fire pump across the street," he said as I helped him off with his coat. "They don't give tickets at this hour, do they? I'm always afraid to walk alone at night in a strange neighborhood."

"This is a safe neighborhood," I said. "And you don't have to worry about a ticket. You have MD plates, don't you?"

"That's true," he laughed. "I don't have to worry, do I?"

He had shaved off his mustache a few months earlier. With his gray-framed glasses and his short hair, he no longer pretended to be stylish. He looked like what he was: a middle-aged physician.

He tested Janet for broken bones, pulled down her eyelids and studied her pupils, and declared her fit. We drank tea and chatted amiably.

"I told Paul that one of the unfortunate side effects of Thorazine is sometimes convulsions," he said to Janet. "At least now we know your limits. How much your body can tolerate."

"What other side effects do we have to worry about?" I asked.

"I told you before that I don't like to deal in possibilities. These are complicated, dangerous drugs. But I'm a careful man. I'm as careful as I possibly can be with them."

"I won't have to stop taking Thorazine?" Janet asked.

"No. We know your ceiling now. I'm going to reduce the dosage to eighteen hundred milligrams."

After he left, as we were clearing off the cups and saucers, Janet, in one of her spurts of affection for Dr. Sternfeld said, "I think it's wonderful that he came to see me tonight."

"Oh, it's fantastic," I said. "He gives you such a high dosage that you go into convulsions, and then he comes over to see if you're all right."

"I mean it. It's not every doctor who'd come over at midnight. It's not every doctor who'd feel so personally involved."

One evening in early spring, as I shaved, I looked at my face in the bathroom mirror and thought about my own frustration and unhappiness. I thought about the dreariness of my days, my own dissatisfaction with life, and I was overwhelmed by an old familiar sense of meaninglessness, a sense of absurdity and alienation that I hadn't felt for a long time. For three years, Janet had dominated my life. As Dr. Sternfeld once warned me, I hadn't had much of an opportunity to grow.

Still clutching my cordless electric shaver, I walked into the bedroom. Janet was propped up in bed, trying not to fall asleep while reading.

"If you ever come out of this," I said, "we're going to sell everything we own and go off to Paris to live."

"Paris?" she said.

"It doesn't matter where. I was just staring at myself in the mirror and I had one of those clichéed revelations we always see on television. In just such clichéed words. I saw myself thirty years from now. Still looking in the mirror. Still asking myself why I'm doing what I'm doing. Still asking myself what kind of satisfaction I've gotten out of life."

She nodded her head patronizingly. She was normally much more romantic than I. Or at least she was romantic in a different way.

"But why Paris?" she asked.

"It can be anywhere. You've always wanted to go to Paris, though, haven't you? Call it my romantic gesture."

We did think about moving away from New York. We considered moving to California because I thought I could find work there. But our thoughts about leaving were only dreams. Neither of us believed we could do it.

During the summer, Mary Boyd flew in from California to stay with Janet for a week. They hadn't spent any time together in many years.

"Are you really thinking of moving to the West Coast?" she asked us one evening as we sat around our dining-room table, finishing supper.

"We think about it," Janet said. "We think about getting out of this endless rut we're in. But I don't think I could do it now. I don't think I could leave Dr. Sternfeld. This summer has been the most agonizing time of my life."

"You look all right to me," Mary said.

"It cheered me up to see you. This is the first peaceful week I've spent in a long time. I've just been in extraordinary pain. I'm barely able to fight off my suicidal feelings."

"You could always find another doctor in California," I said. "It's the land of psychiatrists. You can't help tripping over them."

"I've thought about changing doctors many times, over the past few years. It just always seemed pointless to me to start over with someone new."

PAUL

"It would be wonderful to have you live nearby," Mary said to Janet. "We could get to know each other again."

"It would be wonderful," Janet said. "At the risk of being called pessimistic by my husband over there, I can tell you that it won't ever happen."

I had trouble falling asleep that night. I tossed, turned, kicked at the covers, and finally gave up the attempt. I walked into the kitchen for a glass of water. The kitchen light was lit. Mary was sitting at the dining-room table, writing a letter.

"Can't you sleep either?" I asked.

She put down her pen and looked up at me.

"I always have trouble falling asleep," she said.

"I usually don't." I shrugged and sat down next to her. "If you don't mind, I'll just smoke a cigarette with you. Then I'll go back to bed. I have to go to work tomorrow."

I studied her carefully. Janet had told me a lot about her—that both her parents died soon after she was graduated from Ellis; that she had been aimless and restless since then, not able to find a place in life for herself. But I didn't really know her.

"Is Janet really suffering as much as she says she is?" Mary asked.

"It's been an awful summer. The pain goes on and on. I don't know how she bears it."

"Can't anyone do anything?"

"I don't know. On one hand, she's a lot stronger than she used to be. She's more aggressive. She seems to understand more about herself. But she continues to suffer so terribly."

"Maybe it's growing pains."

"Have you ever been in therapy?" I asked. "There's a certain resistance to working out your problems. To growing up posthumously."

"I haven't been in therapy. But that's what I mean."

"I don't know about Janet, though. Her pain is almost unconnected to what she does."

Mary shook her head. We were having one of those unsatisfactory conversations in which nothing conclusive gets said and people end up sadly shaking their heads.

"One thing I always wondered about," I said. "Janet calls you her closest friend. But you're separated by three thousand miles. And you don't even write to each other that often."

"I don't know about being her closest friend. At one time, we were very, very close."

"At Ellis," I said, seizing an opportunity to learn something about a Janet I didn't know. "What was she like then?"

"The funny thing is that I don't remember her cracking up. She tells me about coaxing her out of her room, but for the life of me, I can't remember her being so upset. Maybe I just blocked it all out. I can only remember our good times together. We were both such misfits there. She was so funny, so full of life and energy."

"She remembers the good times also," I said.

"I'm sure she does. It's true that we don't write to each other very often. But when something beautiful happens in my life, I have to tell her about it."

"I know," I said. "You're both romantic in the same way. You both cry at the first sign of spring."

"I suppose that's true. I don't like to think of myself as romantic. I'd rather be much more hard-headed. Ever since my parents died, I've just been drifting along—taking dance classes, teaching dance. I almost envy Janet for being able to live with someone she loves."

"She's always envied you; she thought you were such a beautiful person."

"Hah!" Mary said contemptuously.

"I wish you could stay here longer than a week. Janet's been more like herself since you've come."

"Oddly enough, I've been thinking about moving to the East Coast."

"The grass is always greener?"

"I suppose it is. But it's too big a country. We always end up in the same place we started."

"No more suicide," Dr. Sternfeld had told me before the summer. "At least I can guarantee you that we'll have no more suicide attempts."

I had been sitting in his waiting room thinking about Janet's newest series of hallucinations. She had recently bought a pair of sunglasses, but characteristically, she had questioned the wisdom of her purchase, changed her mind, and cancelled the order. Soon afterward, she had hallucinated a young girl wearing the same gold-rimmed owlish glasses she refused to keep. Dr. Sternfeld zeroed in on this hallucination. What did it mean? Why was the girl mocking her? Why were the elders always laughing at her?

Dr. Sternfeld was a psychiatrist, after all; he dealt in the business of insight and self-awareness. He believed that a person's problems revolved around their self-image. He said that his long years of psychiatric experience had taught him that we all share a common difficulty—the problem of coming to terms with the conflicting ways we see ourselves. He hammered away at Janet, trying to get her to realize that she mocked herself, to realize that the elders and the girl with the sunglasses were projections of the part of herself that judged and criticized everything she did and was.

Janet even listened to him. But she realized something that went beyond his words. All her life she tried to do everything "right." She let other people determine what she should do, how she should act, what she should feel. Even those people who had set themselves up to help her had judged and directed her. They had looked at her feelings, had determined them "sick" or "inappropriate," and had tried to wipe them away. They had punished her as severely as she had ever punished herself, filling her with drugs, shooting electricity through her system, and locking her away.

Without much strength and without any conception of who she really was, Janet had grown depressed. The hallucination of the young girl was constantly mocking her for thinking she could ever be "normal like everyone else" and she, of course, agreed with the young girl's conclusion. She thought herself hopelessly trapped, without the power to break out of her world of sickness, drugs, and caretakers.

So when Dr. Sternfeld followed Janet out of his private office and told me that I no longer had to worry about a suicide attempt, I was surprised.

"No more suicide?" I repeated.

"At least we can say that," he insisted. "Don't you think Janet's grown stronger? Can't you see a difference in her manner?"

"Her voice sounds firmer on the telephone, if you mean that," I said. I couldn't figure out if he really wanted me to answer his questions.

"No. I mean deeper than how her voice sounds. In her manner. How she says what she says."

"I think I know what you mean," I said, although I wasn't certain that I did.

"Anyway, I can safely say there'll be no more suicide attempts. And no more hospitalizations. I think we've turned a corner these past few months."

He was wrong, for a change. A few months later, on September 10, 1970, at three o'clock in the afternoon, Janet attempted suicide. Dr. Sternfeld wasn't surprised, of course. He pointed out that she had phoned him soon after she swallowed her overdose of pills. He called the whole attempt a plea, a signal that she wanted to go into the hospital, but couldn't bear the pain and sense of failure in requesting it. But I was tired of calling a duck a goose. It was a suicide attempt, dammit. She just about died.

At noon on the afternoon of Janet's suicide attempt, I ate lunch with my father. I told him about Dr. Sternfeld's newest sense of optimism, but my father looked at me skeptically.

"How much more can you take?" he asked.

"Oh, come on," I groaned.

"I mean it. Can you take another year of this? Five years?"

"Oh, look," I said disgustedly. "We have this same exact conversation every six months."

"I'm not as patient as you are. I like to see results. How many years has she been going to that charlatan Sternfeld? How much money has he soaked out of you and Janet's parents?"

I could have answered his questions. In four years Janet had had nearly four hundred fifty sessions, almost twenty thousand dollars worth of therapy. But I saw no reason to feed his anger. My father didn't believe in psychiatry. Despite his new wealth and sophistication, he was still the son of his blustery, hot-tempered immigrant father. Aggressive, high-strung, filled with terrible fury, my father had spent most of his life wrestling with enormous torments and rages. When he grew into middle age, he mellowed and finally settled into a wary peace with himself.

"If it makes you feel any better," I said, "I've almost had enough."

"Every man has a breaking point," he said.

"That's not quite what I mean. I just hardly care what happens to me anymore."

"I sometimes think about what I would do in your place. Everybody talks about a generation gap. But what am I? Almost sixty? I haven't given up living yet. I still want the same things out of life that you do."

"What would you have done in my place?"

"I would have run away from the whole thing a long time ago."

"I don't know if you would have. You would have gotten trapped by responsibility, like me. And don't forget, I love Janet."

"I wouldn't have gotten trapped," my father insisted. "You know me. I would have listened to those 'experts' up to a point. And then I would have blown my top."

"If you dislike experts so much why did you drag me to so many people for my stuttering?"

"That was more your mother's doing. She made me feel guilty. But I thought Ilse Levin, the psychologist, did you some good."

PAUL

"She was a nice enough lady. I question how much good she did me."

"She helped you indirectly. She was really for me. Not for you. I was so hot-headed then, I wouldn't listen to anybody. She sat me down and said, 'Leave the kid alone, for God's sake. Stop hovering over him. The stuttering isn't so important. Just let him grow by himself. He'll grow out of his problems and turn out all right.' "

"You listened to her," I said, "and we lived happily ever after."

My father wrinkled up his face. "If you believe in happy endings," he said. "I remember when I was a youngster I always used to see all those Hollywood movies, where everybody gets married and lives happily ever after. I always used to wonder why they never showed what really happened after they got married. Nowadays everybody seems to be running around—in some kind of therapy, doing some kind of exercise—expecting to find that Hollywood-type happiness. But people grow more and more frustrated and unhappy because it's all one big myth. People are afraid to see the truth. It's not really there. There's no such thing as absolute happiness in life."

"This is too abstract for me," I said.

"Then let's not be abstract. What are you looking for? Some miracle to happen to Janet? How much can you stand? Why don't you throw away all those people like Dr. Sternfeld and get away from the miserable way you've been living?"

"It's harder than you make it sound. But I have been thinking along the same lines."

"You should think that way."

"I am. I'm still my father's son."

He stared at me intently. "I don't know. Sometimes I think you are. And sometimes I think you're not."

I spoke to Janet when I returned to my office. She sounded weak and frightened. I hardly even cared. Dr. Sternfeld was always talking about the necessity of Janet's asserting herself. If she wanted me to come home early, she would have to ask me herself. I wasn't going to read her mind.

I thought about where I had hidden her pills. The most dangerous drugs—the Aventyl and Librium—were cleverly concealed behind a row of books in our bedroom bookcase. The giant bottle of Mellaril, too large for the shelf, had presented a problem. Although Janet was no longer taking Mellaril, we still kept them, never knowing when Dr. Sternfeld would want to switch back to them. I had hidden the unwieldy bottle the best place I could, behind the grate of the radiator cover.

Monroe Park II

I was still thinking about Janet when Sid, my father's brother and partner, entered my office. I rustled the papers that were spread across my desk, trying to pretend that I had been busily involved in my work.

"Run an errand for me," he said.

"Oh, come on."

"What are you? Too busy?" He stared at me angrily. "I want you to pick up your aunt and cousins at the Atlantic Avenue station and drive them down to Orchard Street."

I knew that his anger was impersonal. If I had simply asked him for the correct time, he would have contorted his face and glared at me. All my father's brothers and sisters were consumed with a constant, never-ending rage. They fought and feuded with each other throughout their lives. They had built a family business out of the mortar of their fury, though. Their anger was the essence of their being. Longevity ran in the family; without their rage, I often thought, they would all have shriveled up and wasted away.

"I don't know," I said. I was strangely reluctant to leave my office.

"Whaa," my uncle said. He was not the most articulate of men. Most of his conversation consisted of grunts, pauses, and one-syllable exclamations. "I'm telling you to go."

"I guess I can go," I said, feeling suddenly cheap, like a glorified delivery boy. "I guess it won't take very long."

"How's Jane?" he asked.

"Janet," I said.

"Yeah, Janet."

"She's fine. She's okay."

I snatched my coat from the wardrobe closet and bounded into the hallway. I poked my head through the little window in Lillian's front office.

"If Janet calls, tell her I'll be back in a half hour."

"If wifey calls," she mimicked, "I'll give her your message."

"Oh, shit," I said.

I was anxious about leaving. Looking back now, I think I knew instinctively that something was going to happen to Janet. She had undoubtedly laid out clues for me. But I had been too weary and uncaring to pick them up.

Driving back to my office later I became involved in the New York Mets baseball game. But I also thought about what my father had said about happiness. I realized then why I had allowed a man I detested as much as Dr. Lessing to work on my wife. Like so many other people, I, too, believed in the concept of absolute happiness. With all our self-help books, encounter groups, sensory institutes, and psychiatrists, we were either a profoundly unhappy nation, or we had sold our souls to a new kind of devil. Perhaps, with suddenly exploding incomes and constantly growing luxuries, we had misplaced our national purpose and confidence or had simply gone off the track. I knew that all the experts in the world, all the reconditioning of our lives—the behavior experiments on our criminals, the psychoanalysis of our children, the drugging of our lost and unfortunate—wasn't going to help me. Putting my life in someone else's hands was never going to improve the quality of my days.

When I came back into my office, I discovered that Janet had tried to take her own life. Like Dr. Sternfeld, I wasn't even surprised. It was the only part of herself she had left to take.

A Day in the Life, Revisited

And so I waited. Even after Janet broke out of her five-day coma, I continued to sit in Monroe Park's plastic lobby, waiting to see how firmly this new miracle of rebirth would take hold. I had plenty of time to review the events of the past four years. But my mind was blank; there was little to review or make sense of. Part spectator, part unwilling participant, I had doled out pills, marched through mental hospitals, and learned a great deal of psychiatric jargon. But I never had any meaningful place in anything I did or experienced. I learned something about love, something about passion, something about the human mind, and something about my own strength and courage. But now I was frightened about the future. Janet, in taking an overdose of pills, had betrayed the fragile balance of trust that had always held us together. I didn't know if I even wanted to stay with her.

A week after the suicide attempt, Dr. Sternfeld came to the hospital to visit Janet. He spent a half hour talking to her in her room, and then wandered downstairs to speak to me.

"It looks good," he said.

"I know. I just spoke to Dr. Caine this morning. He seems quite pleased at how well she's recovering."

"Usually these things go up and down," he said. "But Janet's recovery was relatively smooth. Her kidneys are still functioning well, thank goodness. The jaundice has just about disappeared. Her body temperature is almost normal."

I tapped out a cigarette for myself and he held out his hand, gesturing for me to pass him one.

"I thought you'd finally stopped smoking," I said.

He shook his head. "I stop and I start again."

I lit my cigarette and blew smoke up at the off-white ceiling. We sat at right angles to each other, on identical bright yellow plastic chairs.

"It's odd," Dr. Sternfeld continued. "One of the first things Janet talked about when she came out of the coma was going to California."

"We've been toying with the idea for a long time."

"I know. She's been telling me."

"Do you think it's a good idea? After what's just happened?"

"I think it's a good idea, Paul."

"I wouldn't do it if it were just for her. It's more for me. I'd like to break away from the dreary life we've been leading. I just want to go someplace new and relax and think about myself for a change."

"You have to take risks in life, Paul. In this case, I think the risk is a wise one."

But as I watched him swivel back and forth on his plastic chair, I couldn't shake the feeling that he wasn't telling me the whole truth about how he felt about Janet leaving New York. I thought that he was eager to get rid of her. She was finally too much for him; too much pain, too much work, and too much disappointment.

I liked Jake Sternfeld. He was in all respects a very charming man. I didn't particularly blame him for Janet's suicide attempt. From my point of view, it wasn't even his fault that he had clung to her well past the point where he could ever do her any good. I wasn't angry at him, only saddened by the arrogance of a profession that believed it knew so much more about human emotions and longings and motives than it could ever possibly comprehend. With all his charts, psychiatric papers, theories, and pills, Dr. Sternfeld believed that he knew Janet and that he could predict what she would do. But he didn't know her. He knew only a boneless, soulless, shell of a person, as lifeless and one-dimensional as the clear, typographic print on her hospital reports. And he could only predict how this paper-thin image of a person would act and what it would ultimately do.

"I'm not even going to test for brain damage," he said. "I don't really think we have to worry about it."

"Brain damage," I said, horrified.

He thinned his lips into an indistinct simulation of a smile. "You know that she took almost five thousand milligrams of Mellaril," he said. "That's more Mellaril than I've ever read about anyone taking. That makes her almost a medical curiosity—the fact that she survived such an enormous overdose. We have no real backlog of information; we don't even know what kind of body damage to expect. And, of course, with an overdose of tranquilizers in general, and with a coma, a certain amount of brain disintegration is always a possibility."

"She's been out of the coma for three days. Wouldn't brain damage be apparent by now?"

"Not necessarily. The brain is a very sophisticated and complicated organ. A few cells die and you might not even notice a change in her behavior. But with someone as extraordinarily bright and inquisitive as Janet, even a slight deadening of intelligence would be disastrous. As I said before, though, I don't think we have to worry about it. I wouldn't recommend going through the expense of testing her. As far as I can determine, it's not really necessary."

"Why didn't you mention possible brain damage before now?"

"You had enough to worry about, didn't you?"

"I suppose I did. If she took such a high dosage, how did she survive it?"

"I don't know. On the one hand, she's always been highly resistant to drugs. That's why I've always had to give her such high doses. On the other hand, nobody really knows what goes on inside a person's brain when they're in a comatose state. If you wanted to be romantic, you could say that she fought a final, knock-down, drag-out fight. The life force against the death wish, so to speak. And ultimately, she made a monumental subconscious decision. The life force was obviously victorious."

"Is that romantic?" I asked.

He laughed. "It's certainly not medical."

Ten days after her suicide attempt, on September twenty-first, Janet was transferred from the medical ward to the locked psychiatric ward. The afternoon before her transfer, the psychiatric resident, a silly-looking young man who had a pimple on the edge of his nose which wiggled whenever he spoke, came into Janet's room to examine her.

"Am I going to the fourth floor?" she asked.

He looked at her chart and shook his head. "You were originally assigned to the seventh floor when you were admitted. That's where you're assigned now."

"I'd rather go to the fourth floor."

She was propped up in bed. The half-empty I.V. bottle which had been detached from her veins three days before, was still in its metal stand near her bed. The long rubber tube dangled limply over a metal arm, looking old and spent, like a wasted organ of the body. I sat next to Janet, perched on the edge of her hospital cot.

The resident studied his chart again. "It really doesn't matter which floor you go to," he said. "At one time the seventh floor was for the more disturbed patients. But we're so crowded now that we no longer make any distinctions between floors."

"I still want to go to the fourth floor," Janet insisted.

"She's always been assigned to the fourth floor," I offered. "She has friends on the fourth-floor staff."

PAUL

The resident leaned over the bed, studying Janet for a telltale clue to the workings of her mind, I suppose. I watched his face in profile. His red pimple wriggled and twisted as if it had a life of its own. Finally, he stepped back and shrugged his shoulders.

"It's okay with me whichever floor you go to," he said. "I just have to go over to the nurses' station and check it out."

The machinations of Janet's transfer were as complicated and as flurried as a bedroom farce. The third-floor resident psychiatrist had to ask the seventh-floor resident psychiatrist to ask the fourth-floor resident psychiatrist if it was okay for Janet to be shunted from the second floor to the seventh floor to the fourth floor. He phoned upstairs through the intercom system. He didn't cup his hands over the microphone or he pushed the wrong button, because his words were amplified throughout the hospital.

"I have a chronic schizophrenic," he called out, "acute psychotic episode. Postsuicidal condition. Requests transfer from the seventh to the fourth."

There was a moment of static-filled silence and then a garbled voice replied, "Okay with me."

Janet and I exchanged glances.

"Is that me?" she asked.

"He's certainly nothing, if he's not direct," I answered.

"What do you expect in a hospital?" she said. "Competence? And discretion too?"

She stayed on the locked ward for only two weeks. Still categorized as "postsuicidal," she was a constant source of anxiety for the hospital staff. They insisted that I continue to pay sixty dollars a day for a private-duty night nurse in order to make certain that she didn't swallow her comb or hang herself with a torn strip of nylon panties or otherwise damage herself in the wee hours of the morning when no one was readily available to check on her.

Janet remained in startlingly good spirits, though. During the five days of her coma, she had undergone a mysterious and profound change. A knot of despair had broken apart in her mind. For the first time in ten years of psychiatric experience, she no longer felt comfortable in the hospital. She felt herself an outsider, in fact, as much of a detached witness to the day-to-day hospital activities as I had always been.

Ten years' worth of psychoactive drugs had been steadily pumped out of her system, sliding out through a catheter and settling into a plastic container beneath her bed as a gruesomely muddy, sour liquid. She could actually concentrate her attention on finishing a book. She could taste her food, move her bowels regularly, and she could sink into a normally placid restful sleep.

I came every afternoon to visit her. To the disgruntlement of the hospital staff, I stayed well into the evening, bringing her a nightly food snack in order to fatten her up. I enjoyed being with her. Despite a sense of confusion about the future, I was enormously pleased that she was still alive. She had lost seventeen pounds in five days. I called her the sexiest skinny woman I had ever seen.

Throughout her two weeks of hospitalization, her spirits continued to rise. But I was still wary. Living with Janet had taught me to be skeptical of her moods, and I waited patiently for her inevitable collapse. Dr. Sternfeld warned me not to be fooled by her sudden explosion of ecstasy and peace. After an unsuccessful suicide attempt, people fall into an oddly tranquil state of mind, he claimed. The suicidal act seems almost to cleanse them of their torments and pain; it gives them a momentary lift in spirits and pushes them out of themselves, into a suddenly wondrous world.

Even he had to admit, though, that Janet's joyous spirits seemed to go beyond the usual "postsuicidal uplift." She was more than free of pain. She was free of ten years of "sickness," institutionalization, and psychiatric domination. In her typical, excessively romantic fashion, she thought herself alive for the first time in her existence. She was involved in an exquisitely bittersweet love affair with life.

If I had once dubbed her Miranda, her new state of mind dwarfed even the most romantic outlines of my earlier metaphor. The world was "newer" and "braver" to her; the people in the world were more "wondrous" than they had ever appeared before. And, although I understood nothing about an "inevitable postsuicidal depression," I knew enough about life to understand that she was heading for a terrible disappointment. She would never be able to sustain her heroic romantic vision of living. But her disillusionment, which was properly intense and soul-shaking, was to be a very long time in coming.

The smoothness of her short hospitalization was marred by only two episodes. The first involved her eyesight. A few days after her transfer to the fourth floor, she went down to Monroe Park's fenced-in courtyard to play volleyball. Reaching backward for a ball, she lost her balance, collapsed onto the cement, and momentarily lost consciousness. After being carried to the ward, she discovered that her eyes could not readjust to the dim indoor light. She was nearly blind.

PAUL

She attempted to phone me at home, but she couldn't read the numbers on the dial. She asked another patient to dial the telephone for her.

"Why'd they let you go outside?" I raged into the receiver. "They know you haven't recovered your strength yet."

"There's no point in getting angry at the hospital. I wanted to play volleyball. I wanted to get outside into the sunshine."

"Have someone examine you."

"I already asked to see the medical resident. But you know the hospital. It will probably take two days before he comes up to look at me."

"Look, Janet. Insist on seeing him immediately. You've just gone through a terrible physical ordeal. You're by no means recovered from it."

"I will insist on it. I was just suddenly very frightened. But I think my eyes are getting better now. Shapes and forms are a lot clearer to me."

"I'd be going through the ceiling by now. What do you think caused the blindness?"

"It's probably a temporary reaction to the overdose of Mellaril. I don't think it's permanent. Otherwise it would have shown up as soon as I came out of the coma."

The hospital concluded that her temporary loss of sight was "hysterical," rather than physical. A doctor came to see her in the afternoon, lifted her eyelids, peered into her pupils, muttered something unintelligible, and informed the staff that he could discover no physical damage. They allowed her to go back to the courtyard the following day. Once again, on returning to the ward, Janet suffered a four-hour bout of blindness. The nurses decided that they better not feed her "hysteria"; they barred her from going outside again.

Characteristically, the hospital diagnosis was incorrect. We discovered later that Mellaril was known to affect the eyes. Janet's overdose had affected her retina; a number of retinal cells which normally absorb light had been bleached white. It took two years and a miracle of physical regeneration—other, previously dormant, cells slowly began to take over the functions of the ones that were permanently destroyed—before she could see normally again. At first, she was almost completely blind in dim light. In the months that followed her release from the hospital, when we ate dinner together at dimly lit restaurants, I was forced to cut her meat for her.

But Janet was determined to let nothing, not temporary sightlessness, not even harassment from the nursing staff, destroy her rarely achieved sensation of peace. She reacted to the day-to-day burden of her failing eyesight far better than I did. Her suicide attempt had just about destroyed my willingness to suffer with her anymore. I didn't know if I had any strength left to deal with even a momentary physical calamity.

She continued to glow with life. Although she had waited on the fourth-floor ward for over a week, Dr. Sternfeld had not yet visited her. Against her better judgment, she phoned him and they immediately broke into their typical hospitalization dance. She insisted that she had to see him. He hedged, promising to visit her as soon as he could. She pleaded. He berated her for interrupting a conference with another patient, for phoning him in general, for not "using the hospital." She hung up the telephone feeling abandoned and upset.

In the early evening, while I sat with her in her room, she told me that she wanted a few moments of privacy, that she wanted to close her eyes and try to sleep.

I strolled into the hallway and stood near her door, discussing the weather with Mrs. Hand, Janet's private-duty nurse. Mrs. Hand was a plump little West Indian woman with a soaring musical voice and a ubiquitous laugh. She laughed at Rags who could contort his body into exotically twisted patterns, at Harold who constantly organized his fellow patients into impromptu dances or performances, at the hordes of addicts who now crammed into Monroe Park in a city-financed methadone program, at the old people who came into the hospital as part of the Medicare program, even at Janet, when she complained about the insensitivity of the staff.

Mrs. Hand's laughter was basically good-natured and I even considered it somewhat noble, far better than the part fearfulness, part authoritarianism, part earnestness of the regular hospital staff. Her laughter was an attempt to hold her distance from the hospital, almost as if she was determined not to take the sometimes frightening manifestations of pain all around her very seriously. But she could afford to laugh, after all. She was free to come and go as she pleased.

"When I first arrived in this country," she said, "I took my psychiatric training at a big hospital in upstate New York. It was nothing like this hospital."

"How was it different?"

"Oh, it was much, much better. The trouble with this hospital is that the patients have nothing to do all day. They're bored. At least where I was they could walk outside on the grounds. We had a whole lot of activities for them to do. Every six months each patient went before a panel of psychiatrists and the panel decided who could be transferred from the locked buildings to the less secure buildings, how much freedom they could have. Some of the patients were even allowed to go into town by themselves."

"That's real freedom," I said.

"It was so much prettier, also," she said, ignoring my comment. "The grounds were lovely. They were all manicured and mowed. It was a much prettier atmosphere."

"You don't think they should put mental hospitals in the middle of cities then?"

She chuckled. "I come from the Islands. I don't think they should put anyone in the middle of cities."

I heard Janet call to me and I turned toward her room. Framed in the doorway, she seemed suddenly frail and insubstantial, as if all her good spirits had flooded out of her. She motioned me into her room. She appeared badly shaken.

"I just had a terrible experience," she said, trying to ignore Mrs. Hand, who had followed me inside. "I lay down on my bed and I closed my eyes. Suddenly I saw Mike. He was standing in front of me, calling out to me."

"It was probably a dream, Janet," I said. "Or one of those half-dreams, half-visions people get just before they fall asleep."

"No. It wasn't. It was a real hallucination. I know what a hallucination is after all these years. He was standing there, like you are now. I could practically reach out and touch him."

Mrs. Hand slid out the door and returned a few seconds later, dragging along one of the nurses. The nurse, a pretty young woman with an unbelievable mop of frizzy blond hair, posed in the doorway, glaring at Janet.

"You say you heard voices?" she said. "What did they tell you to do?"

"Not really voices," Janet said. "I saw a vision of a friend of mine. A boy named Mike who's been dead for almost six months now."

The nurse disappeared. Janet sat down heavily on her bed.

"I was just lying here thinking about my conversation with Dr. Sternfeld," she said. "About how lonely and abandoned I felt. And suddenly I saw Mike."

"Don't panic over it," I insisted. "I still say that it was some kind of a half-dream."

"It wasn't. It was Mike. He was perfectly real. Sometimes I think about how terribly much I miss him."

A Day in the Life, Revisited

The ward psychiatrist, a glum-looking young man in a well-tailored sharkskin suit, appeared in the doorway.

"You hear voices?" he asked Janet. He carried a folder of papers underneath his arm.

"Not voices," she said, suddenly getting angry. "I already told the nurse. I had a vision. A hallucination."

He looked at me and then at Mrs. Hand. "I want you both out of the room," he said.

"I'd rather stay with her," I said.

He shook his head. "Out. She's still potentially suicidal. I want to talk to her alone."

He shooed us out and closed the door firmly behind us. I walked down the hallway to the door of the dayroom. I turned around and tramped back to Janet's room. I leaned my head against her door.

"You had a sexual relationship with this fellow Mike?" the psychiatrist was asking.

"No. He was a friend of mine."

I heard the sound of papers rustling. "According to your old hospital records, one of the nurses thought you were . . . uh . . . unduly intimate with him. She considered your relationship with him to be basically unhealthy."

"I told you. He was a friend of mine. I loved him deeply. That was all."

"Well, that's neither here nor there," the resident continued. "When he spoke to you, what did he tell you to do? Did he tell you to harm yourself?"

"No. He just called to me. He just spoke my name."

"You say he's dead. Did he ask you to join him?"

"No. I told you. He called my name. Maybe it was only a dream, after all. I don't even know."

"Let's be perfectly clear about this. Did he tell you to do any damage to yourself? Did he tell you to do away with yourself?"

I was startled by a hand on my shoulder. The blond-haired nurse stood next to me, glaring angrily.

"What do you think you're doing?" she demanded.

"What does it look like I'm doing? I'm listening at the door."

She stepped back in surprise, showing me a row of even white teeth.

"Get away from here," she roared. "You're not supposed to be standing around in the hallway."

I walked down the hall to the bathroom. As I urinated, Harold came over to me. He was a small, bearded, well-groomed man in his early forties. I had heard that outside the hospital he ran a successful art gallery.

"You're not a patient?" he asked.

"No. I'm Janet's husband."

He bobbed his head up and down. He practically dominated the hospital. I suppose he was what was called a "manic-depressive," in his most "manic" state. He was always in motion, organizing parties, helping the staff, fixing the television set, teaching the old people how to paint pictures. From a distance he appeared perfectly rational. But up close, talking to him as I was now, his conversation was somewhat disjointed and confused, almost as if his outpouring of energy was designed to cloud his mind.

"One thing all of us wonder," he said. "Her bandages. The bandages on her feet. Did she cut herself there?"

"No," I answered. "She took an overdose of drugs and she was in a coma for five days. They had to cut into her ankles to find an uncollapsed vein for the I.V."

"Oh," he said, still waving his head. "We thought she cut herself."

I zipped up my fly and tried to move past him, but he blocked my way.

"If you're not a patient, what are you doing here?"

I was weary and intolerant. "What are you doing here?" I asked.

"I'm a patient. I belong here, don't I? You have no place here."

"I'm visiting Janet. She's my wife. Remember?"

"How is she doing? Is she feeling better?"

"She's feeling remarkably good."

"I'm glad. She seems like a nice young lady."

I finally shifted past him, but before I could open the bathroom door, he grabbed hold of my arm. He screwed up his face in thought.

"They tell me to expect a big depression. Which I do. But they're giving me something called Lithium, and they say with any luck I'll be out of here in a few weeks. Do you believe it?"

I turned to look at him. "If Janet could feel good," I said, "anyone can."

I wandered around, then walked back to Janet's room some time later. The door was wide open. Janet was propped up on her bed talking to Mrs. Hand, who sat next to her on a straight-back chair.

"What happened?" I asked.

"Nothing really. He asked me the same old questions. What do the voices tell you to do? Things like that. I had to convince him that I wasn't going to attempt suicide as soon as he left the room. He wasn't bad, though. He told me that he was born in Budapest. He called it the most beautiful city in the world."

A Day in the Life, Revisited

"How do you feel?"

"I'm a little shaken up. And I'm very tired. But I feel better."

Mrs. Hand began to laugh. "You should have seen the nurses' station," she said in her musical voice. "The nurses were running back and forth. You're still on a suicide watch. They were afraid you were going to harm yourself."

"My God," Janet said. "I feel marvelous. A hallucination or a dream or whatever it was isn't going to change my feeling about myself. I wouldn't even think of suicide now. I feel alive for the first time in my life."

Mrs. Hand stared at her skeptically. "No matter how good you feel, you'll always have to be careful, Janet. You're a schizophrenic and you'll always be a schizophrenic. No matter what happens to you in your life, you'll always have to take special care of yourself."

"You don't understand . . ." Janet started to say.

"What don't I understand, dear?"

"Nothing. If I want to get out of here soon, I've learned enough to know when I ought to keep my mouth shut."

"That's right, dear. Just listen to what the doctors and nurses have to tell you and before you know it, you'll be feeling much better. And you'll be able to leave."

Janet had weathered the hallucination, but it had shaken me up. I couldn't stop my mind from dwelling on the incident. The next morning I phoned Dr. Sternfeld.

"It doesn't sound like much to me, Paul," he said.

"I suppose it doesn't mean much. I just can't stop myself from worrying about it."

"Look. The mind is a strange contraption. There are ten million reasons why she could have hallucinated Mike. You'll have to learn that you can't keep studying every little thing she does or feels. And you can't play psychiatrist. The important thing is that she feels strong now. If her strength and good feeling last a few months longer, I'd say that we're out of the woods. But you can't anticipate the future."

"We still plan to go away," I said.

"I still think it's a good idea. No matter what happens. I don't really expect her to have any more trouble."

"And if she does have trouble?"

He sighed. "This is the jet age, isn't it? No matter how far you go, you'll never be more than six or seven hours from New York. Isn't that true? You can always speak to me."

"Are you going to visit her in the hospital soon?"

"I already spoke to her about that," he said evenly. "I told her

PAUL

that I would see her as soon as I could. But I don't think it's even necessary for me to see her in the hospital. I expect to release her in less than a week."

I hung up the telephone with mixed feelings toward Dr. Sternfeld. It was almost as difficult for me to give him up as it was for Janet. Despite my skepticism toward him, I had depended on him for a long time. In four years, he had become a bridge between Janet and myself. When she was depressed or frightened or angry, I had always told her to call him. "I don't know what to do for you. Take another pill. Call Dr. Sternfeld."

I was frightened. It was easy for Janet, suddenly so full of blinding life and hope, to view her years of misery as some distorted, alienated nightmare. She had been taught that her pain was a "sickness" as unconnected to her being as an attack of measles. She had believed that her "sickness" would simply pass away one day and that, like a person exorcised of an evil spirit or cured of a chronic disease, she would finally be free to resume a "normal" life. It was harder for me to forget the pain of the past. I continued to watch her for signs and signals of "sickness" for a long time.

She never hallucinated again. Her visions of animals and knives and Elders and laughing men and women slid back into the gloominess of her mind where they belonged. If the visions continued to whisper to her, they whispered subliminally, as all our old fears and dreads and lonelinesses continue to whisper to all of us. She thought of Mike often, and as she told me in the hospital, she continued to miss him terribly. But she forgot about her hallucination of him almost as soon as the vision faded away.

She took Mrs. Hand's advice, listened to all the nonsense the doctors and nurses had to say to her, and toward the end of 1970, she was released from Monroe Park for the last time.

"It's nice to finally get out of this whole gruesome hospital world," she said, as the door of the ward closed behind us.

The elevator creaked open and Dr. Lessing, papers fluttering beneath his arm, charged out the door. He brushed past us, turned sharply around and performed a burlesque double take when he saw Janet.

"You know," he said to her, "I thought it was you."

We let the elevator glide down without us.

"What do you mean?" Janet asked.

"It's very funny, isn't it?" he said. "A few weeks ago a colleague of mine said, 'Dr. Lessing, there's an unusual case you'd really be interested in seeing. Some young woman just took five thousand milligrams of Mellaril and she's still alive.' So I went down to look at her. I saw her lying in bed in a coma and I remember telling my colleague that she looked terribly familiar. But I couldn't place the face."

He began to laugh.

"That was really me," Janet said.

"Yes. It was you, wasn't it? I'm pleased you recovered so quickly. You're really something of a medical curiosity, aren't you?"

He waved to us, jammed his papers into his armpit, and unlocked the door to the ward with one of his tangle of keys.

"You'd think he'd know my face after all these years," Janet said.

"He probably didn't recognize you without the conducting cream on your temples. Without the electrodes attached to your scalp."

She made a horrible face. "Oh. That's an awful thought."

Outside, in the late-afternoon light, she pressed her eyes closed.

"Are you having trouble seeing?" I asked.

"No. I'll have trouble when I go into dim light again. I'm just blinking my eyes because the world looks altogether different to me. As if I'm seeing it for the first time."

I swallowed down a cynical comment. "It's good to be alive?" I asked.

"You can't imagine how good it feels. After I took all those pills, I was certain that I was going to die. I just sat in our living room, waiting for my mind to slip away into nothingness. But I didn't even get sleepy because I had taken tranquilizers, not sleeping pills. When I woke up from the coma, I was truly happy to find myself still alive. I felt like a person who was rising from her death bed. You can't imagine how beautiful everything looks to me. The smallest, simplest things. Even the noise and dirt of this city."

I steered her down the street, toward our car. We heard the distant whine of a siren and a few moments later, we watched two red fire engines chase each other.

"Are we really going to go away from New York?" she asked.

"If you still want to go. If you continue to feel okay."

"Of course I'm going to feel okay. Where are we going to go? California?"

"I've been thinking about Paris again."

She looked at me in surprise. "Why do you always think about Paris?"

"Isn't that where Americans typically go to find themselves?"

She stared at me to see if I was joking. I was at least half-joking.

"I called Paris a romantic gesture once," I said. "But as long as we want to go someplace to relax and to spend time together and to think about ourselves, why shouldn't we go someplace radically different? What have we got to lose?"

"You don't have to try to convince me. I've wanted to go to Paris all my life."

"I've been thinking about it. I figure that we can rent an apartment in Paris and use it as a home base. We can travel around Europe until our money runs out. Or until I can find some kind of work."

She held my arm tightly. "You're getting me very excited."

"Right now you're so sloppily sentimental," I said, "it doesn't take very much to get you excited."

We sold almost everything we owned. Over the next six months, we unloaded our car, our hard little orange couch, our two maple bookcases, our upholstered wing chair, and our matching bedside tables. I stayed at work through the busy season; we arranged for passports and vaccinations; and in March 1971, almost a year after I had idly brought up the idea of living in Paris, we were ready to leave for Europe.

I can't even say that our plans seemed in any way romantic or unrealistic to us then. In four years, between Major Medical, Blue Cross, our parents, and my own labor, we had laid out nearly forty thousand dollars in medical bills. None of our possessions meant anything to us anymore. Pain, which had dominated our life for so long, had also wiped away any desire for status or worldly success or the gathering of things. We didn't see the throwing off of our possessions as a rebellious gesture; we were still children of the middle class, after all. But we flattered ourselves into thinking that we had learned some small lesson from our unhappy experiences. We were determined at least to pull back into ourselves and to keep our life lean, simple, and free of pretension and judgment. We were again starting anew. And it seemed fitting to us that we begin our brand new existence with a clean brave adventure.

In December, four months before we left for Paris, Janet insisted that we take in a kitten that someone had offered to us.

"What are we going to do with the damn cat when we go to Europe?" I asked.

"We'll take her with us."

"Oh, come on, Janet."

"We can. I've checked on it. All she needs is a current rabies shot. We can bring her into every country except England."

So, our suitcases packed, our cat carrier purchased, our airplane tickets to Paris in hand, we cleared away the last departure from New York.

On the morning of March fifteenth, the same day w our apartment, Janet had her last session with Dr. Ste his waiting room trying to ignore the easy listenin ~~~~ that streamed endlessly out of the portable radio balanced on the ledge over the door. I had recently organized and packed away our medical bills and receipts. In five years, Janet had visited Dr. Sternfeld four hundred twenty times, a total of eighteen thousand dollars' worth of "therapy."

I heard Dr. Sternfeld's office door creak open and I saw Janet motion me to come inside.

"I just wanted to say good-bye and to wish you all the luck in the world," Dr. Sternfeld said. He stuck out his hand and I shook it stiffly.

"I was just telling Janet that she could call me anytime she wanted. After all these years, we've grown to be more than doctor and patient." He laughed. "We're almost friends by now. I almost know her better than I do my own wife."

He hugged Janet in his typically awkward, tentative fashion and he escorted us to the front door. When we walked out into the street, Janet was crying.

"Why are you crying?" I asked.

"You wouldn't understand."

"Are you crying because you're happy or sad?"

"Neither. I don't know how I can ever thank Dr. Sternfeld."

"For what?" I asked.

"For saving my life."

Driving back to our apartment, I considered my own feelings of gratitude. There was a time, in the midst of Janet's most overwhelming pain and panic, that I would have practically laid down my life for Dr. Sternfeld if I had thought it could save her. I was a sucker for good-byes myself. I felt suddenly warm and mellow toward him. In truth, he had dedicated almost ten years of his life to Janet. And in a way, he had saved her life. Or so I thought at that moment. I was later to wonder why, after nearly a thousand sessions with him, she knew so abysmally little about herself.

I parked my father's car in front of our house. A small moving truck had pulled into our driveway, but the moving men were nowhere in sight. We were transferring a few odd pieces of furniture—our bed, Janet's childhood rocking chair, an antique secretary—to my in-laws' house for storage.

Mrs. Kramer, our landlady, intercepted us at our front door.

"I want you to move that truck out of my driveway," she shouted at me.

"I can't do it," I said. "The men aren't here. They arrived early and I assume they went for lunch."

"I want you to move it," she repeated. She was a thin-haired woman with a loud voice, the manners of a busybody, and the ability to sustain herself in a constant flurry of rage. "You're going to crack my pavement leaving it in the driveway."

"Look, Mrs. Kramer," I patiently explained. "I told you that the men aren't here now. When they come back, we're going to load a few items into their truck and then they're going to leave. It's a small, light truck. It can't do any damage to your driveway."

"I want it moved now. If you don't move it, I'm going to call the police."

"I don't care what you do," I said. "Call the Royal Canadian Mounted Police, for all I care."

She did call the police. Fifteen minutes later, as Janet and I were stacking our cartons of books and dishes, two policemen burst through the open door of our apartment. It was a strange moment for me, eerily reminiscent of the evening Janet had gone into her Thorazine convulsions.

"What's going on here?" one of the policemen asked.

"Don't you know?" I said.

"We don't know. We just got a message that someone made a complaint."

The other policeman studied the wreckage of our cartons and furniture suspiciously.

"Do you live here?" he asked.

I showed him my driver's license. He shrugged his shoulders.

"Go upstairs and talk to my landlady," I said. "You can find out why she made her complaint."

Janet and I followed them outside. Mrs. Kramer was leaning out of her kitchen window waving her arms at the two policemen. When she sighted Janet, she began to windmill her arms even more frantically.

"She's crazy," she shouted, pointing down at Janet. "Ambulances coming. Police cars screeching at all hours of the day and night. This is a respectable neighborhood. What do you think it is? Pitkin Avenue?"

My own temper, which I had repressed for four years, came raging out of me.

"Who the hell do you think you're talking about?" I yelled back at her. "You vicious old whore. Why don't you climb back into your crypt with your broomstick and voodoo dolls."

The younger of the policemen grabbed my arm and pulled me aside. He was younger than I, with a broad rosy face, modishly long hair, and a bristling mustache similar to my own.

"What are you getting so excited about, buddy? It's not worth arguing with her."

Mrs. Kramer was shrieking at no one in particular. "Did you hear what he called me? A vicious old whore. I ask you, is that any language to use in front of a respectable person?"

I took a deep breath and shook my head.

"I guess there is no point in arguing with her," I said. "I'm just irritable from the strain of moving."

The policeman clapped me on the shoulder.

"That's the right attitude, buddy. Just relax and let things happen. Take it from me. Bend with the wind, like the Zen people say. You live longer that way."

An hour later, after I had transferred the last of our sparse possessions into the moving truck, I said to Janet, "I bet you didn't know I had such a terrible temper?"

"I wasn't really surprised," she said. "I know your father. But I was a little frightened by it."

"That's what life is all about," I said.

"I was more frightened for you. It must be very painful to have so much anger locked inside of you."

We spent our last week in New York living at my parents' apartment. I continued to go to work each morning, clearing away my papers and organizing my file cabinets so that someone else could understand them. The night before our departure for Paris, I was overcome by an attack of fear and doubt.

"What are you so frightened about?" Janet asked. We were crammed together in the narrow convertible bed in my parents' den. It was nearly 2 A.M. I had been trying to fall asleep for the last hour and a half, tossing and turning so fitfully that I had finally roused Janet from her sleep. Our airplane flight was set for 8:30 this same morning.

"Aren't you frightened?" I asked.

"Of course I am. We're making a tremendous new step. But at least I can fall asleep."

"I always get frightened before I go someplace new," I said. "I even used to get scared before weekend holidays on Long Island."

PAUL

She sat up in bed. "This is a lot more traumatic than going to Long Island."

"I know it is. I keep having all kinds of strange thoughts. I'm afraid I'll never be able to speak French, for instance."

"You'll pick up the language in no time." She yawned and stretched her arms over her head. "All you have to do is live in Paris for a few weeks and you'll practically be talking like a native."

Janet spoke almost fluent French. She had gone to a French dramatic class in high school.

"You don't know me and languages," I said. "I've got the original iron tongue."

I was flirting around the reasons for my fear, though. It was easy for Janet, who had never really had any life before now, who had always felt herself alien to the rest of the world, to throw off the routines of the past four years and to slide smoothly into a new existence. It was harder for me. As unhappy and dreary as my life had often been, it had also had its pleasures and satisfactions; it had at least been clearly defined. I was anxious about the future now, and I was having second thoughts about our decision to leave New York.

We kissed and I rolled over on my side and lay perfectly still, pretending to fall asleep. In a few moments I heard Janet's breathing resume its slow steady tempo, and I carefully pulled aside my covers and slid out of bed.

I strolled into the living room, switched on a lamp, curled up on my mother's royal blue couch, and lit a cigarette. The past six months had moved far too quickly for me, and I suppose I was having trouble absorbing everything that had happened. Janet had broken out of her coma radiant with energy and life, and she had not collapsed again as I had thought she would. She approached the world with an imperturbability now. But even as I brooded on the couch, I knew that her peacefulness could never last.

Jenny, our cat, leaped up on the sofa and settled down next to me. Part Persian, part alleycat, Jenny had a pedigreed animal's disdain for her mixed-breed owners. She had never quite forgiven us for dragging her away from her mother and brother and, by her temperament anyway, she was stand-offish and somewhat unfriendly. But, like most kittens, she knew instinctively when someone she lived with was troubled or unhappy, and she pressed herself against my leg, draping her round little face across my knee.

I stubbed out one cigarette and lit another.

A few months from now, while camping in the Normandy woods, I would settle into a homemade bed in the rear compartment of a

A Day in the Life, Revisited

Volkswagen bus and brood again about the future. Jenny would curl up next to me and I would stroke her furry body, overcome by a sudden sense of sadness for the utter simplicity of love and the damn difficulty of loving. The European adventure, which Janet and I had once envisioned to be so vivid and exciting, would turn before our eyes into a treacherous aimless experience. We would be locked together by as many bad memories as good ones, and we would discover ourselves to be separated by such a wide gulf of suspicion, resentment, and rage, that neither of us would believe we had the strength or courage to reach across it.

Now, I yawned, and threw my arms over my head, elbowing Jenny, who poked her head at me, blinked her eyes contemptuously, and slid wearily across the pillows. Without the benefit of foresight, I couldn't really anticipate the traumas of the next few months. But I suppose I could already see the outlines of my coming struggle with Janet. I felt suddenly old and rootless, as if even my most recent memories of our life together were floating off into a void. On the verge of what I saw to be a brand new life, I wanted very badly to reach backward for some solid sense of meaning and tradition. My family roots were incomprehensible to me, wandering back into strange little Eastern European villages, moving through old-fashioned conventions and customs that I couldn't even stretch my imagination to see. I had always been taught to substitute the glossiness of the American dream for tradition, to substitute competitiveness, success, and the amassing of money and possessions for emptiness and alienation.

I thought about a book I had just finished reading which had deeply affected me and which had taught me something important about myself and my relationship to Janet. I had started *Tender Is the Night* three and a half years earlier, when I first brought Janet for outpatient shock treatments. But I had found the novel painful to read then and laid it aside, picking it up again the previous night. The reputation of F. Scott Fitzgerald, the great twentieth-century romantic, had recently been damaged by the publication of *Zelda*, the biography of his wife. Like me, Fitzgerald had endured a torturous complicated relationship with an unhappy "psychotic" wife. But according to Zelda's biographer, he had actually helped destroy her; he had subtly invalidated her worth, ridiculed her ambitions, stolen her writing for his own use, infantilized her, and finally institutionalized her for life.

In *Tender Is the Night* Fitzgerald attempted to redo his life. Superficially the fictionalized story of the middle years of his marriage, the novel was also Fitzgerald's metaphor for the Jazz

PAUL

Age, when a dream of blind pleasure and high-styled living, turned, as dreams always seem to, invariably sour. But in the book Fitzgerald created an odd new role for himself and he slipped a strange ending onto his own story that, in life, he was never able to reproduce: He transformed himself into a psychiatrist and through Dick Diver, his doctor-hero, he sustained Nicole, his fictionalized wife, took good care of her, and ultimately saved her. At the end of the novel, Diver, after manipulating his wife into a love affair with another man, felt free enough to leave her. With a shattering shakeup of his life, he abandoned more than Nicole; he abandoned the pretensions of his flurried expatriate existence, the bitterness of his wasted ambitions, and the sad futility of his dream of love. He returned, as Fitzgerald's alter ego always does, to the simpler, firmer, sourly inadequate traditions of his childhood home.

I identified with my vision of Fitzgerald. When I finished his book, I found myself filled with a shadowy sense of melancholy, for in my own way, I had created my own fantasies about Janet, and I had incorporated her into my own dream of love. My father, in a moment of bitterness, once called her my "magnificent obsession" and although I argued with him, I knew that his romantic metaphor was somewhat accurate. What had tied me so obsessively to Janet during all our years of pain? Why had I never given up on her? Out of stubbornness, dumbness, guilt, or a deep subtle refusal to face reality, I had blindly bounded along, doing what my senses and nerves had forced me to do.

In *Tender Is the Night*, Fitzgerald made Nicole reveal to Dick Diver something profoundly important about himself. But Fitzgerald had been unable to translate what he learned into action. He could no more throw off his dreams and ambitions than he could abandon his obligations toward Zelda. He had undoubtedly done her wrong, had transformed his confused feelings into a bitchy denigration of her. But he had remained haunted by her also. And, even after he had given up on her, he had burned out the rest of his short sorrowful life, still searching for what she had once symbolized to him, mystery and glamour and love.

I could empathize with how badly Fitzgerald wanted to throw off the burden of his wife and I could share his fantasy of bringing her to a firm level of happiness and peace so he could finally leave her. But Fitzgerald had never been able to tolerate the sin of being unhappy, and he had scurried away from pain, moving from one wasted life to another. He believed all the myths of the careless Jazz Age, as he embodied these same myths, and finally he was trapped by them, as well. He looked at Zelda's pain as being distant and distinct from his own pain, as being "pathological" and "sick"; his refusal to see her as being anything more than a distorted alien reflection of his own dream finally destroyed him.

So what had I learned from Janet? I was skirting the question as I smoked cigarette after cigarette in my parents' living room. Janet and I had endured an unreal life for the past four years, a life dominated by pills to wipe away unhappiness, doctors to explicate suffering, and hospitals to lock away the irrationality that threatened our love. There had always been something faintly moral in the way Janet had been treated, almost as if her pain were a sin against a new regime of happiness and normality, as if her pain had to be broken apart and stacked neatly away, like clean little rows of houses. The idea of madness or schizophrenia or mental illness had terrified both of us in our different ways, and we had both run away from it and from ourselves. I had sought to sustain her in any way I could. And like Fitzgerald, I had created my own fantasies of freedom and peace and love to sustain myself. I loved her deeply. But the dream of happiness and release that had locked us romantically together for so long was beginning to wear away.

I could only see the outlines of the changes in myself at that point. I knew I could never lead the same life I had lived before. I came away from the unhappy experience of the past few years with a softening of my ambitions, a belief that openness and meaning and love were far more important than things, and a determination never to allow my life to be judged or labeled or analyzed by standards other than my own. But I couldn't really see any of the profound changes in myself. Like Fitzgerald, I was a child of my time. I had witnessed in Janet more suffering than I had ever imagined I would see, but I still couldn't recognize her pain as being bound up with my own. The terrible revelations that Janet and I were later to experience, revelations that would focus and make meaningful the events of the last four years, were still a long time in coming.

I wandered back to the bedroom and climbed gingerly into bed. In the blackness of the room, I could barely make out the shadowy contours of Janet lying next to me. She stirred as I settled under the covers and she flung her arm out toward me.

"Haven't you gone to sleep yet?" she asked.

"I was just sitting in the living room."

She rolled on her side, facing me.

"What were you doing?"

"Just thinking about myself."

She fell right back to sleep. I lay on my back, held her hand, and finally closed my eyes. But my mind continued to run through the memories of the past years and I don't think I ever really fell asleep myself.

In the morning, my parents, Janet's parents, and some friends saw us off at the airport. I learned later that after our departure Janet's father had shaken his head and muttered, "I hope they know what they're doing."

As we were lifted off the ground, I leaned back in my window seat, watching a congregation of little cars, houses, and people shimmer off into the paleness of the clouds. Just before I boarded the plane, my father hugged me, kissed me, and whispered in my ear that he loved me. It was a reflection of how warped and alienated my feelings had been for so long a time that, as I thought about his words, I was surprised.

Janet

PART 3

Paris

It was in Paris, in the spring of 1971, that I first realized I had been fucked over.

Horse-chestnut trees bloomed on the boulevards, students gathered on the Boul' Mich to face angry barricaded *flics* equipped with plastic shields and helmets, a frail reminiscence of May 1968. The stores said *Tabac, Boulangerie,* and *Pharmacie,* the concierge called our cat Mignonne, and men traveled home for dinner on bicycles with fresh breads under their arms. The *Herald Tribune* was gone from the news kiosks by nine o'clock, Le Drugstore drew chic Parisians in droves, and countless cafés opened onto streets I had seen a million times in books and movies and paintings and in my mind.

It was the rive gauche, St.-Germain-des-Prés, concerts at the Conciergerie, and afternoons with children in the Luxembourg Gardens. It was the Louvre, Montmartre, and Ile Saint-Louis. The Seine flowed with fine ageless languor under the bridges I never believed could be true. And, in our rented studio, four French floors above the winding and narrow rue des Sts-Pères, I listened to the morning sounds of Paris float upward, ate fresh *croissants* and *confiture,* and was sure it was not real. I had wanted to come to Paris since I was ten.

"I am in a Truffaut film, Paul," I said.

"No, you're here, in Paris, with me. It's real, we're real. The ordeal is over."

I left New York in a spirit of spontaneous adventure, exuberant, freed finally of the miseries that had pursued me for ten years. No one was able to explain the miraculous disappearance of my symptoms after I came out of the five-day coma. But then, no one, not Dr. Sternfeld or Paul or I, seemed to care to try. I was "well." Wasn't that enough?

Life had never seemed so dear, so clear, as through my unfogged mind the sounds and sights of Paris commingled in an uproar of romantic joyous play. But soon after we arrived the buoyant feelings began to change; it seemed to me that I was angry—all the time. It would seethe and bubble inside me, this black rolling anger and I would strike out—at Paul, at our cat Jenny, at myself. The dream had again turned ugly. My anger, unexplainable, unfathomable, haunted me like a guilty secret and the specter of my mental-patient past seemed to engulf me in an identity I was afraid I would never truly shed.

I couldn't understand and I cried to Paul and to myself, out of incomprehension and fear. Why did I feel so angry? Was I—good Lord, no!—getting sick again?

Here I was declared "well," released from treatment—and as lost and scared as ever. Often, I felt so consumed by this anger I had been taught to call sick that I felt myself slipping away to my dark place again. But something in me made me hold on, tenacious; made me cling to my affirming vision of myself as I had clung to life during the five days of my coma.

Soon after we arrived, on a calm, soft, spring day, Paul and I had a tremendous fight. I don't remember what we fought about. I remember only that I was filled suddenly with a rage so black and thundering, it pressed my ears and my chest to overflowing. I did not know myself, or Paul. The inky black squid of former days was inside me and I couldn't stand the horror of it, or the pain.

"I'm leaving," I said, terrified of my own audacity in walking out, frightened somewhere in the back of my mind about what Dr. Sternfeld would say, if he knew.

I ran out, ran crying down rue des Sts-Pères to the river, down to the sloping shore, tears choking my throat, blinding my eyes. I sat down on the cool ground next to a sleeping wine-quiet old man, drew my knees up to my chin, and watched the flow of the Seine. All I could think was, "I hate him, I hate him, I want to die." I whispered the words over and over to the water, wishing, at the same time as I planned to jump in, that Paul were there to hold me and tell me everything would be all right.

I watched the Seine as it flowed by, making slow ridges near my feet. Looking into this river was like looking into myself. I saw its swirls, its depths, its rocks, and its swelling beauty. This Seine, it wasn't good or bad; it just was. "What is wrong with me," I thought, "that I always want to die? What is wrong with me that I fill with blackness to overflowing and want to scream and hurt Paul and cut my wrists?" I watched the Seine again, as it flowed and flowed.

"For aeons, since there have been human beings," I thought, "there has been this river. There has been this pool of suffering." It was as if a light came into the darkness that was in me at that instant.

Paris

is what they were, superficial trappings. The hallucinations, th delusions, the anxiety states, even the wrist-cutting obsession, and, worst of all, the debilitating vision of myself as helpless and sick—I had learned most of these in my years as a mental patient. They were real, in the sense that they reflected some of my pain. But I could shed them, like clothing, only I never knew it. And when I did, like after the suicide attempt, I still had the real me to face—all my pain and fear still intact, only hidden. And, superficially normal, Dr. Sternfeld declared me cured, nothing more to worry about, the world would be rosy. Welcome to the Land of Mental Health.

What a cruel hoax that had been.

I had never been sick and I wasn't well now. The whole idea of my illness and my eventual cure were inventions of my psychiatrists. I thought and remembered and my anger poured out, wild and raw and cleansing. I remembered, bitterly, the years of drug-taking, dependency, shock treatments, self-denigration. In the succeeding months I reviewed my own ten-year history, going over the details with a new view, seeing it all, truly, for the first time.

The day in September that I took the pills was a blur. But I remembered the months preceding my suicide attempt: Mary's week-long visit in August, Paul's short summer workdays, my threats of suicide, Dr. Sternfeld's grave decision that keeping me out of the hospital was "a risk we had to take," Paul doling me my daily ration of pills each night and hiding them in the bedroom while I crouched outside wondering how long it could possibly go on. I remembered my growing distance from Paul, from my mother and father and my friends, the knowledge that grew in me in spite of all my resolves, that one day soon I would take my life. It would not be a suicide *attempt;* even if it failed, I knew, it would not be an attempt. I remembered only one thing about the day itself and that was an overriding sense of relief at having made a decision. I was going to take control of my life, even if I had to die doing it.

After five days in a deep coma, I remember waking, not with the sickening sour sense of a failed suicide attempt, but with a tingling joy-shouting feeling. "Thank God I am alive!"

And I was alive, truly, for the first time, perhaps, in my life. My mind was clear; my symptoms gone. I read *The New York Times*; I read an entire book, Yasunari Kawabata's *The Sound of the Mountain*; I saw a whole movie. People's voices came through clear and precise. My hands and legs did not shake and I moved my bowels without a laxative. For the first time in eight years I was without drugs and it felt fantastic. Even the sudden onset of pains in

weeks after I took the Mellaril did not dampen my
was frightened at the partial loss of sight, but I knew I
through. I was alive.
e had been amazed at my first cure four years earlier,
they w̶e̶r̶e̶ ̶ ̶unned by this one. How had it happened?

"You never know what goes on in their heads when they're in a
coma," a nurse had told Paul.

"You do not feel depressed anymore?" the third floor doctor
asked me.

"I never was depressed," I told him. "Dr. Sternfeld says I was
never classically depressed." How many times had I gone through
this with Oscar Lessing and countless self-important floor doctors? I
watched the doctor nod his serious head, knowing he didn't believe
a word I said.

"You still have to be careful," a doctor said. "In cases like yours
there is often a letdown after the elation at being alive. We must
watch out, because this feeling good can often be more dangerous
than the depression."

"Of course you feel good now," Mrs. Hand, my private-duty nurse
had said. "But there is one thing you must remember. Wherever you
go, whatever you do, however you feel, you will always have to take
care; you will never be like the rest of us; you will always be
schizophrenic."

Her words had struck an instant of sheer cold terror in my heart.
And I had been thinking I was going to join the human race again. I
toyed with the idea of telling her that Dr. Sternfeld said that I was
not schizophrenic, then thought better of it, realizing that she would
never believe me. She had read reams of charts on me, an
accumulation of seven years of reaffirmed diagnoses. Anything I
said would only serve to reconfirm for her my sickness. I wondered,
struck, what Dr. Sternfeld said when he spoke to his colleagues
about me. Did he say, "She's not really schizophrenic, although the
hospitals keep insisting that she is"? What was schizophrenic
anyway? I thought again of Mrs. Hand's prophecy and shivered.

To my parents it was just a plain miracle, though underneath
their pleasure and relief I sensed a fearful suspicion that I would get
sick again. I, too, had that fear lurking around in me, thinking, "If I
got well, what is to stop me from getting sick again?"

Dr. Sternfeld, who was not surprised, but immensely pleased at
my good spirits, had brushed that fear away. Well, why not? I could
ask now. The whole thing, my so-called sickness, was mostly his
invention. And he would always, always, he told me, be there for
me, waiting for the time when, as all humans do, I would fall down,

hesitate, when life would get to be a bit too much for me—and I would come to him again, thinking that I was getting sick. Only now I knew I would never ever go to a psychiatrist again. It was they who had made me into an emotional freak with their treatments and therapies and left my real pain untouched, to surface, as it had in Paris, to frighten me—but not this time—into submission.

I remembered and told Paul, about a session with Dr. Sternfeld shortly after I was released from Monroe Park. I had just realized how close to death I had come and that the reason all the bottles of pills were in our bedroom was that Dr. Sternfeld insisted that Paul dole them out to me and hide them.

Paul interrupted me. "Sternfeld said he was awfully glad it was the Mellaril you found, not the Aventyl. The Aventyl would have killed for sure, he said."

I stopped. "He really said that?"

"Yes," Paul said.

I continued with my story. For months I had been telling Dr. Sternfeld how afraid I was that I was going to look for the pills and take them. He had said it was a risk *we* had to take; he kept giving Paul huge bottles of pills, all kinds, to keep and hide from me. This Saturday I was suddenly really really mad.

"You know you almost killed me," I said to the doctor.

"Nobody *does* anything to anybody, Janet. You know that. I did not force you to take the pills; I didn't want you to take the pills."

"But you put them close to me; they were a constant source of temptation."

"But *you* swallowed them," he said. "The responsibility is yours alone."

"I kept warning you, telling you how afraid I was of taking the pills," I said.

"You didn't want to go into the hospital again did you, Janet?" he asked, without waiting for an answer. "Then this was the only other way. You were very agitated and depressed. It was a risk we had to take."

"*We*," I shouted. "*You* didn't take any risk. It was *my* life, *my* life *we* were risking."

Then he didn't say anything. He just looked at me and I could tell he was angry. I was afraid again, afraid he would leave me. Goddamn it, I didn't even need him but I was still afraid he'd leave me. He knew I was afraid too. Finally, he said, "I realize you are angry, Janet. But you know as well as I that this hostility comes from sources deep inside you. I think we should discuss it and find out what it means."

what it "meant," I realized. And, coming so close to the
as afraid to face it; so I slipped back into an old pattern of
g my feelings, as if they were all symptomatic of my
distu...nce, as if they had no meaning outside of revealing my
sickness. Jesus, I had been accusing the man of criminal irresponsi-
bility and neglect that nearly ended in my death! But I had backed
down. I had let him con me again. And three months later, as Paul
and I were leaving for Paris, I had thanked him—THANKED
HIM!—for saving my life. My God, had I been duped!

The months passed, a blur of vivid insights, moments when the
truths I was seeing hurt me and I almost wished I could accept the
easy fantasy of sick again and go to a doctor, or take a pill to cure
my soul-pain.

Looking back on my life I could see that in spite of my brilliant
conformist façade I could never accept what was mapped out for
me, whether school, marriage, or secretarial work. Yet I did not
have the tools that would have enabled me to assert my differentness, challenge my family's and society's expectations, and go my
own way, whatever that would have been. I could not express my
angers; I could not say, "The hell with you all." I fought and fought
to be someone else, anyone, as long as it wasn't me. That agonizing
birth process was called mental illness—and I nearly died trying to
become myself.

I suffered greatly those years; much of my pain was the pain of
growing. That I do not regret. I hope I will have growing pains all of
my life. But the suffering I endured because I was a mental patient I
could never forget or forgive. The memories of my humiliation and
degradation as a prisoner of drugs, hospitals, and psychiatric jargon
continued to haunt me and would, I knew, forever.

But I was finally able to say, I do not believe I was ever sick. Lost,
yes; suffering, yes. Troubled, desperate, and pained, yes. But not
sick. My so-called sickness was an invention of the psychiatric
profession—of Dr. Berman and Dr. Kurtzman and Dr. Sternfeld, of
all the doctors who treated me during my ten-year career as a
mental patient. The fact that I—and my parents and my husband—
believed in my sickness for so long attests to our own need to
believe experts and to the effectiveness of the scare tactics,
brainwashing, and public relations of the American psychiatric
profession.

Little by little, I ripped away the façade of jargon and mystifica-
tions and saw that out of my pain and groping the doctors had
produced a mental patient, unable to survive anywhere but in a
so-called mental hospital. I was finally able to say to Paul, "They

fucked me over, royally. There is no such thing as schizophrenia, not outside some psychiatrist's imagination. There is pain and people's odd convoluted ways of trying to survive in the world. That's real. Not mental illness."

I don't know why my mind flashed clear that afternoon near the Seine, just as I don't know what really happened during the five days I was in the coma. I think, though, that during those five days I came into contact with the core of me. Stripped, I think I fused with my real self. I must have realized, somewhere too deep for words or remembering, that I wanted to live. When I awoke, I felt as if I were being born. I couldn't use pretense anymore. I knew only that I had to get away from Dr. Sternfeld and my past or I would truly die. I didn't know why I knew that, at the time, but I acted on it just the same. My realizations, in Paris, were the culmination, the final illumination, of what I only sensed when I woke up from the coma.

I never had been schizophrenic or even mentally ill. The doctors had called me that. They had looked at my behavior, looked at the symptoms I had assumed to hide my pain, decided I was unacceptable, and given me a label. Nothing I could say or do, then, would erase it. Eventually, I came to believe it myself. I accepted the drugs and shock and hospitals because I believed it. I identified with the other people who were called mentally ill and soon you couldn't tell us apart.

The anger that had surfaced in Paris was the real feeling, years of frustration at being used and never being able to speak out. It was not a symptom. I was not getting sick. And Lord, it felt good to rage at real demons, finally.

Yet, the question came and came again. Why, at that moment was I able to see so clearly, after ten years of indoctrination into my fundamental worthlessness? Where did I get the strength to sustain my vision and integrate it into my life during the next treacherous months? Where did I get the strength? Why that particular moment? I don't know. And to this, as to other mysteries of human suffering, glory, and struggle, there may be no answers.

Certainly my love for Paul and his for me sustained us both, as it had for years. Luck surely played a part. But really it was a certain vivid confluence of thoughts, dreams, and seasons in my mind—the time was right. And would we really know anything more if I were able to give a name, a label to the miracle of rebirth and liberation that happened to me in Paris? I think not, and this way the awe remains, as it should, because the process was a mystery. It cannot be defined. I was free.

But something was still unfinished. I knew I would have to

confront Dr. Sternfeld, sometime. On a late August evening I got very drunk over dinner. With all my new insights and strength I needed something to quell the old spirits of fear and dependency that were writhing inside me as the operator put through my transatlantic call. I knew Dr. Sternfeld couldn't hurt me anymore, but the old terrors of his power seemed as real as ever.

"I want to ask you something, Dr. Sternfeld," I began, and the words came pouring out, a torrent of reproach, bitterness, and disillusionment, smoothed by red wine and calvados.

"You treated me for eight years. Why didn't you ever tell me I'd be angry when I was well?"

I filled his silence with angry words.

"Why didn't you ever tell me what to expect from life, from myself?" I cried to him over the phone, wondering if, after traveling thousands of miles, scrunched through transatlantic cables, my words were coming to him meaningful and strong.

"Why didn't you prepare me for living? Why didn't you tell me I would be suicidal? Why didn't you warn me? You took away the only two things I had—my symptoms and yourself—and you let me go out, completely unprepared, into this shitty, stinking world. Why?" The tears were pouring down my face, salt, hot, cleansing. I felt naked but strong, facing Dr. Sternfeld as an equal, with truth, for the first time in eight years.

"I don't understand what you are asking me, Janet," I heard his calm guarded voice through the fluted receiver.

"What do you mean, you don't understand?" I said, my voice rising tight in anger. "I am asking you how you could treat me for eight years and not prepare me to live a normal life, how you could send me out into the world with *no* skill for survival. I am telling you you perpetrated a hoax, a farce on me—and I am asking you why."

"Are you drunk, Janet?"

"Yes. I am drunk, but I have never thought clearer in my life."

"You sound very upset, Janet. Why don't you take some Thorazine and calm down? You can call me again and we'll talk about it."

"I don't want to call you again and I don't want to calm down. I am perfectly lucid. I don't need a Thorazine. What's the matter, Dr. Sternfeld, don't you like what you're hearing?"

"I think you are too agitated for me to understand you, Janet. At least take a Valium."

" 'Take a Thorazine, Janet. Or a Valium. Or a Stelazine. Or a this or a that. Calm yourself, Janet. You're very agitated. You mustn't become upset.' " I mocked him, anger seething inside, frothing out.

" 'Come in and we'll talk about your feelings when you calm down.' "

"You're very sarcastic and hostile," Dr. Sternfeld said.

"You're damn right I am. And I have good reason to be. I am telling you that I am angry and you want me to take a pill and talk to you about it? This is my *life* I am telling you about. I'm saying you fucked me over and made me into an invalid. I'm saying I almost died because of you and now, that I'm alive, I'm lost because you never prepared me for living in the real world; and you want me to take a Thorazine and discuss it with you. Don't you hear what you're saying? I'm a human being talking to you, but you only hear the patient. You only want to see symptoms, not real emotion."

"You are out of control, Janet."

"So what if I am? What are you going to do about it? Put me in a hospital? Give me shock treatments? Give me more drugs? Bury me? Don't you ever get out of control?"

"I'm going to hang up now, Janet. When you come back to New York you may call me and we can talk about this."

He hung up but I wasn't finished yet.

"Oh, damn it, Paul, he always said he cared about me and I believed him. But if he really cared he wouldn't have put me through the tortures of shock and hospitalization. He wouldn't have sent me to Franklin Central to teach me a lesson. You know, he didn't hear what I was saying on the phone. He heard my accusations and anger as *symptoms*. He didn't hear *me* at all. 'Take a Thorazine, Janet.' He's a goddamn creep; he's nothing better than the seamiest pusher on the streets." I was still crying, now in Paul's arms. The truths were coming fast and I knew it would take time to assimilate them.

"Ten years," I said. "And now where am I? I'm a labeled psychotic with a mental-hospital record. I don't know how to begin to live on the outside without doctors and pills. Good Lord, Paul, he turned me into a fucking invalid, all in the name of Mental Health."

"You're not an invalid," Paul said. "You're a free woman, finally. And if you're a little scared and tentative and pessimistic, why, welcome to the human race."

I smiled, in spite of myself.

"I loved him a lot, Paul," I said. "For a long time he was all I had."

"I know, Jan."

"And it's hard to let go. It's hard to be strong."

"But you always have been strong. And now, at least you have real anger to cope with. The worst you can do is freak out. But you know what that is; you're luckier, in a way, than most of us. You're not afraid of your craziness, you know it's just another part of yourself that you have to learn to live with."

"I used to think the psychiatrists were going to exorcise me, in a way," I said. "It's funny. I remember now, all the doctors I ever knew, in any hospital or on the outside, were always afraid of me and of the other patients. It was almost as if we showed them something they couldn't look at in themselves. As soon as someone started acting weird, *experiencing* their pain, quick, it was a shot of Thorazine, shock treatments, or, if they happened to be on the outside, lock them up. Only, they would always tell us we were acting sick, and somehow that made it okay for them. They could stay calm and removed; they never really had to relate to us at all—or to their own madness. They could always say it was a one-shot psychotic episode. They hid behind their line of demarcation: they were healthy, we were sick. And we—we felt guilty, ashamed for just being alive."

"What do you think the doctors at Monroe Park would say about you now?" Paul asked.

"Probably that I'm a schizophrenic in permanent remission," I said, almost laughing.

"They'd never admit they could have been wrong?" Paul asked.

"No, I don't think so," I said. "Their livelihood depends on the existence of schizophrenia and related medical hallucinations."

We sat quietly, listening to the night sounds of Paris float up through our open window.

"I'm not going to be afraid anymore, Paul," I said finally. "And I'm not going to lurk around, hiding what I've been through. In the hospitals they treated us as less than human; they taught us to be ashamed of what we were and to hide what they did to us. They taught us to hate ourselves and each other and to doubt our truest instincts, to feel guilty about our incarcerations. They wanted us to be ashamed and to keep silent. Well, I'm not ashamed or guilty anymore. Just angry. I used to feel different from the other patients; I used to want to think of myself as somehow better than they. I was sick but they were crazy; I was voluntary, but they were committed. I hated them because they were all miserable, lonely, peculiar, helpless people and I didn't want to be associated with them. I wanted only to forget about them and my own hospitalizations. Now, I feel a sense of kinship with them; it is the people who categorized us and diagnosed us and made us outcasts that I despise—not my sisters and brothers. I thank whatever God there is that I have escaped the fate that was planned for me and that I am finally free. If anything is a miracle, it is that I am intact and

calling the guards doctors, the tortures treatments, and the humiliating experience of being a mental patient therapeutic. They are saying that the psychiatric labels that degrade and imprison people are diagnoses. They are the Mental Health Professionals.

They are Dr. Berman and Dr. Maynard and Dr. Lessing and Dr. Sternfeld—and very often they do not need to resort to legal measures to oppress and imprison their patients. They need only the "faith" of the family and the patient.

Looking back on my ten years as a mental patient, it is the fact of my own collaboration and that of my parents and Paul that I find most astounding and disturbing. Why, why did we go along with the doctors' designs? I asked my parents why they had consented to my hospitalizations. "We didn't know what else to do," they said. "We didn't want to put you in the hospital, but Dr. Berman said it was necessary. He said you would surely kill yourself. And you acted so strange; we wanted to do what was best. We didn't know where to turn."

So they turned to the expert, the person whom society designates the arbiter of acceptable behavior, the witchhunter, the psychiatrist. And they continued to listen to psychiatrists, never stopping to question what gift it was that gave these men the right or power or knowledge to decide their daughter's fate. They listened to the doctors at Oceanville and for eight years they listened to Dr. Sternfeld. In spite of the fact that they saw me continue to suffer, that they loathed the places into which they put me, despite the fact that I became more miserable and cut off as the years went on, they listened to the psychiatrists. And I did too. That is the worst part. They were afraid to listen to themselves, to their decency and love and sensibility. I do not blame them. They were victims, too. They had been scared and indoctrinated into having "faith," into believing that the experts had the answers. The doctors said, "She is mentally ill. That means she is ours. Only we can cure her." And, unwillingly, lost, we all believed them, believed they only wanted to help. But their help was imprisonment and torture and we allowed the semantic niceties of treatment and hospital to continue to fool us.

We must explode the myth that emotional turmoil indicates the presence of illness. We must reject the myth that only doctors and other mental health workers can treat this *illness;* that is incorrect and constitutes a monopoly, helping only the treaters, not the *treated.*

Those millions of us who have undergone psychiatric oppression in its many forms—from private therapy to legal commitment to lobotomizing, and the many stages in between—have undergone a kind of *brainwashing* as an integral part of our experiences. We have been taught not to have any faith in ourselves and to put all faith in the experts. Our faith constitutes *their* power. Without attributing universal malintent and evil designs to the profession, I say that given the kind of power, literal and psychological, that a mind-doctor has in this country, given the absolute power over people's lives that hospital personnel possess, I say that it is a very rare individual who can survive with her or his humanness and sense of fallibility intact.

For many years mental health professionals of all rank and persuasion told me I was sick. I believed them, my parents and Paul believed them, and we allowed them to perpetrate indignities upon me because we believed that their knowledge was great and their intent honorable. They only wanted to help.

But help is not help when it does violence to a person's body, mind, or freedom; it is power abused; it is medical responsibility distorted; it is liberal ethics convoluted. It is not help.

I have learned from my own suffering that we must come to accept our many-faceted selves. That to alternate between highs of ecstasy and lows of despair, to indulge in fantasy and vision, to act self-destructive or lethargic, to refuse to conform, to lunge forward in spasms of creativity only to retreat to depths of inactivity, to cry, to mourn, to suffer, to create new visions—is to be human, not sick.

Epilogue

Epilogue to the HarperPerennial Edition (Janet)

Twenty-one years have passed since that desperate September when I nearly died from an overdose of Mellaril, sixteen years since the publication of *Too Much Anger, Too Many Tears*. Paul and I have been married for twenty-five years. We are still in love, still friends. We live, as we have since 1971, in a small, pleasant village on the Hudson River, in Westchester County, about an hour's drive north of New York City. Miranda, who was three when *Too Much Anger, Too Many Tears* was published, is in her second year of college. Bethany, who wasn't even a fragment of a dream for us in 1975, is fourteen and in her first year of high school.

We have lived the last sixteen years without psychiatrists, drugs, shock, hospitals, or suicide attempts, although not without some pain and struggle—and not without a lot of love. Like many people, we have been occupied mostly with the dailiness of life. In spite of the publicity we received from *Too Much Anger, Too Many Tears*, and our involvement with the ex–psychiatric inmates movement, our life has been what Paul described in his original Epilogue as "outstandingly normal."

We've had much success: a happy marriage, two extraordinarily wonderful children, friends, cats, and activism. We've worked, cried, laughed, fought, and tried to be good and loving parents. We've vacationed in the Adirondacks; gone to see the New York Mets; watched our kids play flute, piccolo, softball, and soccer; played cards and Trivial Pursuit; joined the synagogue; and participated in nursery school events. Paul became a volunteer firefighter, I finished college. Outstandingly normal.

Writing *Too Much Anger, Too Many Tears* was a way to give meaning to our experiences, harness our anger to social change, and connect with other people whose lives had been disrupted by psychiatry. We wrote in the belief that wasting our experience and insight would be a terrible sin. We believed and trusted that through education, political action, litigation, consciousness-raising, and grassroots organizing, we could contribute to efforts to change the powerful and oppressive entrenched psychiatric system.

But *Too Much Anger, Too Many Tears* is as much a story about the mystery of rebirth as it is a polemic against institutional psychiatry. Miraculously, I survived more than one hundred electroshock assaults on my brain with very little memory impairment. Miraculously, too, I came out of a five-day coma after a massive overdose of Mellaril with no lasting physical damage. I emerged physically unscathed from nearly ten years of taking tremendously high doses of drugs like Thorazine, Prolixin, and Mellaril, drugs that routinely cause an irreversible brain damage syndrome called tardive dyskinesia. My body functioned adequately; my children were born intact.

After ten years as a "mental patient," I was able to free myself from the pernicious belief that I was "sick" and doomed to live a life bounded by drugs, hospitals, and psychiatric diagnoses. Contrary to almost everyone's expectations except mine and Paul's, I did not get "sick" again. Paul and I gathered the threads of our life and became, somewhat to our own amazement, rather conventional. Two kids, four cats, and a house in the suburbs.

I felt like a phoenix, rising from my own ashes, exhilarated and grateful beyond words for the gift of life. Neither Paul nor I tried very hard to decipher the "why" of this mysterious rebirth; we just accepted it. And, in the wake of post-Paris euphoria and the busyness of raising children, going to school, and working, I paid almost no attention to an even more intractable mystery: Why had I cracked up in the first place?

When we wrote *Too Much Anger, Too Many Tears*, we chose, for several reasons, not to talk much about my life before my encounters with psychiatry. Although our story was personal, our intent was political. We felt that it wasn't important why I had the problems I had. What was important was how those problems led me to seek what I thought would be help and how that "help" turned into a nightmare of drugs, psychiatric diagnoses, and hospitalizations.

But even if we had wanted to tell about my early life, we would have been hard put to do it. I had almost no memories of my childhood. Compared to the textured remembrances that formed Paul's personal motion picture of his life, I could remember nothing but a few, barely focused, still pictures that seemed to be from someone else's life. I could not have reconstructed what I felt or experienced for most of my childhood or adolescence. For a long time, I thought that my near-total amnesia about my childhood had been caused by shock treatments, but, as I have recently discovered, I was wrong.

I did have pieces of memories, but these odd, disjointed fragments, vividly colored, poised in my mind like the wrecked stained-glass windows of an ancient cathedral. They were dramatic and evocative, but they had no discernible relation to one another or to me, although I knew, intellectually, that they were true and that they were parts of my life. These memory pieces were also deeply at odds with the ordered, picture-book landscape that I had constructed and had been taught was my childhood.

If someone had asked me about my past—and Paul, as well as others, certainly had—I would have answered:

"My father was a New York City high school principal and a well-respected writer and educator. My mother was a typical 1950s housewife who abandoned her career to have children and support my father's ambitions. My brother was six years older than I, a brilliant misfit who knew the names of all the dinosaurs when he was three. I was a perfect child, smart and popular. Everybody loved me. We lived in Brooklyn. I don't remember ever being sad. No one ever yelled or got angry in my house. I went to camp in the summer and we visited relatives on Sundays. We were a perfect family."

But the memory fragments I had did not fit neatly at all into this picture. They seemed to be pieces of a jigsaw puzzle that had inadvertently strayed into the wrong box. I remembered my father beating me black and blue on my bare buttocks every morning before I went to school, for days at a time, because I wouldn't drink my orange juice. I remembered being terrified to close my eyes at night, fighting sleep, because of a glowing, leering, bushy-tailed fox that lived in the tree just outside my bedroom window. I remembered burrowing under the covers with my radio, its vacuum tubes glowing, telling myself that if I tried hard enough I could make myself so tiny that I could move inside the radio and never have to come out again.

I remembered being (and hating being) my father's perfectly submissive "secretary," taking his messages, bringing his drinks, sitting on his lap, being paraded in my pajamas for his friends. I remembered years of Thursday nights when my mother went shopping for the evening and I felt sick to my stomach and my braids were awry. I remembered climbing to the top shelf of the living room bookcase, when my parents weren't home, retrieving the heavy volumes of Havelock Ellis and Krafft-Ebbing, reading them in the bathroom, and throwing up.

And I remembered, as an adult with children of my own, rummaging around in the basement of my home, finding the mildewed fragments of poems I wrote when I was eleven or twelve years old, describing, in agonized verses, my longing to kill myself. I knew I had written them, because I recognized my child's handwriting and the paper, but I had absolutely no idea why. How could I, the perfect child, have wanted to die so much that when I was only twelve these words were nearly burned into the paper? This desperate, hurting child had been me, yet I hadn't even a trace of a remembrance of her or of the grief and pain and despair that drove her to long for death.

Sporadically, I tried to ferret out some truths about myself, make some connections between the static, idealized, and almost mythically unblemished picture I had of my childhood and the disconnected and discordant memory images that I sensed were true and real. Mostly, though, I accepted that I was, emotionally, an orphan, cut off from my past, unattached to my roots. I didn't feel any connection to the child I had been told I was, and I couldn't seem to find the right threads to tie me to the child I felt I might have been. Paul and I started *Too Much Anger, Too Many Tears* where we did because my life, as I remembered it, began the summer before I went to college.

In the past two years, all that has changed. I have been given a second gift, an excruciatingly painful but liberating one: I have started to get back my childhood memories. In pieces, chunks, and flashes, the way a jagged stroke of lightning illuminates a room, I have begun to remember events and feelings that have been buried for decades. Unbidden, unrelenting, unexpected, these memories are returning, violent streaks of sound, color, and texture. They are called "flashbacks," and at times, driving in the car, walking down my street, reading, eating, talking, I find myself impaled on a shard of memory, paralyzed by grief, hurt, and pain—so long buried, so potent when unearthed.

The memories come, and continue to come, curtains of secrecy ripped aside, decades of blindness swept away. With each new memory, with each moment in time brought to agonizing consciousness, I find myself nodding in appalled recognition. "Yes, that is how it was," I say, as tears stream across my cheeks.

With gruesome clarity, I am remembering what I kept from my awareness for more than forty years. As a child, and as an adolescent, I was sexually molested by two close male relatives, one a boy, the other a man. Like millions of women, I am an incest survivor.

When I started to remember, I wanted only to hurt myself, to run away, to die. I cried, I denied, I raged. More than anything else, I wanted this not to be true. I thought about my children, remembered how fragile they were, my no-longer little girls. I imagined them violated and terrorized and betrayed—and the pain was nearly unbearable.

For months, as memories washed over me, the enormity of the truth of my childhood threatened to undo my life. My insides were raw, I felt as if I were bleeding inside. I was disoriented, moving foggily through an undelineated, unfamiliar world. I held on to Paul for dear life. And I cried. All the time, I cried. I didn't want this truth. I didn't want this connection. What I wanted was not-to-know again. Couldn't I close my eyes and wake up again, not-knowing?

"This can't be," I told myself. "I must be making this up. I am really crazier than anyone thought." I wanted to be crazy, to be sick, to be dead. I wanted to cut my wrists, take pills, jump off a dam, lie down on the tracks as the train pulled out of Grand Central station. Anything to blot out this knowledge. "How could this be?" I asked myself, over and over, an incantation against evil. "How could this have happened in a nice, upstanding, middle-class Jewish family from Brooklyn? A 'perfect' family. Incest?" I wanted to die—anything but to be that terrified, violated little girl who tried desperately not to close her eyes at night and who dreamed of suicide when she was twelve.

Almost two years have passed since my memories began to return. I don't cry all the time, or even most of the time. I still hurt a lot, but I know that I am healing, from the inside out, slowly, but cleanly, wounds open to the light instead of festering in darkness. I have joined a self-help group of incest survivors. We talk about our hurts and our angers, our sense of separateness and shame. We reveal our secret pasts and try to find courage for the future.

Incest was the central fact of my growing up. Stark, brutal, unimaginable; it is the key. From the time I was a small child, through my adolescence, I had no escape. I did what I could to get through the seductive and often violent abuse that existed, year after year, under a facade of calm and eminent respectability. I think I left my body while I was being molested. Children do this; they do anything they can in order to survive.

Years after the abuse was over, I could still leave my body at will. I remember sitting with a group of young women, all of us wrist cutters, in the dayroom at Oceanville Hospital. We were laughing about how we could leave our bodies during doctors' rounds and watch from the ceiling as the pompous, self-important fools went about their business, none of them ever realizing that we weren't there at all. None of us identified ourselves as incest survivors, even to ourselves, although we all bore the stigmata. Of that group of eight, three women are dead—suicides—and another has recently shared her history of incest with me. They did not survive the double assaults of incest and psychiatry.

A former Miss America who was sexually molested by her renowned humanitarian father and who regained her memories in her forties, wrote that while she was growing up and being molested, she was "the day child and the night child," and that neither knew of the other's existence. She was leading two parallel lives in one small body. When I read her description, I recognized myself, realizing with a jolt what a fragile protection I had created in not-knowing and how close I must have come, like so many other incest survivors, to truly splitting off into pieces. I have come to have great admiration for the child I was and for the millions of other warrior-children: for their strength, resilience, and sheer determination to make it through.

When I find myself overcome by sadness and rage, trying to integrate my knowledge, trying to heal, I tell myself that I've already been through the hard part. I survived incest and I survived psychiatry. I can certainly manage to survive the remembering.

And, in fact, the remembering, with all its pain and dislocation, has been truly a healing balm. Finally, everything makes sense. I understand, as I never expected to understand, the *why* of my life. Although the days of the squid and the Elders are long past and it has been years since I seriously thought about cutting my wrists, I have never, in all these years, been far from despair. I have been plagued by unexplainable angers and I have struggled, always, to maintain my equilibrium when I felt as if there was a black pit in me that could open at an instant's notice and swallow me up. Always, I was a breath away from falling into a reservoir of unstoppable, eternally renewing tears. I have had to work myself through never quite disappearing feelings of self-hatred, fear, shame, helplessness, rage, and humiliation.

I have never understood where these feelings came from. I never understood where all the pain came from or why it never went completely away, flooding me periodically like some great, undeterred, natural force. I never understood why my body went numb and panic rose in my throat at my first tentative teenage sexual encounters. I never understood where the squid came from, or the Elders, or the Girl with the Sunglasses. I never understood why I couldn't seem, ever, to be free of the mad, wild, unrelenting desire to die.

Now, finally, I understand.

At the source of all this pain, at the core, there is the sad, frightened, wounded little girl who was me. Regaining my memories has given me a chance to find this child, and to shelter and nurture and protect her—at last.

Astonishingly, for the first time in my conscious life, I feel whole, with a real possibility of being free from the demons of my childhood. As long as they were hidden, blotted out of my consciousness, I could never face the pain head-on. Now, when I feel those old, scary-familiar black feelings, I am able to say, with sorrow and rage, "I know what this is. I know where this is coming from. Hold tight. It will pass." And it does.

So, as a failed suicide attempt turned into a life-giving chance to escape from the clutches of psychiatry, these emerging memories have given me a chance to put the pieces of myself together and move on. The core of pain remains; I don't think it will ever go away. But I am healing.

And again, strangely, I am called upon to share my personal story in the belief that some good can come out of it. Again, the personal is political. Because incest is political, just as institutional psychiatry is political. Both are about the abuse of power and the betrayal of trust. Both have flourished in an environment of secrecy and shame.

For many years, the institutional psychiatric system operated virtually unscrutinized. No one with influence cared to know what was really going on inside mental hospitals and clinics and when an occasional horror story surfaced, it could be discounted as an aberration in an otherwise benign and smoothly functioning universe. *Too Much Anger, Too Many Tears* helped to debunk the myth of psychiatric wisdom and beneficence and focus attention on the abuses inherent in the system. Paul and I are hopeful that this new edition will spark renewed scrutiny of the psychiatric system and renewed activity to eliminate its endemic abuses. We are hopeful, too, that more incest survivors, like ex–psychiatric inmates, will take courage and break out of their isolation to come forward to share their pain and their memories.

When Elizabeth Packard was being tormented in the early 1860s by the superintendent of the Jacksonville Asylum, one of the inmates questioned why the administration was so intent on making her life miserable. "They discern that I am a truth-telling woman," she replied. "And they are afraid." What we have told in *Too Much Anger, Too Many Tears* is also the truth. It is a frightening, horrifying truth, albeit a common one. We do not know if the perpetrators of psychiatric violence and sexual violence against children will be afraid when they read this book. At the very least, they will have been put on notice that their activities are under scrutiny. If the truth does not, of itself, bring about change, perhaps it will at least cause some sleepless nights.

Of course, we need to do more. We need to work for the elimination of forced "treatment" and involuntary "hospitalization" and for the creation of humane caring environments for people in pain. We need to protect the vulnerable and powerless: children, the elderly, the poor, the abused, the friendless, and the disenfranchised. These are the people who are hurt by psychiatry, and who end up drugged and shocked and incarcerated. And we need to look inside ourselves and acknowledge the part we play, as a society and as individuals, in the perpetuation of abuses like psychiatric violence and incest. We need to ask ourselves: Have we given over our powers of judgment and discernment to doctors? Have we implicitly accepted the myth of mental health and illness? Have we abrogated our responsibilities to care for each other? Have we colluded in keeping secrets?

We hope that *Too Much Anger, Too Many Tears* has touched you and

EPILOGUE

made you think about power and the abuse of power, and that reading this book has changed forever the way you view sanity, madness, psychiatry, mental hospitals, psychiatric drugs, shock treatments, and "mental patients." We hope, too, that you will never allow yourselves or anyone you love to become a victim of institutional psychiatry. If we have been able to do that, we will feel, truly, that the effort of self-revelation was worthwhile.

September 1991